HAWKING & STONE (1965)

Claire Ingrams

ALSO BY CLAIRE INGRAMS

The Perils of 1925
The Debacles of 1935
The Enigmas of 1945

The Yellow Glass (1955)

Copyright Claire Ingrams 2019

CONTENTS

Title Page	1
Also by Claire Ingrams	2
Copyright	4
Part 1	7
1. A Blast from the Past	9
2. I, Rosa Stone	16
3. The Funeral	22
4. Introductions	32
5. The New Investigation	39
6. Mushrooms	50
7. Bill Hawking	58
8. Rendezvous at the Pub	66
9. Coast Cottage	73
10. Old Harry Cole	83
11. Dungeness	100
12. Dinner at Shore House	108
13. Come to my Senses	118
PART 2	123
1. Developments	124
2. Mayfair	135
3. Verity Flinders	147

4. Absolute Rubbish	154
5. Wrong Turns	162
PART 3	169
1. The Mrs Dyminge Lectures	170
2. Hawking & Stone	175
3. The Psychiatrist	183
4. Picnic in the Shingle Garden	196
PART 4	207
1. Big Sticks & Loot	208
2. Busted	217
3. Stories & Facts	228
4. The Flat Over the Laundrette	241
5. Bad Karma	250
PART 5	257
1. Bluebells	258
2. A Done Deal	267
3. What Shall we do About Verity?	277
4. The Bigger Boys	293
5. To the Horizon	302
6. The Second Funeral	319

PART 1

1. A BLAST FROM THE PAST

On Monday the invitation to the funeral arrived through the morning post. Inside the envelope, addressed to myself and my brother in a madly loopy, elderly hand, the card was not edged in black – as one might reasonably expect – but in emerald green. I wondered whether he would have wanted this show of eccentricity, being, outwardly at least, the very essence of the good, conforming soldier. But, then, she had known him best, of course.

So, he was in my mind all day while I did . . oh, all the things that I have to do these days, the things that I can't even remember doing two seconds after they are done, that pile on top of each other like an overfilled sandwich that one can't get one's mouth around . . until the afternoon post stopped me dead in my tracks. I was out back when Mr Grimes, the postman, brought it into the shop.

"Good afternoon, Mrs Stone," he called out, "delivery for you".

"Thanks, Mr Grimes. Please leave it on the counter, will you?"

I was much too busy to come out.

I thought he'd gone, but:

"Which one's the counter this week, then?"

I was hot and bothered. Why did everyone have to make things so difficult? Just put the damn letter down. It would be a bill, they always were. Unless somebody else had died, of course.

"Put it on a chair."

"There are a lot of chairs, Mrs Stone."

"Oh, for goodness... Any chair will do."

The shop doorbell jangled instead of a goodbye. I suppose I'd snapped, because Mr Grimes was usually punctilious in the extreme; a nice London postman who tipped his postman's hat and made a point of addressing me as Mrs at all times.

When I emerged, I had the twins with me, one on each hip. They were getting heavier by the minute, my fat, black-haired babies and I wondered just how much longer I'd be able to go on carting them about. No, that's not true. I didn't wonder at all, because I *couldn't* wonder, really. My mind hit the familiar, blank wall. The future was simply unimaginable; just keeping them fed and changed was as much as I could do, was actually so much more than I could do, and the idea that they might keep on growing and actually want to do outrageous things like crawl or walk was .. well, thankfully, my brain wasn't capable of such feats of imagination any more.

Now, what had I come into the shop for? I spied a neat, brown package on the purple rattan chair with the dodgy seat that I was pretty sure hadn't been there before. Had I ordered something? I couldn't remember doing so, but that didn't mean a thing; I could have ordered the entire contents of a bankrupt stately home, owners and dogs included, and not have remembered. I lay the twins down on a faded quilt in the shop window, wedged them in with the telephone directories that I kept for that specific purpose and picked up Mr Grimes' delivery. It was small, but had a nice weight to it.

The package was addressed to Miss Rosa Stone, The Arcanium, World's End, Kings Road, Chelsea, London and, that being my name and address, it had found me. I could infer nothing from the string because it was lavishly sellotaped, as so often nowadays, but somebody had taken care with the wrapping and I had some trouble ripping it open. Layer upon layer of brown paper and then what looked to be a silk scarf yes, it was a Hermes silk scarf complete with horse paraphernalia, and a substantial wodge of cotton wool under that. I stuffed the lot into the capacious pocket of my kaftan; I'd had to learn to be thrifty and, of course, the cotton wool would come in extremely useful with the twins.

So, what had I got? Well, I liked it; it was satisfying, somehow. A small, glass owl, chunky, with bubbles captured inside like a bottle of Lucozade. A small, bright yellow, glass owl. I cradled it in the palm of my hand, tracing the beak and feathers with a fingertip. It said Scandinavian to me, previous decade Scandinavian, around the 1955 mark. And then I gasped. If my brain had been functioning, I'd have twigged straight away. The owl was made of uranium glass.

Then all hell broke loose as Jessica began to wail and Benjamin, never far behind, joined in, and a figure rapped on the window and I dropped the little owl like a hot coal and just stood there, literally rubbing my hands like some Lady Macbeth, as if I *still* believed that the bright yellow glass was impregnated with deadly amounts of uranium.

The figure rapped once more.

"How much for the two in the window?" It was Sam, my little brother, camera slung round his neck, pockets stuffed full of film. "They're noisy, but I can see they might appreciate in value."

"Oh Sam," I was so relieved to see him, "Major Dyminge is dead and now I've been threatened. Someone's got it in for me; I can feel it in my bones."

I kicked the little owl under the chair and peered down at it, as if it were a mouse that might take it into its head to scuttle under the wide skirts of my kaftan. I was consumed with a powerful urge to get out of there and wash my hands.

"Look after the babies for a sec, would you?"

I dashed into the back room of the shop. Then I dashed straight back.

"But don't, whatever you do, touch the yellow owl under the chair. In fact, pick up the babies, skirt round the chair, put them in their pram and push them outside. Out in the yard, I mean."

"Ja wohl, mein Fuhrer. Jeez, Rosa, you get bossier by the day. Look after your own kids."

But he'd got them into the black pram, swathed in blankets against the February cold, by the time that I'd scrubbed up and composed myself. We wheeled them out to the sooty scrap of back yard and they subsided, as they always did when sitting facing one another in that great, black galleon of a pram. Each seemed to find the other endlessly fascinating and, if they hadn't been wrapped up so tightly that they looked like mummified potentates from the East, they would have been investigating one another's toes, gurgling with laughter.

"Thank goodness for the pram," I headed back in. "D'you fancy a cup of tea? Come and talk to me while I fill the kettle."

"Isn't it cold for them?"

For a nineteen-year old boy, Sam was shaping up well on the uncle front.

"Nah! You're supposed to give them masses of fresh air; the more, the better. Come on in, I'm freezing."

Sam negotiated tins of Brasso, boxes of vintage perfumes, piles of lace and linen and all of the plain old dusty junk that constituted my main living quarters and ducked to avoid the string of wet nappies suspended over the electric fire. Something must have caught his attention because he turned, crouched and focused his camera. The nappies, the junk and the view through the back door to the pram should have made an edifying sight.

"Are you doing a project on the London slums at your art school?"

He laughed, but he didn't deny it. Then he perched on a packing case, his dark, curly head bowed as he played with his camera, looking so young and handsome and, somehow, right for the so-called Swinging Sixties. Having a shop on the Kings Road I was surrounded by youth and beauty, even though it didn't always make it as far up the road as the Arcanium. I was in pole position to watch other people swing.

"There you go," I passed him his tea and cleared a space to sit down.

"So," he said, "the death of [1]Churchill and Major Dyminge, eh? All at once."

"Yes.. I hadn't thought of that. The end of an era, I suppose." I blew on my tea. "Of course, the Major was very old, but I'm still sorry."

"You were closer to him than me. What with your famous *Yellow Glass Adventures*".

"There's no need to put them into italics. Just because you were too young and insignificant to take part. Major Dyminge was a wonderful man, Sam. The *best* of men. After all, Major Dyminge saved my.."

"Life," he chimed in.

"You're just jealous because you haven't had any adventures of your own."

"My whole life is an adventure, man. One far-out adventure."

I laughed.

"No that's just the pot, idiot; I think you may be confusing real life and mind-altering substances."

"Have you got any cake?"

"No, Dad never comes to see me any more and I can't afford cake."

"You could, like, make one. Maybe."

"Ha! It's me you're talking to, Sam."

He whipped his damn camera up and snapped me there

and then. God, I hated it when he did that.

"Don't you dare." I made an ineffectual effort to snatch the camera from him, but he was too quick for me. "Not when I'm in the same kaftan I wore all through the pregnancy because I *still* can't fit into anything else and my hair's so tangled, I'll probably have to chop it off and I smell of sick. You give me that film, Sam Stone, or I'll never forgive you."

He raised a charismatic, v-shaped, black eyebrow at me,

"Don't worry; nobody'll be able to smell the sick when it's printed up. I can see the caption now: 'Unmarried mothers of the 1960s; the problem persists.'"

"You little.."

He was getting too close to the bone now: yes, I was on my own, but more than that, I was tired, I was old and I was fat. If I had the energy I might cry.

"Ah, come on . ." All of a sudden, he backed off. "You know I was only joking, Rosa. I'll snip it out when the roll's finished, if you're that uncool with it."

"You'd better."

He got up to inspect a moustachioed tailor's dummy in a Guardsman's red parade jacket. It used to sport a Busby, too, but it had become infested with small, black flies and I'd had to put it out for the dustmen before the flies migrated to the rest of the shop. Not that I was, in any way, pernickety about the stuff I sold; I liked to be as inclusive as possible. Everything was interesting to me and I found it much harder to weed out the dross than to polish the dross up and stick it in a cabinet at an enterprising price.

"So, why the paranoia, Rosa? Any connection to the hair and the vomit, by any chance?" Sam made one of those charming circling gestures with his index finger next to his brain.

"Aargh! I'd forgotten about that. Honestly, I'm starting to wonder whether [2]Dr Spock was the right book to follow. It's all very well being against rigid rules for childcare, but he doesn't seem to account for some of us having work to do the next day. It's got so that I can't hold anything in my head for longer than it takes to boil a kettle. Come."

I got up and beckoned him into the shop, kneeling to point out the yellow owl under the chair.

"Now, take a look at that, Sam. You won't know this, but that's uranium glass, that is, and it just arrived in the afternoon post out of nowhere. It's a blast from the past. I think it might be a threatening message."

"What, that little bird? You really have got a screw loose, Rosa."

He scooped the owl up from the floor and waved it in my face,

"Ooh, hea*vy*! To-whit to-whoo, I'm coming after yoooo.."

I, instantly, felt foolish. What was the matter with me? Ten years ago we'd established that uranium glass was made with tiny amounts of uranium oxide in order to produce a bright shade of yellow and that it was simply impossible for it to hold a quantity large enough to do anyone any harm (despite the apparent threat to export toxic amounts worldwide, which had turned out to be a hoax, anyhow). Moreover, why assume that there was any kind of sinister message behind the package? People sent me bits and bobs all the time. Granted, there was generally a note included . . I stuck my hand into my kaftan pocket and retrieved the scarf and cotton wool that had swaddled the little glass owl. No, there was nothing else there, nothing I'd missed when I'd unwrapped it. All the same . . I eyed the cotton wool uneasily before chucking it into the waste paper basket . . *that* was going nowhere near my babies' bottoms.

2. I, ROSA STONE

You would probably like to know how I came to find myself on my own with two children and running a junk shop at the age of twenty-nine. I wish I could explain. I cannot, in all honesty, say that I decided to take any kind of radical *stand* (against the bourgeois concepts that bind middle-class society etc). Really, [3]they were just things that happened when I was supposed to be doing something else, to mangle an expression. Which is a pretty bad way to bring children into the world, isn't it? Pretty selfish, slovenly, and irresponsible and a whole raft of other words that I'm just too tired to care about any more. Actually, they're not my words either, but the words that, if you took a straw poll, have been applied to me the most; applied by those closest to me. So, they should know.

Although, now that I've got that out of the way, I'm not about to apologise for any of it. I mean, that would imply that my two beautiful babies should not have been born and I'm not having that. I may not be a fully paid-up member of the counterculture taking anti-bourgeois stands, but I'm certainly not having that. My twins are by far and away the best thing to have happened, not just to me, but to the entire world. Everyone thinks that of their own offspring, but I know it's true. I'd known it from the minute I found out that I was pregnant. I was filled with such crazy joy that nothing my family tried to scold me with made an iota of sense . . . And, then, for it to be twins. How magical and astonishing. How incredibly clever my body had turned out to be. I mean, I'm a clever person, with unusual abilities, but what an amazing sensation it was when something *so* clever happened without me thinking about it at all.

What I was supposed to have been doing (and had been trying to do, believe me), was to act. However, making much headway in the acting profession proved harder than expected. I'd stuck it out at drama school, despite feeling that they'd got me all wrong from day one; I saw myself in the [4] Sarah Bernhardt, tragic heroine mould, whereas they seemed to have me down as more of a Jewish [5]Hattie Jacques. My actress aunt, Aunt Kathleen, had warned me about the business, but it still took me a few years of struggling to get the tiniest parts imaginable for her advice to hit home. She'd been right, luck was *so* much more important than talent; having the right face at the right time, and I, with my mass of curly, black hair, my long skirts and my Junoesque figure, was all wrong. As the Sixties progressed, I only became more and more wrong. It would have been terribly lowering if I hadn't had the shop to concentrate on.

So, thank heaven for The Adventure of the Yellow Glass, because the Arcanium really began with that, back in 1955 when my interest in glass and ceramics of all kinds was well and truly piqued. I started to collect hand-blown glass from the new wave of small studios that were springing up all over the place and found that I didn't have to hold on to it for very long before it gained in value. I also began to amass a valuable collection of old clothes, handmade lace and linens and found, again, that I was just that important fraction ahead of the Zeitgeist because a new , who'd grown up with machine-made fabrics, suddenly began to appreciate the old techniques that they were about to lose altogether. In short, I found that I had an eye.

Therefore, those of you who have followed the fortunes of my family in previous adventures and who may have jumped to the conclusion that my wealthy, mercantile parents splashed out to get their only daughter set up in her own London shop are wrong, quite wrong. I found the premises and I pay the rent myself. So there. Yes, I may have accepted the offer of a private nursery nurse in the days after Jessica and Benjamin were born – and what an insufferable, uniformed horror *she* turned out to be; very much like the real [6]Mary Poppins of the books, not that saccharine invention that Julie Andrews played in last year's film – but, other than that, Rosa Stone is her own woman.

And Rosa Stone's Arcanium has been a success, by and large. I feel that my brother's behind-the-scenes snapshot of nappies and chaotic junk – the London slums one – may have given entirely the wrong impression of my business. It's just that it's going through a rough patch. When I opened up it was all order and cleanliness personified because I, actually, have a genuine talent for order. I enjoy categorising and sorting, just as I enjoy facts and figures and history and connections and .. well, most things. I am insatiably interested in almost everything and I have the kind of photographic memory that compartmentalises it all in my mind with even more dexterity than I can achieve physically. But *you* try having twins. You try making the early morning starts, in order to get to Bermondsey or Portobello markets, when you haven't slept and the babies are crying in the back of the car. You try being so tired that your supersonic memory goes completely kaput and you have no idea whether it will ever recover; in fact, you're so damn tired that you don't care whether or not it recovers because all you care about is getting a proper night's sleep. Just one decent night's sleep is all I ask; that's not too much, is it? Apparently, it is.

That evening, after I'd shut up shop, I treated my little brother, Sam, to a beer at the Man in the Moon pub across the road. It was dark as death and, despite my old fox fur coat, bitterly cold when we wheeled the twins over, but Seamus, the welcoming Irish landlord who had become a bit of a friend, had a roaring fire going inside and it was all very cosy (and good for my electricity bill). The Man in the Moon wasn't a fashionable pub because, as I said, the beautiful hordes who traipsed up and down the Kings Road looking for [7]Mary Quant's shop, or hoping to join the Beatles shopping, didn't waste much time hanging around World's End. The pub still belonged to the locals at night. Only the sound of revving sports cars in the distance reminded us of what we were missing.

A group of old codgers were huddled round a newspaper doing the football pools, but nobody else much was there, except for an antiquarian acquaintance of mine. Mr Summerby was retired from the trade – he'd been an expert on antiques from the Far East and run a well-known shop in Chelsea for many years – but was now becoming a bit of a fixture propping up the bar in the Man in the Moon, his dog lying at his feet. He was an amiable man, with a mop of pale hair and a marked country burr that belied a sharp and knowledgeable brain. I had once brought a vase to the pub that I'd thought might have been Ming Dynasty, and he'd laughed so much he had nearly fallen off his stool.

"Ah, come here my little beauties."

Mr Summerby was fond of babies and had a tendency to coo.

"Are they ready for a drop of ale in their bottles, Rosa? It'll put heart into them."

This was a continuing theme; he had been pushing alcohol on them since they'd been born and I often wondered whether it might have been the only form of sterilisation around when he was a baby.

"Stop it, you'll have turned them into alcoholics before they can walk."

I set the brake on the pram with my foot and sat down on a stool at the bar.

"Sit down, Sam."

"Yes, Ma'am."

"This is my little brother, Sam. He's training to be a photographer. Sam, this is Mr Summerby, a fellow antiques dealer."

Sam focused his camera and snapped the two of us against a shining row of draught beer taps.

"He's investigating the slums of London at the moment and keeping a keen eye on me," I explained. "Actually," I nudged my brother, "that's really rude; you should ask before you take random photographs, you know."

"Sorry, sir."

Mr Summerby smiled his mellow smile and dipped back down into his pint.

I sorted out the drinks and bent into the pram to take the babies' mittens off. Mrs Dyminge had knitted them in the softest wool, yellow and white stripes, a row of plain and a row of purl. I was reminded of the Major's death and felt a toast coming on.

"Here's to the old Major," I sat back and lifted my glass, clinking it to Sam's before I took a well-earned gulp. "*Oh, that's better.* The Major," I explained to Mr Summerby, "was a good friend of our family's who's just died. He was quite old – I mean his time had come – but such a brave, kind man. I don't know whether I've ever mentioned it, but the Major saved my.."

"Life," Sam chimed in, unnecessarily.

Mr Summerby looked interested, so I told him the story of how I'd stowed away in a boat as a child during the war, and Major Dyminge had rescued me from drowning.

"We'll be going down to Kent for his funeral on Tuesday."

"This coming Tuesday? That's such a drag," My brother interjected. "I've got college on a Tuesday. What time?"

"11 o'clock at the church in Hassels, you know, near where their old house fell off a cliff. You'll have to skip college, Sam; Mrs Dyminge has invited you and that's that. I'll drive us all down."

"Dyminge," Mr Summerby mused, "an unusual name. Now, I used to know a girl who married a Dyminge." He set down his pint and fixed cobalt blue eyes on mine, as if he'd seen something extra interesting in me. "*He* was a military man."

"A girl? I don't think you can mean Frances. A lot of wild, white hair and likes gardening? Wrote some detective stories that did quite well in the Thirties and Forties?"

"Frances, yes. That *was* her name," he exclaimed. "Frances Carlisle, the vicar's daughter. She had a rope of soft, brown hair down her back and we picked primroses together in the woods."

Sam made a face at me, surreptitiously, but Mr Summerby wouldn't have seen it because he looked to be completely away with the fairies, as my mother used to say.

"I've never known her maiden name," I said, "but the bit about the primroses sounds feasible."

At that, my children decided to hijack the conversation, so I grabbed some peanuts from the bowl on the counter and hustled Sam out of the pub, waving goodbye to Mr Summerby, who must have been a lot older than he looked and was still wandering the Elysian primrose paths of yore. Possibly accompanied by a young Frances Dyminge; although it was difficult to envisage Mrs D ever being young.

Then my brother disappeared back to the rat-hole digs in South Kensington, that he shared with another student, and I fed and bathed the twins and put them to bed. After which, I whisked up a little light, but nourishing, supper, watched [8] The Wednesday Play on the telly and did my accounts. Who am I kidding? I finished tucking up Jessica and Benjamin, sat down for a minute and lost consciousness until the regular 2'oclock time bomb exploded. Dr Spock had let me down again.

3. THE FUNERAL

When Sam showed up at the shop on Tuesday morning, he had a tiny girl with him. She had the plentiful blond hair, pointed chin, enormous soot-rimmed eyes and skinny legs that so many modern girls seemed to possess. She was wearing a large-brimmed, floppy, black hat, a little black coat and a very brief black shift dress with black, diamond-patterned tights. She was mainly legs and looked much like a stick insect dressed for a funeral.

"This is Verity," he said. "She can fit in the car, too, can't she Rosa?"

If she took the hat off, Verity could have curled up in the socket for the cigarette lighter.

"Hello Verity," I said, trying to sound relaxed and sociable, when I was actually extremely fraught and wearing an ensemble that I'd had to cobble out of a curtain at seven that morning, when I realised that I couldn't fit into my one presentable dress.

"It's very nice to meet you .. any friend of my little brother's .. but, I hope you don't mind me asking .. were you a personal acquaintance of Major Dyminge's? I mean, I think this funeral may be invitation only." Even to my own ears, I sounded prehistoric.

"Verity isn't coming to the funeral, bozo. I want to photograph her on the marshes."

She peeked out at me from under her vast hat.

"I always wear black," she volunteered. "[9]I'm in mourning for my life."

If I hadn't been wearing a curtain, I'd have smiled at her appropriation of Chekhov, but, as it was, I was highly irritated.

"Well, *we're* in mourning for our old friend Major Dyminge, who, I think you'll find, is actually dead."

Verity looked shocked to her core, like she might be about to burst into tears, and my brother put his arm round her and pulled her into his shoulder.

"Now look what you've done. You can be such a bully, Rosa."

Verity shivered in his arms. I felt like I was the wicked witch of Somewhere. I opened my mouth to answer back but suddenly didn't have the energy.

"Sorry Verity. I didn't have much of a night's sleep."

Was that a triumphant gleam in her eye? It was gone so fast that I couldn't be sure, hidden behind her exaggerated, mascara-caked lashes. She burrowed deeper into my chivalrous brother's arms.

"Okay, there's room for you both in the car. But you sit in the back with the babies, will you, Sam? They know you." It was an order. "Sit in the front with me, Verity."

I wanted the stick insect up front where I could keep an eye on it.

We made it to Kent without killing one another, just. My [10] Hillman Husky was an old model, so Sam had to clamber through the side-hinged rear door and sit on the bench seat – which was generally folded back so that I could transport furniture – with Jessica and Benjamin beside him, wedged into their basket. I managed to ignore any complaints coming from the back, while trying to find the A20. I noticed that Verity kept extremely quiet when he suggested that she might like to take a baby on her lap. My efforts to engage her in conversation were also mainly met with silence, as if she might never forgive me for being so snappish. So, because I'm cursed with uncontrollable curiosity, I was forced to take the direct approach.

"What's your surname, Verity?

"Flinders."

"And how old are you?"

"Seventeen."

That surprised me; the clothes and paint-box make-up had led me to believe that she was quite a few years older.

"Do your parents know that you are out and about, travelling in cars with strange photographers?"

"They don't care."

"Oh," that seemed sad. "Well, don't worry, you're quite safe with us, even if my little brother is a bit of an idiot."

"Oy, I heard that."

"A very nice idiot. Hey, Sam!" I called, "Verity's only seventeen, so no funny business, d'you hear?"

Nobody answered; embarrassment had probably stunned them into silence. I could, vaguely, remember being like that myself at their age, but hallucinatory tiredness had loosened up my inhibitions.

"And she's not staying the night in Kent. Do I make myself clear? You're putting her on the train this evening, if I have to come with you myself."

My goodness; what *was* all this that came spewing out of my mouth? I must have become a mother when I wasn't looking.

"But the light . ." He protested. "The light'll be gone by the time they let us out of church."

"That's not my problem, Sam. Nobody asked you to bring your model down to Kent with you. And, anyhow . ." I thought about it, ". . you'll be expected at the wake, so I'd just put thoughts of snapping Verity in the marshes out of your head."

"Sorry, Verity," I glanced sideways at her. "It may not be much of a day out for you."

Miss Flinders' chiselled little profile didn't look too happy under her hat, so I tried a more cheerful, less nagging mother approach.

"But, looking on the bright side, I'm sure you'll be welcome at the wake. What's the betting our father will be doing the catering, eh Sam? I promise you, Verity, it'll be worth the trip down just for a taste of his chocolate buns."

That went down like a lead balloon; inexplicably (because, really, who *isn't*?), she didn't seem to be a chocolate bun kind of a girl.

In the event, Verity was needed to make up numbers in the church. It was all very sad and, indeed, odd. You may have noticed that I am, officially, now the most boring woman in the world and ascribe everything to lack of sleep, but really, it went beyond that sweaty, hallucinatory kind of odd that tinged my entire life. It was all just, plain, *odd* and getting more so by the minute.

We reached my parents' house on the beach in time for the funeral cavalcade. The Dyminge's house, Coast Cottage, being right next door, the Major was already parked up by the sea wall in a glass-sided funeral car, his coffin draped with the Union Jack and topped with his old cap. Grey clouds glowered over the great expanse of St Margaret's Bay and the tide was high, spitting at the two white houses on the shingle. The door of Shore House, my childhood home once the war was over, and the house where Sam had been born, stood open.

"Hello! Anybody at home?"

There was a crunch of shingle underfoot and the funeral party emerged from the Dyminges' cottage. My father was on one side of Mrs Dyminge, with his arm around her shoulder, and a tall, nice-looking, fair boy in a dark suit was on the other. It took me a moment to recognise Bill Hawking. His mother and mine brought up the rear. I waved across the low, stone wall that separated the houses, but instantly felt silly; waving seemed far too cheery for such a sombre occasion. Yet Mrs

Dyminge didn't seem to mind.

"Rosa, dear, how *wonderful* to see you! And Samuel, too! And these must be the twins," she broke free of her escort and half-ran, half-stumbled in a loose gait across her gravel garden to reach us.

Mrs Dyminge must have been at least eighty but she was still straight-backed and her white hair was still thick and escaping all attempts to subdue it in the sea wind.

"I've been absolutely *dying* to meet them."

I may have gone a little pink at her choice of words, but she seemed un-fazed. In fact, she seemed rather on the happy side of fine.

"Golly, aren't they divine!" She exclaimed. "I'd have loved to babysit, if only I didn't have to go to this *thing*.." She paused, as if searching for the right words for her husband's funeral. "You know .. this *sad* thing."

I glanced at my mother for help, but she only shook her elegantly be-hatted head, enigmatically.

"But never mind," the Merry Widow continued cheerfully, "it will all be over soon and we can have a lovely party."

I don't think there was a person there who didn't look a touch uncomfortable.

"And who is this pretty girl?" Mrs Dyminge even greeted Verity with joy. "I don't think we've met, dear. I do like your hat. Is it a Millicent?"

A Millicent being a hat that my mother, Millicent Stone (a fashionable milliner in her day), had made back in the Dark Ages when everybody wore hats.

"Come on, Frances," my father came over, retrieved Mrs Dyminge and began steering her in the direction of the car. "Time to make a move."

We all obeyed him simultaneously, with some relief.

"Yes, it is," Verity suddenly spoke words out loud, all by herself. "It's vintage Millicent. How frightfully clever of you to notice. She's so *out*, she's *in*, you know."

Behind me, my brother sniggered.

Anyhow, we progressed to the church in Hassels village. The Union Jack draped over the coffin had suggested some sort of army presence, but there was none; no crossed swords, nothing. The men from the funeral directors disappeared into thin air once the car was parked, as if they, too, had expected a formal military send-off. Which left hardly enough hands to bear the coffin from the car. Yes, I said it was sad. My father and Bill Hawking took one end, then Sam was conscripted to the other. Being quite strong, I was about to lend a shoulder, when a bald, middle-aged man in an RAF uniform volunteered himself. I'd never seen so many gongs on one jacket.

"Thank you, Gabriel dear. So glad you could make it," Mrs Dyminge smiled broadly.

"So sad," the man murmured. "Such a loss. Will be deeply missed."

She seemed rather taken aback by such sentiments and hesitated in the church porch looking confused, as if not sure what else might be required from her. I averted my eyes and busied myself with the pram; she was evidently losing her marbles and it was painful to see.

"Hello, Frances."

She turned to greet an old man in a wheelchair.

"Peter! Oh, Peter," she cried. "Guy's gone. Did you know?"

He reached up and took her hand.

"I did. You sent me a card, old thing."

"Did I?"

"Mm. Gabe and I were dashed sorry to hear the news. How are you bearing up?"

That blank look crossed her face again and then she smiled,

"All the better for seeing you, Peter. Shall we dance?"

He gave a loud snort of laughter.

"I'm afraid my dancing days are done, Frances, but you can wheel me in, if you like." She took hold of his chair. "Look to your laurels, [11]Stirling Moss."

They disappeared into the darkness of the church and Sam and I eyed one another.

"I hope I die before I get old," he said. "They're all completely barking."

I had to agree.

The service was simply pitiful: the place was freezing – despite the curtain I was wearing, topped off with my fox fur coat – hardly anyone was there and the with-it, young vicar had obviously never met the Major. Then, my father over-compensated by singing the hymns in such a bellowing voice that it was a relief when he woke the twins up and I had to take them out in disgrace. It was dispiriting, somehow. Especially because the Major had been a man of such spirit.

However, that was when things began to take an even stranger turn. Yes, I was wheeling my bawling babies around ranks of gravestones carved with the name of Dyminge, rocking the pram back and forth, when the specific oddness that had, so far, hung around the thin shoulders of Mrs Dyminge, started to become general. To begin with, a flash of white caught my eye. It was moving, in a darting fashion, between the grey branches of bare, winter shrubs and trees. I thought it might be a dove, except that I wasn't sure how much darting doves do. It seemed to be circling the church in a low-lying manner. I'd learnt to keep the pram on the go if I wanted to quieten Jessica and Benjamin, so I was also going round and round the church, my breath steaming in the February cold. Yet, every time that I looked up, there it was; that flash of white in a sombre, grey day. In the end, I lost patience.

"Come out, come out, whoever you are!"

There was a rustle and a scuttle and the interloper disappeared; diving for cover I supposed. I was intrigued, so I wheeled the pram past the coffin-shaped hole in the ground that had been prepared for the Major and out to the road beyond the church. I looked up and down the road, but all was quiet; that thick, winter quiet that feels so tangible that you could stick a fork in and pull out a chunk. There were just a few cars parked against the narrow pavement: my Hillman Husky, my parents' ancient Crossley, a lovely maroon Citroen DS, a plain green van and a Ford Cortina. A couple of bikes were propped up against the church wall. The empty funeral car had obviously gone home for lunch.

Behind me, Verity Flinders was standing by the church door. She was blowing her nose with a black handkerchief, like one of those mourners one hears about in more emotional parts of the world, who has been rented for the day. Honestly! Others of our sparse funeral party were starting to emerge from the church now, too, and I sighted my mother by the empty grave, where she stood alone with her thoughts.

"Sorry about the noise," I whispered. "I think Dad's singing disturbed them."

"His singing would waken the dead," she whispered back, promptly covering her mouth with a gloved hand when she thought about the company she was keeping.

"The massed ranks of Dyminges," I couldn't help laughing, recalling that [12]Stanley Spencer painting where the dead clamber out of their graves in their nightshirts, "emerging from the earth to still the voice of the heathen Jew."

"Ssh, Rosa. There's a time and a place."

"Sorry."

"Lovely service," the old boy in the wheelchair appeared at our side, pushed by the RAF veteran and we both nodded, over-enthusiastically.

"Rosa, you remember Lord Peter Upshott, Tristram's father? And Air Chief Marshal Sir Gabriel Adair." My mother took a flying leap at the introductions and it all came out in a great rush.

That was who the man in the chair was. We'd met, but not forever and a day. He was sort of family. My mother's younger sister, Kathleen, had married Lord Upshott's son, Tristram. However, I didn't remember his father being at the wedding. No, Lord Upshott was more of a mythical character to me; my mother's old employer and Major Dyminge's partner in so many adventures. It was difficult to reconcile all that with this thin, old man in a good suit and a wheelchair. He was like a heron folded into a sitting position.

"Of course, I was only a child when we last met, but I remember you *well*," I lied.

"Millie's little girl, all grown up." He exclaimed, politely. "And these must be your grandchildren, Millie.."

My mother – a tiny, elegant woman in her late fifties – had, long ago, learnt a certain 'savoir faire' with the upper classes (rising from poverty to become the country's top milliner had required her to do so), but something ambiguous flickered in her eyes at that moment. The mask slipped a fraction. Was it insecurity, or snobbery that I could read on her face? Suddenly I knew that she would do *anything* not to have to admit that her grandchildren were born out of wedlock in front of this man. My hackles rose. What was so wonderful about her own match with a Jewish market trader that I should have to feel inferior in front of a couple of old queens? (I'd heard the rumours . . and besides, I'd been to drama school.) Would she disown her own grandchildren if she could?

She was saved from further embarrassment by the arrival of my father with the grieving widow safely tucked under his wing. He parked her between Bill Hawking and my brother, who had been friends since childhood, and came over to us.

"Has anybody seen the undertakers?" He asked in as low a voice as he could muster.

"I think they might have gone," I replied. "I couldn't see their car in the road."

"What? Are we supposed to cart him back out to the grave? I thought that was their job."

"Well, the funeral bier's got wheels, hasn't it? Perhaps we could roll him out," I suggested.

"Poor Frances," my mother sighed. "How undignified."

"I'm not sure she'll mind too much," I glanced over to where she seemed to be sharing a joke with the younger element.

"Well, we have to do something, fast," my father pointed out. "We can't stand out here chatting forever. Look. Your Reverend is on his way and Major Dyminge is still lying all by himself in the church."

The with-it young vicar was, indeed, picking his way through the graves towards us, prayer book in hand.

"Come on, lads. Time to roll up your sleeves again," my father bellowed across the churchyard, collecting the Air Marshal on his way.

"It just gets worse and worse," I muttered into the pram.

I was right. A shout went up from the church.

"Oh, Jerzy," my mother sighed. "Can that man not use a normal tone of voice for once in his life?"

But other voices began to join in.

"What the.."

"He's not.."

"What d'you mean he's not..? That's his coffin, isn't it?"

"But where..?"

I'm afraid I abandoned the pram where it stood and dashed into the church.

"What's happened? What's happened?"

"He's gone." Sam had his camera up to his eye. "He's been coffin-snatched."

"Oh, my *God*."

It was true. The Union Jack lay tumbled on the floor and the lid of the coffin was open. Major Dyminge had vanished.

4. INTRODUCTIONS

Old pals were dropping like flies, but Dyminge was a different kettle of fish, to mix metaphors with wild abandon. Communication between the two of us had always been sketchy when we were apart; he hated the telephone so, and we mixed in such different circles; Gabriel and I happily settled in Norfolk and Dyminge down in Kent. Yet, when push came to shove, that had never mattered. The old boy was a constant in my life; just knowing that he was down by the sea, beavering away on odd projects of his own. It had seemed enough to hear from Frances every now and again and to imagine them all, a superannuated team of adventurers, washed up on the shore together.

The news of his death hit me hard, I admit it. Yes, he'd been some years older than myself and I knew that life had not always been easy for him .. but he was a tough character, you know. Tenacious. Wouldn't countenance any financial help when one offered it. Bit one's hand off, point of fact. But he was like nobody else in my life and I suppose that meant that when I was with him a different part of myself emerged blinking into the world. I think that he encouraged something in me that was halfway worthwhile. I felt peculiarly wronged by his death (he had died in his sleep, apparently, felled by a massive stroke). He should have held on harder, kicked up more of a storm, given Death a better run for his money. Because, if Guy Dyminge had gone, then he'd taken that worthwhile part of Peter Upshott with him.

Gabriel had driven me down in my Citroen, singing tunes by the Beatles and the [13]Kinks. The Air Marshal has always been a fiend for a bit of popular culture (and the sweet man likes to keep my spirits up). My breathing is on the iffy side these days, the cigarettes having affected my lungs as well as my legs, so I didn't join in.

Frances seemed to be taking things well. The service was a gloomy number, but what can one expect from these do's? I've been to enough of them and they all make one want to become a Hindu, or an Orthodox Greek; I don't know, something with a bit more colour and oomph to it, a bit more smoke and mirrors. Anyway, my old housemaid – shouldn't really mention that when she's been a star in the fashion firmament for so long – Millie, was there, looking as chic as ever and barely a day older than when we last met. Of course, she's a relation by marriage now (although I was *desperately* hoping that she wouldn't ask me about my son Tristram because I can't help feeling ashamed that I've absolutely no idea where he is, or what he's doing). And her offspring: a rather eye-catching, courteous boy and considerably older daughter, Rosa, the latter of whom I remember as a precocious child (in a not entirely attractive way), but who is now an earth mother in a flowing purple velvet robe and flea-bitten fox fur and only requiring bare feet to be one of the [14]larger Pre-Raphaelite women holding a pomegranate. Christ .. what's the matter with me? I'm burbling on like the campest old gossip when all I really want to do is to get to the crux of the matter. Which is that he'd departed. I mean *really* departed. Guy Dyminge had upped and left his own funeral.

It was strangely upsetting, whichever way one looked at it. My first thought was straight out of a [15]Hammer Horror. Was Dyminge actually dead when they nailed him into his coffin? Had the flag draped on top masked the sound of his frantically beating fists? It didn't bear thinking about and yet one couldn't *not* think about it. I felt an urgent desire to discuss this point with somebody, but who? I suppose that Dyminge, himself, would have been my candidate of choice. I decided I'd do better to keep quiet.

"Oh my *God*. You don't think that the Major wasn't dead, after all? That he'd been in some kind of a coma and then woken up just before he was about to be buried alive?" It was Millicent's daughter, Rosa.

A chorus of disapproval met her remark:

"Oh Rosa, how *could* you?"

"*What* a thing to say."

"What if Frances were to hear you'd said that?"

"Engage brain before mouth, bozo."

I made up my mind to speak to her at the wake. If there was still going to *be* a wake.

◆ ◆ ◆

A friend of my parents had died, ok? So, what I was going to do was to bum a lift down with my sister, show my face at the funeral for the minimum amount of time I could get away with, borrow Bill's wheels and then take this bird – the daughter of an advertising supremo I'd done some work for – to Romney Marshes, or Dungeness. I had it all planned. My idea was to do an [16]Ansel Adams on the wildest parts of Kent and then stick something as Sixties as this chick in front of it. What's the word? Juxtaposition? [17]Parkinson may have done it, I don't really know, but I thought I could try something newer with it, less formal and posed than the old guard, then flog it to the fashion mags. Or put a ciggie in her hand and use it to advertise fresh air.

Then it turned out I'd be expected to stick it out at the wake afterwards, too, but that really *was* a drag, so I cornered Bill after the service, the first chance I got.

"Hey, Hawking, I can still have your Morris Minor, right?"

"Hello to you, too, mate."

"Yeah, yeah. But the Morris is still in the frame?"

"It's back at your parents' if that's what you mean."

"Aargh; you didn't bring it here, you bozo?"

"No, I came with Auntie Frances. She needs looking after."

"Certainly does. By men in white coats."

"What did you say?"

Bill was like the old lady's grandson (though no relation), and he was touchy about her. His granddad had been her old gardener before her house fell off a cliff and there'd been some slippage in the status quo.

"Nothing, Hawking." I reassured him. "Take it easy."

Verity sidled up to me.

"Hi Sam," she cooed, hooking her arm in mine, "who's your friend?"

"Bill Hawking," he introduced himself, stepping forward like he was going to give her hand a shake. "Sam and I went to the village school together."

"This is Verity," I disengaged my arm. "She's a London bird, daughter of an actual tycoon in the advertising industry; she doesn't want to hear about village schools, Hawking."

"I'm Sam's model," she said, and I could tell he was impressed.

"Yeah, and we're going to do a recce today, which is why we need the car before the bloody light goes.."

Old Mrs Dyminge suddenly appeared at my elbow, smiling in that un-hinged way she'd been doing all day.

"Nice service," I said.

"Was it?"

"Fab," Verity contributed.

"I just can't get over how pretty you look in a Millicent, dear. As pretty as a picture. I can't think why the younger generation don't seem to want to wear hats when they could look so darling in them."

Bill, Verity and the old lady all laughed together, while I wondered just how long it was going to take before the Major went into the ground and we could split. My father was obviously thinking along the same lines:

"Come on lads," he came thundering past. "Time to roll up your sleeves again."

I didn't mind shifting the coffin if it meant we could get a move on. But it turned out that wasn't going to be necessary.

The lid of the coffin was open, we could see that for sure the second we went back into the church. I ran down the aisle, guessing how the light was falling; I didn't need a light meter. I snapped the empty box from all sides.

My sister was close behind.

"What's happened? What's happened?"

"He's gone," I said, clicking away, mind on my job. "He's been coffin-snatched."

Yes . . I stopped and gave it a bit of thought . . *Coffin-snatched*! This had the makings of a genuine scoop. I could see the headline in the *Daily Kentish News* with my photo underneath. Or, maybe I should try one of the Nationals; you never knew, if it was a slow day they might use it. I'd give them all a try.

Then Rosa came out with a real gem, something about the Major not being dead after all and waking up just as he was going to be buried alive. Wow!

"Engage brain before mouth," I said, automatically.

But what I was really thinking was, never mind *Coffin-snatched*, what about *Buried Alive*? Bull's-eye! Which newspaper was gonna turn that baby down?

◆ ◆ ◆

"Just one more push, old girl," he'd said. "Stand up straight. Find something black to wear, if you must. Keep smiling through."

"But you won't be there. How can I possibly do it all if you won't be there, Guy?"

"Don't be a weed, Frances; we've had far worse times

than this."

"But, that's the point. We had them together, don't you see?"

"Oh, good grief, this is wearing thin, it really is. I mean we've had days of this whining and wailing behaviour. We're British, Frances, show a bit of decorum. Nobody wants to see a tear-stained face at a funeral."

"Don't they?"

"No. Well, I certainly don't. Didn't."

I crawled out from under the bedclothes and sat up, pushing my hair from my face. It was the day of Guy's funeral and, if I didn't make a colossal effort, I was going to let him down. It all felt quite impossible.

There was no need to open the curtains to know that it was as black as night outside, despite it being seven in the morning by the bedside clock. Late winter; a spiteful season when winter's claims to spring proved nought but lies, and my husband of over fifty years had died. It shouldn't have come as a surprise at his age, yet it did. Guy had suffered periods of debilitating illness for some little while, yet nothing that had indicated the coming of a fatal stroke. I had tried to get him to Doctor Morris, but he had assured me that he was simply suffering the usual privations of old age. Should I have pushed more and made him get seen? Pushing Guy had always been such an impossible task and old age did nothing to change that fact. He was himself to the last: difficult, impatient, involved in things of which I knew nothing. A law unto Guy Dyminge. So, yes, the end had been swift and shocking and I could make no sense of it. Especially when he kept coming back.

"I thought you were dead, Guy? The doctor said so, I'm almost sure of it. He told me that you'd gone and then he gave me these pretty green and black pills."

"I am. Probably. No, I'm sure I am. That's why you're so upset, Frances."

"So .. it's right that I should be upset?"

"Yes, of course. Just don't overdo it, old girl. Try to see

things as they are for once, eh?"

"You're gone, but you're not gone. Is that it? Will you be living on in my heart sort of thing?"

There was no reply.

The last however-long-it-had-been-since-Guy-departed had been a true black hole, from which I could retrieve little, if anything. Millicent and Jerzy had been as kind as ever and my Sweet William had come to visit, but most of it had vanished. I don't know who arranged the funeral; I don't *think* it was me. But funeral there was, and it would appear that I must attend.

Some kind soul had laid out a black skirt and jacket on the Lloyd Loom chair and a lovely dark green scarf. They were brand new and much finer than anything that I possessed. I put them on. Everything was so strange; even my dressing-table looked utterly unfamiliar. Where was my silver-backed hairbrush? My bottle of Yardley's *English Lavender*? Surely the can of hairspray by the mirror, the pressed powder and the pink lipstick weren't mine? No matter. I sat down and applied them all, as if to somebody else's old face and hair. Then I went into the kitchen and made a strong cup of Nescafé – about half a cup, to leave room for the gin – and waited for it to cool down a touch before I took my pills.

After that it seemed to be fairly plain sailing. There were two beaming babies and a girl was wearing an exquisite Millicent. Um.. Peter Upshott was doing a lot of sitting down. [18]*The Lord's my shepherd*, of course, and then something I hadn't heard before, called [19]*Coom baa yar*, which the vicar appeared to be jolly enthusiastic about. And then Guy's body disappeared from his coffin. And I conked out.

5. THE NEW INVESTIGATION

Mrs Dyminge had fainted in the church and we were all at a loss as to what to do next, until my mother took charge.

"Rosa, get the twins into the car and then come and help with Frances. Samuel, put that blessed camera down and go and find a phone-box. Call the police and tell them to come to St Aethelred's straight away. Jerzy, guard the coffin until they come and don't let anybody touch anything"

My mother was at her best in a calamity.

"Yes, Sam," I added, "stop taking pictures, you horrible ghoul. You should be ashamed of yourself."

Then Verity piped up:

"Art knows no boundaries," she declared. "A true artist is never afraid to cause offence."

"Bravo!" It was Lord Upshott. "Aren't the Young wonderful?"

I'd forgotten that he was still there and had no idea whether he was being rhetorical, or expected an answer to his question. I wheeled my children back to the car feeling suitably old and bourgeois.

I missed the arrival of the police – in a pale blue mini, apparently – because I'd been ordered to drive Mrs Dyminge back and put her to bed in my parents' spare bedroom. Once she'd been carried to my car she came round fast, but her speech was slurred and groggy and I was worried that she might have had a stroke, like her late husband.

"No, dear. No shtroke."

"If you're sure? We could always drop off at the hospital. I don't mind at all."

"No hoshpital. Absholutely fine."

So, I drove her straight back to Shore House, although, once out of the car, she tried to stumble back to her own home and I had to divert her on the front path.

"Really, Mrs Dyminge, you shouldn't be on your own at this time. Not when you've had such a terrible shock. Let us take care of you."

"Shock?"

"Yes." She didn't appear to understand me. "The Major disappearing and everything. It's shocked us all; goodness knows how shocking it must have been for you."

"Oh, don't worry about that," she patted me on the arm and then leant on my shoulder to whisper. "Guy's not gone at all, dear Rosha. No, he's shtill here." She gave a girlish giggle and put her finger to her mouth. "But .. sshhhh."

She was so convincing in her madness (there seemed no other word for it) that, for a moment, I actually believed her.

"You can't really mean it?" I was wide-eyed. "Oh, Mrs Dyminge , was he in a coma? About to be buried alive in his coffin when he came to and realised his dreadful fate? Truly?"

I swear, she straightened her back and looked at me as if I were the one losing the plot:

"No, dear, come come. I'm afraid the Major passed away last week .. at least, I think it was last week. Anyway, he's definitely dead. I know it's hard, but we must face facts. Now. Let's go in, shall we?" She nodded towards the door. "I feel it *must* be time for a drink."

I discovered a pair of brand-new, metal cots beside the bed in my parents' room, which gave me pause for thought. If I'd been allocated a spare bedroom and a proper night's sleep, I couldn't help feeling grateful. The ructions over my pregnancy had got us off to a bad start. Maybe my parents had decided it was time to play Granny and Grandpa. It struck me that I'd reached the stage where I was more than willing to swallow my pride, if it meant an unbroken night's sleep.

Jessica and Benjamin had been fed, changed and put down to sleep – and Mrs Dyminge was on her second gin and tonic – when everyone else arrived. Personally, I felt completely shattered by the events of the day. I rummaged in my handbag for some scent to dispel the smell of nappies that I felt sure trailed in my wake, spritzed *Fracas* everywhere I could think of, and went hunting for some funeral baked meats. I was in the kitchen, just taking the lids off a stack of cake tins when I heard voices.

"This is very kind, Mr Stone. I rather thought the wake might have been cancelled, what with one thing and another.." It was Lord Upshott's uniformed friend.

"Man must eat," my father declared.

"And you've come all this way, Gabriel," added my mother.

"Of course, there's nothing like death to give one a ravenous appetite," said Lord Upshott. And then, "Whoops. Sorry Frances, I didn't see you there."

"Peter! Dearesht Peter. What a lovely shurprishe."

I dropped a tin of flapjacks on the kitchen table and scooted into the drawing room, not wishing to miss a thing.

"Shouldn't you be in bed, Frances?" My mother suggested.

"Bed? Pooh. Don't want to mish a party."

My mother gave me one of her looks; one of her 'now look what you've done' looks. Well, I couldn't see how it was my fault. Nobody had told me to keep Mrs Dyminge away from the gin. But Lord Upshott seemed oblivious.

"That's the spirit, Frances. I can't believe how well you're taking all this, y'know. You're a lesson to us all, quite frankly."

I decided to take Mrs Dyminge's example – seeing as she was such a lesson to us all – and poured myself a large one before circulating with the bottle. It looked like Sam and Verity had managed to do a bunk. Bill Hawking and his mother, Sadie, had joined us and a couple of old men from the local fishing fraternity, the Major's friends from the Coastguard pub. It still made for a sparse attendance when one considered how much food my father had prepared. He was famous for his enormous spreads, but had really gone to town on this one: every kind of cold cut and delicious chutney and pickle imaginable, smoked salmon, tiny cucumber sandwiches, golden sausage rolls and latkes and that was before the contents of the cake tins emerged. Someone had to make a start on it all, so I piled my plate high and went to sit on the window seat overlooking the bay.

It was all of four o'clock now, but night had set in and the Cap Gris Nez lighthouse blinked at us out of the vast black. Our small party seemed tired and glad of the food and warmth, as if we'd travelled far and finally found shelter. People chatted in a polite, desultory way, interspersing their conversation with longer pauses than usual, while they ate and, no doubt, pondered the events of the afternoon in their minds (probably reluctant to voice their real thoughts while Mrs Dyminge was sitting on the sofa). Mysteries are tiring and this one had a painful edge to it. Assuming that he really *was* dead, then Major Dyminge should have been quietly laid to rest. It was so wrong that his body should be somewhere unknown, presumably being handled by persons unknown. So wrong and so horrible at the same time. And why? Why on earth should anyone *want* the corpse of an old man? What would they *do* with it?

"It's pretty nasty, isn't it?" It was Lord Upshott, wheeling himself up to join me at the window seat. "Disturbing and all that."

"It keeps going round and round in my head," I said. "I mean, I know that the body is nothing after death, in terms of the real person.. I'm not religious.. but I hate it, anyhow. It's so *wrong*."

He crumbled the last golden flakes of his sausage roll between long, bent fingers, looking thoughtful.

"Actually, I don't agree that the body *is* nothing, you know. I saw my share of the dead in the war - the first show - but I could never get used to them lying about like so many pieces of meat; they deserve the same respect as the living. Perhaps more. They can't stand up for themselves, after all." He set his plate down next to me. "And Dyminge was such a brave, honest soldier all his life. There was nobody like him. He would save a man's life in a twinkling of an eye and get cross if you praised him for it."

I took a gulp of my gin and tonic, feeling it zoom straight to my brain; tea would have been better for an exhausted mother, but Mrs Dyminge had led me astray.

"Yes, he was a good man. You may not know this, but he saved me from drowning when I was a child. He did his best to save my uncle, too," I could sense myself becoming maudlin, as I always did when I thought of the death of my Uncle Albert – the very worst period in my life so far. I suppose that, in trying to rid myself of that familiar ache, I overcompensated and my voice came out high and falsely bright:

"Always assuming the Major really *is* dead."

Our eyes met.

"Ah .. the buried alive thesis," he replied, quietly. "I must admit that something similar had crossed my mind."

"Really?" I'd thought it was just me saying the unspeakable out loud; stumbling about in my usual tactless manner.

"Mm. You never know .. well, *I* don't. I mean to say, people are always quick to seize the sensible option, but I'm a great believer in keeping an open mind. And Guy Dyminge ..

he could be a surprising sort of chap. Wouldn't put it past him to hop out of his own coffin and take to the hills."

I was agog.

"*Really?*"

"Yet, why wouldn't he want to hang around, I ask myself? That surprises me, quite frankly. One would think he'd like to say hello to his old pals, take a glass at his own wake. Tell me, Rosa," he leant forward in his chair, as if we'd become conspirators, "how much of your mother do you have in you?"

"Um.. fifty percent?"

"That's not what I mean at all. No. Bravery, derring-do, get up and go, sheer bloody gumption; that's what I mean."

I looked over at her, organising cups of tea in her smart little black suit and sky-high heels. Steering Mrs Dyminge away from the gin bottle and pushing black coffee on her. It's always problematical to imagine your parents when they were young and without you, but my mother was a small powerhouse and had, most likely, always been so. Even when she'd been a parlour maid sweeping the stairs. We were chalk and cheese, of course, and utterly unlike each other in every way, but he didn't have to know that.

"Gumption is my middle name, Lord Upshott."

"Excellent," he replied. "You can call me Peter. Charming scent, by the way."

There was a hiatus while Mrs Dyminge was taken upstairs to lie down and we all hushed and made sympathetic faces at her but, once she was gone, the room visibly relaxed, as everybody felt set free to discuss the extraordinary vanishing of her husband.

"What did the police say?"

"Oh, you know the police. They never give much away if they can help it."

"If only we hadn't left him on his own in the church."

"Mmm. But it's not the kind of thing you expect to happen, is it?"

"And the newspapers turning up, too. How on earth do

you think they got wind of it?"

"Who knows. Poor Frances."

"Yes, *poor* Frances."

Peter and I returned to our chat, cloistered from the rest of the party by our position at the window-seat in the far corner.

"I really do think that Frances is made of sterner stuff than they seem to think. Just because one is old doesn't mean one has no backbone," he said. "Rather the reverse, actually."

"Well," I wasn't quite sure how to put this to my new friend, "she's been a little .. changeable. A little .. all over the place. Not doolally, exactly – I wouldn't want to suggest that – but sort of up in the air, you know?"

"Oh, that's just Frances. That's just what makes her such a darling."

I wasn't entirely convinced, but never mind.

"Now," he said, firmly. "Are we agreed that we need to look into all of this? That we can't just sit back while the old man is knocking about, dead or alive?"

"Yes," it came out in a fervent hiss of assent. "Oh, my goodness, *yes*." I couldn't remember the last time anybody had asked me to look into anything and, really, there was nothing I liked more in the whole wide world. "You can count on me, Peter."

"Wonderful. We may not have a lot of time to talk because I can't see this shindig going on much longer; it's not exactly choc a bloc. Gabriel and I are staying at a hotel for the night – I'll give you the telephone number – but it's occurred to me that this may be a top-hole opportunity for a bit of a snoop, what with Frances being out of the way. What about you nipping over to the Dyminges' cottage at some point this evening and finding out whether he was up to anything? He was always beavering away on peculiar projects of his own, you know and he had a hell of a brain; sharp as a tack when he was in his own ball court. What do you say?"

I was a little confused, what with tacks and ball courts,

but got the general idea.

"You'd like me to be your eyes and ears?"

"Bingo!"

Owing to my rapidly dwindling stores of energy, there was no delaying the start of my new investigation; I must go while still fired up with excitement. Which meant that Peter and Gabriel had no sooner said their goodbyes than I ducked out of Shore House and jumped over the low wall to Coast Cottage. I'd brought a torch and the Dyminge's spare key, which had hung on a hook in my parents' kitchen since time immemorial.

Nobody had drawn the curtains, so I could see my way in clearly. The front door opened directly onto the small parlour (as Mrs D always referred to it). Coal was stacked up in the fireplace and everything looked tidy and shipshape, although there were two vases of dead flowers on the mantelpiece, either side of a collection of knick-knacks. I lanced the torch over them: ochre pollen from shrivelled lilies had spotted the cheap, souvenir ceramics from various seaside towns, a well-polished silver-plate award from a crime-writing society and a bright yellow, glass egg cup with daisies picked out in white. I caught my breath. Uranium glass, if I wasn't much mistaken. Still, this was no time to get side-tracked.

I passed through the kitchen – somewhat less tidy than the parlour, with cups and plates stacked up in the sink and an empty bottle of gin glinting, greenly. There were two glass-paned back doors, one to the narrow, outdoor space that divided cottage from cliff, where I knew the bins were kept, and one, the window obscured by a drooping, flowery, curtain affair, that led to Major Dyminge's inner sanctum. The door was not locked; however, it was at that stage that I began to feel like a trespasser. The Major's workshop was common knowledge, yet I'd have been willing to bet that nobody had ever visited it. Possibly - recalling the Major - not even his wife.

It was pitch black and I couldn't find a light switch, so I aimed my torch. A red, tartan rug had been tacked against the window, but it was cold and the sea somehow made its presence felt more than it had in the rest of the cottage. I swung the torch upwards and realised that the roof was made of corrugated iron, nailed on none too well, and I was in a kind of outhouse. The place might have been snug when the single armchair was drawn up to the little gas fire, I supposed. But not now; now it had that extra forlorn atmosphere that close, working spaces have when they've been abandoned by their people. Not only that, but there was a definite sense of work interrupted, of flow cut short. On the Major's desk, papers – weighted down by a ship in a bottle – shifted in a draught. A stack of magazines was coated in the ash from a saucer, against which the Major's pipe still leant, as if buried in windblown sand. No, nobody else had come visiting. I was the only trespasser.

There had, evidently, been a lot of work going on. I wondered whether the Major had been working on several projects before his heart attack. He'd been writing, that was for sure; many pages of foolscap were covered with a crabbed squiggle that would have been difficult to decipher even if every third or fourth word had not been crossed out with black ink. There was a title, however, deeply underlined. *The Something, Something of Radar Engineering and its Application to Something.* Interesting. Then there were lots of drawings that seemed to have been done with a compass and a black pen with the finest of nibs. There were circles swirling outwards at different widths to one another: some with inches between each arc and others where the space between the circles was so tiny as to be on the verge of becoming an India rubber ball of ink. I rifled through them, frowning with the effort to understand.

Several disembowelled radio sets had been stacked on top of one another beside the desk, the largest an old, mahogany number from the days when a wireless was a substantial piece of furniture. I'd sold one or two of these dinosaurs in the shop and they fascinated me. They looked like time machines which, with a flick of a dial, might transport one from Stornoway to Ceylon. There were headsets, too, all jumbled together in a basket on the floor. I stooped to pick one up and studied it by torchlight, mystified by its size and grandeur. It was a crazy circlet of many wires, spiked and sculptural. If it had been a crown, it would have been a crown of thorns. I bent down again, to see what he had stored beneath his desk, and discovered an old television set and a melamine container full of those round pads that people stick on their corns and a woman's bathing cap that had been cut into several pieces.

It was all highly thought-provoking, yet the strangest items of all were still to come. I could so easily have missed them because they were well-hidden under a giant welder's helmet. I just lifted the visor, absent-mindedly, because my thoughts were full of black circles and spiky wires, and chanced to find them hiding underneath. Five little, yellow-glass bottles with glass stoppers, lined up on an ebony-lacquered tea tray. They looked so .. feminine in that overtly male room. Actually, do you know what I thought of? Sherlock Holmes and the Limehouse opium dens, Chinese men with pigtails and the sweet lassitude of opiates beside the stinking Thames. Rather unkind, really, when one thinks how the Major had saved my life (did I tell you?), to instantly suspect him of being a drug fiend. Nevertheless, since I was in full spying mode and quite unable to stop myself, I immediately overcame any qualms I might have had over sticking my nose into unknown narcotic substances and removed the first stopper. Wow! Now *that* would never have crossed my mind, not in a month of Sundays.

It was *Chanel No 5*. I've a good sense of smell - sharper since my pregnancy, in fact - and there could be no doubt about it; that bouquet of aldehydes (that smell like a whoosh of sparkling air) and French flowers. The liquid in the second bottle was brown and I approached it with a little more trepidation (brown being a colour that would haunt any mother of two children who have just started on solids). I needn't have worried, because it was *Youth-Dew*, Estee Lauder's smoky concoction of cloves and burnt toffee apples. What wonderful taste in perfume Major Dyminge was turning out to have had. My nose was pretty sure that the rest of the bottles contained Guerlain's *Vol de Nuit*, *Diorella* and Yardley's *English Lavender*. How baffling. The association of the Major with the world of fine fragrance was like barging into Buckingham Palace and finding the Queen knocking back pints of Guinness. It just confirmed my theory that you could never really know anybody.

I replaced the welder's helmet over the bottles, wondering whether I was doing the right thing. I mean, what if Mrs Dyminge knew nothing of her husband's predilections? What if the Major's surprising hobby un-manned him in her eyes, so to speak? Yet, I wouldn't have liked to have taken them; I stocked a selection of vintage perfumes in the Arcanium and knew how costly they were. It would have been stealing and, anyway, perhaps she might grow to enjoy them in the future, herself. Once she'd got over the shock.

At that point, I sensed that my knees were about to crumple with exhaustion. I must put all thoughts of perfume from my mind, along with open coffins and corpses roaming the Kent countryside. I grabbed a couple of circular pictures and the manuscript about radar and went home to keep my long-awaited appointment with sleep.

6. MUSHROOMS

I went to the phone-box in Hassels High Street, dialled 999 for the fuzz, gave them the essentials and hung the receiver back up on the hook, rootling around in my trouser pocket for coins. Then I got the number of the local paper from the operator, told them I'd drop the film round later for them to develop and extracted a promise that I'd have exclusive rights if it went national. This was a first for me and I wasn't sure whether I was getting it right, but I tried to sound like an old hand. The man on the other end was one of those wheezing, Kent blokes with a seen-it-all attitude: like corpses disappearing from their coffins halfway through the funeral was all in a day's work for Hassels village.

I returned to the church and found that the village policeman had arrived in a blue mini and was taking a couple of statements – not mine because I was itching to get away with Verity – when, who should turn up but the Press, with a photographer with a damn fine camera, a [20]Graflex Super Speed Graphic.

"Hey, hey, hey!" I tried to intercept the first one on his way into the churchyard, but they both carried on walking, as if I weren't there.

I lowered my voice, "Listen, mate. I'm Sam Stone. It was *me* who rang your editor and gave him this story. Listen.. I've got the rights on the picture. He promised me."

"Who promised you, lad? If it was old Benny on the

blower, he's the caretaker. D'you think the editor answers the phone of a Monday lunchtime?" he sneered.

"Too busy down the Red Dragon," the other laughed.

I wasn't giving up without a fight.

"Oy, stop them!" I shouted in mock-alarm. "They're journalists. The local paper, maybe. Someone *do* something."

The policeman didn't seem remotely interested, but Dad heard the noise and bellowed down the aisle, from where he was guarding the empty coffin:

"What's going on? Newspapers, is it?"

"Jerzy? What's this?" Mum appeared by the church door, taking stock of the situation fast (as she does). "Oh, *no* you don't. We're not having Major Dyminge's funeral desecrated by gawkers. How dare you? Think of the poor widow. You've got a nerve just turning up like this to a private function. Who tipped you off, I'd like to know?"

The photographer simply stuck his camera over her head (not difficult, seeing as she's a dwarf), and used his flash.

It was time to split, before it all got even more heavy.

We hitched a lift along the coast with a lorry delivering something to the [21]new nuclear power station at Dungeness. I'll say this for Verity, she didn't whine about the wheels; in fact, hitching seemed to give her a kick. I was relieved to see the cloud lift as we got nearer and a bright blue winter sky emerge; I've noticed before that Dungeness seems to have its own weather system. Windy, though.

"Gosh," Verity clambered up and down the ridges of shingle after me, "I wish I hadn't worn this hat."

"Don't know why you did, you bozo," and I turned round, catching her by surprise, snatched the hat off her and threw it at the sea, like a plastic frisbee.

"Sa..am."

I ruffled her yellow hair and she couldn't prevent herself from looking pleased.

"You're much more beautiful without it, girl."

She wasn't, actually. That beautiful. But she had a certain elfin, child-like vibe going, along with an edge of forlorn darkness, that was attractive. She was small, for a professional model, but I'd been looking for a [22]Shrimp to my Bailey and this one might just work, I thought. Temporarily. Because the light was so good, and I like the sea and we'd escaped that dreary scene, I decided to give her a kiss.

"Oh, Sa..am."

She snuggled in and it was nice; it felt powerful, like I'd made the right decision when I took up photography. I wondered how far she'd go.

I made the most of the couple of light hours we had and snapped her every which way. She was good at it, too; opened her big, grey eyes wide against the sea wind and let her hair go bananas, sank into the shingle and made shapes for the camera. Her cheeks were pink and she really did look pretty. When I thought about the crap she was liable to come up with in conversation, it was excellent to discover that my hunch had been right; that she was a bird who was good at playing.

"Trees, windmills, scare crows," I shouted and she gave it all to the lens.

I even had her against the nuclear power station as the dark came down and all the lights began to blaze into the sea. It felt excellent. Elemental. I wasn't ready to stop.

"Um, Sam. It's getting rather chilly."

I rummaged in my trouser pocket and leered at her.

"I've got something to keep you warm."

She giggled and looked coy.

I tried my jacket pocket. There it was.

"We've got 'shrooms."

"Um.. 'shrooms?"

"Magic mushrooms, you daft bird."

I brought out my dented, tobacco tin full of shrivelled Liberty caps. People think you have to go to Mexico for mushrooms, but I'd picked those beauties on Denge Marsh at the end of the summer. They didn't look much, but they were a hell of a lot cheaper than amphetamines.

"Oh, you mean *psychedelic* mushrooms. Oh, I've had those loads of times."

"Yeah? Then you're up for it? It's going to be one crazy trip with the weird vibe of this place. I mean, would you look at that new black and white-striped lighthouse - if that's not Op Art, then what is? And the nuclear setup? It's the end of the world here, yeah? In more ways than one."

She looked over at the power station and then shivered.

"It's just .. that I'm kind of cold, Sam."

"Man! Are you telling me you'd rather go back to my parents' pad and sip sherry and talk about corpses? Like, really?"

And I picked her up in a great, big hug and swung her about.

"C'mon, Verity. See these fishermen's sheds on the beach? Well, I happen to know that they don't always lock them and some of them have got, like, big soft ropes and nets you could wrap round you to keep out the cold."

I put her down, grabbed her hand and started tugging her up the dunes of shingle, over to where the sheds were scattered here and there among rusty winding gear, just black rectangles in the deepening dark now.

"It's gonna be a *gas*."

And it was. We found ourselves a shed, only it was so dark inside that it was kind of impossible to see when I closed the door, and those ropes were all scratchy and damp to the touch. Bulky, canvas covered objects protruded into my back. I shifted them to make room, then went in for a kiss and cuddle before she started 'Sa . .am'-ing me again. That was nice, but she resisted going any further, so I thought it was a good moment to share the 'shrooms.

We were finally starting to generate some heat when they kicked in.

"Um .. Sam .. um .."

I noticed she was panting and thought, at first, it was passion. So, I carried on.

"NO!" She screamed in my left ear. "It's too dark .. it's horrible .. I hate it .. Let me OUT."

I stumbled to my feet and tried to find the door, but it had gone somewhere.

"Hey, don't sweat; it's alright, Ver."

I was moving incredibly slowly, but the shed was moving too, spinning round and fooling with me while I tried to follow the door. Each time I got to the edge of it, it spun away again.

"Help me," she squeaked. "Help me, Sam."

"Got you, you bastard."

I burst out onto the beach, dropping to my knees before the universe of wonders out there. A full moon had risen and was pulsing, rainbow rings of colour pinging from it like little rockets going to the stars. The heavens were showing their true face.

"Look Ver, it's a bloody miracle," I *had* to share it with her, aware of my own generosity.

She leant on my shoulder, but she seemed to be crying. Was it in awe at the fab colours? At the sight of the sea breathing purple and scarlet breaths at the moon?

"I love you, Ver," I heard myself say. "You're sort of beautiful."

But, mysteriously, she began to run away from me, making a weird honking noise, like a stranded seal, and falling over now and again.

"Come back! Didn't you hear? I love you."

I set off after her. We ran for a while, past the lighthouse and the railway tracks and over to the flooded gravel pits. I thought she was having a laugh, like before. Making pictures for me. That was why I'd brought her there, after all.

When, out of the night, there came a bloody great siren and it wasn't just a noise, it was coloured indigo and felt jagged. Solid. It struck me on the back and sent me flying, but not into the air. It sent me flying into the gravel pit and the freezing water came up to meet me and I let out my breath, but there was nowhere to find another one. It was unbelievably, painfully, icy. I couldn't keep my head above water because the cold came for me, dragging me under.. and that was when I saw it. Its eyes were open and its face was white as a peeled thing. Just before I lost consciousness, I sensed our legs entwine. It was like a jellyfish preparing to suck me up. But it was no jellyfish. Somebody had got into the water before me. Somebody dead.

When I came to, I was off the Ness and inside somewhere and Verity was leaning over me, rubbing at my shoulders with a blanket in an annoying way.

"What happened?" I was wearing somebody else's clothes. "Did I black out? Where are we?"

"You fell in the lake, Sam. I managed to pull you out with a long piece of wood that was lying at the edge and then I brought us to the only place with a light on."

"You mean..?"

"The lighthouse, yes. He's been fab. He's got a telephone and everything and he's rung up your parents and they're on their way now."

"What?" I sat up, shrugging her off with the blanket. "What did you want to go ringing my parents for? Of all people."

Her face fell.

"Well.. I don't know anybody else in Kent. I mean.. did I do the wrong thing, Sam?"

I sighed, getting up from the old armchair I'd been sitting on and testing my arms and legs. They all worked; I was kind of shivery, but alright.

"Never mind. Thanks for getting me out." A terrible thought struck me. "Where's my camera? It didn't..?"

"I don't think it was with you. No, it definitely wasn't. Um .. sorry."

It had been slung round my neck when I went under. My beautiful [23]Topcon RE Super, the roll of film inside and the two other full rolls I'd put in the camera case must've slipped off my neck into the water. It'd all be soggy toast by now. Lying on the bottom of the gravel pit with the dead man. Ah.. him. A nasty great shiver passed through me, as if I'd swallowed an iceberg. I'd forgotten about the dead cat.

The lighthouse keeper came down the winding stairs and I'd just begun to thank him when a car horn tooted outside; it was my dad in the Crossley. He was probably wondering why I'd been falling into flooded gravel pits in the dark.

"Hey, Dad," I greeted him. "You're a star for coming out in the middle of the night."

"What time of night, son? It's only six o'clock, you know. The last guests have gone and we were just beginning to clear up."

"Only six? *Man*, I thought it was later than that," I got into the seat next to him, marvelling at how the 'shrooms could distort time, itself. If it was really that early, the siren had probably been for knocking-off time at the plant. "We got carried away, didn't we Verity? With the shoot, I mean," I explained, giving her no time to answer from the back. "Like, it was going so well that we didn't notice how dark it was getting and then I tripped over and fell into the pit and.. worst of all, my camera's gone, Dad. My beautiful Topcon. Can you believe it?"

"Ah, Sam. Bad luck. Still, your mother will be glad that you don't seem to have hyperthermia. You haven't got hyperthermia, have you, son? You can feel all your fingers and toes?"

"Yeah, yeah."

"I'm relieved." He glanced at Verity in his mirror. "And you, Miss Flinders? I hope you're not too cold? I understand that we have you to thank for pulling this crazy boy out of the pond?"

"Um.. that's ok, Mr Stone, I used a big stick; I didn't have to go in the water."

"Well, you're a brave girl, whatever you did and we're immensely grateful."

My old man never knew when to stop.

As we drove back along the coast, I studied the full moon. It was no longer psychedelic, but pale and reserved. It was keeping its secrets. I reckoned I might do the same.

7. BILL HAWKING

The evening after the funeral that never was, I was having a quiet pint with a man from work when Sam Stone walked in. He looked his usual, cocky self, scanning the Coastguard until he saw someone he knew. Unfortunately, that was me.

"Hawking!" He yelled across the bar. "What are you drinking, mate?"

I raised my pint and he made a sign that he was getting me another and did his small man strut over to the bar to chat up the barmaid. He'd ditched the sober suit and tie of the day before and had on a leather jerkin number, with a floor-skimming, woolly scarf around his neck. I could have placed a bet on it that some girl had knitted it for him; maybe the pretty one he'd been with at the funeral.

Sam and I had been friends since before we could talk. Since before either of us could sit up in the pram, they said. Before there'd been any choice in the matter, anyhow, or I reckon I'd have thought twice about hanging around with a fiend like Sam Stone. We were neither of us twenty yet, but while I'd been working at Dover Library since I was fifteen, Sam had been allowed to stay on at the Grammar forever and then pushed off to some airy-fairy London art school to learn how to put his finger on a camera and snap the shutter. And, while I'd been earning a decent enough wage to pay my mum bed and board, he'd been ingesting as many illegal substances as his student grant would allow, like a pelican gulping down ten fish at one sitting. I was pleased to see him; I always was, although I knew I shouldn't be.

By the time he tore himself away from the barmaid, my fellow librarian had pushed off and I was alone and at his mercy.

"Who's the Square?" He enquired, setting the drinks down on the table and making himself comfortable.

"Len from the library and he's a nice chap. He's a [24] Dylan aficionado."

"A Dylan freak? You're getting desperate. You really should come up to London, Bill. See some life." He took a gulp of his short.

"What're you drinking?"

"Ginger wine."

"Ginger wine! That what they drink up in London, is it?"

"It only costs tuppence and it works. I'm an indigent photography student, remember."

"Indigent!" It was a nice long word but, in his case, completely untrue. "You've got a nerve .."

Stone's parents were rich, never mind that the state was paying for him to take snapshots and he'd never done a proper day's work in his life.

"Never done a proper day's work .." he parroted, twisting himself a roll-up. "I can read your mind, Hawking and *man* is it dull."

"Well, thank God I can't read yours. I'd hate to think what's in there."

He leant back in his chair, looking solemn.

"Depravity," he said. And then, "You know .. mushrooms?"

I had an idea where this was going and I didn't like it. If Sam thought he was going to drag me out of bed at two in the morning to drive him to Denge Marsh again, just so he could fry his brain for free . . .

"Never again," I said, because I'd been stupid enough to fry mine, too and hadn't made it to work that day.

"Nah, not that," he said, "wrong time of year, anyhow, you bozo. I just need a bit of advice, actually. From a fellow shroomhead."

"I like that. It was just the once and it's never happening again, I'll tell you that now."

"Listen. Stop being a pillar of moral rectitude for once in your sad life, Hawking and just . . listen."

He had caught my attention.

"Right," he took a big drag of his roll-up and then leaned in, blowing the smoke out in my face in the process, "what I was wondering was . . your opinion on shroom trips. As somebody who, I take it, had a blast on our previous foray to Denge Marsh; as in stripping buck naked and singing [25]'Heartbreak Hotel' at the top of your voice."

It was difficult to deny, being the truth.

"Yeah, what I was wondering was . ." he continued, " . . when you were, like, at the height of the trip, did you ever see anything which you'd have sworn was real – *really* real, like you sitting in front of me now – but disturbed you. Disturbed you enough to stop you sleeping the night after. So you couldn't just walk away from it, literally and the other way. Couldn't even go back to London and college the next day."

"Ah. I think I'm getting your drift. You thought you'd get high last night and you had a bad trip."

"But it wasn't a bad trip, not at all. The bird I was with, Verity, she might have got the heebie-jeebies, but I was cool. In fact, super cool, because I fell into some freezing water and was actually being shocked out of the high when I saw this . . disturbance."

I started to laugh:

"Only you, Sam, could think it was just fine to get high on psychedelic mushrooms on the same day as a funeral in which the corpse has disappeared. As if that's not weird enough, why not heap weird on weird and make a night of it?"

"Oh, ok." He looked thoughtful. "So you reckon that the coffin-snatching sort of triggered something in my brain which made me see this .. apparition. Yeah. That must be it. Well, thanks, mate. Fancy another one?"

"No, I've got to be off."

"You've actually been a big help for once in your pathetic existence."

"Glad to be of assistance. By the way .." I had stood up and was belting my mackintosh. "What did you see?"

"A dead man. In the flooded gravel pit by Dungeness. All white and bloated, he was. Yeah, he drifted by and sort of wound his legs round me. They were solid, just as solid as yours' and mine. Freaky, eh?"

"Whaaat?"

I plummeted back down into my seat. Which was when his sister appeared.

"Hello, Bill," she said." "Hello, Sam. What's freaky?"

"Hello. Rosa." I managed, still dumbfounded by what Sam had said.

"Are you talking about Major Dyminge? Can I join in? My parents have decided to play Granny and Grandpa, so I've been walking along the beach and found myself at the pub. Accidentally on purpose. What are you two having?"

"Oh, we were just going, weren't we, Hawking?"

Sam shot me a look; one of those looks that would like you to shut up. But I wasn't having it. What he'd said was far too big to shut up about:

"You saw a dead body in one of the flooded gravel pits at Dungeness? Yesterday evening? And you haven't mentioned it to anybody until now?"

"You whaaat?" Rosa Stone plummeted into the seat next to me. "Oh my God, Sam. It wasn't Major Dyminge, was it? He hadn't been dumped in a gravel pit like an old fish head?"

"Well thanks a million for that, Hawking. What I said was confidential. If I'd wanted to tell my sister, I would have done so, mate."

He gathered up the ends of his enormous scarf and tried to look dignified as he made his escape.

"Oh, no you don't," she caught him and pushed him back down in his chair (and she was a strong woman). "You are going nowhere, Sam Stone. You'll tell me what this is about if I have to wring it out of you."

He sighed loudly, and then he told her what he'd told me. His sister looked aghast.

"You take a seventeen-year old girl to Dungeness in the dark and give her drugs? Then.. it sounds like you do nothing whatsoever to protect her when she suffers a bad trip? Dad said she looked just terrible when he took her to the train station."

"And *then*, as if you haven't done enough for one night, you find a dead body in the water and don't even *think* to call the police? I'm so angry with you I don't know what to do with myself. You say it wasn't Major Dyminge, but it was still a person, Sam. I mean, dead men have mothers and wives, brothers and sisters. People will be sitting at home hurting as they wonder where their father is, did that never occur to you? You go straight home this instant and call the police, do you hear me? This *instant*."

"But.. I didn't know if it was real, Rosa. Like, was I hallucinating, or..?"

"Rubbish." She interrupted. "I can't think what's got into you. That's complete and utter rubbish. If somebody bumps into you in freezing water, don't try and tell me it's a hallucination; you know full well it isn't. Go on, off with you, you little.. Now."

Well, that told him. He scarpered out of the pub as if his trousers were on fire.

"Sorry, Bill," she was breathing heavily, her bosom rising and falling as she did so, and had flushed rosy pink in the face.

It probably wasn't the right moment, but I have to admit that it did cross my mind to wonder why I'd never noticed how very beautiful Sam's big sister was: voluptuous and magnificent and .. just gorgeous.

"I seem to be becoming my mother," she added, and took a big breath.

I felt awkward and couldn't think what to say all of a sudden. I cursed myself for the millionth time for being so damn shy.

"How are you, anyway? What are you up to these days?" She asked, reaching across the table for her brother's half-finished glass of ginger wine and chugging it back.

"Oh, fine, thanks. Still at the library, you know."

How boring could I get?

"How wonderful. I'd love to work in a library. Ginger wine." She licked her lips. "An interesting choice."

"Very cheap, apparently."

"Is it? Now that is worth knowing. Yes .. being surrounded by books; I couldn't think of anything better. I bet you get to read all the latest stuff. What did you think of [26] *The Manchurian Candidate*? I sell a few books; just a shelf, really. Old ones, of course, because it's an antique shop. Well, not strictly an antique shop. All sorts, you know. Kind of a cave of wonders .."

She didn't seem to be difficult to talk to.

"Talking of wonders. What's your take on yesterday? Horrible, wasn't it? I haven't seen Mrs Dyminge today, but I should think she's absolutely reeling .."

"I'm finding it difficult to comprehend, to tell you the truth," I confided. "I drove over to see Auntie Frances this morning, but she wasn't feeling so well and had gone back to sleep. We didn't get to chat."

She made a kind of snorting noise:

"Hangover, probably."

"Eh?"

"Oh.. no.. sorry, Bill. I didn't mean the alcoholic kind. No. I meant, a sort of hangover of misery from the shock. Yes, that's what I meant."

"I just hope the police can sort it out."

"Find the body, you mean?"

She was pretty blunt, like her brother, but she seemed.. straighter.

"Yes," I replied, "find the Major's er.."

She looked long and hard at me and I felt increasingly hot under the collar, being studied by those searching, dark eyes. Eyes which stood out against her delicate, white skin, lightly dusted with freckles. Should I offer to buy her a drink? Would she think I was too young to be drinking with her in a pub? I was still worrying when the conversation took an unusual turn.

"That's *if* the body was a body in the first place."

"I beg your pardon?"

"I've probably said too much.. I usually do. It's just that you strike me as being an awful lot more sensible than my brother, if you don't mind my saying so, Bill. I've always really admired your mother, Sadie, you know. She's such a strong, independent woman. I've thought of her a lot since I had the twins."

My mum? My unmarried mum (which made me a.. well, just ask the kids in the village what that made me and they'd tell you, quick enough). How did *she* fit into all of this?

"I wonder whether I could entrust you with a secret? Because I think your experience at the library might come in very handy."

"Well.. I'm not sure what you're talking about, but I'm always glad to be of assistance."

"Spoken like a true librarian," she laughed and then, quick as a flash, became serious again. "Right, well, here goes. It's about yesterday; Major Dyminge's disappearance from his coffin. Some of us – myself and Peter, to be precise – we feel that it needs investigating. Properly, I mean, not a little police effort, but an in-depth investigation such as might be done by MI5, or somebody; just to pick an organisation out of the air, you know. Because it's horrible. It's *so* horrible. And we loved the Major so very much, as I'm sure you did .."

Loved was too strong a word. The old man had been cranky and rather intimidating. Quick to put down Auntie Frances when he found her irritating, too. Yet .. if you needed help with making a fighter plane out of balsa wood, or finishing the tough Meccano set you got for Christmas, there'd be nobody better than the old Major.

"What do you think? Will you help us?"

There wasn't really any thinking to be done.

"I'm still not completely sure what you mean, but I'll do whatever I can if it helps Auntie Frances," I replied.

And I was sincere about that, even as I found myself mesmerised by Sam's sister's beautiful brown eyes.

"Wonderful," she whispered, placing a milk-white hand over mine. "Thank you, Bill."

"There's just one point," I came up for a breather, still about strong enough to resist drowning. "Who's this Peter?"

"Lord Peter Upshott," she replied. "But all *that's* beside the point. He was Major Dyminge's best friend. They had many adventures together, just like this one."

"This one?"

"Mm. I find that they seem to run to a time-table, like buses. One gets to recognise the signs."

"Really? I don't think I've ever had an adventure."

"No?" She smiled at me, such a tender smile. "Well, all aboard then. And no ringing the bell until the bus has reached its destination."

But then she looked across the pub and sat up straight.

"Aha! He's here," she began to get up. "When I said I'd come to the pub 'accidentally on purpose', well .. I lied. Come on, Bill; we can't make him come to us, not with all of these tables and chairs in the way. Follow me."

8. RENDEZVOUS AT THE PUB

"*Chanel No 5?* Guy Dyminge? Hardly."

"I know, I couldn't believe it."

I scrabbled around in the bottom of my packet of crisps, but there were only salty crumbs left.

"Would you like some more crisps, Rosa?" Bill Hawking spoke up for the first time since we'd moved across the pub to sit next to Peter Upshott.

"Thanks, Bill; that's most kind of you."

He set off for the bar and Peter immediately turned to me:

"Rosa, dear, why the devil did you invite that young lad to our rendezvous? He looks completely wet behind the ears."

"Poor Bill; honestly, he's nowhere near as young as he looks. He's the same age as my brother and he's been working at the big library in Dover for years. They've got simply wonderful archives there, you know, and it occurred to me that he might come in useful for research purposes. It was spur of the moment, really. Shouldn't I have involved him?"

Peter looked dubious and, watching Bill on his way back to us with the crisps, I wondered whether he might be right. While being tall and rather dishy, in a willowy kind of way, Bill had that sort of downy, fair hair that's generally darkened by adulthood and, with his short back and sides and neat mackintosh, he did look rather like his mother had just wiped his face with a damp hanky and packed him off for a day at school.

"Rosa tells me you work at the library, Bill?" Peter wasted no time in interrogating him. "Do you have a specialism?"

"Well, sir, if I'm not shelving, they usually put me on the front desk."

"As in .. dealing with library tickets?"

"That's right, sir."

Peter looked, meaningfully, at me.

"But I expect you understand all of the systems, don't you Bill?"

It was obvious that he was an intelligent boy and if all he did was take library tickets and date stamp books all day long, that seemed a terrible waste to me.

He looked thoughtful.

"Do you mean the archive systems? The reference sections and the microfiches? Yes, I know how they all work."

I flung a triumphant smile at Peter.

"But I couldn't do anything to jeopardize my job, you do understand that? Nothing against the law, or underhand in any way, I'm afraid."

That certainly limited our horizons. However, Peter just nodded, thoughtfully.

"That's fine, dear boy. We wouldn't want to make you do anything that you'd rather not. After all, you do have one magnificent advantage .."

"He has?"

"Legs," he said. "Like most things in life, one doesn't value them enough until they're gone," and then he laughed. "So, we're all set. The three musketeers. Shall we shake on it, Compadres?" He stuck out his hand and we took turns to stand up and give it a formal shake.

After which, Bill looked shyly at me and proffered his.

"We will find Major Dyminge," I vowed, as I took his hand in mine, "if it's the last thing we do."

Talk about tempting Fate.

"Anybody fancy another snifter?" Peter asked.

"Thanks, but I really do have to go. My mother will be wondering where I am," Bill replied, innocently. "It's been nice to meet you, Lord.. m'lord .."

"Just Peter does the trick. And the same to you, Bill. I want you to know how grateful we are that you've joined us and how much we will value any help given. Rosa and I will be keeping in touch via the telephone because I've got to get back to Norfolk, but please do take my number from her and use it if anything important crops up; anything germane to the investigation, you know. We need to keep in regular communication, so that all areas are covered, as my old friend Dyminge would have said. Stations at the ready, alright? And keep it all under your hat, particularly the perfume angle."

Bill looked pleased but perplexed when he left the pub, as well he might.

"A sweet youth, if a touch clueless," was Peter's verdict.

Unlike us, I thought.

"Well, Rosa, if you'd be so good as to fight your way to the bar again, mine's a whiskey and soda. And whatever you fancy .." he handed me a pound note and I went off to buy the drinks.

When I returned, he had the circular drawings that I'd filched from Major Dyminge's study fanned out on the pub table and was scrutinising them, intently.

"Of course, Dyminge's interest in radar goes a long way back, to well before it was in the public eye. In fact, if he hadn't been tempted off the path of sense by the sound mirrors fiasco, he might even have got there before the other boffins and invented it all by himself."

"Sound mirrors?"

"Early experiments in tracking enemy aircraft from before the war. They turned out to be a dead end and put the kybosh on Dyminge's army career in the process. It was all very sad."

He took a sip from his glass, before continuing, reflectively:

"Well, it was and it wasn't. Guy Dyminge's great quality was his tenacity; the old boy had the tenacity of a terrier after a ferret. Nothing could destroy that. We have the proof right here, in front of us, don't you see? Because he continued to work in the same area. Where the rest of us might have been put off by shame and disaster, Dyminge just carried right on."

"Yes, I can see that," I thought about him disappearing into his workshop for the years and years that it had taken me to grow up and move to London. "And, of course, radar *now* is a very different matter from when it first began. I have to admit that I don't know much about it, but I should think its moved streets ahead of tracking planes over the English Channel. It's probably being used to track the distance to the moon by now."

Peter slammed his glass down on the table and made me jump.

"Yes!" He exclaimed. "To go out, out, out . ." he held up the diagram with the greatest gap between circles, ".. but, also, to go in, in, in . ." He shuffled the papers to find the dark pattern where the gaps had all but disappeared.

"In, in, in?" I asked. "In, in, in to what? To the centre of the earth? Into matter, itself? Into the atom?"

"Yes, indeed. Those are all intelligent ideas, Rosa .. and I'm not suggesting for one moment that you are wrong, but ... Look at this black picture. I mean to say; doesn't it remind you of anything?"

I considered it. When I'd first seen it on the table in the Major's workshop, I'd thought of an India rubber ball, but now that I looked at it more closely, I could see that it wasn't nearly spherical enough for that. It had a squashed aspect to it that had, perhaps, made me think of the texture of rubber, yet it was loosely frilled around the edge, much like a cauliflower.

"It's not a cauliflower, is it?"

"No, I would say not, although a cauliflower also has the kind of .. hmm, *organic*; now would that be a proper word? I'm frightfully ill-educated. Only got to Oxford on a sports blue and learnt as little as you can get away with at public school, which is very little indeed, I can assure you. Organic, curving, natural: these are all words that I associate with this particular thing. The thing which is not a cauliflower."

I hated it, but it looked like I was going to have to give up.

"No idea?" He seemed disappointed. "Oh, well, perhaps it's just me, then. A cauliflower would probably work as well in my case. If one were substituted for the other."

A light bulb went on. It was going to seem rather rude to suggest it, but then, I'm afraid I often am rather rude.

"A brain," I exclaimed, and he smiled. "It's a cross-section of a brain."

"Yes, I'm pretty convinced that it is. So .. we must ask ourselves what old Dyminge was up to with radar engineering and the brain?"

"Oh my goodness; that changes everything." I could almost feel the pathways of my own brain starting to fire up, to fizz with energy after their long, maternity-induced, hibernation. "The perfume. The body snatching. Everything."

"Perfume? Body snatching? No, I'm afraid I'm not following you, Rosa. You will have to explain in words of less than two syllables."

"Well, this is only a theory – not even that – just the first glimmers of a theory, but .. look .." I scrabbled in my handbag for my bottle of *Fracas* and then spritzed it into the air.

We both leant forward to sniff the fragrance without even thinking about it.

"Do you see what we did? We introduced the perfume to our brains by sniffing it. We directly introduced a foreign body to our own bodies. Major Dyminge was testing something out."

"So, the *Chanel No 5* was part of an experiment and not a fetish at all. I must say, I'm rather relieved."

"Yes. The *Chanel* and the *Diorella* and the *Vol de Nuit* and the *Youth-Dew* and the *Yardley's English Lavender*. What's more .." it struck me as I spoke, "I should have noticed it right away, but I was too surprised by the whole combination of the Major and fine fragrance; they are all quite different. From one another. I mean .. *Chanel No 5* is a bright, airy floral, of course we all know that, but *Diorella* is not. *Diorella* is a green chypre with citrus top notes. *Guerlain's Vol de Nuit* is a woody, cold oriental, while *Youth-Dew* is a warm, amber-ish oriental. Then, *Yardley's English Lavender* is aromatic and herbal. So you see, if the Major was measuring the effect of our sense of smell on the brain, somehow using radar, he was experimenting with fragrances that have been deliberately finely calibrated to be poles apart from one another."

"Wowzers!" Peter sat back in his wheelchair and stared at me. "I have no idea what this all signifies: whether what he was doing has been tried before, or could be applied to anything else, but I will say one thing. You're a clever girl, Rosa Stone."

I may have smirked, or looked like the cat who got the cream, but do you know, I think I deserved to do so. I *am* a clever girl - well, woman - and it had been far, *far* too long since anybody had noticed.

"I think I need to go home to Norfolk and think all of this over, my dear, but we've made a jolly good start. Oh, look, the Air Chief Marshal has just come in, right on cue." He waved at his friend, who had been standing by the door looking lost.

"Let's both think this over and see what else we can come up with; you have my number and I have yours. I shall take the drawings and manuscript, if I may. I'd like to get a proper squint at them, and see if Gabriel has any ideas, too. Just a sec, though. I nearly forgot. I seem to remember your saying something about the body-snatching being explained. How so?"

Peter's friend was nearly upon us, so I leant over the old man and whispered in his ear:

"Somebody wanted his brain, don't you see? And now they've got it."

9. COAST COTTAGE

I woke with the horrors. Something utterly dreadful had happened, but I wasn't sure what it was. If it was as bad as the way my head felt, then it must have been very terrible indeed.

"You were intoxicated, Frances. In the most shameful state at your own husband's funeral. *My* funeral."

"Aagh." I was drooling into my pillow, incapable of speech.

"How could you? How *could* you?"

There was a knock on the bedroom door and I made a noise at it. Surprisingly, it was Millicent with a cup of tea. What was she doing in our bedroom?

"Good morning, Frances. How are you today?"

I made a supreme effort and hoisted myself up in bed. One of my eyes was glued shut, but the other eye managed to register that I was not, in fact, at home, but in one of the Stones' spare bedrooms.

"We're all feeling awful, so how you must be I can't imagine."

It wasn't just me, then. Had we all got drunk as skunks and made fools of ourselves? What kind of funeral was it? I was drawing a complete blank.

"I've already been on to the police first thing because

we all know we have to keep them at it. They do their best, but they can't be allowed to let it slide. Although, as I said to Jerzy, why they should when they've got little enough to investigate in Hassels – just the odd burglary on a good day, I'd have thought, nothing on this scale . . I doubt if there's been anything on this scale in these parts for . . oh . . all of ten years, really."

The police? Scales? I thought it might be best to drink my tea. It was good and strong and hit the spot. When my voice came out it was in a froggy croak:

"Thank you, Millicent. So kind. I think, perhaps, I'd better take my pills with the liquid. Would you be a dear and fetch me my handbag?"

"Pills?" Her face took on a peculiar expression. "What pills would these be, Frances?"

"Oh, you know, those pretty [27] green and black pills that the doctor doles out to all and sundry when they are going through a bad patch. They will be in my handbag, dear."

She snapped open the clasp of my black handbag and fished the pills out.

"Hmm. And how many of these have you been taking, may I ask?"

It seemed a little high-handed, but I didn't like to be rude.

"As and when, dear. You know, in difficult times. When the need arises."

She was peering at me in a searching manner, so I made a stab at calculating how many I'd been having.

"Two. Three. Four . ."

"Five. Six . ." she continued, before putting them back in my handbag and snapping it shut.

"I say!"

"Frances, you may not thank me for saying this, but you have been taking more than enough of these things. And adding alcohol on top; that'll do it every time. It's a wonder you haven't killed yourself. I think I shall have to confiscate them."

"Well, really! The doctor said.."

She didn't wait to hear what the doctor said, but took them out of my handbag once more and put them in the pocket of her red apron.

"One, in *really* bad times, just to take the edge off. You just let me know when it feels that bad and I shall come over with it. Although, we might try a nice chat first. And Frances.." she picked up my empty cup and went to leave, ".. lay off the gin."

Well, honestly! If I hadn't been feeling so dreadful, I would have upped and left Millicent's spare room, then and there. However, as it was, I promptly fell back asleep and dreamt that a dragon was rubbing its green, scaly skin all over me and awoke several hours later feeling hot and itchy and cross.

I may have been ever so slightly short with Millicent when I left Shore House, but she's a tough, little character and just smiled sweetly at me, in between feeding spoonsful of mashed carrot to Rosa's twins, who were sitting up in their high chairs looking exactly like small Buddhas.

"A nice chat, Frances," she called out, as I went to leave. "Remember. Any time, day or night."

Then Jerzy foisted a large, brown paper bag of goodies left over from the wake upon me, which made it a trifle difficult to leave with my nose in the air.

It was getting dark again outside. I stood looking out at the sea for a stretch, but it was damp and chill and did me no good. I sensed myself descending, beginning to lack hope that I would ever see light again. Anxiety, that cold companion, put her hands over my eyes, so that light and cheer and all sense of future were obliterated. The stupidest questions invaded my thoughts as I stood on the beach. Who am I? *Why* am I? And (last and most disgracefully): If I can't drink gin, then what *can* I do? When I turned my back on the sea to go into our little cottage - *my* little cottage, now - I believed that I was at as low an ebb as I was likely to be. Ha!

The front door hadn't been properly locked with the Yale and the mat had become rucked up, as it used to be when we had a dog. Who could tell *where* my mind had been on the day of Guy's funeral? The parlour was fearfully cold, so I knelt to put a match to the spills of twisted newspaper that I store by the coal fire, inveigling them between the coals before I'd even taken off my coat. Standing up, I noticed that the lilies on the mantelpiece were all quite dead.

I dragged myself into the kitchen to unpack Jerzy's bag of food and store the contents in the larder. How shaming it was to see so many cups and plates piled up in the sink, and an empty bottle of gin on the draining-board, taunting me. I sat down at the kitchen table and put my head in my hands. How does one go on when all of one's co-ordinates have gone haywire; when all maps have been torn into a hundred little pieces?

Yet, even as I sat there, at my lowest ebb, something highly unusual began to happen to my brain. It began gradually, yet gathered force, flooding me with sudden, unexpected, strength. For, sitting there with my head in my hands, the most vivid pictures of forests and flowers popped up into my mind: lemons on warm hillsides, wood smoke and pine, roses and lavender. It was extraordinary how rapidly the pictures worked upon me. They were so real, those scenes, so tangible, that hope leapt, unbidden. Perhaps my late father, the vicar, had been right and there was a God? Perhaps Guy was tramping pine-scented hills with rosemary and honeysuckle entwined around the brim of his old army cap? I lifted my head and sniffed the air, luxuriously, like an animal. Heavens, the scent was as real as anything could be. I opened my eyes. Wait a minute...

The shabby old curtain that I'd made to keep out the draught was loosed from its rail, so that I could see that the door to Guy's workshop was hanging off one hinge. I jumped up and ran into the outhouse. Horror upon horror, all was smashed and .. desecrated. Shards of yellow glass littered the floor, mingling with screws and cogs: the workings of the old radio sets that Guy had liked to collect. Papers and periodicals had been ripped into bits, books heaved off the shelves, their spines bent backwards. Even the armchair that had seen better days, the one we'd bought in a sale in Hythe, had been eviscerated, its innards spilling out in a mass of wool and horsehair. It brought back memories of another such scene, one that had happened long before, just as the war was ending. Again, it was so unexpected, so shockingly personal and yet .. this time it smelt divine. One hears of dreadful substances being thrown about in cases of vandalism - paraffin, acid, or far, far worse - but expensive perfume was a new one on me.

I staggered out and collapsed onto the kitchen chair once more, while a strange numbness began to take hold; as if I simply didn't have it in me to care any more. If there had been gin to hand, I would have drunk it, because why on earth not? Why should I not drink myself to death? What did it matter? At that moment, I really couldn't see a single argument against it. When there came a knock at the front door.

I dragged myself out of the kitchen and into the parlour, smudging away tears with the sleeve of my cardigan, before I opened the door. There on the front step, his white hair shining in the dark, stood my late husband, Guy. With a dog.

"Good evening, Frances," he said, "I hope I'm not troubling you."

But it wasn't Guy. Guy had never hoped not to be troubling me (rather, it had been his mission). Guy had not spoken with the comforting Kent burr of my youth. The visitor came from long before Guy, so long ago that even I found difficulty believing it had ever been. It was a boy from my childhood, Edwin Summerby.

"Edwin. Gracious me. What are *you* doing here?"

"I shouldn't have come. It was too soon."

He seemed to take fright, no doubt at the ghastly vision

of my haggard, old, tear-stained face.

"Forgive me," he replaced his cloth cap, as if to go.

I pulled myself together, fast.

"Nonsense," I exclaimed. "Now you are here you must come in. Old friends should never be turned from the door. Please *do* come in." Pleasantries poured from my mouth all by themselves. "Goodness, what weather we're having; you must be freezing. Trains and buses can be so badly heated .. but I see you came by car. And you've brought your dog, how delightful. Come in, come in; I've only just lit the fire, but it's taking well, look."

Edwin was staring at me, seemingly unconcerned about the fire (although his dog, a butterscotch mongrel with pricked ears like a wolf, looked very pleased, indeed, to see it).

"I'll tie the dog up outside," he suggested.

"You certainly won't. Bring it .. him? .. in."

He relented and brought the animal in, un-hooking the leather lead from its thick neck.

"Now, behave yourself, Canaan," he said, whereupon the dog promptly slumped in front of the fire, sighing dramatically.

Edwin and I gazed at one another for a bit, taking in the ravages of time and searching for the young people we had known. We had not met for a lifetime, yet he appeared strangely unaffected by age: still strong-looking and still the possessor of a thick head of pale hair, of clear blue eyes and unlined skin. I daresay *he* had plenty to take in.

"Please, do sit down," I gestured to one of our old, chintz armchairs; the one with less patches. "I shall make us a cup of tea. No, please don't trouble yourself. I'll only be two ticks."

He had made as if to follow me, but it was imperative that I keep him out of the kitchen.

"This is exceptionally kind, Frances," he called out, while I searched for clean cups and saucers. "I know I'm imposing on you at a terrible time."

Ah, he knew about my husband's death. It all went

quiet, while the tea brewed in the pot and I hunted out a couple of Jerzy's delicious, little iced buns. I laid the tea trolley with a clean cloth and the makings of our tea and wheeled it through.

"I must admit," he said, "I saw the funeral. Yesterday. I'm so sorry for your loss."

"Ah . ." I was going to have to play this by ear, remembering practically nothing of the day before besides my own, shameful, behaviour. I felt a little panicked. How much had he seen? But he seemed to feel the need to explain *himself*, which was helpful.

"I live in London," he began. "Chelsea. Just by chance I happened to discover, recently, that we have a friend in common. Rosa Stone."

"Dear Rosa? Goodness me, what a small world."

"That it is. Anyway . . she happened to mention that a Major Dyminge had died and that she was coming down to Kent for his funeral. Her brother was there and she gave him the date and time, and said that the funeral was taking place at St Aethelred's in Hassels, which, of course, I know well."

He took his cup of tea and looked into it, hard.

"And . . I thought to myself, well, how many Major Dyminges could there be? In our part of the world, too. So . . I seized the moment, Frances, and drove down. I hope you don't mind. I mean . . I didn't wish to infringe upon your mourning in any way. I didn't come to the service, no, I just hung about outside, hoping . . well, hoping for a glimpse of you. That was all. Just a glimpse, after all these years."

Golly, I felt rather flattered. Except . . I so hoped he hadn't seen me rolling around intoxicated, making an utter fool of myself.

"It was wonderful," he lifted his eyes from his teacup and looked me full in the face and I remembered the blueness of his eyes, as blue as Guys' had been.

Wonderful? Perhaps my behaviour hadn't been so bad, after all.

"Rosa was outside, wheeling the pram around the church and I thought she might have seen me because she called:

'Come out, whoever you are'.

"But I was far too ashamed of myself; an old man creeping about at another man's funeral. What a seedy way to behave. I only hope that you can forgive me, Frances. It was just that it was all I had to go on, so I seized the moment."

It was difficult to know how to respond, somehow. If I hadn't known better, I would have said that he seemed rather . . ardent. But, of course, that couldn't be right. I took a bite of iced bun while I tried to think straight.

"Ah . . Edwin . . I cannot see that there was anything seedy in your behaviour. No. You should have made yourself known and joined us and . ." I rather ran out.

"That's exceptionally kind of you, Frances, and far more than I deserve," he rattled his cup and saucer for a bit, deep in thought while, absent-mindedly, leaning over to offer the dog some bun.

"But, even an old yokel such as myself knows it wasn't the right way to go about things. And, I would have waited for a better time before I came to see you, only . . I felt I might be able to help you with your loss."

What a very peculiar day this was turning out to be. If I hadn't known better, I would have said that he seemed rather . . oh, I'm repeating myself. But he did. He really did. Ardent.

"Ah, Edwin . . how thoughtful. But, you know, I'm sure time will do that. It's painful, of course, but we all have to go through it, to endure. In fact, I believe that it's essential to have a period of grieving and not stint yourself in any way; to allow time to do its job."

I noticed that he was beginning to look a fraction puzzled.

"Well, of course, but . . such a loss is not given to us all. I'd say it would be hard - cruelly hard - to endure *this* loss; even harder than in the ordinary way."

He seemed very insistent. My late husband had had his moments, of course, and we had loved one another dearly, in our fashion, but I couldn't feel that even Guy, himself, would have considered his death to be so much worse than anybody else's. He'd been a very old man, after all.

"So, when I saw the article this morning over my egg and bacon at the Red Dragon, I realised that I had to find you again, that there was absolutely no time to lose."

"Article? I'm sorry, you will have to forgive me Edwin, but it's been a trying time and .." There was nothing for it but to tell the truth. "It's been delightful to see you, but I've rather lost the thread of this conversation."

"The article on the front page of the *Daily Kentish News*, with the big photograph of the empty coffin. The one with the unfortunate headline."

"Unfortunate headline? Empty coffin? I'm sorry to keep repeating what you say, but I really am completely in the dark, Edwin dear."

"Body-Snatched!" He said, and then, "Because, you see, I saw them do it. I was crouching by the back entrance to the church when I saw them leave with the body. It was wrapped in its shroud, of course, but I don't see how it could have been anyone else. There were two men and they carried it into the back of a green van. I had no way of knowing what was going on, believe me Frances, or I would have tried to stop them. I didn't know what it meant, then. I even wondered whether it was official; whether he might be being preserved for science, perhaps. Oh .. who am I fooling? The truth of the matter was that I felt so ashamed of myself for lurking around the graveyard that I left and went back to my B&B. I really had no idea, not until I saw that headline, and it's taken me all day to find your cottage."

For the merest moment, I considered how nice it would be to be completely mad; to not have to know anything more of reality. But, sadly, I was going to have to face facts.

"Let me get this straight," I said, slowly. "The local paper has printed something about my late husband's funeral, something about his body being snatched from his coffin. Am I right?"

"Well, yes. Of course. I understand your confusion, now. You knew nothing of the newspaper article and I've gone and sprung it upon you without warning."

"Nothing of the article? I have to tell you, Edwin, that I knew nothing of Guy's body being snatched, either."

"But you were there," he exclaimed. "I saw you with my own eyes."

"Ah . ." all was becoming, marginally, clearer, "I believe I may have conked out. Oh my . ."

Horror rose up before me, fully-formed.

"Somebody's taken Guy's body!"

My breathing began to change, as if my breath wasn't coming from my lungs, but was coiling in tight circles around my throat.

"Somebody's taken Guy's body!" I yelped, and the tears were rolling down my cheeks and my foot began tapping on the floor of its own accord.

"They've ransacked his workshop and taken his body and now there is nothing left!"

Panic had taken full control and I rocked back and forth in my chair.

"He's gone!" I heard myself scream, in a high, strangled voice. "He's gone!"

Over and over again I screamed.

"He's gone!"

10. OLD HARRY COLE

I'd left Bill and my sister in the Coastguard and was heading home to ring the police, when I heard the screaming. My dad had heard it, too, and was running down the path.

"What the hell?"

I'd stopped dead in my tracks, because it sounded like Mrs Dyminge was being murdered in her cottage.

"Come on son," Dad shouted and he grabbed the end of my scarf, dragging me over the gravel with him.

He unlocked the front door and we rushed in. A man with white hair was bending over the screaming Mrs Dyminge. There was a dog, too, howling like a demon from Hell. My dad yanked the intruder off her, threw him on the floor and sat on him, while I grabbed the poker from the fireplace and tried to keep the ugly mutt at bay.

"He's gone!" Mrs Dyminge screamed. "He's gone!"

"No, he hasn't, Frances. I've got him here, on the floor."

"Back!" I lunged at the dog. "Back off, you bastard."

"Canaan!" It was the man under my father. "Down boy."

The dog immediately sat back on its haunches and began to gnaw on a paw, glancing at me sideways. It looked like it was sharing a joke. I lowered the poker and turned to check out Mrs Dyminge.

The old lady had doubled up in her chair and was panting.

"Let's get a look at you," Dad got off the man and rolled

him round with a kick.

The minute I clocked his face, I realised that he looked familiar.

"Hey! I've seen this cat before. Yeah . ." it was coming back to me. I'd met the man and the dog before somewhere, and not that long ago, either.

"You're Rosa's dealer," I exclaimed. "I met you in the Man in the Moon."

"Dealer?" Dad cried. "What in the name of God have you given Frances?"

"Not that kind of dealer, Dad. Antiques. The old guy knows Mrs Dyminge from way back. He was in the pub when we were talking about the funeral. I reckon he must've followed us down here."

"I'd never hurt a hair on her head. Frances, please, tell them."

"Frances, is this true?"

Dad kept an uneasy eye on the antiques dealer while he went over and set a hand on the old lady's shoulder.

She looked up at him, still wheezing. Her hair had fallen down and her cheeks were wet.

"This is Edwin," she managed. "We are old friends." And then she added, in a murmur so quiet it was almost as if she was talking to herself, "Guy's gone."

My dad pulled up a chair and sat down beside her, taking her hand:

"Oh, Frances. It has upset us all. We can only trust that the police will do whatever they can to get him back."

The antiques dealer heaved himself up off the floor, with some difficulty, and the dog sauntered over to the fire and collapsed, like it hadn't a bone in its body, and the scene went quiet. There was just the crackle and spit of coal in the fireplace, while we stood round the old lady. The fire was blazing now and the warmth of that small room lapped over me, lulling me into forgetfulness. Almost.

"Damn." I'd remembered what I was supposed to be

doing when Mrs Dyminge's screams had diverted me. "I've gotta give the police a bell. Sorry, gotta go."

"What was that?" My Dad pricked up his big ears. "Have you discovered something, Sam?"

"Um, yes and no," I wasn't going to upset the old lady again. "Nothing to do with the Major, though."

"No? Then, what have you been up to, son?"

I was trying to edge past them all to get to the front door, but my father blocked my escape route.

"Hey, keep your hair on. I've done nothing wrong, man. I'm, like, the *witness* to an offence; doing my civic duty."

He looked as if he didn't believe a word of it, but the dealer piped up before he could say any more.

"If you're calling the police, then might I suggest that you report the break-in. That's so, isn't it Frances? You did mention that your husband's workshop had been ransacked?"

"Did I, Edwin dear? When was that? Gosh, I really am losing track. I must pull myself together."

"Someone's broken in? Oy, oy, oy." Dad's face had darkened on hearing of the latest catastrophe to hit Mrs Dyminge. "Come on, everybody back to Shore House. You cannot stay here, Frances; it's not safe. No," he raised his hand against any objections, "no kvetching. Everybody out."

Over by the fire, the dog sighed.

So, we brought her back to the house again and the old guy and his mutt came too, my parents' pad being, literally, open house to every man and his dog. By the time my sister had returned from the Coastguard, the local doctor had been and gone, Mrs Dyminge was asleep in bed and my dad was showing off in front of his visitor. Oh, and the police were on their way over with an offer I couldn't refuse; the offer of a lift back to Dungeness and a cold night's hanging about while they dredged the flooded gravel pit for corpses. Man, what a colossal drag.

Rosa, being Rosa, was thrilled with all the activity, of

course.

"*What's* all this?" She was red-faced with excitement. "So, it was *you* in the graveyard yesterday."

She'd flung herself on the window-seat and was craning towards her friend from the pub.

"You followed us down just to get a glimpse of *her*. How romantic."

Rosa's unfailing ability to shoot her mouth off and make people uncomfortable hadn't deserted her.

"Rosa, please," our mother shuss-ed at her, "Mrs Dyminge is a very new widow, dear. Mr Summerby was just renewing an old friendship."

"Ha! An old passion, more like."

My sister has all the subtlety of a steam-roller.

"And good for you, Mr Summerby. I mean, why not? You're neither of you getting any younger. Time may be running out, after all."

I groaned.

"Anyhow, Rosa," said Mum, "haven't you forgotten something?"

"No, I think I've taken it all in. Somebody broke into the Major's study late last night and destroyed his stuff, and then Mr Summerby arrived and upset Mrs Dyminge by reminding her about the empty coffin and Dad and Sam thought he was attacking her and.."

"Your children, dear. There are two of them, in case you've forgotten, and I think they've waited long enough for their mother to come back from the *pub*."

Mum made the Coastguard sound like the Sodom and Gomorrah of East Kent and I couldn't help laughing. Rosa shot me a withering look before she left.

"Well, where was I supposed to say you were?" I shrugged. "Canterbury Cathedral?"

At that point, the doorbell rang.

"That'll be your escort then, Sam," my sister waylaid me in the hall.

"Just you make sure that you tell them the truth and help them in every way you can, yes?"

"And, why wouldn't I? I have nothing to hide."

"Glad to hear it. Let me know in the morning whether they've found a body. Promise?"

"Who's the ghoul now?"

I had to push past her to open the front door.

"Evening officers. Let me just get my scarf."

◆ ◆ ◆

It must have been a long night on the Ness because none of us heard Sam return. The scrap of paper in front of my bedroom door was the only proof that he'd come back at all.

'Found old Harry Cole in Long Pit. Coppers want formal ident but def him. No camera, sods law. See you, S'

Sam's bed was untouched. It looked like he'd decided to hitch back to town. Was he even allowed to do that when he'd just found a body in suspicious circumstances? I went downstairs to breakfast deep in thought.

My mother was already up and about, business-like in her frilly, red apron. She was mashing something for Jessica and Benjamin. My babies sat up in their high chairs, seemingly bewitched by her; straining to follow her every move with their eyes, like starving dogs. How was it that my mother always seemed to carry an air of professionalism with her, whatever she was doing?

"How did they sleep? I didn't hear a thing."

"Perfectly, the little angels. No trouble at all."

"I don't understand it. Are you quite sure you haven't switched them for someone else's babies? They've never slept through the night at home, not even *once*."

This new, perfect, behaviour of theirs was starting to make me cross.

She waved her spoon at me, airily.

"Ignore them; it's the only way, Rosa. There comes a time when it has to be done."

"Whaat? You haven't been doing a [28]Truby King on them, have you?" I rounded on her. "How could you?"

I simply couldn't believe that she had been leaving them all alone to sob their little hearts out.

"Thirty years of sleeping with your father's snoring has meant I can sleep through anything. Your children are a piece of cake, believe me."

She looked so smug, I could have throttled her.

"But it's *cruel*. How do you think they feel, wailing all by themselves in the dark? In despair; utterly abandoned and hopeless.."

"Abandoned and hopeless, indeed," she scoffed, "I'll give you abandoned and hopeless.."

I sensed the London childhood in abject poverty speech coming up. One apple to share between six at Christmas, if you were lucky.

She inserted a spoonful of mashed banana into Benjamin's mouth and he blinked at the speed of it. At that moment he looked like a fat, baby blackbird; one of those birds that are beginning to dwarf the parent feeding them. However, the speech never came. She wiped her hand on her apron and gave him a smacking kiss on his wide forehead.

"They only cried the first night, anyhow. It was all done and dusted by last night. You can thank me later."

Only then did it strike me how different I had begun to feel with two full night's sleep behind me. I'd been a Dr Spock woman from the day the twins were born, but maybe it was time to ease up on my free and easy methods of childcare. I hated to do it, but I reckoned it might also be time to clamber down off my high horse.

"I expect I can thank you now. Thank you, Mum."

She took her apron off and folded it, carefully, before draping it over the back of the kitchen chair.

"I'm glad to help, love. I know .. we got off on the wrong

foot with the twins.. If you'd just let us contact their father.. I mean, surely it's his duty to help .. who knows, he may have wanted to and you just haven't given him the chance.."

I glared at her.

"No, no, I'm not going to begin all that again, I promise. And it wasn't *all* your fault. I know I can be stubborn; Jerzy's told me often enough."

We smiled at one another. It had been an age since we had even looked each other full in the eyes.

"It must have been hard for you," she said.

"Well, yes."

This was going almost too well. I wasn't fully prepared and sensed myself beginning to liquefy at the edges.

"It *has* been pretty hard, actually."

In the past, I'd have milked this for every drop, yet now I felt peculiarly hesitant; as if something I'd gained might be lost.

"You've grown up, Rosa."

"Grown up? I *am* 29."

"Do you know, I'm not sure how much age has to do with it. My sister, Kathleen, for example, now I don't think that she will ever grow up."

We laughed.

"She doesn't have twins," I pointed out.

"Thank heavens for small mercies. *That* she doesn't." Her Irish ancestry seemed to be coming out in her. "Oh, Rosa," she sighed. "Would you look at these two wee monkeys?"

She gazed long and hard at my children, at their uncannily precocious black hair and round cheeks, at the sheer, undeniable, presence of them. But I was looking at her. My mother had fallen in love with her bastard grandchildren.

I switched on the electric kettle and spooned some tea into the pot.

"You really should get some teabags," I remarked, "they make life a lot easier."

"Teabags, indeed," she snorted. "Making life easier

doesn't make it better, Rosa. They just put the sweepings from the floor in those little bags."

"Well, I can't honestly say that I can tell the difference."

"I can believe that. *You* may not be able to, but *I* certainly would. Now, where's that brother of yours got to? The kitchen will be closing soon."

So, Sam would be getting the full English, would he? I noticed she hadn't offered to cook me anything.

"He's done a bunk. He just came back to leave me a message and then went; his bed's not been slept in at all. I suppose he's hitched back to London."

"No!" She sat down at the kitchen table. "He might've said goodbye."

"Mm."

"What kind of message? Anything to do with the police search?"

I took the scrap of paper out of my pocket and read it out to her.

"Old Harry Cole?" She gasped. "Oh, but that's *dreadful*."

"Is it? Well, I mean, of course it is.. but who *is* old Harry Cole? Should I know him?"

"He was a friend of Major Dyminge's."

I sat up and took notice.

"Yes, one of his odd friends from the Coastguard. They used to play dominoes there of an evening. Oh, how *very* sad."

My mind raced. What had old Harry known of the Major's activities? Had Major Dyminge, all unwittingly, passed secrets to him? Secrets that spelled murder for old Harry Cole.

"About a hundred and a complete dipsomaniac, of course. Impossible to speak to after seven in the evening, and quite difficult to understand at any other time. Cleft palette. He was a gentleman of the road, you know. Just the one suit of clothes and smelt a bit. Well, more than a bit. I always thought it was very charitable of them to let him through the pub door. Still.. harmless. I expect he tumbled into the water when he was in his cups, poor soul. Now.. talking of smelling a bit .. does somebody's nappy need changing?"

I sniffed the air and shrugged my shoulders, as if I couldn't detect a thing.

"I'm not *that* much of a soft touch, Rosa."

All morning the words of the old rhyme kept going round and round in my thoughts:

Old King Cole was a merry old soul and a merry old soul was he.

He called for his pipe and he called for his bowl and he called for his fiddlers three.

I rang Peter later, while the twins were enjoying one of their new experiences, a nap.

"I know old Harry Cole seems a most unlikely candidate for anything but an accidental death," I finished up, "but there *is* a connection there - with Major Dyminge - however tenuous."

"I agree. In the absence of anything else to go on .. I think we have to find out as much as we can about this old fellow."

"You do?"

"Yes. Just off the top of my head, I think we need the answers to two questions."

"Right." I grabbed the telephone pad and a pencil. "Fire away."

"One, what was he doing in Dungeness, a good many miles away from St Margaret's Bay? And two .. did Mr Cole possess a library card? Because, if he did, it might point us towards an address."

So, I looked up Dover library in the phone book and rang Bill Hawking.

"Hey Bill, it's Rosa Stone. What are you up to?"

"Hello Rosa," he sounded quite pleased to hear from me. "I'm just sorting out Literary Criticism in the back room."

"Oh, good. Listen, do you know a Mr Harry Cole? Very old and a tramp, apparently, but that doesn't stop you being a reader, does it?"

He didn't miss a beat.

"I do. We know all the tramps here. They take the seats and we have to winkle them out at closing time."

"Great! Well, he's dead, I'm afraid. They've just fished him out of a flooded gravel pit up by Dungeness."

"Ah. They've found Sam's corpse. I mean .. not *Sam's* corpse .. but .."

I seemed to have embarrassed him. I've always found people who get embarrassed rather fascinating, because I never do. They are like a different species of animal. Still, there wasn't time for my fascinations; we had sleuthing to do.

"Yes, I know what you mean, Bill, and it does look like that's who it is. Only, there's a connection with Major Dyminge because they were friends, apparently, so Peter and I are following all leads and we need your help."

"Now, listen to me, Bill," I gathered my thoughts and then gave them full rein, "is there anything more you can tell me about old Harry Cole? Such as, did he have a library ticket and do you need an address to get one? Or .. might you have a record of the books he got out and know what his reading preferences were? Or .. could he, in your opinion, have been using the library as a rendezvous point? Or .. or .. a secret drop-off .. with letters stuffed in the books, or odd words pencilled in that could only be interpreted with the use of a master code book, or ..?"

There was rather a gap while he took it all in.

"Um."

"Yes? There's not a moment to lose, Bill. Not if we want to find Major Dyminge's corpse intact and give him a proper send-off."

"Um. Right-o. To be honest with you, I'm not quite sure whether Mr Cole *had* a library ticket. Really, we knew him for the bottles he kept trying to smuggle in and .. well .. the smell."

"Oh, I've heard about that. But I think we need to get over the pong. I mean, Major Dyminge obviously got over the pong. They used to play dominoes together and, if you can play dominoes with a brain-box like the Major, I really don't see why you can't read books, or be a spy, or an informer, or .."

"And, if he did have a library ticket, I'm not sure that I'm supposed to be giving out private information about our customers. In fact, I'm positive I'm not. Some of our customers wouldn't necessarily want their reading preferences to get out."

Oh, for goodness sake. What kind of books did they stock at Dover library? If they wanted that kind of stuff they only had to go to the newsagents these days. Bill Hawking was turning out to be deeply disappointing.

"Oh, forget it, Mr Librarian. You carry on sorting out Literary Criticism and using your little stamper."

"I mean, I'd like to be of assistance, but .."

"Stamp, stamp, stamp, Bill," I said. "Stamp, stamp, stamp."

I put the receiver down.

I spent the rest of the day trying to piece together some more about Harry Cole's movements; specifically, why our drunken centenarian should have been wandering around Dungeness. I went into the Coastguard at lunchtime, wheeling in the pram backwards through the swinging door. When I'd lived down here one of my best friends had worked behind the bar, but she was married and living in Bromley, now. Some vestigial sense of women knowing their place compelled me to veer into the Lounge to order a coke from the girl at the bar. The Lounge was deserted. A man in his early forties, the owner of a trendy moustache and sideburns, approached to wipe the table down; I assumed that this was the landlord.

"No dominoes today? I quite fancied a game of dominoes."

What I could make out of his face was not expressive, but I discerned an attitude of surprise in his body language. I supposed that mothers were not meant to spend their lunchtimes in the pub playing dominoes.

"You're Sam Stone's sister, aren't you? You came in yesterday."

He wasn't local; might have been Scottish.

"Yes, I'm Rosa. How do you do?"

"Visiting the parents, are you?"

"Mm.. and dying for a game of dominoes while I'm at it. You must have known our friend Major Dyminge; now *he* was a fine dominoes player."

"Ah.." something dawned above the moustache, "you'll have come down for the funeral. An odd business. Folk round here can talk about nothing else."

"Yes?"

Since the dominoes angle didn't seem to be getting me anywhere, I thought I'd try the straightforward approach.

"Any ideas?"

Unfortunately, he wasn't turning out to be the chatty type of landlord and twitched his moustache at me, possibly in alarm.

"No."

He promptly picked up my empty glass and scarpered. Just my luck to find a taciturn Scot running the pub. I was debating another coke when Jessica – it was almost always Jessica – woke up, took a swift look around the unfamiliar place she'd been transported to while she was having a nice kip and began to bawl. I unearthed her from beneath swathes of blanket and picked her up to give her a swift cuddle. Benjamin was still fast asleep, thank heavens, but it wouldn't be long.

"Oh diddums! Did we wake up in a bad mood?"

A girl with long, auburn hair had sprung out of the woodwork to lean over me and crook a little finger at my daughter's purple face.

"Diddums, diddums," she repeated, curling and uncurling her delicate little finger with its topping of shell-pink nail varnish.

This was not my favourite kind of behaviour and I was about to say something, when I noticed that Jessica had stopped, mid-bawl, and was watching the finger closely, entranced as to what it might do next.

"Wow, thanks. How did you do that?"

The girl straightened up and I could see that she was no more than fourteen, in her blue jeans and polo neck. Shouldn't she have been at school?

"I'm the local babysitter," she said. "Everybody uses me."

This was extremely interesting news.

"Can I?" She gestured at Jessica, who practically held out her arms to be picked up by this vision of loveliness.

"Be my guest."

She gathered my daughter into her arms and promptly winded her.

"Can I buy you a bottle of coca-cola?"

"You don't have to buy it, I'm allowed to help myself, 'long as it's only one," she laughed. "My Dad runs the pub. I'm Suze."

"Rosa. Rosa Stone."

"Sam's sister, yeah?"

This seemed to be my new rôle in life.

"Sam's such a dreamboat," she sighed. "We all fancy him rotten."

"Goodness me," I huffed, "my brother's much too old for you."

"He's younger than Paul McCartney," she said, as if that proved something. And then, which caught me by surprise. "Did you want a game of dominoes? I can get them out for you, if you want."

"Were you listening when I was talking to your father, Suze?"

"Yeah. I always listen to everything round here," she

Claire Ingrams

giggled, slipping off Jessica's sock and playing with her toes.

Bingo, as Peter would have said. This was the girl for me.

"Did you listen when Major Dyminge was playing dominoes with his friends?"

"The old guy whose body was snatched from his coffin? The police came round asking about him this morning."

"Did they? And what did your father tell them?"

She had taken Jessica's other sock off now and a tiny part of me tensed as I watched her make free with my daughter's chubby toes.

"Oh, *he* never sees nothing," she scoffed. "Like .. how much *they* mean to me, how I'd just *die* for them. He thinks it's just me being a teenager and all, but he just doesn't understand. They're like *everything* to me, 'specially [29]Paul, of course. Then Ringo probably. Or George. 'Cos that John's married, only they don't want you to know."

Hmm; leverage.

"They're wonderful, aren't they? Super. A blast. I expect you've got all their records, Suze?"

She scowled.

"He don't let me keep most of my babysitting money. Mean old .. Calls it bed and board. Soon as I'm sixteen he won't see me for *dust*."

She'd spat it out in quite an unpleasant manner, and I didn't doubt her for a second. A short silence ensued while I tried to work out the best method of bribery and she jiggled Jessica about like a dolly. I had to suppress the urge to snatch her away from her.

"Okay," Suze said, as if I'd asked her, "you give me the money for [30]*Beatles for Sale* and I'll tell you what the old men used to talk about. Only don't blame me if it don't mean nothing; I get the money whatever, yeah? Up front."

"*Beatles for Sale* being what ..? Their new LP?"

"Thought you said you liked them. Yeah, it came out in December and I *still* haven't got it."

I felt in my coat pocket and came out with two pound

notes.

"This should cover it. Now tell me what they said, Suze."

She grabbed the money, smiling like a crocodile and, for a terrible moment, I thought she was going to come up with sweet Fanny Adams. But she didn't. She bent forward over Jessica.

"The old guy, he'd pay for all the drinks 'cos I don't think the stinking tramp had no money. The only reason Dad let the tramp in the pub was he knew the old man'd pay and, then, he'd make them sit by the open door, or outside in any old weather. 'Cos of the stink. There was others came and went, locals and that. Only I think it was the tramp the old man knew best. The old man, he'd bring his own set, you know, for the two of 'em to play dominoes, a fancy, pale green one. They'd bend over it, mumbling at one another and the old man seemed to get what the tramp said. Dunno how, 'cos he couldn't talk proper."

So, the dominoes set belonged to Major Dyminge. My photographic memory was not what it was, but I felt sure that I would have remembered seeing a fancy, green set in his cottage.

"Right. Well done, Suze. And is that it? I mean, did you actually hear anything that they said, you know, any *words*?"

She looked down at Jessica and giggled.

"Well, I don't know why Mummy wants to know all about these funny men, do you Diddums? What a silly Mummy you've got, eh?"

Jessica beamed adoration up at her.

"I think the tramp had come out of hospital, that's all I can tell you, cross my heart and hope to die. That he came from over Lydd way and that he'd been in hospital."

"Dover hospital? For his cleft palette?" I was grasping at straws now.

"No," she laughed and lifted her small hand, with its shell-pink varnished nails to do that charming circling motion at the side of her temple.

"Silly Mummy. Not that kind of hospital."

Poor old Harry Cole; he probably *hadn't* been a merry old soul at all.

I had wrested my daughter from the arms of the teenage Beatle maniac and taken us all back home to Shore House. My mother was clearing out her workroom at the top of the house because she had recently sold her millinery business. She had some sumptuous fabrics – taffetas and nets, brocades and shot silks – that she was going to give me for the Arcanium.

"Don't feel you have to rush back to London, will you Rosa? It's been.. nice."

The doorbell rang and she went over to the window and peered down on her tiptoes.

"It's a young man. Oh, it's Bill Hawking. Would you go down and tell him Samuel's gone back to London, dear?"

I galloped down the stairs and opened the door to Bill.

"Was there something?" I asked.

"He took out one book and never gave it back. The library fines on it are mounting."

"You'd better come in. Have you finished work for the day? Would you like some tea and cake?"

"Your dad's cake?"

"Naturally."

He came in and hovered about by the kitchen sink, looking gangly and ill-at-ease.

"What was it, then? The book?"

"The autobiography of [31] Woody Guthrie."

I paused with the teapot lid in hand. Hopping freight trains, life on the lonesome road: it made a kind of sense. Was that how Harry's life had been?

"Thanks, Bill. I hope you won't get into trouble."

"No, I don't suppose I will. There was more, though," he stood up straight for once. "I asked around and found out that his sister joined him up at the library a long time before he ever took out the book. In fact, the Woody Guthrie book was the only book he ever took out. Well, the sister's passed on now, but he's got family. Fishermen. Harry Cole was from one of the fishing families up on Dungeness. That'll be why he was over there."

I cut him a big slice of chocolate cake and handed it over.

"Well I never, Bill Hawking," I marvelled, deciding there and then to fill him in on the rest of the case so far, "we'll make a sleuth of you yet."

11. DUNGENESS

Just before you enter the weird, shingle world that is the Ness, if you're coming from Littlestone and then Lydd, there is a primary school with a low wall surrounding the playground. The children were on their morning break when I parked the car by the side of the road and got out. They jumped about as if they'd been shot from a bottle of fizzy drink. A couple of dinner-ladies in overalls, big bee-hives on their heads – one bleach-blond and the other witch-black – were smoking as they did playground duty. Over in the corner a knot of skipping girls giggled.

"What's the time? Half-past nine. Hang your knickers on the line.

When a copper comes along, hurry up and put them on."

Things had changed a bit since we'd played cat's cradle and got obsessed with crochet.

I walked past the school and then past the rows of Tudor-style, Thirties housing and the entrance to Dungeness lay across the road. It really was like stepping into a different country. Just one sign-post for the pub, advertising the *Best Fish and Chips in the World*, and another for the *Romney Hythe Dymchurch Railway*; both listing sideways in the wind. Then stones and grey sky; miles and miles of both, as far as the eye could see. Which was as far as the new, rectangular block of a building at the head of the bay. The nuclear power station.

The wind was blowing so hard I felt as if I might be able

to give it all of my substantial weight, let it pick me up in my mangy fox fur, headscarf and wellington boots and bear me down to the sea. But I bunched my fists in my pockets and carried on under my own steam. It was so quiet, or perhaps so noisy; the roar of wind and sea had obscured all else and created a parallel kind of silence. The sea was such a long way away; it receded every year, and the shingle shifted and expanded. Old lighthouses became redundant and new ones were built to warn ships of different dangers. The entire area was moving north and east.

When I was younger, there had been sheep grazing on the Marsh, right up by the Ness, but there were none, now. If I'd been a farmer, I don't think that I would have wished to let my sheep graze so close to a nuclear power station. Yet, they still fished here. Fishermen's huts, painted black with tar, still dotted the higher part of the beach, while the boats sat low down by the sea. There was the old narrow-gauge railway track, where they would haul the fish up the shingle dunes.

It was as well that the fishing continued, because it was the fishermen that I had come to see first. The hut I remembered was open and the slippery catch poured into tin buckets. Cod and whiting, flounder and dab and various other flatfish. All looked fresh as could be, the fish eyes so bright they might have tracked me crunching across the beach, and up to the counter, to talk to the fishmonger.

"Morning," he was a big man with a red face and tweed cap and a friendly, comfortable air about him. "What would you like, Miss?"

Buying some fish was distinctly on the cards.

"What's best? It all looks so good."

"Got some lovely Dover sole, fresh off the boat this morning and the boats aren't out that regular this season. First come, first served."

"Any mackerel?" I asked, because the Dover sole looked dauntingly big and probably cost a small fortune.

"Mackerel shoals aren't in yet. They'll be here early

spring, Miss."

"Well, then, Dover sole it will be, please. Er..two."

They all seemed to be monsters of the deep, so I thought two would probably do us. He separated some newspaper from a pile and began to wrap them up, surprising dextrously for a man with such big hands.

"I hear there's been a drowning in one of the flooded gravel pits," I ventured, not being awfully good at bush beating. "What a ghastly thing for you all."

He looked up from his work.

"That got about already, has it? We had the police up here all night long with their lights and vans, but they was asking us to keep it quiet. Just till they knew who he was."

"I thought it was a tramp," I said. "I don't know why, I just got that impression."

"Did you, now?"

"Yes, a very old tramp who liked a drop to drink, was what I was told."

"And who was it told you that, then, Miss?"

He wasn't looking quite so friendly now and seemed to have given up on my fish, altogether.

As I said, beating about the bush has never really been my forte.

"My brother told me that, actually. Because he found the body."

"Ah," he let out a sigh that could only be described as ambiguous.

"It was old Harry Cole, wasn't it?" I blurted out.

He didn't reply, so I tried to reassure him.

"Don't worry. Really. My brother isn't the talkative type and he's gone back to London, anyhow; he'll have forgotten all about it by now. It's just that he told me and.. well.. I have a reason – a very specific reason – for wanting to know how poor old Mr Cole really died." I came to a shuddering standstill. "I'm Rosa Stone, by the way. How do you do?"

"Eric Cole," he said.

"Oh, my goodness," I practically fell out of my wellington boots. "I had no *idea* you'd be a relation. I'm so sorry, Mr Cole. I've gone and put my big foot in it again."

"There's only a couple of fishing families left here, Miss Stone. Not surprising you'd run into one of us." He pushed back his cap and scratched his head, still looking blank. "Seems like you know more'n me. It really *was* old Harry then? In Long Pit?"

"I'm afraid my brother was certain of it. He knew him from the pub in St Margaret's Bay."

"That's a way off from here, Miss, you sure about that?"

"Yes, he's well-known around our way."

"That'd be, what, a fair night's walk from there to come home? Seems like a long old way, even for Harry. Still, I reckon he didn't have nowhere else to be."

"He had a friend living by the bay, you see. A Major Dyminge."

"Now, why does that name ring a bell?"

I thought about it; it could have rung a bell for so many reasons. The Major had a certain notoriety in our part of Kent for something he'd done before the war, something that had involved an explosion and a landslide. It had all been very unfair, of course, because the Major had never meant to do any harm, but mud stuck in the countryside in more ways than one.

"Wait a minute," he said, beginning to leaf through his pile of newspapers. "Here it is. Knew I'd heard it recent. He's the old soldier who got himself swiped from his coffin."

He had found the *Daily Kentish News* and brandished the unfortunate headline above his head.

"Yes," I admitted. "Quite horrible. I'm trying to find out why, you see."

"And you think Uncle Harry may've been mixed up in it?"

"He was your uncle?"

"Several times back. Didn't have no children himself,

Claire Ingrams

but was brother to my Great-Grandad Ernie. Last of his generation, last of the next one, too. Here, you fancy a brew?"

He had a thermos flask with him and offered me a spare mug.

"That's so kind. It's cold and windy enough to blow your socks off out here, isn't it?"

"We don't have too many customers here in February," he poured me some tea and even shifted a box out from behind the counter for me to sit on. "The whole place is dying, if you ask me. People aren't shopping local so much these days and they don't care where their fish comes from. Iceland or Kent, it don't make no difference to them."

I took a big slurp of deliciously strong, sweet tea and brought him back to the subject in hand.

"So, if you don't mind - at such a sad time, and all - could you describe your Uncle Harry to me? His character and the kind of life he led, that sort of thing."

"He was a tramp. You said so yourself. Spent his life on the road in holey boots. He didn't do nothing except drink and walk and beg where he could. He was always light-fingered, too; I caught him stealing from me once, didn't make no difference I was family. And he got worse. Latterly, he would've sold his sister for the price of a glass of whisky, would Harry."

I couldn't work out Eric Cole's attitude to his great-uncle.

"But there must have been more to him than that. There's more to everybody."

"That's Christian of you," he gave me a lopsided smile. "My old mother would've said the same. She always had a soft spot for Harry. He was a lazy, good-for-nothing and not always right in the head, neither, but I'll tell you something, Miss; he wasn't stupid, was Harry. He taught himself to read, because he didn't get no schooling to speak of. They didn't let him in school owing to his cleft palette, but when it came to putting himself up for cannon fodder nobody said no to that. Oh, no. He volunteered from the off in the First World War and saw most of his mates from the Ness and Lydd way die. Only reason he lived was he was buried up to his neck in the mud and Jerry thought he was a goner. Buried in mud for days he was, and wasn't never the same man again. Mental. Not always, but liable to go that way."

I was getting a picture of him; some understanding of why he and the Major might have got on.

"Did he have anywhere where he might have kept possessions? Only, I'd be interested to know the whereabouts of an old set of dominoes and a library book. The dominoes set was pale green, and the library book was about the singer, Woody Guthrie."

"Why, did Harry nick them?"

"Well, the set originally belonged to Major Dyminge, but hasn't been found among his things. I don't think Harry stole it from him, though; I just wonder whether he might have given it to Harry one of the last times they met. The book is the property of Dover library, but, don't worry, I'm not concerned about that. I'm just grasping at straws, really. Just trying to find anything that might help with finding the Major."

"Look, Miss, I can ask around and if you give me your phone number, I'll let you know if we find them, but I don't hold out much hope. Being a tramp, the road was his home. If he did have anything to call his own, I'd say he'd have squirrelled it away somewhere on his route. Under a tree, or a patch of brambles, like."

"Yes, you're probably right," I sighed.

I couldn't walk the road from Dungeness to Dover looking in every ditch, after all. This was turning into a fool's errand, especially when one considered that old Harry Cole had probably just drunk himself to death.

"I suppose, given what you've said, it wasn't unlikely that he would have drunk too much, stumbled home all night long and lost his footing by the flooded gravel pit. And, then, he probably wouldn't have been able to swim."

"Harry could swim," he said, "Harry could swim for England in his day. He used to pick up bits of work on the lifeboat, when he could. They don't take you if you're not a swimmer."

"But he was awfully old."

"He was, but he could take his liquor . ." He seemed to be warming to his theme. "You don't live that long, drink that much and walk that far, without being a strong old sod. What's more, he knew the Ness like the back of his hand."

He looked me square in the face and it struck me that he *had* cared for the old man. I was glad.

I left Eric Cole's hut with the wrapped Dover sole in a plastic bag. I wanted to see exactly where his great-uncle had fallen into the water and drowned. I clambered back up the beach and scanned inland. It wasn't difficult to find, owing to the cordon of yellow tape, flapping in the wind, and the single police car parked nearby, a pale blue mini. However, it took me a while to reach, since walking over deep shingle can be strenuous and my wellingtons kept sinking and gathering stones. When I did get there, a hulking, great police officer promptly got out of the small car to warn me away.

"Nothing to see here, Miss."

I rather agreed; only little ripples scudding across the surface of the deep, grey water and the winter-brown vestiges of rushes and weeds. Any signs of a struggle would have been erased by the persistent winds. I wasn't Sherlock Holmes, but as far as I could make out there were no incriminating blood stains, nor oddly bent grasses. I waved my fish at the policeman and passed on my way, back across the shingle dunes towards civilisation.

There had been little to learn and even less to see, and yet I felt quite different. I was possessed with the strange certainty that old Harry Cole had not met his death by accident.

All the long way back in the car, I thought about those two old soldiers. Those two old men who'd been knocked badly by life, but had only ever wanted to serve their King and Country. They'd had much in common. I pictured them playing dominoes outside in the cold because one of them reeked. That was all that most people would have said about the poor man: he reeked, he stank, he ponged. The little, yellow bottles of perfume rose up before me. Could it have been *because* he smelt that Major Dyminge sought out Harry Cole? Those two sat in my mind's eye all the way home, bent over their game in the cold and rain, one still brim-full of ideas and secrets, and the other willing to do anything, anything at all, for the price of one more drink.

12. DINNER AT SHORE HOUSE

Boy, did it feel good when Rosa congratulated me on asking around at the library. I couldn't think of much else all evening, despite it being beef stew for tea, with dumplings. As I was lying on my bed that night, writing up my journal, I made a private vow to find out more.

"Would you like a hot chocolate, Bill?" It was Mum knocking on my door.

"No, thanks Mum."

I glanced up from my writing and noticed she was dressed up to the nines. She had her dark hair all piled up and lacquered and was showing an awful lot of long leg.

"What's that?" I gawped. "Are you wearing one of those mini-skirts?"

"D'you like it?" She did a twirl in the doorway.

"People's mums aren't supposed to wear those. You'll make a laughing stock of us."

"Oh, Bill," she laughed, "you're such an old-fashioned boy. As if I've ever cared what people think. C'mon, admit it, I've got the legs for it, haven't I?"

I thought I'd die of embarrassment.

"Well, I'm off out now, so don't wait up, Bill, will you love?"

I'd forgotten she was going out, probably with the girls from work.

"I mean it, Bill. There was no need for you to stay up that last time, no need at all. I'm a big girl."

She hadn't come home until gone two in the morning and I'd been on the verge of dialling 999. What on earth could she find to get up to in our sleepy, old village? It beat me.

I turned the page of my journal and started a list:

FACT 1. Major's body removed from coffin. Place: St Aethelred's church, Hassels, Kent. Date: Tuesday 2nd February 1965.

Why? R Suspects Major of scientific advance re: radar imaging (x-rays?), effect on <u>BRAIN</u>, adaptations to olfactory sensation. Why useful? Who might want info? How did they hear about it?

ACTION: Research brain, neuro ... (?) Look in Psychiatry (Reference) and allied library sections. Any magazines/scientific journals?

FACT 2. Bodysnatching witnessed by a Mr Summerby. Credible witness? Two men, green van, no number plate id.

ACTION: Find out what police know. How?

FACT 3. Major's workshop ransacked night of funeral/ early morning after. <u>After</u> visit by Rosa.

Assuming bodysnatching and search of workshop perpetrated by same suspects, what might they want to find in workshop? Did they find it?

ACTION: Ask Auntie F if anything missing. Offer to help clear up? With R?

FACT 4: Body of Mr H Cole found in Long Pit, Dungeness by Sam, night of Tuesday 2nd February 1965.

Police conducted proper id? Any marks on body that might suggest violence/cause of death OTHER than drowning. How long had he been in water?

Connection with Major: regular meetings at The Coastguard and dominoes. Death accidental? Co-incidental? Connected with Major? Murder?

ACTION: Find out what police know. How?

I chewed my pencil for a bit and added another sentence to my last ACTION.

Find out whether Auntie F knew H Cole.

There, that all seemed fairly comprehensive. I had that satisfactory sense of order snatched from the teeth of chaos that shelving books often gave. It didn't help me sleep, though. Midnight had been and gone by the time I heard the car parking outside. I leapt out of bed to peek between the curtains. A light-coloured mini was by the kerb, headlights still on and engine ticking over. The car door nearest our house opened and one of my mother's long legs emerged, then an arm shot out and pulled her back into the car. I clearly heard her giggle and then sigh, as some male person made free with her. I froze in sheer horror.

Breakfast was a queer affair, what with me pretending to read the local paper and Mum, humming softly in her curlers, while she unwrapped the bread for my packed lunch.

"Ham and tomato as usual, love?"

My feelings welled up in me, constricting my throat.

"I hate ham and tomato," it came out in a strangled falsetto, "I never want ham and tomato again."

She looked astonished.

"What's up, Bill?"

I threw down the paper and went to snatch my mac from the hook, before storming upstairs to get my briefcase. I bent to retrieve my journal from under the bed and slung that in.

My mother just didn't seem able to understand me – maybe she never had – because she'd begun humming again before I even got to the outside door.

"Well, please yourself," she said, and it felt like the last straw.

I strode out and scrabbled at the door of my Morris Minor with my key, conscious that I'd have to sit in it for at least half an hour, being much too early for work.

I was in a state of turmoil all day and was busy making a complete hash of Literary Criticism, when a colleague motioned to me.

"Phone for you, Mr Hawking."

It was Rosa again.

"Hey Bill," she breezed, "how's Lit Crit going?"

"You don't want to know."

"Don't I? I always want to know *everything*," she laughed.

It relaxed me to hear her voice, somehow. Cleared my head, too.

"Actually, I've been thinking about you know what," I said, glancing round the library to make sure nobody was listening, "and I've jotted down a few particulars."

"Great, because I've also been busy and I think we need to meet up, which was why I rang. Would you like to come to dinner? You know, Friday night dinner at my parents' house."

"Um. Wow. Yes." I was so happy, I couldn't think of anything else to say, until it occurred to me. "But, Rosa, it's Friday *today*."

"I know, that's why I asked you. Seven o'clock, then. Be there or be square."

Sam had never invited me to dinner with his parents, so I felt somewhat honoured. There was fish for dinner – which I'd always understood to be a Christian tradition on a Friday – and a showy, silver candelabra took pride of place on the dining table. What with the electric lights being off, the candle flames and crackling blaze in the fireplace, it all made for an exotic atmosphere. I was given to understand that Mr Summerby, the witness at the church, would be joining us, as he was staying with the Stone family for a short holiday. Rosa told me that Mr Summerby was one of the world's foremost experts on antiques of the Orient. I reflected that *this* Mr Summerby should be a most credible witness. A thrilling sensation crept over me; that I might finally be joining the Bohemian society of which I had so often dreamt. I was still in Dreamland when something poked me under the table in an unexpected place. I must have jumped a mile high.

"Canine," Mr Summerby said.

And it was. A yellow dog with yellow teeth grinned up at me between my legs.

"If you don't mind, Edwin, I'll shut Canaan in the drawing-room," Mrs Stone suggested. "I can see fish being too much of a temptation."

She shooed him out.

"Fish, meat, vegetables," Mr Summerby ruminated to the table at large, "the dog's a gannet. He'll eat anything and everything."

"Yes," Rosa agreed, "he loves a pint of beer."

I studied my cutlery, suddenly blank as to which knife and fork to use first. I felt sure that some stimulating, intellectual conversation would begin at any moment.

"In fact, he likes crisps almost as much as I do," Rosa continued.

"Come, come," her father interjected. "Nobody likes crisps as much as you do, Rosa."

It was at this juncture that Auntie Frances appeared. She came and sat down next to me, squeezing my hand under the table. Hers felt icy and all bone.

"I say, what spectacular Dover sole," she exclaimed. "Wherever did you get them, Jerzy?"

"He didn't, I did," Rosa corrected her. "I bought them from the fish stall at Dungeness."

"That was an awfully long way to go," Auntie Frances

spread her serviette on her lap. "I've always found the boats at Kingsdown jolly satisfactory."

"Kingsdown," mused Mr Summerby. "It's a long time since I've been there. Now, what was the name of that nice pub on the beach?"

The conversation flowed from pubs to the price of cod nowadays to whether sea-kale was, actually, worth eating. Not having known that sea-kale was edible at all, I waited to see what the consensus might be before I made my contribution.

"Definitely NOT," I said, with confidence.

The room went quiet as they all turned in my direction, no doubt waiting for me to expand upon my trenchant views on sea-kale. At which point it struck me that it was the first time I'd opened my gob since the dog had goosed me. My cheeks began to prickle in the old, familiar way. Sam was right not to have invited me to dinner. I wouldn't invite me to dinner. I'd be a damper on any sophisticated soiree.

I pushed the remains of my meal to the edge of my plate and stood up.

"Um .. Thank you for having me, Mrs Stone, Mr Stone."

I mumbled some tripe about having to get up in the morning for work and made a dash for it.

Rosa caught up with me just outside the front door.

"Hey, Bill. What's the matter?"

"Um .. just gotta go .."

"But I need to talk to you. About our case."

"You don't need me, Rosa. I'm just a boring librarian."

"Of course, I need you. You're vital to all this. Besides .. you can't go now; you're my guest of honour for the evening."

She grabbed my arm and pulled me out of the cold and back indoors.

"You crazy boy, did you think we were going to force feed you sea-kale?" She laughed, her warm body so close to mine. "You haven't even had pudding. Nobody misses pudding at my parents' house. Why d'you think I'm the size I am?"

"But you're beautiful," I said, just like that.

I couldn't believe the words had come out of my mouth.

"You're not so bad yourself."

Was this flirting? Nobody flirted with me.

"But you're far too young for me, sadly. Come on, you idiot. Pudding will get cold."

I took a quick look at my journal in the downstairs toilet, before we all went to sit in the drawing-room for coffee and brandy. So, I had the facts fresh in my mind when Rosa finished with the coffee cups and came to sit next to me on the window-seat. I gave her a brief summing-up, before she shared what she had learnt on her trip to Dungeness.

"I'm not sure that qualifies as actual fact," I pointed out, with regard to what was, in my opinion, just a strong hunch that Mr Cole had been murdered in the flooded gravel pit.

"Oh, don't go all librarian on me again, Bill. I have extremely good instincts. Old Harry Cole simply knew the lie of the land too well to go tripping up and falling into the water, however drunk he may have been. Especially when there was a full moon and he would have been able to see his way home clearly. Now, a heart attack, I grant you, that might have caused him to fall, but how can we get hold of the pathologist's report? You know, we're not doing too badly, considering, but I think we can agree that without some kind of 'in' with the police, we're at a strong disadvantage."

She looked thoughtful.

"What we need, Bill, is to make contact with the police officer in the pale blue mini, because he seems to be present at all of the important bits in our investigation."

"Pale blue mini? I've seen one of those recently."

"Really? Well, think hard, Bill. I mean, how many policemen can there be in East Kent driving one of those? I can't believe they're standard issue. Now . ." She changed the subject. "The most useful point you just made was the one about asking Mrs Dyminge about Harry Cole. That's definitely got to be done as soon as poss."

We both glanced towards Auntie Frances, who had just stood up to refuse a brandy.

"Look, she's going up to bed," Rosa began to prod me, "corner her while you can, Bill."

"Night night, all. See you in the morning, my dears," Auntie Frances was already halfway out of the room.

I, more or less, sprinted across the drawing-room to catch up with her as she paused at the bottom of the staircase.

"Auntie Frances!"

"Bill, dear. How very nice to see you here tonight. How are you?"

"I'm just fine, Auntie. How are *you*? Can I give you a hand up the stairs?"

"I must admit, stairs seem to be growing steeper. A helping hand would be most appreciated."

I took her arm and guided her upwards. When we reached her room, she sat down on the bed with a small groan.

"Um . . would you mind if I asked you something, Auntie?"

"Ask away . . I can't vouch for the answer being 'compos mentus', though."

"How well did you know Major Dyminge's friends? His pub friends, from the Coastguard."

"His pub friends?" She looked blank. "Well, I wasn't really ever invited to join them, Bill. Not that I gave two hoots about that because beer and dominoes have never been my scene, as they say nowadays."

I might have known that'd be her answer. Still, I supposed it was worth a try.

"Except for his batman, of course."

For a bewildering moment I thought of Batman and Robin.

"Batman, Auntie?"

"Yes, in the War, you know. The East Kent Regiment. Harold Cole."

I returned to the drawing-room, triumphant.

"Mr Cole was Major Dyminge's batman during the First World War. They went to France together. Auntie Frances always had some trouble understanding everything he said, due to the cleft palette, but he and the Major were thick as thieves. They'd always played dominoes together, even in the trenches. The Major still had the old set from the war and would take it to the pub in a bag. The set had originally belonged to Harry, but he'd given it to the Major after he'd done him some service and they'd always referred to it as 'Harry's set'. What's more, it wasn't just your regular dominoes. It was Chinese dominoes, apparently. Auntie Frances said they had a system."

"A system?" Rosa opened her eyes, wide. "Oh, *wow*, I love a system."

"She said she'd always wondered whether they communicated through the game."

We both went quiet for a sec, while we digested this new information.

"You didn't tell her he was dead, did you, Bill?"

"No, I thought I'd spare her that, just at the moment. She's got enough on her plate." I considered our conversation. "Not that she even asked *why* I wanted to know about him; she was so tired, she wasn't really her old self."

"She hasn't been her old self since the Major died. We're all so worried about her. Still, at least she steered clear of the drink tonight."

"How d'you mean?"

"Oh, Bill," Rosa sighed, "you really *are* young, aren't you?'

◆ ◆ ◆

I went to sleep with the boy's voice in my head, asking –

quite out of the blue – about Guy's batman in the war. And, when I slept, I dreamt that Guy and I returned to that so-called sanatorium; the asylum near Albert where they had imprisoned Harold Cole. Poor, young Harold who couldn't speak properly, who had been buried in the mud of the Somme for all of those days and nights, until Guy had managed to go back and dig him out. Somehow, Guy had known his batman wasn't dead. When he found him, however, he'd been raving. At first, they had brought him to the field station where I nursed. We cleaned him up, of course, gave him food and water and bandages, but there wasn't really much we could do for him, not when there were so many other young men clamouring for our attention. We barely noticed when they put him in a straitjacket and carted him away from the battlefield.

In my dream I was that young field nurse once more, falling in love with the gruff soldier who came looking for his batman, only to discover him gone. It was Guy, of course, who hatched the plan to get him out of the asylum. He persuaded me to go with him on my day off, I remember, to look after the boy. I was filled with trepidation; have always been such a coward. But Guy hadn't cared a jot, had marched into that place and pulled rank, as if he were the head of the entire British army. Guy had never cared. So, we got him out, poor young Harold. For all the good it did him.

13. COME TO MY SENSES

I loaded up the car with the piles of wonderful textiles that my mother had given me. The twins were already wedged on the back seat. They weren't too happy about the situation and were complaining, bitterly.

"Will you be able to drive with all this racket going on?" My father asked.

"Drive, eat, run a shop: I'm, pretty used to it by now, Dad."

"Why don't you stay a mite longer, Rosa? It's so nice for us and I'm sure you could do with the break," said my mother.

"No, no, I must get back. The Arcanium can't stay closed indefinitely."

But I was sorely tempted. Staying with my parents had been like staying on that island of Lotus Eaters. If I remained much longer, I might be persuaded into handing my children over, altogether, while I gorged on cake and went chasing after adventure. It was time to return to the mainland. I hugged them both.

"You will let me know if they find him?"

"Of course, we will."

I switched on the ignition and set off for London, not looking back in case I changed my mind. I paused in my journey only once and that was to post a letter to Bill in the pillar-box in the village.

Dear Bill,
Have come to my senses and am going back to the Big Smoke. I am the mother of two small children; nearly forgot. You have been a sterling musketeer, but don't feel you have to carry on for my sake. After all, you have Lit Crit to attend to.
See you,
Your friend Rosa.

It was over two weeks before I got a letter back.

Dear Rosa,
There have been developments.
Cordially,
Bill (Hawking)

I wasted no time in ringing Dover library, but a brusque voice informed me that Mr Hawking no longer worked there. What seismic eruptions could have occurred to drive Bill from his job? I had a terrible feeling that they might have something to do with me. Should I get his mother's telephone number from my parents and ring her up? Then again, would that inflame some family situation of which I knew nothing, and make things worse? I wasn't at all sure what to do next and, as the most impatient person in the world, this was painful. It was sheer luck that the shop happened to be busy that day, or I might have gone completely bonkers with frustration.

I had sourced a consignment of the most beautiful sari material in orange and pink and draped them over two dummies in the shop window, which had generated a flurry of interest in my collection of fabrics. The wife of a record producer had wandered in after cushion material, and then three students from Chelsea College of Art, who were making a film. I doubted the second group had much money to spare, but one of them gave me the number of a props buyer at the college who was interested in setting up some sort of long-term rental agreement. This was good news, indeed – any steady source of income was cause for joy – although I wondered why I hadn't thought of contacting them before. I didn't have long to wonder because the answer to this question began to wail at me from the back room for supper.

I had, therefore, just shut up shop for the day and was boiling up carrots and swede in some stock from a ham-bone, when the phone went.

"Rosa," went an extremely far-back voice, "I bring news."

It was my poshest connection, Lord Peter Upshott.

"Hey, Peter."

"Mmm. Listen. Your little lad at the library has turned up trumps. We've had some confab in the last few days, but I'm afraid his hard work has brought the boy bad fortune. He is no longer stamping tickets, but alone and adrift in the wicked city."

I promptly turned off the gas under the saucepan and cleared a chair.

"*Really*? He sent me a brief note saying there'd been developments, but I've only just found out that he lost his job. So, the two things *are* connected. Oh dear."

"Indeed. From what I can gather, he managed to obtain some information from the police by dubious means."

I must have drawn in my breath at the idea of Bill Hawking doing anything halfway dubious in his whole life.

"Yes, I'm afraid so; I wasn't able to get the ins and outs out of him, but whatever it was, it was obviously effective, because we now know that the police are treating the old boy in the pond's death as Murder, with a capital M. What's more, they haven't forgotten our friend, because they are also investigating a link with Dyminge's disappearance. It seems they have an eye-witness at the pub, a young girl, who saw a canvas bag affair pass from Dyminge to Cole at what must have been their very last rendezvous for beer and skittles."

"Chinese dominoes."

"*Chinese*? How interesting."

"Yes. Possibly with some kind of coding involved within the game."

"Mysterious-er and mysterious-er. Nevertheless, right up Dyminge's street, of course. Why didn't you tell me this before, Rosa? And what's made you give up the hunt so easily and go to ground, by the way? I have to tell you that Millicent would never have succumbed so fast."

This was a bit much; telling me off when I had forced myself to do my duty against the prompting of every bone in my body.

"I'm a mother, Peter. What was I supposed to do? They're only little and I've got no man and no help at all and my living to earn. I had to come back to London and face facts, I had no choice."

There was a pause on the end of the line.

"No man, Rosa? I naturally assumed that your husband was back at home keeping the fires burning. Did he do a runner, my dear?"

"Well, no. Not really. In actual fact, he was never even informed of the race. The twins were an accident but, when I say that, I mean an accident of the most glorious, important kind, that I am not, remotely, ashamed of."

"Hmm. Well, bully for you. Sort of. Very modern of you, I'm sure."

"So, you see, I should *never* have agreed to become involved in all of this. I was simply caught up in the idea that I might be allowed to have another adventure .. and, then, the theft of the Major's body genuinely upset me, and .."

"No need to explain. No, I can see that I dangled temptation in front of you at Dyminge's wake. Not the first time I've dangled temptation and, hopefully, not the last," he sighed, rather wistfully, down the line.

I wasn't sure what to reply.

"Goodbye, then, my dear. All good wishes and so forth." He hung up on me.

Never - even at school - had mashed carrot and swede looked so dreadful. This, then, was my life. I sat down in the shop that evening, still damp from being splashed at bath time, hungry – though too listless to do a thing about it – and I bent over and put my head in my hands to cry. But, just as I did so, something caught my eye. It glinted yellow at me from under my chair. I stretched down and picked up the little glass owl, the one that I'd received through the post on the day that I got the invitation to Major Dyminge's funeral. It didn't seem frightening any more; I wondered why that might be? Any deadly powers it might have had were gone. I turned it this way and that, and then I got to my feet and found a pencil and a label in the drawer. I priced it up at a hopeful five pounds and put it in a glass cabinet with a chipped Staffordshire shepherdess for company.

PART 2

1. DEVELOPMENTS

I'm not sure I'd have bothered seeing her again, only I bumped into her on the pavement outside the [32]Pheasantry in Chelsea and she invited me to a party at her parent's pad, and her dad was a prime work contact. She was wearing her little black coat and looked even paler than usual; so black and white, she might have been a negative.

"Say you'll come Sam," she stood on tiptoes and laid her head on my shoulder, wafting the smell of booze and pot at me.

"What've you been up to, Verity? Have you been in that dive?"

The Pheasantry had got pretty run-down, nowadays, although it still had a grubby little nightclub in the basement.

She giggled, arching her back and turning her face up, as if I was going to kiss her. I didn't.

"You've *got* to come because I'm going to be eighteen."

I'd forgotten she was so young.

"And my parents will be splashing out. There are going to be some frightfully groovy people there. *Please* say you'll come."

If she was that desperate, I supposed I might make the scene.

"Yeah, alright. When and where, Ver?"

She clapped her hands and gave me the address of a pad in Mayfair.

"And you can bring a friend, if you like. Just not a girlfriend," she giggled again, pie-eyed, "I want you all to myself, Sam Stone."

I raised my camera and shot her, before I carried on home to my digs.

I'd got a lot on my mind, mainly money worries and was seriously contemplating having to bite the bullet and find a part-time job. A real downer, if ever there was one. The camera I'd rented from college was nothing compared with my old Topcon and I felt frustrated at having to work with below-par equipment. I was desperate for a [33]Polaroid colour camera, but my dad was holding out on me; hadn't been 'happy with my behaviour' on my last visit, apparently, and thought I needed a lesson in making do with what I'd got. Man, didn't he know this was the Sixties? Why 'make do' when you didn't have to?

Then, the guy I was sharing digs with had turned out to be an uptight Square who couldn't deal with a few dirty ashtrays around the place, and had quit to share with someone else. Which meant I was having to pay the whole rent from my grant. Life was so unfair.

I turned my key in the lock and walked in, up the narrow stairs that climbed over a launderette and into my two rooms that shook whenever anybody used the big dryer. The Square had slept in the main room, where the kitchenette was, and I'd taken the smaller room – my bedroom cum darkroom – which I'd thought was pretty damn generous of me, considering we went half and half with the rent. But no, the odd dirty plate on the floor and empty bottle here and there and he'd lost the plot. Some people just weren't cut out to be Artists.

I dipped a hand, gingerly, into the stacked washing up bowl, trying to find a mug that wasn't growing green stuff. There didn't seem to be one. Nothing in the cupboard worth eating, either. *And* it was bloody cold. So unfair.

I was wondering whether to go and see my sister again, when somebody knocked on the downstairs door. I nearly didn't answer it in case it was the landlord. However, they kept on knocking, as if they'd seen me come home.

"Alright, alright, keep your hair on; I'm coming."

I opened the door and, who should be standing there, but Bill Hawking.

"Bugger me, what are *you* doing here?"

"Hello, Sam. It's me, Bill."

"Yeah, I can see that."

I peered through the dusk at him. Belted mackintosh, polished shoes, short back and sides; all present and correct and yet, he looked different, somehow.

"Have you got any bread on you, by any chance, Hawking?"

◆ ◆ ◆

I ended up treating him to an Italian meal at a local trattoria, Barino's, opposite South Kensington tube station. It was my first taste of Italian food. I liked it; the sauce was like no mince I'd ever had before. And the red wine sitting in a wicker basket felt suitably exotic for my new start.

"I can't believe you've never had Spaghetti Bolognese," Sam Stone crowed.

"Nope," I was finding it took an awful lot of concentration to wind the spaghetti around my fork; one lapse and it squiggled away.

"We'll be here all night, at this rate."

He poured us another glass of red wine, found he'd emptied the bottle and held it up to the waiter for more. He was certainly generous with other people's money.

"So. You've lost your job, you bozo," he laughed. "How did you manage that, then?"

I had gone over and over this on the coach up to London. I wasn't about to tell Sam the whole truth, yet, what *should* I tell him? It had all developed so shockingly fast, that I was still dazed.

What had *actually* happened was this. Firstly, I'd remembered where I had seen the blue mini, which was slap bang on the pavement outside my own house. Then, by pure coincidence, I'd driven home a bit early from work and found a policeman's helmet sitting on the kitchen table.

So, needless to say, I charged upstairs and caught them at it. At which point I'd had a real rush of blood to the head, during which I yanked this enormous policeman out of my mother's bed and thumped him. Me. Bill Hawking, Deputy Librarian. I remember Mum screaming and, then, I'd run out of the room and out of the front door, only he – Constable Davies, or Barry, as she calls him – had got his trousers back on and come after me. At which point, he caught up with me on the corner of our road and tried to calm me down with a cigarette. Not that I smoke, no, but the cigarette had been pushed on me anyway, which gave me pause for thought. I looked at his hand and clocked the wedding ring. It dawned on me that the constable might be trying to hush me up.

At which point, I discovered that I had the nerve to blackmail him. It was an opportunity and I grasped it, without a moment's thought. Well, it was most probably the lack of thought that had actually made me grasp it. Still, I am surprised at how easily it came to me, especially when you consider how genuinely shocked I was at my own mother's behaviour. I simply insinuated that I would tell his wife what he'd been up to if he didn't come up with certain information, and that turned out to be all that was needed. The copper came straight out with it.

Mr Cole had been bludgeoned on the back of the head before he drowned in the flooded gravel pit in Dungeness. They had found blood and hair on a wooden stake hidden nearby in the rushes. What's more, they were working on a connection with Major Dyminge owing to the exchange of a canvas bag – from the Major to Mr Cole – as described by the landlord's daughter at the Coastguard pub. Indeed, the best possible time of death for Mr Cole was reckoned to be within twelve hours of that meeting.

However, this proved to be just the start of the fall-out from my rush of blood to the head, because my mother promptly dumped the policeman in a phone call the very next day. Possibly as a result of the lecture I'd given her about dallying with married men, given her sensitive position as an unmarried mother in a small village. I pointed out the stigma we'd had to endure – the names in the playground and so forth – and how important it was to maintain our respectability in the community. I was pleasantly surprised to find that she came round to my way of thinking so fast; making the appropriate phone call to Constable Davies the minute he'd got to the station for his day's work. What I hadn't taken into account, though, was how Constable Davies might feel about the situation. For it turned out that he was the sort of man that didn't like to be bested by anyone.

I am now going to insert a short parenthesis, if that's the right word (those of us forced to leave school at fifteen having to educate ourselves). At the library we try to stock a wide selection of suitable magazines and periodicals, which are available to our customers in the Reference section. Tidying these up in a lull, I had unearthed a backlog of copies of a periodical called *The Amazing Brain*, which actually did deal with matters to do with that organ – from the current thinking on how it works, to the popular Jungian theories to do with memory and the unconscious and the even more popular theories of Mr Freud. I found it a mishmash of practical science, explained clearly for the layman, and some more esoteric ideas that might attract the fashionably susceptible crowd. There was, for example, a long article in the second edition that appeared to be taking astrology seriously. Well, I freely admit that, in the interests of our investigation, I'd borrowed all the copies I could find, had slipped them into my briefcase and taken them home to have a better look. Borrowed them from the Reference section, where no borrowing was allowed, of course.

What's more, Constable Davies – having a professional nose for snooping – had noticed the big pile of them on the floor beside the settee and the 'Property of Dover Library, Not to Be Borrowed' labels on the front. So that was how I got the sack. He came to the library, got hold of my boss and made such a big stink about me thieving their property that they sacked me on the spot. End of parenthesis.

It was odd; my mum was more upset than I was. I suppose she felt responsible. I didn't have the heart to keep giving her the cold shoulder over her behaviour when she was so upset about it all. We talked, long into the night, over hot chocolate and I told her pretty much everything: everything that had happened since Major Dyminge disappeared at his own funeral. She's not all short skirts and late nights, my mum, and if I've given that impression, I've done her a disservice. Sadie Hawking is a sensible woman, on the whole, and a tough one. She's a woman who gets through life with a smile on her face, whatever hardships come her way.

"D'you know, Bill?" She said. "I think the time's come for you to move on. It's a big world out there and you need to see a bit more of it than you've seen so far. Getting sacked with no references, well, I never heard anything so unfair in my life, what with the years you've given to that place, but still .. The more I think about all this, the more I reckon it may've been just the kick up the bum you needed."

"I've not seen that much of Rosa Stone, not since she's grown up," she continued, "but I trust that family, I really do. They've been generous to a fault to our Frances. Why don't you carry on with this 'investigation' of yours? Go up and see Rosa and Sam. Get a taste of London life. Swing a bit while you're at it."

"Honestly, Mum!" This was going too far. "What am I going to do for money?"

"Get the coach up, 'cos it's less dear and you're not going to need a car in London. Then, if I were you, I'd crash at Sam's pad."

When I talked to my mum, it often felt like I was talking to somebody younger than myself.

"Crash at Sam's pad," I scoffed.

"Yeah, and then get a job sorted out. 'We've never had it so good', remember?"

"That was near on ten years ago, Mum."

"Yeah, but from what I hear there's jobs growing on trees in London."

There you go; that was what *actually* happened.

"So, you've lost your job, you bozo," Sam laughed. "How did you manage that, then?"

"It was all my own decision. I'd been there long enough."

"Oh yeah? Quick work, though; they couldn't wait to see the back of you, eh?"

I let the spaghetti have its own way for the minute and started to talk very fast.

"That's just Dover library for you, Sam," it rattled off my tongue. "It's such a desirable place to work; there's a long list of people after a job there, so they didn't mind me going straight away. Gave me fantastic references, of course. What are you having for sweet?"

"Don't mind if I do, Hawking," he clicked his fingers for the waiter with alacrity. "There's this pudding with coffee and chocolate and cheese.."

"Cheese? Ugh! I'll leave that one to you, mate. Listen. I need a place to stay for a bit. Just while I get myself sorted out with a job, you know."

"Aha! *Now* I see why you've been splurging. You're after my spare room. Well, as it happens, you've come on the right day. My flatmate has just ditched me, leaving me with all this week's rent to pay. Half the rent up-front gets you the biggest room with a kitchenette all included."

"Wow!" I couldn't believe my luck.

He raised his glass and chinked mine.

"To Stone & Hawking," he toasted.

"Hawking & Stone," I replied. "It's got a better ring to it."

My high spirits lasted all the way through coffee and the walk back; all the way up to the moment Sam led me into his flat, in fact.

"It's all yours, Hawking, for the derisory of sum of £2 2s 5d per week. You don't happen to have it on you, by any chance?"

"More than two pounds a week!" I was flabbergasted. "You must be joking.. I don't mean to be.. but this is a slum."

The flat was in Cale Street, which looked like a nice enough area, close to South Kensington tube station with lots of useful little shops. Nothing outside gave any clue as to what you might find on the inside. The room Sam showed me was the front room, although it had no windows. There was a torn settee, roughly painted black floorboards with no rug and a flimsy kitchenette in the corner. I caught movement out of the corner of my eye; too small to be a rat, I reckoned it was a mouse scurrying about by the sink, where several weeks' worth of dirty plates offered a choice of menus. Filled ashtrays and yet more stained mugs littered the floor. The flat was a slum and it stank.

"It's up to you, of course, but I'd grab it while the going's good. I mean.. you must have heard of Rachman[34], Hawking? Even in the wilds of Kent, they've heard of Rachman. Landlords can just throw people out on the street if they want, 'cos of the price of London property. You don't know how lucky you are to have found a pad in a neighbourhood like this."

Sam Stone had a habit of assuming everyone but him was as thick as a brick.

"Yes, I've heard of Rachman; I do read the papers, thank you very much. So, I know all about the [35]new Rent Control Act. Don't think you can pull the wool over my eyes, mate."

"Aww .. come on, Bill. It's not so bad here. Just needs

a bit of a tidy up and a lick of paint. It'll be fun; you and me. I'll show you the sights. Introduce you to some London birds. Two pounds a week, all in. How about it?"

"This room doesn't even have a proper bed to sleep on."

"I'll find you a mattress, no sweat. Come on, Bill. If you think this is bad, you should see where Rosa's shacked up; now that really *is* a slum."

It was the smell that greeted me first when I woke up the next morning. Stale cigarette ash, soiled settee covers, rotten food and who knew what else. Our house at home smelt of those blocks of air freshener that people hang up in toilets; lily of the valley and bleach. It was so dark, too. What front room didn't even have a window? I swivelled my legs sideways off the settee and felt a slight headache, from the red wine of the evening before, behind the eyes. I discovered I was still wearing my vest, which was still tucked into my trousers. I had my socks on, too. I'd been worrying about the mouse, obviously; that and bed bugs.

It was cold, so I got a jumper out of my suitcase and put it on over my vest, before trying the gas on the top of the cooker, experimentally. I was pleasantly surprised to find that Sam must have been feeding the meter, because a flame leapt up under the match, so I got a kettle going. Not being able to bring myself to sniff the half pint of milk in the fridge, I made a couple of black Nescafé's and put a heaped teaspoon of sugar in both.

"Sam?" I knocked, lightly, on his door before opening it a crack.

"Hey man, good to see you," he sat up in bed with a big grin on his face.

"Thought you might fancy a coffee."

"I just had, like, the best dream ever. I was in Las Vegas, playing snooker with Elvis and Frank Sinatra."

"Pool."

"No, that bit came before, with the bikinis."

"They don't play snooker in America, it's called pool."

I handed his coffee over and took a look at his room. He'd papered his walls with photographs, every spare inch. Mostly, they were black and white and of girls, or landscapes, or both. I moved closer to study them and discovered a clutch of pictures of Rosa and her babies stuck over the gas fire. She had her hair down, over her shoulders, like one of those black shawls that Spanish women wear to church, and her dark eyes stared out of her white face at the camera, as if she had an important question to ask it. He'd caught something true about her, but it needed to be studied properly before I could say what.

"I hate to say it, but these are quite good, Sam."

"You an expert, Hawking?"

"No, not at cameras. But I've been using my eyes all my life, and these look .. real, somehow."

"Well, that's a start I suppose."

He shrugged the covers off and leapt out of bed, stark naked. I backed out of the room.

"What are you up to today, then?" He called after me.

"Not sure. Cleaning up by the looks of it. And buying some milk."

"Wow! You're better than having a wife."

I ignored that remark, largely because I'd just noticed something; there *was* a window in my room, and quite a big one at that, only it was black all over. It wasn't paint, it was my first experience of London soot.

While Sam was at college, I scrubbed and scrubbed at that window, until the glass was clear and I could see straight across the road to the butcher's shop opposite. If I opened it and leant out, I could even see real, red London buses going past the end of the street and hear all the noise of real, London people and cars and life in the city. It was exciting to be here; to be grown-up and away from Kent and the library and just at the beginning of a brand-new life. Even though my room looked even filthier now daylight had been allowed in, I was happy. I emptied the pail of black water in the bathroom that I found down the hall and then set to work again. I washed everything in the sink and then filled the sink again with all the dishes and ashtrays from the floor and washed them. And when they were done, I even went into Sam's room to get *his* dirty dishes and ashtrays. I opened his curtains, noting that – ashtrays aside – his room was tidy: darkroom equipment and labelled boxes of negatives and prints all stacked in an orderly manner.

I went over to take another look at his photographs of Rosa. What it was, I decided, was that she looked lonely. In every single picture. Lonely and a bit scared. She hadn't seemed at all like that in life – just the opposite, in fact – but Sam's photographs looked honest, somehow. I stood there for a while, feeling puzzled. Then another photograph caught my eye.

It was Major Dyminge, no shadow of a doubt. Old Major Dyminge in his battered hat making his way out of the pub, his friend beside him. It might have been closing time because there were others close behind. I reckoned Sam must have been sitting on the sea wall and had framed his picture with the Coastguard entrance. It was dark, sure, but Sam had used a flash and it had just caught the whites of the old tramp's eyes, so that they squinted directly out of the photograph at me. Harry Cole was as dishevelled as I remembered him. He held a shapeless bag and a book under one arm. I reckoned a magnifying glass would reveal whether it was a book about Woody Guthrie.

2. MAYFAIR

Sam had been invited to a party and asked me along. A real London do in a city that was behaving just as it was supposed to behave. For, when we came out of the tube station, we found that it had begun to snow; thick gusts of the stuff whirling round and round the streetlamps. We turned a corner and walked into a Square with a generous garden in the middle, where the snow was beginning to lie. I felt as if I'd stepped into a novel by Charles Dickens.

"This is Grosvenor Square," Sam said in a superior voice, like a native city dweller showing his country cousin around town. "And that modern block there is the American Embassy."

There were a couple of policemen stationed outside, shoulders huddled in their capes, shuffling their feet against the cold.

I waited for more information.

"That's all I know, actually."

"So, these friends of yours, Sam, they must be pretty well off to live here?"

"Loaded, man. I've done the odd pic for Dave Flinders, you know, the advertising man, and hung out with his daughter, Verity. It's her eighteenth."

"Verity? Is that the fair girl who came down for the funeral? The model?"

"Mmm .. except she's a phoney. She's not a real model,

Claire Ingrams

more of a sponger off Mummy and Daddy waiting for the right man to marry so she can make a career of it."

This was a bit rich coming from Sam Stone who, as far as I could see, knew nothing at all about how the world really worked for ordinary people.

"Blimey, if that's the kind of thing you say about your friends, I wouldn't want to be your enemy."

He laughed.

"Oh, lay off the clichés, Hawking. Verity's kosher .. I expect. She's nuts about me, so she can't be that thick. Come on vicar, let's go and nab ourselves some champagne."

The door was actually opened by a butler and there were black and white tiles on the hallway floor and a sweeping, gilded staircase, burgundy striped wallpaper and oil paintings and everything a reader of Victorian novels could hope for. The butler reached for our coats, but Sam shrugged him away from his leather jacket. I handed him my damp mac with a smile - to make up for my friend's rudeness - but the butler seemed to like that even less.

We took a glass of champagne each from a maid, dressed in a rather skimpy outfit, standing at the foot of the stairs and then we started the long climb upwards. I was still in a dream; anticipating a ballroom and a string quartet. It wasn't until we got to the top and the door in front of us swung, mysteriously, open, that the real nature of the party became clear.

The screech of an electric guitar came at us, full on, like a punch in the guts. It was loud enough for earache. A real-life pop group was jigging away and bodies - many, many bodies - were jumping up and down and shaking their manes of hair like they had fleas. Lurid, unpleasant colours were projected into the room, exploring faces and sliding about over the walls. It was extraordinarily hot and any available air was acrid with the unmistakeable, vegetable smell of pot.

I was very sorry indeed to say goodbye to my dream evening and, had I been given the chance, I think I might have turned right round and tried to navigate the tube home. However, the shriek put an end to that. A girl gave an almighty shriek and all of the manes of hair turned to peer at us, proving to have faces.

"Sam! You've come. My darling Sam!"

The pretty girl from the funeral launched herself at the lad and began to kiss him, hard, on the mouth, right there in front of everybody. What we'd call a snog at home. I felt embarrassed for him, that and downright jealous because she *was* really pretty and, what's more, she didn't seem to be wearing much at all over some strappy, black undies. She had bare feet and her long, blond hair hung loose and, when she finally let Sam go, I could see that her face was painted with silver stars down one side, like a panto fairy.

"Mummy! Daddy!" She shrieked again, decibels above the guitars. "It's my boyfriend, Sam!"

I just had time to catch the look of horror passing over Sam's face, before a trendy-looking couple bore down on us, him with a Mexican bandit type of moustache and shirt open to his navel and her with the tiniest dress I'd ever seen on an adult; a cut out triangle of white paper. I didn't like to stare, but I was pretty sure that it really *was* paper. A woman wearing a [36] paper dress was a new one on me. If these were Verity's parents, it was certainly disconcerting to realise that I'd come dressed as her grandad. Although, more than anything else, it was the hair that made the biggest impression: what with the generous amounts of it all around, shaking its stuff, the lacquered, blond arrangement on Verity's mum's head and the black curls sprouting from just about all of the parts of her Dad that I could see. With my short back and sides, should I, perhaps, pretend to be in the Army?

Of course, they ignored me and drew Sam into warm embraces.

"Hi Sam, glad you could make it. I don't think you've met my wife, Clementine," he pronounced it in the French way. "Clementine, this is the young snapper I was telling you about. Come with me, hot-shot; I may have something for you."

And that was the last that I heard from Mr Flinders, for the time being, because he put his arm around Sam, pulled him back into the crowd of hair and disappeared.

Mrs Flinders, however, was ready to make friends. She extended a pale arm, silently, and dragged me onto the dancefloor. I wondered whether she might be slightly drunk because she continued to make no effort to talk, but remained uncomfortably close, shaking mildly in her chic, little dress and waggling her elaborate edifice of hair every now and again. Her face, while beautiful, was completely inexpressive.

"Fantastic party, Mrs Flinders," I did my best to communicate. "I hear it's Verity's eighteenth."

Her face remained blank as I mumbled something boring about her lovely house. She just stared into my eyes, scarcely blinking. I shuffled from one foot to the other, as best I could, getting hotter and hotter in my jumper, shirt and tie. It felt like aeons later that she stroked my hair and, moving her pale lips in a lopsided way that might have been a smile, let me go.

I'm no dancer and this type of party was new to me. My library friends and I would sit quietly at parties, nodding knowledgeably over a pint of bitter, while listening to something authentic and often acoustic. You know: [37]Peter, Paul and Mary or [38]Pete Seeger, or Dylan. Then we'd discuss the deeper meanings behind the lyrics, somebody would get het up about [39]Vietnam and I'd find that everybody else had, mysteriously, paired off. This bunch didn't look like they'd be at all interested in . . well, anything. They seemed closed off in their own little worlds. You didn't even get an 'excuse me' out of them if they barged into you. It was enough to make a person feel invisible. So, I gave up not long after Mrs Flinders had left and backed up to stand against a wall and let pink and purple lights wander all over my face. Every now and again, a head of hair would hang back to reveal the face of a pretty girl – or boy, for that matter – but I couldn't see how you'd get to meet them. It was becoming obvious that I couldn't rely on Sam to come and find me, nor to introduce me to any of his friends. Well, that was no surprise; he'd be smoking pot, or taking something else in that line by now. I noticed a door on the opposite wall and decided to make a beeline for it.

It opened into another big room, but with a balcony, swathes of curtains tied back to show the white gardens below. This was where they'd put the grown-ups. I wondered whether there had ever been another time in history when the young and the old had looked like such different species of human being. There were old men in dinner jackets holding cigars and ladies in strings of pearls, curly hair-dos glued to their heads, all very upright on the stuffed chairs. Proper conversation was being had, some of it in French, I noticed, guessing that these might be older relations of the chic Clementine Flinders. It was if the orgy next door didn't exist. I was probably the only person under fifty there. I stuck to the outskirts of the room, trying to look like I knew what I was doing and where I was going, until I stumbled upon a tray of oysters on ice and some more glasses of champagne on a side table. I picked up a glass, but the shellfish gave me pause for thought.

"Go on. There's an 'r' in the month," somebody actually spoke to me.

It was a tall, dark man in black-rimmed glasses, and a dinner jacket, smoking a cigarette. A stunning, middle-aged blonde in a long, jade-green gown swept up to us and picked out an oyster shell, downing the contents in one. I may have gawped.

"What kind of noise annoys an oyster?" She asked, unexpectedly.

"I've forgotten, darling," replied the man.

"A noisy noise annoys an oyster."

"They must be pretty, damned livid, then," he remarked, to nobody in particular, because she'd already gone.

He stubbed out his cigarette and then took off his glasses, found a pristine white handkerchief in his jacket pocket and gave them a wipe. Then he shot a sideways glance at me.

"Do we know each other? I have a feeling that we might."

"Well . ." I felt quite overwhelmed with shyness, "I *did* recognise the lady in the green dress . ."

"Did you? I'd have thought you might be a shade young to recognise Kathleen."

She was the beautiful lady in the cat food commercials, with the diamond collar and the miaow. She was also Sam's famous aunt.

"So, you must be . . "

"Tristram Upshott," he held out his hand to shake mine. "I believe we've met in Kent."

"Gosh, yes," it came flooding back just who he was, "you're Sam Stone's uncle."

"Married to Millicent's younger sister, Kathleen, yes."

I shook his hand gladly, pleased to meet somebody who was connected to home.

"I'm Sam's friend from the village, William Hawking. Um . . Sam's here, somewhere. He knows these people better than I do. I really don't know anybody here at all."

Boy, did I sound lame, as usual.

"I'm glad you don't. They're quite foul."

I was startled.

"Are they?"

"Mm. Delinquent children and his French wife's haute bourgeoisie relations, with a sprinkling of poisonous media types stirred in for good measure."

"Really?"

"David Flinders owns a conglomerate of advertising companies and he's courting the telly people at every opportunity, like the world and his wife. We're only here because he's had my wife dressing up like a cat for some time now. Care for one of his oysters? No?"

We stood in silence for a while.

"Where did you say Sam was, William?"

"I'm sorry, I don't know. Mr Flinders took him away the minute we arrived and I haven't seen him since."

Sam's uncle had one of the most unreadable faces I've ever seen but, even so, I had a sense that he wasn't best pleased about what I'd said.

"So, you don't know anyone here? And, presumably, nobody here knows *you*?"

"That's right. But don't worry about me, or anything, Mr Upshott. I'm having a super time."

"I bet," he seemed sceptical about this statement.

The conversation died again. My shyness can be so powerful that it simply kills the power of thought and language, as if I'd never spoken a word of English in my life. So, it took me quite a while of wrestling with my inadequacies before I was capable of noticing that he seemed on the twitchy side, himself. He lit a cigarette, took a couple of drags and then stubbed it out. Then he fiddled with his cufflinks. Then he looked at his watch. Then he took his glasses off and put them on again. Several times. I must have been boring him, unbearably.

"Well," I began, "nice to meet.."

But he cut me off before I could go any further.

"Listen. Hawking. Let's go and see if we can find Sam, shall we?"

It was funny how he put this so mildly and yet it felt like an order.

"Right," I jumped to it, flooded by a sense of relief that I'd been given something to do.

"Follow me," he said, "and try to 'gee up' a bit."

I blinked and straightened my shoulders, but took no offence. They seemed to have brought back National Service.

"Good man. Let's give downstairs a go first."

We went back down the gilded staircase, past the oil paintings and towards the girl in the French maid's outfit, who still stood on the bottom step with her heavy tray of champagne glasses.

"Excuse me," Mr Upshott addressed her. "We've been sent downstairs to get you. Apparently, they're running out of champers up there."

She did as she was told and hurried off as fast as her tray would allow.

"But we weren't.." I tailed off.

He sighed.

"It's always nice to have some elbow room when you do a clean sweep. This way, I think."

We turned left into a smallish, darkish room. There was a piano in the corner, a rather flash-looking record player and some reel-to-reel recording equipment. There were framed photographs all over the walls, many from well-known advertising campaigns featuring girdles and chocolate bars, gum and holiday camps. Signed pictures of famous actors and actresses, too, but Mr Upshott didn't stop to look at them. We passed on, through a door at the back of the room and then down some carpeted steps, landing up in a cloakroom stuffed full of coats. There was a strong smell of damp wool. Some disinfectant, too, which smelt familiar.

"Seems we've found the coats. But where've they put Sam, we ask ourselves? Let's look for the butler."

There was another door, so we took it, finding yet more steps, narrow this time and covered in lino. There were small puddles of water on the lino and the stink of disinfectant grew stronger. He stopped on the stairs for a sec and cocked an ear.

"Ah.. splashing. Can you hear?"

I could. I'd never heard of such a thing, but it was becoming clear that the Flinders family had installed a swimming pool in their basement.

"You didn't bring your trunks, Hawking?"

He didn't wait for a reply, but pushed through some steamed-up glass doors and came to a standstill.

You had to peer because of the thick steam rising from

the water and hanging in the hot air but, from what I could see we'd barged in on [40]Elvis in 'Blue Hawaii', because it was straight out of a film. It was a tropical paradise of palm trees and bikini-clad girls lounging by the pool, under a complicated arrangement of strip lighting. Of men with impressive chest-hair smoking cigars as they dangled their toes in the water, or gathered to talk business under a banana palm bar affair. It was hard to take it all in, especially in such overwhelming heat; I was going to have to take my jumper off if I stayed much longer.

"Bill!"

It was Sam, over by the bar, amongst a close-knit group of men (who I didn't much like the look of; Mr Flinders' associates looked more like a gang of hoods than a group of advertising men at play.) As for Sam, he was splayed out on a sun lounger, wearing one of those necklaces of tropical flowers and his tiny underpants. He got up, with difficulty.

"It's my dream, man. The one I had this morning, yeah? I'm, like, a shaman, I can predict the future."

It was obvious that Sam Stone was stoned out of his mind. I turned to see how this was going down with his uncle, but his uncle had disappeared.

Sam was performing a strange, wonky kind of dance as he made his way around the edge of the swimming pool, towards me.

"Come and meet Davy baby, Hawking. He loves me." He gave me a sort of leer, wobbly perilously close to the edge of the pool. "He's gonna give me all this work and make my name. Bailey's gonna have nothing on me, man."

"Well, that's great mate." I wasn't going to begrudge him his moment.

"Yeah, groovy or what?"
"Groovy, I'd say."
"Yeah."
"So, where's Verity, then?"
"Who?"

"Your girlfriend."

"What, that dimbo?" He wagged his finger right in my face. "I can do so much better, man. I mean, even Dave thinks she's a dimbo, and he's her father. Have you *seen* the chicks here, Hawking? I'm travelling light, it's the only way to go."

I couldn't say I was surprised by these remarks – this being classic Sam Stone behaviour – but I felt sad for the girl; it was her eighteenth birthday party, after all.

I peered through the steam and found her. She was all alone, sitting on the edge of the pool with her feet dangling in the water. I couldn't be sure, but it looked like she might have been talking to herself.

Sam's devilish, v-shaped, black eyebrows shot up and he grabbed my arm.

"Coming for a swim, then?"

"Don't go all barmy on me, Sam; I'm not exactly dressed for it, am I?"

"Man, you are one square prude. Just strip it all off and jump in, that's what all the beautiful people have been doing."

"What? Like, no clothes? They haven't, have they?" I shot a quick look around; it was difficult to see what with the steam rising from the pool, but I tried.

"Not everybody needs 'shrooms to let it all hang out. Some of us are just naturally cool with our bodies."

I began to sense where this might go.

"C'mon, Sam," I backed away from the swimming pool, "leave me out of this."

With every backward step I made, he came closer, jigging about in that buzzed way of his, and I had an ominous feeling that he wasn't going to wait for me to strip off before he pushed me in.

"This is not funny, mate .. I mean, what would your uncle say? I bet he doesn't want to see you behaving like a complete idiot."

"What uncle, bozo? What are you talking about?"

"Your posh uncle, the one who's married to that actress.

He's here somewhere. Well, he was a minute ago. We were looking for you, for some reason."

"My uncle, the spy?"

"What?"

"He's a fucking spy, man."

"Who's a fucking spy? I didn't invite any fucking spies to my daughter's birthday party?"

Dave Flinders had crept up behind Sam, like a particularly furry spider in swimming trunks.

"What the hell are you talking about?" He spat.

Judging by his face, Mr Flinders wasn't a fan of spies. He looked from one to the other of us, as if trying to work out who was to blame.

"Um," Sam was doing his jazzed jig on the spot, "like, um .. take it easy .."

Mr Flinders, realising he'd get no sense from him, turned to me and I felt myself begin to blush and then stammer.

"I'm sorry, M . m . mister Flinders, I d .. don't .."

I was saved by an oddly familiar shriek and a commotion over by the pool.

"Aargh! Help, help! I can't .."

It looked like Verity Flinders had fallen into the swimming pool and, judging by her wild flailing about, nobody had taught her to swim. It only took a sec to realise that not only was the crowd of onlookers too stoned or pissed to do anything to help, but they actually seemed to find it funny. I slipped off my black slip-ons, ripped off my sweater and took a running jump.

There wasn't much of her, although she kicked and struggled against me as much as the water, giving her a momentary strength. I suppose I must have clasped her to my body and dragged her to the edge of the pool, where a hand descended to tug her out. It was all over very quickly and I, instantly, felt foolish, anticipating a moment in the spotlight. But, by the time I'd pulled my soggy-trousered legs out, and got to my feet, that moment appeared to have passed and the crowd had moved on to the next big thing. Never a word of thanks, not a clap on the back, nor even a smile. In fact, Dave Flinders just scowled at his daughter, as if thoroughly disgusted at her behaviour. I went up to the girl.

"Are you alright, Verity?"

She blinked at me, as if I had never held her close, as if some enormous distance had grown between the two of us. Silver stars still twinkled down one side of her face. She was wet through, of course; a drowned pantomime fairy.

"Yeah, I guess so. Like, thanks though. Whoever you are."

I stuck my hand out.

"Bill Hawking, Sam's friend."

And then, she did the funniest thing; she selected my little finger and shook it, briefly, almost as if the whole hand would have been too much for her.

"Come," she said. "Let's lift and separate. I'll find you a towel."

3. VERITY FLINDERS

The girl took me to her bedroom. Not that I knew it was going to be her bedroom. She paused just before she opened the door.

"I think I know you," she said. "You and Sam went to the village school together."

"Yes, that's me."

I remembered what Sam had said at the funeral.

"Although I know London birds don't want to hear about village schools."

"Yeah? I wish *I'd* gone to the village school."

I couldn't think what to reply. A brief, unwelcome, vision of being backed up against the playground fence and called names came and went.

That's when she opened the door and I realised that it was her bedroom. I'd always imagined girls' bedrooms to be tidy places with white counterpanes and flowery wallpaper. Verity's was black and very, very cluttered. Books and clothes and magazines were strewn all over the bed and the floor.

"I've got my own bathroom," she gestured to a door, "you'll find towels there. I'll get you some clothes to change into in a minute. Dave won't miss them."

I stripped off my soaked clothes and dried myself off with the biggest, softest towel ever, reflecting that I'd never met anybody who called their parents by their first names before. Imagine the look on Mum's face if I started calling her

Sadie. Then, I hung around in the bathroom for a bit, hoping Verity might pass the clothes through a crack in the door. When that didn't happen, I had no choice but to re-enter her bedroom wrapped in her towel.

She was sitting cross-legged on her bed, hugging a teddy bear, not seeming to have noticed that own her own clothes were soaking wet.

"I only got out of hospital in November," she said, addressing the bear. "Did you know?"

Assuming the question to be aimed at me, I shook my head because, of course, I knew practically nothing about this girl except that Sam, and her own father, thought she was a dimbo.

"Psychiatric, that is."

I may have grasped my towel with a firmer hand.

"It's funny, really. I never know who knows and who doesn't. All those groovy people downstairs, I think 'do *you* know, or don't you?' Because, if they *do*, then why doesn't anybody ever say anything?"

I hesitated to reply, until I thought of what Mum might say.

"Perhaps they're waiting for you. To say something."

She looked up and laughed.

"Like an announcement? I'm a loony everybody, don't you know? Absolutely crackers. Hear voices all the time in my head and they won't shut up. Such a loony, they had to wire me up to a machine and give me electric shocks. Like, snap, crackle and POP!"

And then she started to cry, hiccupping as she went.

"Sam doesn't want to dance with me. Hic. Nobody does. Hic. And it's *my* party."

Suddenly, I'd had enough. I just saw red. I sat down on the end of her cluttered bed and years of frustration at all the pretty girls I'd witnessed losing their hearts over my shit of a friend came pouring out of me.

"Sam? Sam Stone's a bloody fiend, Verity. He's a bloody

monument of selfishness. He's my friend and he always will be, but *please* don't let Sam Stone hurt you. He's not worth it. Not for a beautiful, young girl like you, with all your life ahead of you. Especially when you've already got your fair share of problems."

It simply poured out.

"Please, Verity, please just promise me one thing?"

She'd dropped her teddy bear and had stopped hiccupping.

"Just don't knit him any more scarves. No more bloody scarves. I'm begging you."

"I didn't. I mean, I haven't."

"Oh, ok. Well, just don't."

She wiped her eyes and got off the bed.

"I'll go and get the clothes, then."

I took a good breath when she'd gone. What the hell was happening to me? I was a sober librarian, surely, so where was all this embarrassing passion coming from? I hardly knew myself any more, sitting on girls' beds wearing towels. Not that I was on Verity's actual bed because there was so much clutter on it. I shifted a buttock and pulled out a magazine. Lo and behold, it was a copy of *The Amazing Brain*, the periodical that had enabled Constable Davies to get me the sack with Dover Library. It was the latest edition, bent open at the astrology page and I was searching for my sign when Verity returned.

"I'm Aquarius, though I hate water. What are you?"

"No idea," I scoffed, because men don't know their star signs.

"Hmm. Capricorn, I'd say. Or Virgo."

"Virgo? No chance. It's all a load of tripe, anyhow."

"Here, you can have these," she passed me some of her dad's clothes. "They might be a bit big, but I expect they'll be warm. You've got a coat downstairs, haven't you?"

I went back into her bathroom and got changed, while she shouted at me through the door.

"It's Capricorn, isn't it? Admit it."

"Ok, I suppose it *might* be."
"Ha! Listen to this:

You will be experiencing passions that you serious Capricorns never suspected might exist. The very ground is shifting beneath your cloven hooves, but you must not let them bury you. No more a ruminant, but a creature of action, let your brain expand in new directions. The time has come to stop being a scapegoat.

Are you experiencing passions, Bill Hawking? Is it me?"
It was the first time I'd heard her laugh properly and the first time she'd called me by my name.
"Modest, aren't you?"
She'd changed into a black jumper twice the size of her when I came out of the bathroom, and was studying her own sign with the awed seriousness most people might reserve for their bibles.

"Beware the water, Aquarians! What was your friend has become your foe. Your birthday signals a new departure. You must listen to what the voices are telling you and set your amazing brain free. Let all of the day to day concerns that tie you to your corporal form be gone. Go wild, water-bearers."

"Wow, did you hear that, Bill? 'Beware of the water' and I've just fallen in! And Sam fell into a lake by that beach in Kent and he might have drowned if I hadn't managed to pull him in with a big stick. This is just mind-blowing."
"Long Pit on Dungeness? It was *you* that saved Sam's skin? He told me about the mushrooms and the body in the water, but he managed to leave that bit out."
She gave a sharp intake of breath.
"The Body in the Water."
I stared at her; I swear I'd never seen someone look or sound so terrified. She had clasped her hands to mouth and her enormous, pale eyes were almost bulging out of her small face.

"Do you mean..," she whispered, "that there *was* a body in the water?"

"Yes. Yes, there was. I'm sorry. I shouldn't have mentioned it. Please just forget I ever said anything."

Her terror was transmitting itself to me and I felt all shivery. What kind of idiot was I, to have brought dead people into the conversation? Please tell me she wasn't about to lose her marbles.

"I . . I saw it . . the dead man floating in the dark. I thought it was my crazy mind, you see. I was so . . freaked out. Again. I . . told Clementine when I got home from Kent and, then, she told Dave and they made me go to Dr Ambrosia's clinic. I hate Dr Ambrosia. And . . . I've only just got over it, really."

A tear slid down her cheek, over the painted silver stars.

I felt miserable; wanted to give her a hug and let her know it was going to be alright, but I knew I couldn't do it. I was just too damn shy. Well, I reckoned there was one thing I *could* do.

"I don't suppose . . I mean, you probably won't want to . . and I'm not even sure I really know how to, but . . It being your birthday and everything, I was wondering whether you'd like to . . to have a dance? Downstairs. With me."

As it turned out she didn't, but my suggestion got her downstairs before the end of her party, where proceedings had slowed down, thankfully. The band had packed up and gone and the uncanny lights been turned off, but a record player had been found, from where a French girl was singing in a low, sweet voice, as if everything else had been a mistake and the world was the most innocent place, after all.

"[41]Francoise Hardy, my favourite!" Verity exclaimed.

"Shall we?"

I extended my arms, no doubt awkwardly, but she didn't notice.

"Where's Sam, do you think? I need to find Sam. Wait

there .. um .. Bill."

And she was gone. I wondered how many more people were going to dump me that night.

In the room next door, the older guests had mostly taken their leave of the party and staff were clearing away the dirty glasses and the tray of oyster shells. Somebody had drawn the curtains and shut out the snow. I enjoyed thinking of it, all 'crisp and white and even', London urchins building snowmen in the morning. But I was tired now; longing for Sam to come and retrieve me, so we could go home to bed. I sat down on a well-stuffed armchair and closed my eyes. I was just nodding off, when a sharp knocking noise, roused me. There it was again, an urgent rat-a-tat-tat from the window area.

I got up and, finding myself all alone in the sitting-room, went over and drew back one of the heavy curtains. Tristram Upshott was crouched on the window-ledge outside and we met each other eye to eye, uncomfortably intimate. I took a step back in surprise.

"Let me in," he mouthed. "It's bloody cold out here."

I turned the catch and lowered the top half of the window enough for him to clamber over and jump into the room. He brushed some flakes of snow from his dinner jacket, but still looked remarkably debonair, if slightly blue about the face.

"Well, that was a stroke of luck, finding you still here. Thanks Hawking. You haven't seen my wife anywhere on your travels, have you?"

"Um, no."

"She's probably taken the car and gone home by herself. Not for the first time. No matter. Where are you going? Fancy sharing a taxi?"

"Well, I was just waiting for Sam."

"Hmm. I hope he's put some more clothes on by now. Right. I'll be off, then."

He went to go, which was when I noticed that he had

something stuffed down the back of his trousers.

"Ah, Hawking, one tip, if I'm not butting in. Steer clear. Pass it on to my nephew, would you? Steer *well* clear."

He adjusted the back of his dinner jacket and strolled away.

I must have dropped off on the comfy chair again because, when I woke up to find Sam shaking my shoulder, the curtains were wide open and a watery, morning sun shone on the pristine, snow-covered gardens below.

"Come on, Bill," he said, "let's split. I can't hang around waiting for you all day."

4. ABSOLUTE RUBBISH

The last time that we'd met, he and my beautiful Aunt Kathleen were flying off on a world tour in a plane that they'd built themselves. We had all gone to see them off at Lydd airport at an extremely early hour.

"Give my regards to the Statue of Liberty!" I'd hollered.

"Oh, Rosa, don't," said my mother. "How in the heavens could a tin can like that make it to America? Of all the daft things my little sister has done, this must be the daftest. My heart's in my mouth, it really is."

But I had known they would make it. How could they not, with him at the controls? Tristram Upshott would make a success of anything once he set his mind to it. My Uncle Tristram was, truly, the best and bravest man that had ever lived.

We'd all received postcards to begin with, but then they'd petered out. I only found out that they had actually made it to America because a mutual friend, who was out there working on the Space Programme, had told me. My family were beyond hopeless at staying in touch.

So, I was caught completely unawares when he came into the shop on Monday morning (yes, I was wearing my pregnancy kaftan, and yes, it may have had patches of sick on it, because the previous night had been one of epic length and colic).

"Hello, Rosa, how very nice to see you."

He looked pretty much the same as he'd always looked, which is to say handsome in a well-cut dark suit, with just a smattering of grey in his dark brown hair. An unfamiliar pair of heavy glasses only enhanced the effect; as if he were a modern intellectual imparting wisdom to the masses on the telly. My delight at seeing him come into the shop was tempered by a strong desire that he should leave immediately, thus giving me time to turn into a better version of myself, before he returned to begin all over again.

"Golly, Uncle Tristram. You're back."

He gave me a hug and I sucked my stomach in hard enough to take my breath away.

"It would seem so, Gypsy."

I made a vague gesture towards one of my many chairs and he sat down. Monday mornings weren't my busiest and we were alone in the shop.

"Was it wonderful, amazing and fabulous?"

"It?"

"The world."

He laughed.

"Yes, it was. You should try it some time."

"If only. Still . .," I tried putting a brave face on it, "you haven't met my babies, have you?"

"No."

"They're wonderful, amazing and fabulous, too."

"I'm sure they are. Not that I'm an aficionado. I tend to prefer them when they're capable of understanding the rules of cricket."

"That would be never, then," I joked, but he didn't find it funny. "Well, they're over there, in the window. Taking a nap between the telephone directories."

I gazed over at their mops of shiny, black hair and rosebud faces, eyes scrunched shut in deepest sleep and my heart gave its usual lurch.

"Ah, how very interesting," he'd got up and was peering down at them. "I'd say they take after their father's side of the family."

"W.. what? I can't think what you mean."

"Ah. It's not in the public domain, I see. Consider the subject dropped. Any chance of a cup of tea for your old uncle?"

I was beyond rattled, and immediately set to work with the kettle and teabags, painfully alert to the sound of him wandering about in my shop, whistling and picking things up. He stuck his head under the string of laundry to survey my sordid back room, then, swiftly, withdrew it.

"I ran into that brother of yours at the weekend," he called out. "How's he getting on, would you say?"

I returned to the shop with two mugs of strong tea and set them down on top of the chessboard with a missing queen.

"Fine, I should think; he tends to fall on his feet. He's doing this photography course at the School of Art and he's so talented it's ridiculous. He has loads of 'groovy' young friends and ravishing-looking girls running after him and, as I think you can tell, I'm not remotely jealous."

"Understood." He took a sip of his tea. "I gather he knows Verity Flinders."

"The stick insect? Oops, sorry, I mean the lovely, petite Verity with the blond tresses and the legs. Yes, he does. I don't know how well, but he brought her down to Kent for Major Dyminge's funeral."

"Right. News reached us about the disappearing Major, poor old fellow." He lit a cigarette and blew a long stream into the air. "He disapproved heartily of me, of course. Probably had a point."

I thought about it.

"Well, I should say that it wasn't you, *personally*, that he disapproved of. I mean, he'd had a tough time with the Establishment and you were working for MI.."

"Quite so," he interrupted.

"And, are you still? Spying? Tell me you are, Uncle Tristram, that they've realised what a stupid mistake they made and they've welcomed you back with open arms and given you a promotion and you will soon be the top spymaster in the whole of Great Britain and..."

"Rosa," he was laughing, "you never change. It's delightful."

"Is it?"

An absolute surge of joy nearly knocked me over, and, for the merest moment, I couldn't speak.

"No, but seriously, Rosa. Even if that daft scenario had occurred, I shouldn't tell you, as you well know. Not that it has. No, I've been taken on in the City. Dusting my bowler hat off, as we speak."

I didn't believe a word of it. Not one word. Uncle Tristram and I had worked together – in a classified capacity – and if he wasn't back in the Secret Services, possibly sniffing out information about the stick insect, I would eat my own bowler hat. If I had one.

We went for a walk later, when it became apparent that absolutely nobody was going to come and spend money in the Arcanium that day.

"Monday is a pint of milk and a packet of fish fingers day," I explained. "Not a day for interesting shopping. Now, you should see it on a Saturday.. "

"You can't move for customers wanting to buy broken chess sets?"

"Exactly."

How like a spy to notice the missing queen.

We walked all the way to the river, me pushing the twins in their black pram while I wormed information out of him about my aunt and her new role in a popular television quiz show, where she wore an evening dress and flirted with [42] David Jacobs. Knowing my uncle's lack of tolerance for chit-chat, I found myself waiting to see whether the stick insect might re-surface in the conversation. I'd had a hunch about Verity Flinders, and I felt quite smug that my old instincts were not completely dead.

"Well, I'm glad to hear that your brother's prospering, Rosa. He's a presentable young man. I'm not surprised to hear that Verity Flinders has taken a shine to him."

My ears pricked up.

"You don't know the Flinders family, by any chance?" He enquired, in a nonchalant manner.

We'd stopped at a bench and I was unearthing my daughter from her blankets, recognising a light in her eyes that signalled imminent danger. I put her on my shoulder, then got Benjamin out and dumped him on my uncle's lap before either of them had a chance to protest. Tristram Upshott was family, after all.

Jessica and I arranged ourselves beside him.

"No, I don't know any of them. Should I?"

"It was at a party for Verity that I ran into Sam." He scrutinised my son. "David Flinders, her father, is a well-known advertising man. He's behind your Aunt Kathleen's cat commercials, you know. Fished, or Pissed, or something."

"It's called DeLish-ed, as you well know. I love her in those commercials; I'd buy it like a shot, if I had a cat. Those matching diamond collars and the little miaow she gives at the end."

"Please don't remind me."

"So, Verity's dad is a big cheese in the advertising world?"

"Mm, he's been merging and acquisitioning advertising companies like there's no tomorrow. I say that in my capacity as a humble cog in the City machine, of course, not the fellow with the miaowing wife who takes his shilling. No, I've run into Flinders several times in my professional capacity and never enjoyed the experience."

"Oh."

Then again, perhaps he really was working in the City.

"Did your brother meet the girl through her father, or vice versa?

"I really couldn't say."

Why on earth was he so interested?

"It's just that I'd advise steering clear, that's all."

"Well, I can't say I liked her. I know she's only seventeen, but I sensed something dark about her.." I was warming to my theme. "For instance, she and Sam took drugs on the Ness and I assumed it was all down to him, but what if *she* brought the drugs with her? What if *she* forced him to take them and then pushed him into the gravel pit where he saw the body? Honestly, there's something world-weary beyond her years about that girl." The full implications were coming, thick and fast. "You don't think that she's trying to drag Sam down into the gutter with her, do you? To wreck him body and soul?"

He appeared to find that amusing.

"I hardly think he needs any help with that, Rosa."

"I don't know what you mean. Sam's only a nineteen-year old boy, you know. He's an innocent out there in the big, bad world."

He stifled a laugh.

"Oh, Gypsy, I see your talents are still working overtime."

All of a sudden, he picked Benjamin up and put him back in his pram.

"Off you go, baby, you're distracting me. Let's just rewind a fraction, Rosa. Did you mention the word 'body'?"

So, I told him everything while we headed back to the shop for the twins' lunch.

"And, as you can see, I've got my hands full with the children, but Bill and your father may still be on the case for all I know."

"My father, humph," he snorted. "Why is *he* still meddling in other men's business? I thought he was growing flowers in Norfolk while he lapsed into senility."

As my mother would say there'd never been much 'love

Claire Ingrams

lost' between Tristram and Peter Upshott.

"And William Hawking, indeed. What a team. Old men and milk-fed boys take on the world."

I glanced at him.

"I didn't know you knew Bill, Uncle."

"We met at the Flinders' party. I've rarely met a man so lacking in confidence and charisma."

"That's pretty harsh; Bill's a kind, intelligent boy. He's got a slight crush on me, but," I gestured to my stunning outfit, "who can blame him."

I'd unlocked the shop door, but he didn't follow me in.

"Don't do yourself down, Rosa. Charming British self-deprecation is all very well in its place, but you'll find that the rest of the world tends to take it at face value. This can't be the easiest of times for you, I know .. although quite what you think you are up to in a hovel like this, is beyond me."

I gaped at him. He couldn't, surely, be talking about the Arcanium?

"I don't think I've ever seen anybody bury themselves alive in quite such a *literal* manner. All the detritus – the absolute rubbish – of the last however many years of this dwindling little island, heaped on top of a woman who once had a brain."

I felt the swell of blood on my face, the wave of tears ready to break.

"Christ," he said, "I've overdone it. Kathleen will murder me. I'm .."

"Sorry?" I suggested.

"Look . . all best, and everything. Your children are very .. Goodbye, Rosa."

He took off, striding up the Kings Road and away from World's End.

If it had been anyone else saying those words, I don't think it would have hurt me quite so much. But it was *him*. I was thrown off-balance. It may not have been all his fault, I realise

160

that; can see that it had been building up.

I stopped sleeping altogether. I lay in bed, night after night, pinned on my back by physical exhaustion, while my mind turned cartwheels over which I had no control. It was as if sleep had never been and never would be and every night became an exercise in controlling panic. In the daytime, I trudged through mud. Nothing was of any interest any more: from the sun rising and the coming of spring, to other people, to my children, the vast lack of interest spiralled in ever tighter circles, until there was only me left. Just me, imprisoned in an ailing body. The lack of space was beginning to impair my breathing.

One evening I picked up a pretty, silver pair of embroidery scissors and I cut my hair. Off, off, off; as close to the bone as I could get.

5. WRONG TURNS

My parents came up to get the children and take them home with them to Kent. I was supposed to go back, too, but I refused.

"Promise us, then, that you will go to the clinic. I'm writing the address down on this pad and leaving it here, so don't lose it with all this clutter. I mean, stock."

My mother cleared a space on a low, possibly Regency, table.

"We're so worried about you, love."

There was a clinic run by a renowned Dr Ambrosia – in Harley Street, it hardly needs saying – that some rich friend of theirs' swore by.

"I'll go," I said.

Not that I had any intention of going.

"You mustn't worry about the cost."

I wasn't worried about the cost. I wasn't worried about anything. In order to worry, I would have had to care.

My father stroked my shorn head.

"It suits you, Bubeleh."

Yeah, sure.

I couldn't wait for all of these people to leave, yet, when they did, I wondered why. Oh, it was a relief that the children had gone; but what remained? Nothing, not even shame. What mother gets her children taken from her and feels no shame. Me, apparently.

I was sitting in the shop later that day, turning the yellow, glass owl this way and that in my hand, when Bill Hawking came in.

"I'm so sorry you're ill," he said.

I was surprised by this. Was I ill? How did he know?

"Sam told me."

"Where is he?" I hadn't seen my little brother for ages.

"He's busy working for Dave Flinders, the advertising magnate. I hardly see him, myself, though we're sharing a flat."

I knew something about David Flinders, but had neither the energy, nor the interest, to think what it might be.

Silence descended; it was peculiarly quiet without the twins.

"Can I make myself a cup of tea? Only, I've been walking round trying all the bookshops and libraries, and I'm done in. I'll have to go back home if I don't get a job soon."

I nodded.

"I'll make you one, too, shall I?"

I thought about it.

"No," I said. "Don't. Why are we always making sodding cups of tea in this country? As if tea will do anything except make our bloody awful teeth go even more yellow than they already are. Sod tea, let's go to the pub."

A poster outside The Man In The Moon advertised the 'Underground Theatre Company' for one week only, in the back room of the pub. Probably some anti-commercial, anti-police, pro-sexual revolution collective who got paid in LSD. Not that I was against all that; I'd definitely have auditioned if I still acted. Would it have been a step up from the Arcanium, or a step down? I had no idea, obviously, as to what was acceptable and ambitious and what was downright pathetic. I just knew that I could be relied upon to get everything wrong.

◆ ◆ ◆

Now was my chance to buy her a drink. What had happened to her, I wondered? Why would a woman with such beautiful hair want to cut it all off?

"What can I get you?"

She asked for a whole bottle of Stone's Ginger Wine, which seemed quite a lot, but I wasn't going to lecture her; I didn't want to make her feel any worse than she, obviously, already did. I decided that humour might be better in the circumstances.

"Have you got shares in it? Stones and all that."

It fell as flat as it deserved.

◆ ◆ ◆

Bill brought the bottle over with two glasses. The sticky liquid was the same colour as whiskey, which was helpful. I chugged three down super-fast.

"My parents have taken my children; in case you're wondering where they are."

"I know."

He seemed to be fully briefed.

"Were you sent to check up on me; that I go to the clinic?"

"Sorry, I don't know what you're talking about."

Yeah, sure.

"My mother's been on the phone to Sam, I can tell. And he's sent you because he's too busy taking pictures of detergents, or cigarettes."

That was what I'd forgotten. I cheered up a fraction.

"Mind you, my uncle knows something about the Flinders family and, as near as damn it, warned me off. Well, not me, of course, because I don't know them, but he was definitely hinting that I should tell Sam to steer well clear. Not that I was that surprised, because I picked up distinctly bad vibes around that Verity. You know, she's been pushing drugs on Sam .. most probably."

❖ ❖ ❖

Sam's uncle had done the 'steer clear' routine with me, too, but I couldn't see what Verity had done to deserve her 'bad vibes'. The idea of anybody having to push drugs on Sam Stone was laughable, but I hardly liked to say so to his sister. However, I felt I should defend Verity.

"You know, Verity's not a drug pusher. I don't know where you picked up that idea. She's a nice girl, with a few problems. Oh, and horrible parents."

"Problems, ha! What sort of problems can the lovely, wealthy and unbelievably, outrageously *young* Verity have?"

I didn't want to gossip about personal stuff, certainly not when it involved the word 'mental'.

"Well, nerves, I suppose." No, that wasn't right; 'nerves' made her sound like a nineteenth century hysteric. "You know. Problems to do with the brain."

I'd said way too much.

❖ ❖ ❖

"The brain? You mean she's mad? Well, join the club, young Verity."

He didn't answer, just looked into his glass, unhappily. Poor Bill, he was far too handsome and respectable-looking to be drinking with a woman like me.

"Do you think that might be the problem with all of us? We're all barking, bloody mad. And .." the ginger wine was a lot more potent than you might think, ".. since we all like to believe, nowadays, that the universe is inside us, that puts us in deep, deep trouble. Because, if *we're* mad, then so is the entire show and there is no reason and no morality and no justice and .."

❖ ❖ ❖

"Excuse me, but that's nonsense."

I didn't like to contradict her when she was feeling unwell, but I couldn't let her get away with such nonsense.

"People getting bombed in Vietnam, or starving on the streets all over the world, or just ordinary people like me and my mother – working people who need a proper job to keep going – none of us are inside your personal universe, Rosa. None of us is going to get helped by a bunch of mystics chanting 'om', whatever they might think down the Kings Road. What we've got to do is to get *out* of our heads – and I don't mean swallowing pills, or smoking pot, when I say that – and take action."

This was more like it. This was the kind of conversation I'd hoped to be having in London.

"And kindness, too," I added. "I think kindness is crucial; in fact, it may be even more crucial than taking action."

❖ ❖ ❖

"Taking kind action, then?"

I leant over the table and stroked his nice fingers.

"I don't think I've ever met anyone as sane as you before, Bill. I say .. I've had an idea. Feel free to let me know if you think it's crazy, but .. I think it may fit the bill."

"What's that, Rosa?"

"Well, my idea is this. I think what we should do is go home. *Now*, if you like. And have sex. Or make love. Whichever you'd prefer. I think it would do us both a lot of good."

But I woke up in the night, leant over to look closely at him, and I didn't feel good, not at all. I was pretty sure that

I'd taken Bill's virginity. His eyelashes flickered every now and again, up and down over the fresh skin of his smooth cheek, while he slept. He was a beautiful Adonis dreaming of better things than I could ever offer. He didn't just look young, lying there fast asleep on my dirty sheets, he looked like a child. I had spent hours of my life watching my babies sleep; so long that their rhythms, even the shape of their dreams, had worked their way inside me. This was not right. This was a boy my little brother's age, and I had taken another wrong turn.

I got up and went downstairs to drink a glass of water, but I found that I was standing in front of the oven. So, I turned it on and put my head in it.

My God, the inside of the oven was foul. It was encrusted with hard, black horror, the remains of every meal I'd ever cooked badly. Did nobody think to clean it? Must I do *everything* myself?

"Rosa, what the hell are you doing?"

He yanked me out and pulled me up and into his arms. He was shaking, maybe with the cold, because he was naked.

"I'm sorry," I began to cry into his neck, "I'm *so* sorry to have done all this to you."

"But it was wonderful, Rosa. You've done nothing wrong."

"No, it's all wrong. I'm all wrong, don't you see?"

"You're not, you're perfect," he was crying, too, crying and shaking and still holding me. "I don't know what's happened to you since we were in Kent, but you've taken a knock that you, maybe, weren't strong enough to take just now. I mean, with the twins and all. But I can help you, I know I can."

I pushed him away because he was being ridiculous. What could this boy know about anything?

"Go home, Bill. I'll go to Harley Street, I promise, since that's what you all want. I'll see this Dr Ambrosia at the clinic and he will make me well. You must find a girl your own age and not worry about me. In fact, never think of me again, because I will be perfectly fine. Just go home now."

"What? Let Dr Ambrosia shoot electric shocks into you, like he did to Verity? No, Rosa, you mustn't do it."

Verity again. Why did Verity Flinders keep cropping up?

"Bill, I mean it. You're not wanted here. Go home."

I'd pushed him away, but he was surprisingly persistent.

"No."

"What do you mean, "no"?"

"I'm not leaving you by yourself like this. I'd have it on my conscience for the rest of my life if you did yourself in."

"Oh, for crying out loud." I was getting deeply annoyed now. "You're not responsible for me, Bill. Go on, sod off and leave me alone. Just put some clothes on, first."

He came over all self-conscious at that, as if he'd failed to notice that he was standing starkers in my kitchen. He grabbed an old, linen tablecloth from the ironing pile and draped it around himself. Now he really did look like a beautiful youth from classical mythology.

"I'll sleep down here," he declared. "I'm not leaving you on your own and that's that. Can I make us a cup of tea first?"

Bill Hawking and his cups of tea. Suddenly, I was all wrung out, without even the energy to muster a reply. I gestured towards the kettle and turned to go back upstairs to bed...

"No!" I screamed. "Don't!"

But it was too late. He'd struck the match and a great fireball had erupted into the kitchen before the match had even approached the gas ring. I had forgotten to turn off the oven.

PART 3

1. THE MRS DYMINGE LECTURES

Spring came late, just as I had begun to lose faith. The clues were most probably there, but I'd been in no state to see them. It was winter in my soul, I suppose, and I'd been hunched against the cold for so long that I'd forgotten to raise my face to the sky.

Yes, I must have missed the crocuses, altogether. However, it is quite difficult to miss a daffodil. They are so very yellow. The clouds, too; how unexpectedly frivolous they can become in April, fluffing themselves up and dancing about in a deceptive manner. As if they know nothing of rain. I must have been staring up at them, standing in my garden, lost to the world, when Rosa Stone slipped past.

"Good morning, Mrs Dyminge."

She veered towards her parents' front door.

"Rosa dear. How well you look."

I have to confess that this was an out and out lie. It struck me that I had seldom seen a person so changed in such a short time. It could only have been February when we had last met and yet, look at the girl. It wasn't just her hair, which was now short and curly, but everything about her, somehow. Where she had been so "bonny and blithe and gay", she was now pale and wan and distinctly reluctant to make conversation with nosy, old women.

"Come and have a cup of coffee with me, dear. I'm just about to make a fresh pot and should love the pleasure of your company."

I rather surprised myself with the effusiveness of my offer. Perhaps it was spring that had pushed me.

"Oh," she hesitated, visibly on the cusp of rudeness. "Thank you. How nice. What, *now*?"

"Mm."

She followed me into the parlour and perched on the edge of a chair, as if she might take flight at any minute. I noticed that she kept picking at a loose thread on her skirt. It reminded me of something, of someone; I knew it in my bones. As I got the old, brown coffeepot out of the kitchen cupboard, I considered this new habit of hers. It was only by the time that the coffee was ready and the tea trolley laid that I'd got it. The person that it reminded me of.. was me. The girl must be deeply unhappy.

One of the worst things - and there are many 'worst' things - about being old and, then, having lost your husband, is that nobody tells you anything. Just when a dose of somebody else's misery would not come amiss, they all assume that you should be protected and cossetted and keep you in the dark. I swear I could hear my late husband whisper in my ear as I stirred cream into our coffee:

"Frances," he whispered, "don't stick your nose.."

But it was too late. He was gone and I was not.

"What's the matter, Rosa? I can see there's something dreadfully wrong. Please let me help."

She gulped, then promptly burst into tears. After which, it all came out in a splendid rush. She was old and exhausted and incapable of anything and everything that had once been good about her was broken and gone forever. (Old, indeed. I had to suppress a little smile). She was a changed person who had burnt her shop down by mistake, so that now she had no living and was filled with shame and guilt and wished she were dead because it would be so much better for everybody else.

"There, there, dear," I clucked and patted her shoulder while I considered what I should say.

"In my day .." I began and, while I was aware of a light in her eye that suggested the phrase might not be to her liking, I pushed on, " .. in *my* day a woman with young children had help."

"*Servants*, you mean," she positively spat the word out, like a stray stone in the beans.

"Well, yes, my dear, many did have servants – even the middle classes would have a cook and a woman to do the heavy work, strange as it might seem to us, now. However, if circumstances did not allow servants as such, they had family. Usually lots and lots of family and all living close by, hugger-mugger. The very idea of looking after twin babies all by yourself and running a thriving business at the same time, well, I simply can't imagine how you've done as well as you have."

The martial light in her eye had softened, somewhat, as my little lecture had run its course. I drank some of my, by now, lukewarm coffee and sat back, feeling rather pleased with myself.

"Right, thanks so much for that, Mrs Dyminge, but I have to go now." She stood up. "I have .. things to do. Looking after my children and, oh, *so* many things; a great, thick sandwich of them .."

She ground to a halt, seeming quite beyond reach by the mantelpiece.

I had seen Millicent take the children out earlier, packing them into her car on a visit to the market. It was clear to me that Rosa had lost her bearings, so I let her be for the moment. Contrary to my husband's oft-repeated opinion, I am actually capable of silence.

After a time had passed, she picked up my yellow, glass egg-cup from the mantelpiece; the pretty one decorated with daisies that I'd had for yonks.

"Uranium glass."

"Is it, dear? You would know more than me, being an expert in the field. Talking of which, I must say I'm sorry to hear that you burnt down your lovely shop."

She, instantly, began to sob once more, rather loudly.

"But it's all absolute rubbish," she wailed. "He was right. My shop was just an excuse to bury myself under absolute rubbish because I didn't know how to make anything else happen."

"*Who* was right?"

"My Uncle Tristram," she wailed.

"Oh, Tristram Upshott, he was always a difficult boy. I can't think what persuaded you to listen to him."

She looked astonished.

"No," I reiterated, "if we were all to start listening to men, goodness knows what trouble we'd be in."

"But we do. Women do."

"Well, of course, men think we do. But we don't, not really."

She continued to look baffled and, I must say, I really did wonder what the younger generation thought they were up to. I mean, women having this wonderful contraceptive pill, but *still* thinking they had to listen to men.

"But, Mrs Dyminge, my Uncle Tristram is everything I've ever wanted to be. Of course, I listen to him."

"Ah well, that's a different matter altogether; why didn't you say so before? You wish to be a spy, is that it?"

Her mouth fell open once more. Was I not supposed to know that the son of my husband's best friend was, and always had been, a spy? Good grief, but the Young really did take the biscuit. Did Rosa think that she was the only one to know anything? Did she think that I had never had [43]adventures? Had never stared Sheer Wickedness in the face and bested him?

"Come and sit down, my dear," I patted the faded cushion beside me. "In a minute I shall make you a fresh cup of coffee, but first, I want to say something to you."

Curiosity, visibly, won out over intense reluctance, and she sat back down.

"Now, correct me if I'm wrong, but I can't help feeling that what you need is to be the agent of your own destiny. That's so, isn't it? Because some people just *have* to be, you know. I mean, people like myself can drift a bit, find safe harbour, make our cabins ship-shape and we manage. But others can't just let things happen to them; it hurts them to go on doing that, hurts them deep down. That is the kind of person that I believe you to be. Now you say you want to be a spy, well it might be a little late in the day for official channels .. however, there's nothing to stop you doing what spies do. Investigate. You need something to investigate and I have a missing husband. Dead, of course, but still .. such serendipity! Find my husband, Rosa, and when you've done that, keep going."

Goodness, two lectures in one morning. I was going to have to lie down.

2. HAWKING & STONE

I was wheeling the pram around St Margaret's village one evening when I took the plunge. I hadn't phoned because I simply hadn't known what to say. I was as terrified as I have ever been, yet knew I must make a start. There really was no other option but to live with myself and, believe me, I had considered all other options, in depth. His mother, Sadie, though, must hate my guts.

Seagulls were swooping over the village roofs, screaming blue murder, as I approached Sadie's house. It was in the middle of a dingy terrace, but stood out like a false, new tooth: her net curtains were snowy and her front step shone bright enough to see anyone's face in it. How I did not want to see my own face. If I could have worn a veil, I would. Before I began to cry again, I pushed the doorbell. She answered on the second push.

"Rosa, love, what a nice surprise. You've brought the babies, too. About time. Here, I'll take the front end," and she lifted the pram over the step in one, swift movement, practically lifting me, too, into her narrow hallway.

She continued to talk as she led us into her front room, a gentle flow of words washing over me.

" . . and making my outfit for the May Day parade. Thought I might use real flowers this year, only you can only do that at the last minute . . and this noisy girl must be Jessica . . look at that black hair. Was he Chinese, their dad? Whoops, I've dropped a clanger. Don't mind me, love; just be glad you're not my son. I swear I embarrass that boy so much I don't know how he can stand to be in the same room with me."

She laughed her rich laugh, which I'd forgotten all about, plonking Jessica down on the jazzy carpet.

"Ssh, Jessie, Jessie," she crouched down next to her, "you're just longing to take your first steps, aren't you, my darling." She laughed over the noise. "One of those babies who can't stand being a baby, isn't she? Just wants to be seven and the best at jigsaw puzzles that the school's ever seen."

At which, the dam broke. Heavy, guilt-bearing tears that I could do absolutely nothing about cascaded down my cheeks.

"Hey, whatever's the matter? Is it my big mouth?" She stood up, straightening her short skirt. "Look, here's Bill, come to cheer you up. He had an accident in London with a match and a gas cooker. Nearly blew himself up making a cup of tea in his digs, blooming idiot. If you can look at those eyebrows and not want to laugh, you really *are* in trouble."

Bill's eyebrows were gone and his eyelashes were patchy, too. His right hand had a painful-looking red streak on it, that must have been a burn. Apart from that, Bill looked just the same, in a neat shirt and tie with a patterned jumper over the top that [44]Val Doonican might have worn.

"In .. in your digs? You had an accident in your digs?" I stuttered, swiping at my eyes with the back of my hand.

"He did," she replied, "and, no offence meant, but we haven't half had a laugh over how your brother keeps that place. What with your mother having been in service and all? Fair's fair, though, I expect she had too much on her plate with the millinery business to teach him to look after himself. How *is* your mum, Rosa? Well, I hope?"

I had to sit down before I answered, while she rattled on as if there was nothing at all out of the ordinary about visitors bursting into violent tears at the drop of a hat. Bill produced a proper handkerchief for me, ironed and folded into a perfect square and I began to feel better. I just couldn't get over my relief that Bill was alright, that I hadn't caused him third-degree burns, or worse. Oh, I'd known he was alive, thankfully, because I'd heard on the Kent grapevine that he'd come back to his mother's, but no more than that. Perhaps now I could begin to breathe again.

"Well," she continued, "I will have to love you and leave you because I have to go and get changed for a date. With a very nice gentleman, I might add," and she threw a meaning look at her son.

"Make Rosa a cup of tea, Bill." That lovely, rich laugh bubbled up again. "Only don't set fire to the kitchen."

The small room was warm as toast and the children had dropped off in their pram. I eyed Bill, warily, but he said nothing until the sound of his mother's footsteps had disappeared.

"You could have phoned," he said.

"I'm sorry."

"I've been worried sick."

"Oh. I thought you meant . . phoned to see how *you* were."

"Well, *I'm* alright. I wouldn't want you to worry about *me*. But *you* were in a terrible way."

"What are you, Bill Hawking? Some sort of saint? Besides . . you could have phoned me. If you were that worried."

Suddenly, I saw the funny side.

"We sound just like an old married couple."

His face changed, and then he lunged at me on the sofa, wrapping me up in his arms and banging into the side of my head with his lips.

I jumped up.

"No, you mustn't. Please stop . ."

"I'm sorry."

"I'm just not.."

"No, of course you're not.. I'm so.."

"If you say you're sorry one more time, when I'm directly responsible for your poor eyebrows and that horrible burn on your hand, which looks really painful, by the way.."

"This little thing. It's nothing, honestly."

I glared at him.

"Well, actually, it hurts like hell, but never mind that. Tell me, how's the shop?"

I sighed and sat down again.

"The shop is still a blackened mess. The fire brigade may have saved it, but they left it in a horrible state. Heaven knows how we both survived relatively unscathed. At first, the landlord was hopping mad, of course, and wanted to sue me for negligence or something, not that he knew the full story. However, it turns out that the place should have been condemned years ago and I've actually done him a favour because he can claim some insurance. Anyway, most of my stock has been damaged by the fire. It was absolute rubbish to begin with, of course, but still."

I must have sounded melancholy, because he sat down next to me, so obviously itching to pat me on the hand, or take me in his arms, or seduce me on the sofa.

"Stop it."

"Stop what?"

"It."

We sat, side by side now, not saying a word while I thought things through. There was an idea – a big one – that I'd been mulling over for some days. Now that I knew Bill was ok, that idea had to change, it was obvious. Besides, I owed him.

"Listen, I've been thinking and I have a proposition for you, but it's not the kind you want. And, to be brutally honest, it never will be. So.. if that's too difficult for you, Bill, I'll be on my way."

I hadn't meant to sound quite so tough, but it was probably better than giving him hope. Kinder in the long run.

"Ok," he took it pretty well. "Yeah, ok. No sweat. I can deal with that."

He shifted away from me on the sofa.

"Tell me your proposition, Rosa."

So, there you have it; the beginning of Hawking & Stone.

"Stone & Hawking," he suggested.

"Hawking & Stone," I said. "It has a better ring to it."

He raced upstairs, returning in the blink of an eye with a box file.

"Concentrate, Rosa" he said, which took me aback.

"I will now show you four items," and he opened the file and took the items out, one by one.

Firstly, there was his journal, well-thumbed. Then, there was a yellowing pamphlet detailing the rules of Chinese dominoes. After which, came a periodical entitled *The Amazing Brain*. Lastly, a photograph.

"Your brother took this and stuck it up on his bedroom wall. I've .. borrowed it."

I picked it up. A couple of old men were coming out of the Coastguard. One was Major Dyminge and, next to him, carrying a bag and a book, a man I took to be Harry Cole.

"Incredible, isn't it? By my reckoning, we have a photograph of Harry Cole on the very night that he was murdered. Do you see, he's actually carrying the canvas bag that the landlord's daughter saw Major Dyminge hand over? And, the only book he ever borrowed from Dover library – the autobiography of Woody Guthrie – from which I have ascertained the period of time in which this meeting took place. Yes, because the book was taken out a mere nine days before Major Dyminge died at home in bed."

The photograph was certainly interesting, so why was I not more excited? Was it because *I* should have been the one to find it? Once so fleet of foot, I was now floundering in the mud, lagging behind this boy. How would I ever catch up when my responsibilities weighed me down, so?

Bill must have read what was left of my mind.

"Your mother will help look after the children while you're living down here, you know. Now she's retired she'll probably jump at it, I bet. Mrs Stone will make it much easier for you to take this on properly, Rosa."

"Yes, you're probably right."

When did everything become so hard?

"Oh, Bill," I wailed, "I just don't know whether I'm strong enough to make the phone call. It's like .. begging. Help me, please."

We had agreed on the phone call, that it was the only way to make it a reality. Hawking & Stone, I mean. The phone call was make or break, but I was weakening by the second, any spurious confidence that Mrs Dyminge might have inspired in me evaporating into thin air. Yet, we were pragmatists, Bill and I, that was one thing that we *did* have in common. We had our livings to earn and I had mouths to feed. So, I took a breath, got out my address book and went into the hall to use Sadie's telephone.

"So, you see," I explained, eventually, "for Hawking & Stone to become a proper detective agency we need backing. We need premises and expenses and basic wages for two. To begin with, anyhow; before the cases come in. Equal wages for equal partners."

Lord Peter Upshott didn't even need time to think.

"Caramba!" He yelled down the line.

"Listen to this, Gabriel," I heard him call out to his friend, the Air Chief Marshal. "We're going to set up a detective agency. Yes, a *detective agency*. Private Eyes and whatnot. With Millie's daughter and young thingummy jig. Crikey, I'm so excited I might have a heart attack."

"So, you think it's a good idea, then?" I couldn't quite believe it.

"Crumbs, yes. It's the idea of ideas. Dyminge and I

should have done it years ago. I can't tell you what this means to me, Rosa. It's going to be a new lease of life for us all."

Bill appeared in the hallway and I gave him a thumbs up.

"Whaat?" He mouthed.

"Just let me know what you need and I shall wire it to you straight away, care of your parents' address. And, Rosa.."

"Yes, Peter?"

"Your mother will be so proud."

Would she? Why did he think that?

"Indeed, she will. Now stop all this mucking about and find the old boy. No more excuses. Go on, bugger off the line and find him."

We began in my parents' house, in what had been my mother's workshop at the top of the stairs. Hat boxes were still stacked up high against one wall. On another wall, where she had pinned sketches and fabric samples to a cork board, we pinned our photograph. We had two chairs pulled up to the long sewing-table, a typewriter and a telephone. Bill was dressed in his best suit and tie for our first day, which was making me even more nervous.

"So, we write every phone call down in this little book and that way we can reimburse my parents. I'm not going to be any more beholden to them than I already am."

"I know. You've already told me that ten times, Rosa."

"Just checking you've taken it all in."

"Well, I have."

"Then," I continued, "I will put my mind to this pamphlet on Chinese dominoes, to see whether I can identify any system that might help us with the relationship between Harry Cole and Major Dyminge."

Plus, having once been good at systems, I was hoping to exercise my brain in that area.

Bill had been taking notes, but raised his head.

"Just a sec," he said. "What am I going to be doing?"

"Hmm," I chewed my pencil and considered the matter.

"I suppose it depends on whether you want me to be the boss of Hawking & Stone, or whether you wish to be an equal partner. In other words, should I be giving you orders, Bill? Would you be happier if we did it that way?"

I could see that the library was still in him; years of being told what to do had taken their toll. Personally, being told what to do (and then doing it) had never really worked with me.

"Oh. OK, then," he began to smile. "I get it. You tell me what you're going to do and then I tell you what I'm going to do and.."

"We discuss it. It's a democracy. Which means that we have to be honest with each other and say when we disagree and think that each other's ideas stink to high heaven, without causing offence."

"OK. After all we've been through together, I think we can do that."

"My only proviso being that we never *ever* mention all we've been through together."

He laughed.

"I'll do my best. Ok, so what *I'm* going to do now is ring the office of *The Amazing Brain* and arrange an interview with someone who knows more than us about possible modern connections between radar engineering and the brain. Which would be just about anybody."

"Blimey, Bill," I stared at him, "I'm impressed. Do you think you'll have to assume a fake identity, or what?"

"Possibly," he was thoughtful. "But I'll squeeze some info out of them, don't you worry."

I could see there was no holding him back. Just what had I started? I breathed deeply.

"Ok, Mr Detective. Let's go."

3. THE PSYCHIATRIST

I was not going to blow it. The most incredible woman had come into my boring life and flicked a switch. Rosa was in my head, my heart and my soul. They say love blinds, but that couldn't have been further from the truth. Love had given me eyes, ears and a brain. Nobody could ever have loved another person as I loved Rosa; it just wasn't possible. Because of her, I was now a man. Because of her, I was now going to become a proper private investigator. We would build a business together, case by case, and I would be able to see her every day of my life. I knew she didn't feel quite the way I did, but I was nineteen years old, for goodness sake; if I had nothing else, I had time. I just must not blow it.

I glanced at her neat head – all tiny curls, now – as she bent over the pamphlet on Chinese dominoes, so absorbed in what she was reading. I'd never seen concentration like it. I could do with some of it, myself.

"Do you know, Rosa, I've been thinking it over and I've decided not to use a fake identity when I ring the mag. I'm going to be totally honest and upfront about our investigation."

"Really?" She seemed sceptical.

"Because Lord Upshott's name is bound to open doors for us."

"I'm not sure we should be using his name, Bill."

"Why not? We're using his money."

"Yeah, I suppose so, but .. should I ring and ask him if it's ok, d'you think?"

"If you want to."

If we debated every little step we took, I couldn't help feeling that we'd remain stuck in the mud at first base.

"I just don't know," Rosa's confidence was still pretty low, I could tell. "Oh, go on then. I expect it will be fine."

I picked up the receiver, while she returned to the pamphlet.

"Crumbs, what a coincidence. The tiles in Chinese dominoes are divided into two suits, and you'll never guess what they're called. Civil and Military. Now, with two old soldiers, that must mean something.."

"Ssh," I put my finger to my lips.

I dialled the number for *The Amazing Brain,* which was answered by a telephonist. I was a Private Investigator, I explained, William Hawking of Hawking & Stone, working on a case for Lord Peter Upshott, and please could she put me through to somebody who might be able to assist. It was a question of background information to do with the use of radar and the human brain. The member of staff she connected me to was, audibly, impressed that I was conducting a private investigation on behalf of Lord Peter Upshott etc, and promised to put me in touch with an expert, a Dr T L Robinson, who had recently contributed to the magazine.

"I can't promise Dr Robinson knows anything about radar, Mr Hawking, but he's a psychiatrist with a specialism in psychobiology. If you give me your number, I'll get him to give you a bell."

I scribbled down the psychiatrist's name and put the receiver down.

"Have you heard of psychobiology, Rosa?"

"Um, no, but it sounds promising. Now, the Military tiles are named and ranked by the points displayed on top of them, but the Civil tiles also have Chinese names."

"Such as?"

"Harmony, Goose, Hatchet, Plum Flower, Earth, Heaven, Man, Long Leg Seven, Partition, Big Head Six."

"You said that without looking at the words."

"Did I?" She seemed pleased.

"But .." I considered the Chinese names. "I'm not sure how a secret language could be constructed out of Goose and Plum Flower, never mind Big Head Six .. "

"I hope you're not going to be putting dampers on all my discoveries, Bill. We won't last long, if you do."

Don't blow it, Hawking, I reminded myself.

"Although, they could stand for people," I was grasping at straws.

Her eyes widened.

"That's *such* a great idea. So .. Long Leg Seven could be somebody tall, like, say, my Uncle Tristram. And Plum Flower could be a pretty woman.."

"Like you, Rosa."

"Hmm. And Goose could be Mrs Dyminge .."

I might have taken exception to that, but .. don't blow it Hawking.

"However, the big question is .. who is HATCHET?"

"I'm sorry, I don't get it. Who *is* Hatchet?"

"The murderer, you idiot," she jumped up and down. "Hatchet is the murderer."

Working with Rosa Stone was going to take some getting used to.

A man with a gravelly, American voice so deep it was down in his boots rang me a couple of hours later.

"Dr Robinson here. I was told you wanted to speak to me."

"Thanks for getting back to me so promptly, Dr Robinson. I don't know whether they told you, but my name is William Hawking, of the Hawking & Stone private investigation agency .."

"You're a PI?" He interrupted my flow.

"I am, yes."

"Man. Like [45]Philip Marlowe?"

"Um, sort of. But British, of course."

"[46]Miss Marple?"

He'd wrong-footed me. I had already felt like an imposter, but now I felt stupid, too.

"So, what do you want from me, Miss Marple?" He laughed.

His laugh was more of a rich chuckle than a sneer, though, and I persevered.

"We're working on behalf of Lord Peter Upshott.."

"I don't believe it! *Lord* Peter?" He gave a roar of laughter. "Man, you sure are making my day."

"On a case involving the theft of a corpse.."

"*No!*"

I was struggling to maintain my dignity, while his deep voice was turning falsetto with laughter.

"The corpse of an ex-army officer who was investigating radar engineering, with possible application to the brain," I shouted down the line.

There was unexpected silence.

"Say that again?"

"The corpse of an ex-Army Officer who was.."

"Not Major Dyminge?"

I sucked in my breath with surprise. Could this be a break-through?

"W .. well, yes. The body was that of a Major Guy Dyminge, which was stolen from a cemetery in Kent, February last."

"Listen, man," his voice had lowered in volume and he, most certainly, wasn't laughing any more. "I think you and I need to meet. And fast. Where are you?"

TL, as he asked us to call him shortly after we met in person, came from the US State of North Carolina and was descended from slaves who had worked on the tobacco plantations there. Now in his early forties, he had served in the Marine Corps in the Pacific towards the end of the war. By sheer force of character, and a powerful intellect, TL had subsequently begun his medical training at a public medical school in Charleston and gone from there to the Maudsley Hospital in London. Dr TL Robinson was now, primarily, based at Canterbury Hospital, although he also had clinics at many of the local hospitals. A chapter of a forthcoming book that he was writing had appeared in *The Amazing Brain*, attracting the attention of a reader, one Major Dyminge. The Major and TL had, subsequently, embarked on a correspondence by letter, although they had never met.

"May I ask what the book concerns?" I enquired, notebook and pencil to hand.

"It's about the current loss of faith in psychiatry in many quarters. The unequal balance of power between a psychiatrist and his patient, which a liberal society wouldn't countenance anywhere else. It includes fears about brainwashing and 'totalistic' (sic) forms of social control; Cold War paranoia of the Fifties and how that translates into psychiatry in the Sixties."

I'd been scribbling so hard that I'd had little chance to take part in the conversation.

"Fascinating," said Rosa's father. "Please help yourself to another piece of cake."

"Don't mind if I do."

Rosa, herself, was curled up in a defensive position on the window-seat, face like thunder.

Personally, I didn't feel it was such a bad thing that Mr and Mrs Stone had got involved; an invitation to our 'office' on the evening of our telephone conversation had resulted in Mr Stone opening his own front door and intercepting Dr Robinson before either of us could get down the stairs in time. However, while Rosa was evidently fuming, I sincerely doubted whether we could have elicited so much personal information in quite such a short space of time, not without the aid of Mr

Stone's famous chocolate cake.

"When you say 'cold war paranoia'," Rosa decided to join the conversation, "do you mean American fears that captured soldiers returning from Vietnam had been brainwashed by the Chinese? To slot back into US society as sleeping spies, or unexploded human bombs primed to detonate years later."

"I do mean that, Miss Stone, yeah. Very much a Fifties preoccupation, we like to think, but it's gone nowhere."

"Actually," said Mr Stone, "fears of that type have always been around; certainly, that was the case after both world wars."

"But, would you say that they have ever been anything more than fears?" Asked Mrs Stone. "Does brainwashing really exist?"

"Good question. We could spend all evening debating that. Whether it does, or not, what's certain is that our fear of it has affected how we see psychiatry and the use of pharmaceutical – and mechanical, to a lesser degree – brain interventions. So .." TL grinned, brushing crumbs from his jeans, " .. this has been pleasant, guys, but who's the PI around here?"

"Me," Rosa and I chimed.

"We're Hawking & Stone," I explained. "If you wouldn't mind coming up to our office."

"Your Lord Peter Upshott .." TL sat down by the long table upstairs, "Now, would he be the Labour peer who kicked up a storm about human rights in the House of Lords in the Twenties and Thirties by any chance?"

"You've been doing your research," Rosa said. "Yes, that was him."

"Well, I don't get phone calls like Mr Hawking's every day of the week. Thought I'd better ask around."

"Of course," I approved.

"Now, we're up here, I reckon I should let you guys know that I had no idea Major Dyminge had died, and I'm sorry to hear about it. Can I ask, how did he die?"

"He had an enormous stroke in his sleep. Just went to bed and never got up."

Rosa had sat down beside him, leaving me to hover about by a tower of hat boxes, there being no more than two chairs in our office.

"A stroke," he repeated after her. "Okay."

Rosa picked up on that straight away.

"You don't like the sound of that, TL? Oh, my God, tell me you don't suspect foul play."

The psychiatrist reached into the pocket of his baggy, fatigues-style jacket and got out a bundle of letters. He threw them on the table.

"I'm gonna be honest here, because I like you guys. I like what this Lord Hoohaa of yours did in his day, and I liked the Major and, most of all, I liked your old man's chocolate cake, Miss Stone. Cake like that only comes a man's way once in a blue moon."

We all laughed. I'd been right; involving Mr and Mrs Stone had been no bad thing.

"Major Dyminge was a brilliant guy, but the work he was doing – work that involved the pathways and receptors of the human brain – was risky, in my opinion. It took me longer than it probably should have to register that he was using himself as a guinea pig. When I did catch on, I warned him against it, of course. But, no way would I be surprised to hear that he carried right on, regardless. I'm no expert, but I'm willing to put it out there that if he had a massive stroke, it could well have been caused by his research."

"Oh, no. That's terrible," Rosa exclaimed.

"Did you know him, Miss Stone?" TL turned to me. "Hey, I thought you said you were looking into this for Lord Hoohaa; I don't recall you mentioning any personal involvement."

"Yes, we all knew him. He lived in the cottage next door, actually. His widow is still there."

"What.. the other white house on the beach?"

"Well there are only two. I would have thought you might have recognised the address from the letters you wrote back to him."

"He specified that I was to send mail poste restante to the main post office in Dover."

"That's interesting," I said. "It rather suggests that he was aware of the need for secrecy."

"I think we can take that as read," Rosa replied. "The Major had a long history of clashes with authority."

"You mean he was some kinda activist?" Asked TL.

Rosa was thoughtful.

"I'd say that the word activist suggests group activity of a political nature, which wasn't Major Dyminge's bag at all. I think he'd be best described as a one-man band. And a talented engineer and inventor, of course."

"Yes, I got that," said TL. "I'd never have replied to his first letter, otherwise."

"May we see it?" I asked.

TL selected a typed letter from the bundle and smoothed it out on the table.

30th June 1964

Dear Dr Robinson,

Having come upon a copy of 'The Amazing Brain' periodical in my local library, I read your article, 'Psychiatry at War' with interest. Since then, I have given it much thought. In all honesty, I cannot help but disagree on one very important point and, having felt compelled to write, I trust you will afford my letter equal consideration.

As an engineer and inventor of some experience, with a military background, I find myself unqualified to enter the debate on what you term the 'illiberal relationship' between a psychiatrist and his patient and the undue use of pharmaceuticals. However, I am in agreement with your central contention (one which I under-

stand to be growing among young psychiatrists), that 'lived experiences' play a far greater role in disturbances of the mind than have, heretofore, been acknowledged.

No, where I feel that I must take issue with your thesis, is your unqualified agreement with the sweeping assertion that has been expressed by our American cousins of late; that 'Brainwashing is bunk'. I assure you that this is not true, and, as I see you declare an interest in "psychobiology", your stance greatly surprises me.

Without going into undue technical detail, I can say that my experiments with thermal measurements in radar engineering have convinced me that the physical structure of the brain is in a state of flux; constantly adapting <u>physically</u> to meet new challenges. Moreover, it is clear to me that such adaptations may be manipulated to a remarkable extent by outside forces. Indeed, extensive experimentation on my part has done nothing but confirm the plausibility of so-called 'brainwashing'.

I wonder whether your contention that malign childhood experiences 'disturb the equilibrium' of the brain is still coloured by the vague ideas of the last century? For I tell you that such experiences will have altered <u>the fundamental structure</u> of the brain itself. Why, then, do you contend that the brain cannot be manipulated to admit the presence of a single idea?

I await, with anticipation, your reply.

Major Guy Dyminge

There followed a scribbled request to reply poste restante to the central post office in Dover.

"Wow!" Said Rosa.

"Yup," TL agreed, "it blew my mind. Not that he had me convinced straight away; I mean, I've met enough people with strange obsessions in my line of work to keep me fairly cynical."

"So, you thought he was just another kook?"

"We certainly don't refer to our patients like that, Miss Stone, but..let's just say, I had my doubts."

"But you wrote back, anyway?"

"I did. I don't know what it was, but there was something convincing about his letter."

"The Major was like that; it was as if the things that he knew, he *really* knew.."

"Just a minute," I interrupted. "Let's get this straight. We have here a letter from a man who – as Rosa and I can confirm – wasn't a kook of any description. Who was, in fact, an experienced inventor who had worked on secret projects for the army and probably knew as much about his field as anyone in the entire world. And this man has, pretty much, stated in writing that he knows exactly how brainwashing works. Do you see what I'm getting at?"

"Someone else saw the letter?" Rosa suggested. "Someone who shouldn't have."

"Listen," TL got to his feet. "You guys don't know me from Adam but - hand on heart - I swear that I showed these letters to nobody. Absolutely not another living soul has seen them, until now. I didn't mention them to anyone, either. If there was a leak, it didn't come through me."

He looked honest enough, but I was keeping an open mind. Private detectives need facts, I reminded myself, not impressions. Speaking of facts.

"Of course, we will go through these letters later, Dr Robinson, but can you tell us now whether Major Dyminge ever went into greater detail about his work on the brain and radar? Would it, for example, be possible to use these letters to construct a machine?"

"A brainwashing machine?" Rosa jumped off her stool.

"No way, man."

TL, who had been pacing up and down, stopped in his tracks.

"Look, he was an engineer and I'm just a brain doctor; we were worlds apart. Certainly, I do have an interest in [47]

Katz's work on neurotransmission and the synaptic gap, but there was no way I understood the technical jargon involved in radar engineering, and he knew that. We discussed our thoughts on the processes of the brain, sure, but he never sent me any kind of template for brainwashing, if that's what you're concerned about."

He sounded truthful enough. This investigation business was difficult; perhaps it took experience before a person could get an instinct for truth, or lies.

"Hey, I need to get back now, I've spent way too long here."

We all glanced out of the window; night had fallen while we'd been talking.

He left us his telephone number and repeated his sadness over the Major's death.

"Will you let me know if you find the body?"

We assured him we would and then he left. We listened to him dashing down the stairs. It was obvious that he was relieved to go.

Rosa opened the window and stuck her head out.

"Triumph Herald," she proclaimed. "Convertible. I'm inclined to believe him."

"So, if it had been a Rolls or an Aston Martin you wouldn't?" I laughed.

"A Rolls? Certainly not; it would have been obvious that he was a bloated plutocrat masquerading as a with-it psychiatrist who used the word 'guys' a lot. Just the type to be selling brainwashing secrets to the Russians."

"Well, I think we can agree that somebody cottoned onto the Major's invention and the most likely way would have been through those letters. So, if TL didn't give it away, who did?"

Rosa was still by the window, gazing out at a clear show of stars over the sea.

"I wonder," she said.

"What? What do you wonder, Rosa?"

"I wonder whether this has roots in the Major's past. Whether they ever left him alone. Whether all these years passed and they were still watching him."

Who did she mean by 'they'?

"Just suppose," she swung round to face me, "that he got on a list. Thirty years ago, the powers that be put him on a list and never took him off. And, that Major Dyminge suspected as much; suspected that his post was opened, his phone tapped, etc, etc. Which was why he had his post delivered to the big post office in Dover. That's it! Blimey, Bill, that's it."

"Sorry, I don't.."

But she'd rushed to the telephone and was rifling through her address book.

"Who are you..?"

"He bloody well owes me a favour."

"Who..?"

She waved me silent and began to dial.

"Uncle Tristram, it's me, Rosa."

I couldn't hear his end.

"I'm ringing because I want to ask you something about MI5 and I think you owe me an honest reply. I think you know why."

"Yes, a detective agency."

"With Bill Hawking, yes."

"Yes, he's here, yes. Why? He's my partner and anything you say to me can be said to him."

"The Official Secrets Act? Oh, good grief. I thought you said you weren't working for them any more?"

"Oh, good grief. Ok then. Just a sec."

"Bill," she put her hand over the receiver. "You need to go downstairs for a bit. He won't spill the beans with you here. Just be a love and go and see how the children are, would you?"

I gave her ten minutes, during which I played with the kids, who had taken to crawling super-fast over the floorboards and rugs.

Rosa was writing at the table when I got back.

"What was all that about, then?"

She lifted her head and smiled.

"I was right, MI5 do have a list, although Uncle Tristram has no idea whether the Major would have been on it, of course. But I think he was."

"A list of what?"

"Traitors, Bill. Or people they suspect of treason."

"But, why would they suspect the Major of treason?"

"Because thirty years ago he worked for the Army building secret communications devices. Only, unbeknownst to him, the man he worked under was a German spy. The association tainted the Major's reputation forever more."

"I see .. but what happens if you get put on the list? Did Mr Upshott tell you that?"

"If you get put on the list, your post is intercepted at one of the central post offices and steamed open. A photograph is taken of the contents. This photograph is then put in an unmarked van and driven to the headquarters of MI5. Thirty years, Bill, just think of it; for thirty years pen pushers at HQ have read every letter sent and received by the Major until, last June, they finally struck lucky."

"Because he's invented a technique, or a machine, or some method of brainwashing," I continued her train of thought, "and they must have been on tenterhooks as they got each new letter, waiting for technical knowledge that never came. They knew he could do it, but how?"

"That's right," said Rosa. "They waited and waited .. and then he went and died on them."

4. PICNIC IN THE SHINGLE GARDEN

I rang Peter later that evening to keep him up to date.

"Excellent progress, Rosa," he said. "We're agreed, then, that Dyminge's den was most probably ransacked by chaps on the Establishment payroll looking for more detailed evidence of his brainwashing invention?"

"Yes."

"Which they did not find, owing to you having broken and entered earlier that same night and taken said evidence - in the form of his manuscript and drawings - away with you."

"Yeah, and then given them.."

"To little old me," he interrupted. "Where they remain utterly safe because, besides being several counties away, I simply cannot make head nor tail of his appalling penmanship. Although, I shall lock them up with the family silver the second I get off the phone, no question. Unless, that is, you think we should let this shrink have a look at them? I mean, do we think we can trust him?"

I thought about it.

"D'you know, I'm not sure that it makes any difference whether we can trust him, or not. I'd be inclined to, myself, but the fact is that he doesn't have the technical knowledge to understand them, any more than we do. Well, a *bit* more, I suppose, but.."

"Then, I really can't see how educating ourselves in the dark art of brainwashing is going to help us find the old man."

"The body."

"No, we've discussed this, Rosa. It's not just a body, remember. It's what's left of a brilliant, brave man who deserved to be treated with dignity and respect and not left on a laboratory table somewhere in Whitehall, his brain plugged into electric wires and whatnot, just so that some mindless bureaucrat can warm up the Cold War. We're at a tipping point, don't you see? Just think of [48] the Cuban Missile Crisis.

"Well, I suppose, if brainwashing machines are going to be invented, then it's for the best if *we* get them first. The West, I mean."

"Oh, God help us. Not that old chestnut, again. Don't you understand, Rosa; that's what they always say? That's how all the rotten ideas get taken on. If we don't then someone else will. That's what got Hiroshima bombed flat. What's more.."

I could hear remonstrating in the background.

"No, Gabe, blood pressure be damned. What's more, that's what enables those damned fat cats to spoon up their porridge the morning after, without a care in the world. It wasn't *our* fault, don't you know? We were just saving the world from the Reds, the Bosh, the Japs, the Viet Cong, or whoever the current enemy number one happens to be. It wasn't *us*, oh no, it's never bloody *us*.."

Blimey. I seemed to have touched a nerve.

"Sorry about that, Miss Stone," his friend came on the line. "Peter can get a bit het up about subjects he cares about. Don't take it personally."

"I wasn't going to, don't worry. It's funny, though.." I was thinking out loud, "I had a sort of run-in with his son, Tristram, not long ago – my uncle, you know."

"Of course."

"And that's the first time that I've seen how similar they can be."

"Oh, two peas in a pod, Miss Stone. That's why they can't stand the sight of one another. Two green peas in a pod."

The next day was a Saturday and it dawned as if we had skipped three weeks and landed feet first in May. I was reading a back copy of the Radio Times over a cup of tea when my mother came in with the laundry basket.

"What perfect weather for drying nappies. They'll be done by lunchtime."

"Fantastic," I muttered. "Do you think the babies would like [49]*Bill and Ben, the Flower Pot Men*? Or is it too early."

"I had it on the other day. Benjamin was oblivious, but Jessica seemed to take to the daisy thing."

"Little Weed?"

"Mm. She's going to be a real clever-clogs, that one, you mark my word."

I put down the Radio Times.

"They're both completely brilliant, naturally, being my children."

"Hark at you!"

I watched her as she pottered around her kitchen, straightening the tea towel hanging on the Aga rail and humming. She looked happy.

"Are you pleased that Bill and I have started Hawking & Stone?"

She turned and stared at me, perhaps surprised at the directness of my question.

"Why, yes, I have to say that I am, Rosa. Very pleased indeed, since you ask."

"So, you think we'll make a go of it?"

"Well, that's up to you, of course. Hard work never hurt anyone and I'm not saying it won't be hard. I have every faith in Bill Hawking, though; he was always a serious-minded, hardworking lad."

"Fantastic." She'd managed to get under my skin in record time. "You have every faith in Bill, but not in your own daughter. Well, thanks very much."

"Oh, Rosa, don't give me that look again. We all know how clever you can be, love. It's just .. we haven't seen that much staying power from you. You've got to admit that you could be here, there and everywhere when you were younger."

"So, I'm damned before I've even begun.."

"I didn't say that."

"She didn't say that," my father had come into the room, his thick, grey hair standing on end from the wind.

"How do you know what she said?"

"Because I could hear you shouting from outside."

"Well, I may have been shouting, but *she* wasn't."

"You don't say? Come on, Bubeleh, grow up."

"Grow up?" How I hated it when people said that to me. "I'm old, for Christ sake. Old and on the shelf. Why do you two still talk to me as if I were twelve?"

He burst out laughing.

"Ah, Rosa, how you make me laugh. Old? What am I, Methuselah?"

I just stopped myself from saying yes, that was exactly what he was.

"You are a beautiful woman with everything before you. Your children are healthy. You have new ideas for a new life. Everything is there for you. For the taking, as they say."

"Yes, Jerzy, that was exactly what I was trying to say before she got on her high horse. It's all there, if you work hard and keep at it, Rosa. We had no choice but to make our living as best we could, but *this* .. this is more than just a living .. this is an adventure. Grab it with both hands and don't let go. I know I would."

It was the way she said that word; adventure. Her eyes shone as she said it.

"Now, enough already," ordered my father. "I was speaking to Frances outside and she's invited us all over for a picnic in her shingle garden. Rosa, get the children sorted out, Millicent find the deckchairs and I shall pack a hamper. Chop

chop."

Mrs Dyminge could get anything at all to grow. Have you read [50]'The Lion, The Witch and the Wardrobe'? If you have, you might remember that bit where they step through the wardrobe into Narnia and somebody drops a toffee paper. Next thing they know, a tree has sprouted from the fertile ground bearing a date-like fruit with the flavour of toffee. Well, that's Mrs Dyminge for you; if she dropped a clothes-peg, say, in the gravel (because the gardens in front of our houses are pure shingle and sand), there'd be a tree in the shape of one of those circular clothes horses springing from the beach next morning.

We lounged in our deckchairs, a child on my lap and another on my mother's, in the centre of Mrs Dyminge's low-lying knot garden under the bluest of skies. It was windy, sure, but we would have been surprised if it hadn't been blowing it's best on a spring day by the sea. The shingle garden was formed of perfect mounds of thrift and billowing columbine foliage – green on green – miniature daffodils, blue grape hyacinths and tiny, scarlet tulips, piercing the gravel like slim candles. There was even a vast rose behind us on the cottage wall, already in full flower, pale yellow bunches whipping about in the delicately scented wind.

"My goodness, but it's warm." Mrs Dyminge poured out homemade lemonade for us from a giant jug. "One of those days when an unseen hand has sprinkled the sea with diamonds."

I squinted at the deep blue sea and tugged Benjamin's sunhat down lower over his eyes.

"How lucky we are," my father sighed, waving his arms about, expansively, "to live in such a beautiful place. Surely this must be paradise."

At which point Mr Summerby's dog nabbed his crab sandwich from his hand and we all laughed.

"Apologies, Jerzy," went Mr Summerby, "I seem to have

brought the snake to the party."

The dog waved his curled tail over his back, like a flag and smirked.

"Why do you call him Canaan?" I asked.

"Because that's what he is, Rosa. He's a Canaan dog. A pariah. One of the oldest breeds known to man. I bartered for him with a Bedouin tribesman on my travels."

We all studied the dog with renewed respect; personally, I'd always thought he looked like a Battersea boy.

"Are you much-travelled, Edwin?" My mother enquired.

"Indeed," Mr Summerby set his bottle of beer down by his deckchair and focussed his extraordinarily blue eyes somewhere out at sea. "I found that I couldn't settle after the war, so I took off."

"The First World War?" I asked, because it was so difficult to ascertain how old he was.

"Yes," Mrs Dyminge interjected, "Edwin was in the East Kent Regiment with Guy, if I remember rightly."

"Really?" I pricked up my ears. "You must have known Harry Cole, then?"

"Harry Cole?" He shook his head. "No, I can't say that name rings any bells."

"You must remember young Harold, Edwin. He was Guy's batman," Mrs Dyminge said.

"Ah, but there were so many young Harolds, Frances. So many young men whose futures were destroyed by war. Time has blurred them into a single entity. I don't suppose I might have that last sliver of cheesecake, Jerzy? If nobody else wants it."

I opened my mouth, but my mother was too fast for me.

"Take it," she handed it over. "Tell me some names, then, Edwin; of the places you've been. I've travelled to Paris many times, of course, being in the fashion business, but, other than that, I feel I've hardly seen the world."

Mr Summerby smiled over his cheesecake and took another swig of beer.

"Let's see. China, India, Japan and Siam, of course. From the [51]Sultanate of Darfur in Africa to the [52]Emirate of Jabal Shammar in Arabia and many, many places in-between."

"Jabal Shammar," my mother rolled the words around in her mouth, her eyes closed against the sun.

"He really *is* a world-renowned expert on Oriental antiques, you know," I chipped in.

"You are too kind, Rosa. However I find, nowadays . ." and he threw a shy glance at Mrs Dyminge, " . . that the old adage 'East, west, home is best' has never rung truer."

Mrs Dyminge tucked one of the many wisps of stray hair, that had loosed in the wind, behind her ear.

"More lemonade, anybody?"

Suddenly, my mother jumped to her feet, waking Jessica in the process.

"Is that the phone, Jerzy?"

She didn't wait for a reply, but dumped my screaming daughter in my lap and ran towards the house. Benjamin promptly opened his mouth, on cue.

"Gosh, sorry everyone."

I tried to settle them with some lap jigging, but, when the dog joined in with a peculiar howl, straight from some ancient desert, I had to admit defeat. The noise was so loud that weekend visitors to the beach had stopped in their tracks by the shore to look our way. Any longer and they would hear the commotion from the Coastguard. I stood up with my children in my arms, prior to making a bolt for it, and caught sight of a visitor, standing just beyond our low, white wall, wearing sunglasses. Somehow, I knew that he had been standing there for a while. My knees nearly gave way under me. It was Jay Tamang.

We stepped towards one another and then halted. I turned.

"Dad could you take Jessica and Benjamin for me?"

"Don't," said Jay, softly.

But I, virtually, threw the two warm, solid bodies of my

lovely, loud children at my father and hurried out of the garden gate, without a backward glance.

He looked just the same handsome, young man from Nepal that I had met ten years previously. Maybe his clothes were more with-it, his leather jacket and jeans more authentically American than anything that could be bought in Britain, somehow. We hugged each other, painfully conscious of being watched from Mrs Dyminge's shingle garden.

"Let's walk," I suggested.

"Ok, Rosa, whatever you say."

"How's the Space Programme?" I asked, because Jay was the most brilliant scientist, who had been snapped up by the Americans to help them send a rocket to the moon when he lost his job at MI5.

"Not long now," he said. And then,

"Oh, Rosa, whatever were you thinking of? Why could you not tell me?"

We stopped walking and I hung my head.

"Uncle Tristram told you, didn't he?"

"He rang me last week and I have been travelling since then. How could you, Rosa? When you know I love you and always will?"

Tears started at the corners of my vision, but I swiped them away before they could run. What could I say that might make sense to anyone besides myself? About pride and love and total exhaustion.

We'd had a weekend to ourselves in London before he had gone to the airport and caught a plane to the future. I could see that he wanted to go, and who could blame him? I know I'd have gone like an absolute shot. I mean, building a rocket to the moon; how could I, possibly, compete with that?

"If they are mine, then you should have told me."

At which, I exploded, because I have always *so* much preferred anger to sadness.

"Who the hell else's could they be, Jay? I've not been

sleeping with a regiment of Gurkhas, you know. Of course, they're yours. I've got two babies who look like the Dalai Lama in miniature and I've had a whole year of people skirting the issue. It's been beyond preposterous. 'Oh, what lovely, shiny black hair they have, Rosa.' 'My, but they take after you, Rosa.' As if a Jew looks anything like a Tibetan."

It was actually quite funny, once I came to think about it.

"I mean, when Bill's mother said that thing about their father being Chinese, I was completely flummoxed; not only because she had the gumption to say it out loud, but also because I'd almost begun to doubt the evidence of my own eyes."

"I cannot see that any 'gumption' would be required," he said, with the dignity that I had always loved in him. And then,

"Bill? Who is Bill?"

Jay Tamang was the type of person who was difficult to have a row with, but I persevered and got there in the end.

"*My* children, Rosa; not one, but two miraculous, new beings and you deprive me of the first year of their lives. Am I a monster? Do you hate me? Why would you do this to me?"

He was shouting now and I sensed the visitors to the beach staring at us with growing animosity.

"Of course I don't hate you.. I'm so sorry.."

"Then why..?"

I was feeling increasingly hemmed in and I didn't like it. I tried to explain.

"You had everything you wanted, Jay; the most fabulous new adventure. But I hadn't managed anything until then. I was overwhelmed with feelings, with joy and responsibility.. and it got harder and harder to let you know. Until I didn't want to any more because I, finally, had something of my own.."

"You selfish, *selfish* woman.."

It was as if a starter pistol had gone off. I began to run,

this way and, then, that. I hared along the beach, but was forced to stop at the pub, so I ran up to the road and got halfway, only there were day trippers and cars and .. I stopped, hands on my knees, breathing hard. There was nowhere to go. There was absolutely nowhere to go any more. I turned around and went back.

"You remember Jay, don't you?"

I led Jay into the drawing-room, where my father had deposited the children, and himself, on the rug.

My father got up, clumsily, brushing down sandy trouser legs.

"Of course, I do. Wonderful to see you again, young man," he enveloped Jay in one of his bear hugs.

When he'd let him go, he glanced at the children.

"I'll just .. the kitchen, you know .." and he backed out of the room.

Had he always known who the father was? Had both of them always known?

I took a deep breath.

"This is Benjamin and that's Jessica. Our children."

Jay seemed lost for words, just shook his head and blinked at them, as if he couldn't quite believe that they were real. They blinked back. Then he sat down, cross-legged on the rug.

"Heaven help us all!"

My mother burst into the room, bright scarlet patches livid on her cheeks.

"That was Sam on the telephone, calling from Chelsea police station. They've arrested his friend Verity on suspicion of murder, because her fingerprints were all over the weapon that killed Harry Cole. Sam says there's another set they can't identify and they've picked him up because they think he and Verity may have been re-visiting the scene of their crime when they went to Dungeness."

She put her hands to her mouth and began to sob.

"Murder, Rosa! They've arrested my little boy on suspicion of murder."

PART 4

1. BIG STICKS & LOOT

We sat opposite one another on the Charing Cross train. We had the carriage all to ourselves. My trusty notebook lay open on my lap.

"Admittedly, it stands to reason that if they were able to identify Verity Flinders by her fingerprints, she must have been in trouble before," I allowed.

Rosa gave a cynical laugh,

"You can bet your bottom dollar that she's been picked up for drugs at least once, Bill."

The girl was only eighteen, and a young eighteen at that. I didn't know why Rosa had such a down on her.

"However, we do know that Verity pulled Sam out of the water using a wooden stake that she found at the side of Long Pit; she told me so, herself, at her birthday party. Now, if we assume that was the murder weapon, then Verity has a perfectly plausible reason for having her prints on it."

"Humph."

"You know that's the case, especially since your father has confirmed that Verity said to him on the night in question that she'd used a – I quote – 'big stick' to fish Sam out. So, give Verity Flinders a break, hmm? Considering she may well have saved your brother's life, you've been down on her like a ton of bricks."

Rosa wasn't thinking straight; she was miles away, lost in some problem of her own that I couldn't decipher.

"Would you say I was a selfish person, Bill?"

Yes.

"No, of course not. You're getting a new business started. The twins are only little; they won't remember this stage in their lives and blame you for leaving them with their nan for a couple of days while you have work to do in London."

"I wasn't thinking of that. Oh, never mind," she came back from wherever she'd been. "Where were we? Big sticks?"

"Yes. So, I've spoken to the lawyer and we're to meet him at the police station at noon. Remember, you mustn't get your hopes up about talking to Sam; the charge is a serious one and it may not be allowed."

"Yeah, I've got that. Even though it's difficult to bear."

"Is it?"

"Yeah. My little brother going through hell in a London police cell. Strip-searched and denied cigarettes and home comforts of any kind. He'll be devastated if they won't let him see me."

"Mm. Devastated."

The police station was in Lucan Place, a monolithic mansion-block off the Fulham Road. The lawyer that the Stone family had hired for Sam was already waiting for us outside the main entrance when we got out of the taxi. An old-school sort, florid of complexion and dressed in baggy pinstripes and a bashed hat, he proffered his hand to us both, before ushering us into the reception. We all sat down on a bench and he opened his fat briefcase and got out a leather-bound file.

"They are going to find an interview room for us, Miss Stone and, just to warn you, they would like to have a brief word with yourself, in private."

He turned to me,

"May I ask, what is *your* connection with young Mr Stone?"

"Um, we've been friends forever. Flatmates until very

recently, too."

"The flat in Cale Street? Still got the key, by any chance?" He was sharp, this man.

"Well, I have, yes. Sam made me pay a couple of months upfront, so I thought that Rosa – Miss Stone, I mean – and I might stay there tonight."

He looked from one of us to the other, trying to gauge our relationship.

"We are business partners, Mr Latimer," said Rosa.

"Ah, jolly good," he wrote something down. "Again, just to warn you, you might find that the police ask to take the key to the flat. My client has been kicking up rather a storm about letting them into the premises, apparently."

"What?" Rosa gawped at me. "Why on earth would he do that?"

I could think of a few reasons. Would it have hurt me to have kept my big mouth shut?

"When you say 'kicking up a storm', do you mean that he's been harassed? That he's become distressed, even?" She asked.

The lawyer seemed surprised by her question.

"Not really, no. I've found your brother to be a charming young chap, Miss Stone. Politeness personified. Only the flat search seemed to rattle him. Can't *possibly* think why, myself."

He flung us a keen-eyed, humorous look; he was well-aware of what charming young chaps might stash away in their flats. There were no flies on him.

"To change the subject," I said, as we were still waiting for the policeman at reception to acknowledge us, "do you know where they are keeping Verity Flinders? Not here, presumably."

"Miss Flinders, needless to say, has a lawyer of her own. However, I can vouchsafe that when my client was picked up, he was in her company and that she is, also, being held at Lucan Place."

"Oh, ok. Only, I can testify that she told me about the wooden stake; pulling Sam Stone out of the water with it, I mean. Not only that, but she also told his father about it, on the actual night in question."

"Good stuff, Mr Hawking. Let the police know, when you've got a chance. Miss Flinders has top-notch legal representation, I'm told – way out of my league – who will, no doubt, be in touch with you. Ah, here comes an officer. Let's get the ball rolling."

Rosa remained composed until we found a booth upstairs at Barino's, which was just around the corner from the flat. It was late for lunch and the place was almost empty, but for a few French students smoking over coffee; there were a lot of French people in South Kensington, owing to a big institute nearby. We slipped onto a leatherette banquette.

"The lasagne's very good."

"Anything, as long as I can have a glass of red with it."

I gave the waiter our order, before I enquired,

"So, how did it go? Did you see him?"

She screwed up her eyes, like a child, and began to weep, her shoulders shaking.

"He hates me," she cried.

"Oh, Rosa," I put a hand on top of hers, but she pushed it away.

"He hates you even more."

Damn; she must have told him about the keys.

"He said the police think they're a pair of delinquents who killed an old man for kicks," she sobbed out her story, in fits and starts. "They found Verity's prints on the murder weapon, and then they found Verity with Sam in some nightclub and, when he gave them his name, they connected him straight away with the Stone family who live right next door to the old man whose body was stolen and who was also a close friend of the victim in the pond on Dungeness," she drew a deep breath. "So, they know that Sam knew Harry Cole. It's just too much of a coincidence, they think."

"But it's all circumstantial, Rosa. They haven't got any proof that Sam was there."

Except .. my brain was racing .. except that there was a photograph in my possession that had been taken by Sam Stone on what was very probably the evening that Harry Cole was murdered. Sam had been there to witness Major Dyminge and his friend Mr Cole, bearing his canvas bag and his library book that could be dated with absolute precision, coming out of the Coastguard pub. It was my turn to shudder. Was it possible that Sam, addled out of his brain on drugs, no doubt, followed the old tramp to Dungeness? That he met up with his vulnerable, young girlfriend – so mixed-up and passive and under Sam's thumb – and they bashed poor Mr Cole's head in, for fun? That they even went back later to see what had become of his corpse?

I shook my head to dislodge the terrible, disloyal thoughts that were crowding in. Sam was my oldest friend. No, however badly he was capable of behaving, it couldn't be true; it really couldn't. What a piece of luck, though, that I'd taken the photograph off Sam's bedroom wall. They might be searching the flat at that very moment and, yes, they might well find some pot, or a few pills, but at least they wouldn't find that.

"Would you like an iced coffee for afters, Rosa? I'm having one."

She wiped her eyes and sighed,

"D'you know, Bill, I don't think I have it in me to refuse an iced coffee. Even at a time like this. God, I really *am* a selfish woman."

"That's not selfish, that's positive; it's just bucking yourself up so as to get on with the job."

She laughed and bent forward to stroke my cheek.

"You're sweet."

I wanted to kiss her so badly, but she must have seen it in my face.

"C'mon, then, let's order that iced coffee. You're right; there's absolutely no point in being negative."

She waved at the waiter, but I'd stopped breathing. Negative. There would be negatives in Sam's room; he had boxes full of them there. What was the betting that the police would go through them and find the incriminating picture? My friend could still be in serious trouble.

On the pretext of going to the Gents, I left Rosa stirring vanilla ice cream into her coffee and dashed round to Cale Street. I'd given up my key, but had remembered that the launderette downstairs held a spare. If I was quick, I might get there before the police did.

The launderette manageress was there and knew me well; I had gone down there to do a wash a whole lot more often than Sam. She handed the flat key over and I took the stairs two at a time. All was quiet, so I let myself in. I noticed that my room had degenerated considerably since I'd been living there, but Sam's was still tidy and well-organised. His boxes of negatives were labelled by month, so I grabbed *January* and *February 1965*, emptied the contents into an empty envelope, and stuffed it in my jacket pocket. I went to go, but I couldn't leave like that.

I turned around, went back into his room and rifled through his bedside drawers. There was a paper packet of loose weed, a pouch of tobacco and cigarette papers in the top drawer. Then, I went through his pockets and took a look in the teapot, where I'd seen him stash his mushrooms. There was a small supply of the shrivelled fungi in the teapot and that was it. I confiscated the loot and hotfooted it out. I'd done my best for Sam; if there was more stashed away, I didn't have the time, or the inclination, to look for it. I gave the key back to the lady downstairs and made no mention of the police. If they turned up to do a comprehensive search, it had nothing to do with me.

"Do you have an upset stomach?" Rosa asked, when I got

back.

"Italian food doesn't always agree with me," I sat down, trying not to seem out of breath.

I forced myself to put on a smiling face, without a care in the world. I'd decided that the last thing I wanted to do was to worry her further by mentioning her brother's photograph. It had obviously slipped her mind. If she hadn't been so upset by the morning's visit, I reckoned she would have put two and two together, but I let it lie.

"So, given that they told me to pick the flat key up from the police station this evening, what would you like to do now, Rosa? Maybe pay a visit to your old shop?"

"God, no. I don't think I could take the sight of the poor, old Arcanium, not after the morning I've had. I need some air; it's a lovely day, let's go for a walk. We can clear our heads."

"Good idea."

Quite honestly, I was happy just to be in her company.

London in the spring was new to me. The fresh, lime-green leaves on the street trees almost gave the place a feel of the countryside. Everywhere, visitors on their holidays chatted in different languages, strolling slowly around the maroon-tiled station. There was an air of festivity that I hadn't seen in the dreary days of late winter. Rosa and I walked past the shops and restaurants on Thurloe Street and, then, down Exhibition Road, comfortable enough in one another's company not to have to make conversation. We got as far as the Cromwell Road junction and stopped, the two, great museums directly across the road from us.

"I give you dinosaurs to the left and the costume gallery to the right," Rosa declared, gesturing to the Natural History Museum and the Victoria & Albert. "Which is it to be?"

"Dinosaurs, definitely."

"Really?" She looked disappointed.

"Although, once you've seen one, you've seen them all. Now, costumes.."

She laughed.

"The V&A it is, then."

We waited for a bus to come past and then crossed the big road. To be honest, when I'd lived around the corner, I'd only dropped into the museum for five minutes to ask for a job. After which, thinking it a dusty, old place full of dusty, old remains of Empire, I'd left.

"You might not think it, Bill," Rosa was chattering away, as we entered, "but I simply adore clothes, always have. They have the best costume gallery in the world here. I could spend all day in it, I really could."

I sincerely hoped that wasn't going to happen.

"The only trouble is," she continued, "there's so much other stuff. I can never find my way for all of these Persian rugs and plaster-casts of David slaying Goliath cluttering up the place. Ugh, Judith and Holofernes, no thank you."

We took a left by a lady showing off a head she'd severed from a man's body and found ourselves in China.

"I'd have thought all this would be right up your street, Rosa," I stopped by a glass case to admire some artefacts, "what with the antiques shop."

"Yes, it should have been, I admit. Only I never had enough time to come and study the real thing because I was too busy with the rubbish. Anyway, this is all way above my head; this is Mr Summerby's world, Bill."

The craftsmanship was amazing, so delicate it seemed impossible that it had been made when my ancestors had been stirring up mud pies in Kent.

"How did we land up with all this?" I looked around at the sheer number of ancient objects on display.

"Well, some may have been gifts from the Emir of Jabal Shammar for services rendered, but, by and large, we probably looted it."

"This chess set is loot?"

I gazed down at an exquisite board carved out of opaque, milky jade, of the palest green. *Early Ming Dynasty, circa 1350,* [53]*Nephrite, Xinjiang region.*

"Could be."

She leant over my shoulder to get a better look and I couldn't help closing my eyes to breathe in the scent that she always wore, a perfume of tropical flowers and whipped cream. She gave a start and my lids shot open.

"But that's not a chess set, Bill. That's a set of Chinese dominoes. A pale green one."

We stared at one another, turning the story around in our minds so that it pointed in an entirely different direction.

2. BUSTED

Life was looking so cool, too. I was in with the in-crowd and scarcely bothering to show my face at college. What was the point, when I could learn on the job?

When I started hanging out with Dave's crew, I'd been a glorified message boy, I'll be honest. The money had been good, though, which was the main reason I'd stuck with it. They'd had me on a motorbike bombing all over London to deliver film and samples and whatever the advertising industry wanted to shift. From Wardour Street to Harley Street, Plaistow Road to Park Lane, I was always on the move; it got so the guys on the doors at the Soho screening rooms and the birds on reception at the Harley Street clinics all knew me by name.

"Hi Sam," the beautiful, blank-faced girls with their manes of hair and white uniforms would lean forward to say hello, displaying their assets to best advantage. "*So* good to see you again."

Which was kind of gratifying, of course, but not where I needed to be. No, it was meeting Verity that really managed to get me on my way.

After her birthday party, I was on Dave's radar. The company gave me a Leica to play with – the sharpest 35mm camera you could get – and I began by assisting on shoots. It wasn't too long before I had my first real opportunity. Flinders Associates were making a tv commercial to show on one of the ITV companies' slots and Dave wanted me in Studio 3, Teddington Studios, first thing Monday morning.

First thing on set is very early, indeed and it was still dark when I arrived, around 5. The actors were in the green room, but, being one of the technical crew, I went straight to the tv studio. Dave was already there – every inch the boss in his Savile Row threads – chatting to the money men from the well-known brand of cigarettes that we were all there to promote. He winked at me, but carried on schmoozing. Dave could schmooze for Britain. I went over and hung round the director, but he was busy with the cameraman, talking ten to the dozen and making frames with his fingers. Everyone was so busy being busy it made you wonder whether anything was actually being achieved. A bird holding a clipboard approached.

"Can I help?"

"Hi, I'm Sam Stone, here to do the stills for Mr Flinders."

"Oh, gosh. Well, I haven't, actually, got your name down here," she was obviously new to the job and it didn't take much to fluster her, "but why don't you go and get a coffee? Perhaps you could join Mr Flinders in the viewing room later?"

It looked like she had no idea how integral I was to the process, but I took her drift; she wanted to clear the set, while she worked out what was going on. I decided to find the green room and get in a look at the actors.

They were considerably more clued-up in the green room; one glance at the camera slung round my neck and half the place wanted to be my best friend.

"Hi there," a pretty, young brunette in a mini skirt waved at me from the corner, where a selection of danish pastries and a coffee pot were displayed on a table. "Fancy a coffee?"

"I'm Jo Laine," she shook hands and poured me a cup.

"Sam Stone, set photographer. Nice to meet you. What are you playing in this little masterpiece?"

"Ha-ha. Sweet, young thing, as ever, darling. Terry, over

there with the sideburns.." Terry gave me a little finger wave, ".. has just proposed to me down on one knee in the rain and all that jazz, so we light a celebratory ciggie and the skies miraculously clear and that's us done for the day, as far as I can tell. After that you get the bit where the doc explains how, 'like a breath of fresh air, the brand is good for body and spirit', and points to a chart to prove it."

"Right, so you're a model, Jo?"

"I'm certainly not," she seemed offended. "Drama school trained, I'll have you know."

"Of course. But you obviously *could* be a model; that's what I meant. So, who's playing the doc?"

"Over on the settee, the glamorous blonde in the Chanel suit."

"Yeah right; she looks just like my GP."

"I know. Bonkers, isn't it?"

The blonde actress on the settee must have sensed that we were talking about her, because she looked straight over. Surprisingly, this woman – who was somewhere in her thirties, I'd have said – had none of the easy manner that you tend to get in 'the business', but seemed to be assessing me with her dark brown eyes. Maybe she'd decided to play the siren. I gave as good as I got, staring her down until she raised an elegant eyebrow and turned away.

The bird with the clipboard came into the green room.

"Artistes to wardrobe and make-up, please," she called out.

I was just finishing a second danish pastry, when Dave walked in.

"Sammy! How are you doing, my boy?"

Dave was a touchy-feely type and liked to grab his friends and associates by the shoulders, or mess up their hair. With me, he did both.

"Great, Dave. Really excited to be here. Thanks again for the opportunity."

"Nonsense, you're my little Bailey, aren't you? Any

more in the coffee pot?"

He made himself comfortable on the sofa, while I fetched him a coffee and a pastry.

"I was only saying to Verity the other day; you've found me a right little Bailey in that boy of yours. 'Cos I'm a family man, me; I like to keep family close, if you know what I mean?"

"Right, Dave. Thanks, Dave."

"Talking of family, see much of that uncle of yours, do you?"

"Uncle? What uncle?"

"Ha, ha, very funny; you know who I mean. Son of a fucking lord, no less. Turns out you have some unexpected family ties."

"Well, yeah, but to be honest with you Dave, I don't really know him that well. He and my aunt were abroad for a long time and.."

"Ah, yes, the famous Kathleen Smith. She's been making my day in the cat food commercials; they can't get it on the shelves quick enough, I'm told. Strange, though.. all these connections to my little Bailey."

"What can I say? It's a small world, Dave."

"Yeah, true enough; and a hell of a long way from where I grew up, I can tell you. Well,.." he licked the remaining flakes of pastry off his fingers, "I needed that. Back to work, eh?"

"Right Dave. You want me to take the stills at the end of the shoot, is that correct?"

"I want some in the rain, assuming they get the machine operating, so stay in the studio and take those when you get a chance. We'll do some after, too. Just make sure you get the fag box in shot, nice and clear, so's the brand can be read. I don't want any of the Doc, though; got that?"

"Perfect; you won't be sorry you hired me for this, Dave."

He got up to leave, brushing flakes from his strides.

"Better not be, son. Oh, and Sammy.."

"Yes Dave?"

"Have a word with the Doc before she leaves, will you? She needs a favour done and she's a major client."

"Sorry?" I was confused. "You mean the blonde actress playing the doctor?"

"Playing? That woman doesn't play, Sammy. That's Anna Ambrosia. Dr Ambrosia to you and me."

I left the green room and promptly ran into the cast of [54]The Avengers in the passageway. I stopped, open-mouthed, as they strode right past me on their way to another studio: proper telly stars in their native habitat. The new girl, Diana Rigg, was gorgeous – a real class act – although about 3 feet taller than me, unfortunately. Wow, was I in the groove. I really *would* have to be some species of bozo to cock this job up.

It took a day to wrap and most of that was spent with guys trying to make the rain machine work. In the end, they had to resort to a couple of them up ladders with watering cans. Jo and Terry managed to gambol about like new-born lambs despite getting drenched at regular intervals all day long, and I got some nice pics of them looking elated to be getting married and super-elated to be sharing a fag. By the time they were dismissed, the blonde ice-queen, Dr Ambrosia – all white coat, stethoscope and a string of pearls – had been parked in front of a giant chart to demonstrate the facts and figures. I'd have liked to leave with friendly Jo and try my luck outside, where Dave wouldn't have his eye on us, but remembered just in time that I'd been given orders to wait and have a word with Dr Ambrosia.

After she'd finished her spiel – given in that careful, overly clipped manner that suggested she might have been born abroad – I approached her, but she shook her head at me, as if I'd slipped up in some way.

"I'll expect you in my dressing-room in ten minutes."

So, I gave it fifteen minutes before I knocked on her door.

"You're late," she pointed out. And then, "Heaven

knows where Dave found *you*."

I wasn't used to being spoken to like that, and it floored me.

"Come in, then."

Once I was inside and the door was shut, she turned her Chanel-clad back on me to pick up a vanity case. It was pale-pink, made of a hard, ridged plastic and had a small padlock on it.

"This contains documents that are extremely valuable to my work. Mr Flinders has kindly offered to keep them safe while my premises are being re-decorated," she handed the case to me.

Her flinty manner and clipped way with words didn't encourage discussion, so I took it from her, no questions asked.

"It's vital that you keep it safe, do you understand this, Mr Stone?"

I was surprised, and not altogether happy, to find that she knew my name.

On leaving Dr Ambrosia, I went straight to find Dave, only I couldn't find him anywhere. I caught up with the PA girl with the clipboard.

"Hi, there. I don't suppose you've seen Mr Flinders anywhere on your travels, have you?"

"He left over an hour ago; I got a taxi for him."

"Oh, ok, no sweat. I'd better get going myself then," I shook her hand. "Nice to have worked with you."

"Sorry, who *are* you?"

This bird was so clueless.

"I'm the new David Bailey, don't you know?"

She thought I was being funny, but she had a nice smile, so I grinned back.

"That Dr Ambrosia," I, suddenly, thought to ask, "*is* she the real thing?"

"As far as I know she's a top doctor with a clinic in Harley Street."

"Oh, ok."

She lifted her clipboard over her mouth and whispered at me from behind it,

"Nothing to do with fresh air and clean living, though. Mental cases; I have it on good authority."

"Yeah?" I laughed. "Still, if anyone needs a fag, I suppose it's them."

I rang Flinders Associates the next morning, but was told that Dave had gone to France for a holiday with his wife's family, so I stowed the vanity case in the bottom of my wardrobe with my dirty washing, and thought no more about it.

I was developing the cigarette ad pics – Jo and Terry and the shared fag in all their black and white glory – when there was a knock on the outside door of my flat.

"Hi Sam."

"Verity. What brings you here?"

Her fair hair had grown and was tangling over her shoulders, while her black threads looked grubby at the edges. Seemed like Verity wasn't looking after herself.

"Oh, I was just on my way to the Kings Rd and I thought, 'I wonder what's going down with Sam?' Then I looked up and, wow, it was like karma, because there was the name of your street in front of my very eyes. So here I am. Are you pleased to see me?"

She was talking quite fast, and sweating a bit. Young Verity was tripping.

"I'm kinda busy at the mo, Verity. Just developing some cool stuff for your Dad, as it happens."

"Yeah? Like, a little bird told me you were working for Dave," she wobbled against the side of the door.

"So, aren't you going to invite me in, Sam? Just for a teeny-tiny coffee?"

"Ok," I sighed and let her past me, up the stairs. "Only don't go into the darkroom, yeah? Cos they're not cooked yet."

She started giggling as she negotiated the stairs.

"Whoops a daisy!" She giggled. "Pooh, it stinks in here, Sam."

"That's the developing fluid, you bozo. C'mon, sit down and I'll rustle you up a strong coffee."

She was unable to settle and wandered around the room, while I stirred up the Nescafe. There was a magazine that Bill had left when he went back to Kent, that I'd found under the sofa, and she picked that up and sat down with it.

"Do you read 'The Amazing Brain', Sam? That's *so* weird."

"Nah, that's Bill's. He was sharing the flat for a while."

"Bill Hawking?"

I was kind of surprised that she remembered him.

"Here's your coffee. Get that down you."

"I like Bill," she took the coffee with a shaky hand and managed to spill some on the floor. "Oops."

"Look at the state of you, Ver. What have you been doing?"

I assessed her, with a professional eye: the excitement and the dilated pupils.

"[55]Purple hearts?"

"No, I haven't done anything for ages now. I can't deal with any of it. I'm just not very well."

"Yeah, sure, pull the other one."

She muttered something, under her breath.

"Sorry, what did you say?"

"I said, I'm not going back to Dr Ambrosia. Nobody can make me. They've gone to France and they think I'm at the clinic, but I ran away before I got there and I'm never going back again. Even if I have to sleep on the street."

Dr Ambrosia? Talk of the devil; how many doctors called Ambrosia could there be in London?

"Anna Ambrosia? Blonde with dead eyes and a clinic in Harley Street?"

She spilled her coffee again and one small tear escaped her heavily blackened false lashes.

"I hate her. She and Dave have been having an affair for ages now; they don't even bother to keep it a secret. Dr Ambrosia wants him to leave my mother and marry her, but he won't. Clementine acts like there's nothing going on, but *she's* completely out of it most of the time on uppers and downers. Neither of my parents has any time left for me."

Even though Verity could be a drag, I was sorry to hear all this. Now I looked at her properly, I could see she genuinely wasn't well.

"Hey, Ver," I put an arm round her and she snuggled in, like the unhappy child she was.

It crossed my mind that nobody, including me, had been treating her with any care or kindness.

"Don't worry, I won't send you back to that cow. You can kip down here for a bit, if you're not well and on your own. Bill's gone and you can take this sofa."

"Really? Wow, that's so .. fab," she was slowing down, now, as if she was a car that had been revved to speed on the empty road and was now grinding down to first gear, prior to stopping altogether.

"You're not my girlfriend, though, Ver? D'you get that? You and me, we're mates and that's it."

"Ok, Sam," she'd closed her eyes and I slipped my arm away, so that she fell back on the sofa, half asleep.

"We'll get you something to eat when you wake up, and .."

I was conscious that I hadn't thought to ask her what was up, health-wise.

"Maybe I'll give my doctor a call . ." I said, to myself, thinking of my doctor in Kent, a sensible type and an old family friend.

I took my coffee back to the darkroom, feeling pretty pleased with myself, somehow.

I lost all track of time as I worked, and it must have been quite a few hours later that I emerged to find Verity washing her hair in the kitchen sink with a bar of Wrights Coal tar soap.

"Tea?" I called out, and she nodded.

I was beginning to regret my earlier generosity. I mean, if she was going to this mental clinic, then who knew what was going down. She could be completely barking and go loco in the night. Or – even worse – turn all domestic on me and dig herself into my flat, so that I could never get rid of her. Then, maybe Dave would get nasty and force me to do the decent thing and marry his daughter and..

She wrung her hair out and wrapped it in a dirty tea towel, which was reassuring. Now I came to think of it, Verity Flinders had never shown any disturbing signs of domesticity in all the time I'd known her. Perhaps it was going to be cool, after all.

"There's bread.."

I'd opened the bread bin, but found the loaf had developed small, blue patches. I showed it to her.

"Fab, just scrape them off, will you? I'm famished. Got any jam?"

"Jam, yes. Butter, no."

"Who needs butter?"

I scraped off the blue and cut some big wodges.

"So, what, exactly, is up with you, Ver?"

"Well, nobody is quite sure," she seemed eager to discuss whatever it was. "I do hear voices, but not all the time and I don't really mind them."

Ah.

"I felt pretty blue in the autumn and had a spell in hospital. Then, I'd been seeing stuff and got a little mixed-up, so Dave and Clementine sent me to the clinic. I hate it there because they give me electric shocks, which don't do anything at all, except that I've forgotten some things that I used to know and remembered others that are no use at all. These random thoughts just keep popping up and I never know when it's going to happen."

Electric shock treatment?

"I can't tell you what the things I've forgotten are, of course, but I just have the definite feeling that they've gone, you know?"

No, not really.

"So, it might be manic depression. Or, it might be a bad reaction to doing drugs. Or, it might just be me."

Or, all three.

"Bloody hell."

It was funny, but I found myself looking at her with newfound respect; this bird was a whole lot more interesting than I'd suspected. I lifted my camera and snapped her at the kitchen table, tea towel on her head, mouldy bread in her hand and I knew, in my bones, it was going to be one of the best shots I'd ever taken in my life.

It was two days later, and Verity had dragged me out to a very dark room in the basement of the Institut Français in Queensberry Place for an evening of French chansons, when the police showed up and we got busted.

3. STORIES & FACTS

We had picked up the key to Sam's flat and were standing in the doorway, aghast.

"I reckon he's had somebody else staying on his sofa," Bill said, "because I *certainly* didn't leave dirty sheets on it."

"I suppose it could be the police," I suggested, "doing an exceptionally thorough search."

It was worse than a bombsite, the flat had been ransacked, with dirty mugs and plates, books and magazines, littering the floor.

"I have to say, it doesn't actually look that different, Rosa. I was only referring to the sheets."

"Oh.. well, I'm no one to talk; my digs weren't exactly up to my mother's high standards."

"But this *is* new."

Bill held up a very small black dress, with a tear under one arm, that had been draped over the back of the sofa.

"Verity Flinders," I shuddered.

I still felt a strange presentiment that the stick insect had dragged my innocent brother into her web, or nest, or wherever stick insects called home. Quite why she should have felt the need to murder old Harry Cole was difficult to assess, but her fingerprints were on the stake, and not his; he had told me that the police had verified that fact. I didn't like the feeling that Verity had even invaded Sam's digs, not one bit.

"She probably just needed somewhere to stay," Bill suggested, ever the sweet boy who thought the best of people.

"Hmm. Come on, let's get the kettle on and clear a space. It's been a long day."

I headed into Sam's room, where I was going to sleep. I switched the light on, as the curtains were drawn. It wasn't too bad, just a lot of photographic equipment and pictures on the walls. Even his bed was made. I set my overnight bag on the floor and lay down.

"What I can't understand," I shouted to Bill, as he busied about in the kitchenette, "is what they were hoping to find in his flat? Or, why they're keeping him for the second night running, when they have no evidence that he played any part in old Harry's murder, whatsoever?"

He appeared in the doorway holding two mugs of tea, and with an envelope under one arm.

"Rosa," he said, "I think we need to talk."

Bill sat down on the edge of the bed and proceeded to remind me about the photograph. Then, he opened the envelope and reels of negatives spilled out onto the blanket. He unrolled the coils, held them up to the un-shaded lightbulb over the bed and studied them, one by one.

"Got you. Phew."

What kind of private detective was I going to make, when I could forget the most important piece of evidence? While I was pleased that Bill had saved my brother's bacon by his quick-thinking, I felt deeply disappointed in myself. All I had done was wallow in iced coffee.

"Don't look so down, Rosa. All of this is personal for you; I understand that."

It was going to be tough working with this boy if he kept behaving so impeccably. I drank my tea and tried to engage my brain.

"Ok, so Sam might well have been at the Coastguard on the fatal night, but neither of us seriously believes that he followed Harry Cole all the way to Dungeness for hours and hours – because Sam doesn't drive, remember – and then got his girlfriend to bash the old man's head in for no reason, whatsoever."

"Don't forget the set of Chinese dominoes, though. If the pale green set that Major Dyminge had was made of jade and anything like the one that we saw at the V&A, then it has to be worth a great deal of money. We've been searching for a reason why an old tramp should have been murdered, and it's taken us until now to find it. The dominoes set has to be that reason."

Bill fetched his notebook and sat down once more to scan his notes, flicking through the pages at speed.

"Also, Rosa, I can't help wondering why the set kept changing hands."

"How do you mean?"

"Well, originally it was Harry's, because Auntie Frances said that they always called it 'Harry's set'. He, then, gave it to the Major for some 'service that the Major had done him'; again, according to Auntie Frances. Yet, in this photograph we can be pretty sure that Harry is holding the set in the canvas bag, because the Major has his hands empty. Why, then, did Major Dyminge give the set back to Harry Cole? And was the fact that somebody saw Harry carrying the set the motivation for the murder?"

"Blimey, Bill, we really are clutching at straws. Just because the set was green, it doesn't, necessarily, make it worth squillions. Anyhow, how would Sam know it was worth anything? He's just a nineteen-year old boy with a camera fetish and a squalid flat. You'd have to be .. I don't know .. an Edwin Summerby to judge the value. Perhaps we should ask *him* about it."

Bill's face had gone all peculiar; as if he'd tuned in to a strange radio station and heard something that he'd never expected to hear.

"How much do you know about Mr Summerby, Rosa?"

"What? Oh, come off it. He's a perfectly respectable retired antiques dealer who I just happened to get to know in my local pub in London."

"Who spoke first?" Bill's concentration had become so intense that he was rather scary.

"Um. Me, probably. It usually *is* me who starts conversations with complete strangers. Although.."

I pictured our first meeting in The Man in the Moon, across the road from my shop. Some quality that had been slumbering in my brain woke up. I could see it all, as if I were there; the sparse, early evening crowd, my friend Seamus – the Irish landlord – the shining taps and Mr Summerby, there in his usual place. He'd been sitting on a stool at the bar, of course, the yellow dog slumped at his feet. There'd been a magazine open on the counter in front of him.. no, not a magazine, a catalogue: Christies or Sotheby's, I think. I'd ordered a drink for myself and, then, he had looked down at the twins, two tiny bundles asleep in their pram.

"Are they ready for a drop of ale in their bottles?" He had asked, and we'd laughed.

"Him. It was him."

"So, we think that there may have been a possibility that he wanted to make contact with you because he knew of your connection to Major Dyminge and Mr Cole? How?"

"Seamus could have told him where I came from. Or, he may have had more of a connection with his old stamping ground than we have assumed. But, one thing's for sure; if he was using me as a source of information, then, at that point, he hadn't got the dominoes set."

Bill and I went quiet.

The low rumble of machines in the laundrette downstairs was an ominous background to my thoughts; as if an evil presence were approaching. I shivered and drew Sam's blanket around my shoulders. Fragments of conversation from the picnic in Mrs Dyminge's shingle garden returned.

"Edwin Summerby denied any knowledge of Harry Cole when we had our picnic, but I think he lied," I said. "I think that they *all* knew each other from way, way back. That they were three boys who grew up in the same area of Kent towards the end of the last century.

"Guy Dyminge, Edwin Summerby and Harry Cole," Bill began to write.

"Local boys with different backgrounds, but who were allowed to kick a ball about on the beach, or climb trees in the woods. One of them, Edwin, knew a girl called Frances Carlisle, the vicar's daughter. They picked primroses together and he never forgot her. For all we know, he may have been serious about her, may have wanted to propose. But, then, everything changed, because the 1915 war was upon them and they all joined the East Kent Regiment to fight for their Country."

"Guy became an officer, but we don't know about Edwin. What we do know is that Guy kept his friend Harry close; he knew about Harry's problems, of course - his cleft lip and his trouble with speech - but he also knew that, underneath, he was an intelligent young man. So, Harry became Guy's batman when they went out to serve in France. And, in the evenings, in the trenches, Guy and Harry would play Chinese dominoes with a set that Harry had, somehow, acquired.."

"We can't say how Harry got it, but we can suspect that Harry, who was always light-fingered according to his great-nephew, may have stolen it. He could, even, have stolen it from a fellow soldier who had always had an interest in precious objects from the East and an eye for value; from his old playmate, Edwin."

Bill continued to scribble, as I pictured the scene.

"Only, then, the set changed hands again, because Guy 'did Harry some service in the war'. I think he may have saved his life. So, Harry gave Guy the set to say thank you; after all, I can't see Harry having any idea of its value. No, Harry would only have stolen it because he wanted to play dominoes."

"Then, when they met up once more, as old men – after a lifetime of adventures for one, and a lifetime on the road for the other – they reverted to their old pastime, one that may have meant more to them than a simple game, and took to playing Chinese dominoes in the Coastguard."

"However, Edwin Summerby never forgot the precious set that had been stolen from him in the war. The idea of it festered inside all the time that he travelled the world to find antiques to sell in his famous shop. I think the jade set was the treasure that got away."

Bill stopped writing and smiled,

"You're good at stories, Rosa."

"Of course. I've had experience of them."

"If you do the stories and I do the facts, we might even make a go of Hawking & Stone."

It had grown dark and the single lightbulb that dangled from Sam's bedroom ceiling gave out the palest glow. The rumblings from the launderette below had ground to a stop.

"That's it," I said, suddenly confident. "I think we've found Hatchet."

"The murderer?"

"Yeah. We've just got to place him there."

"We have; it's tenuous in the extreme, otherwise."

He yawned and stood up, closing his notebook.

"It's late, Rosa, maybe we should turn in."

"We should go to bed?" I couldn't resist it; seeing the hope rise in his face. I may not be a very nice woman, I'm afraid.

"See you in the morning, Bill."

"Oh. Right. See you then. Goodnight," he backed out of the room and closed the door behind him.

I was so tired, and yet it was impossible to sleep with so much churning away in my head. So many pictures. So many words. So many characters. All fighting for a space in the night.

I saw pleasant Mr Summerby trailing old Harry along the coast, trudging mile after mile, hour after hour. But, no, Mr Summerby had a car, why walk when you could drive?

That was it; he'd stopped to offer Harry a lift.

"I say, it's not Harry Cole, is it?" He would have wound down the car window.

It would never have occurred to Harry that nobody could have recognised him after the life that he had led. Mr Summerby, on the other hand, looked remarkably the same. Did he offer the tramp a drink? Get a silver hip flask of whisky, or brandy, out of the glove compartment?

"This calls for a tipple, wouldn't you say? Meeting up after all these years. Here, take it all, do. Now, let me give you a lift. Where are you off to, old boy?"

I rotated in Sam's sheets, restless and hot, trying to block out the image of the stake crashing down upon Harry's skull, of the old man toppling into the water. Was he already dead? I clung to the hip flask and the night in the Coastguard, hoping he was too drunk to know what was happening to him.

Time passed and still no sleep. I saw fields that became trenches, the wide sea shrink to a drowning pool. Young Mr Summerby and Mrs Dyminge tripping through the woods to pick primroses, turning as they heard me approach, their faces vastly aged under wigs, shrivelled like trolls. Verity Flinders appeared in my mother's hat. Then, I was at the edge of the flooded gravel pit staring down into the water and Mrs Dyminge floated to the surface, a bloody gash striping her forehead.

I opened my eyes. My breathing was quick and tremulous and fuelled by a sense of horror.

Where the ceiling met the wall, a magic lantern show of buses and cars paraded around Sam's four walls, illuminated by street lamps. A strip of London was projected up, above the top of the curtains and I watched the shadows travel the room, forcing myself to cling onto the here and now.

I became aware of a scraping sound. Was it a mouse? Not a rat, surely? The sound was coming from Bill's room.

"Bill?" I called out, nervously.

There was no reply. The scraping continued, small but determined, until I heard the front door to the flat open.

Somebody was breaking in. I heard their footsteps pad into the room.

"No, you don't!" Bill shouted. "Stay right where you are and don't move a muscle. I've got the carving knife."

I jumped out of bed and ran into the room, switching the light on as I went.

Bill was holding an ordinary kitchen knife at the throat of my uncle.

"Uncle Tristram? Whatever are *you* doing here?"

"Christ!" He exclaimed. "You two nearly gave me a heart attack. I'm going to have to sit down."

He was in a black polo neck and black trousers, a rucksack on his back. In fact, he looked exactly like a person should when setting out to burgle a flat. Only the glasses were incongruous; not that burglars couldn't be short-sighted, probably, it's just that they never were in films and tv.

"I'm sorry, Mr Upshott, I didn't know it was you," Bill, actually, apologised.

"Ha!" I exclaimed. "Well, it's not what one expects, is it? One's uncle breaking and entering one's little brother's flat in the middle of the night. Just what are you up to, Uncle Tristram? I think you have some explaining to do."

"'One's little brother's flat' is a touch clunky, I think you'll find, Rosa."

It was unbelievable how clever he was at twisting everything around, so that he had the upper hand. However, I wasn't going to let him get away with it, not any more.

"Skip the grammar lesson. Just *what* are you doing here?"

He lifted an eyebrow and there was a gleam of a smile, instantly suppressed, as if I'd, finally, done something of which he approved.

"Any coffee on the go? It's a long story."

Bill had cleared away his bedclothes and he and my uncle

were sitting, side by side, on the sofa. I was on the floor, wrapped in a blanket and cradling a mug of coffee.

"I don't work in the City," said Uncle Tristram.

"I knew it. You're back with MI5."

"I don't work for MI5."

"MI6?"

He shook his head.

"I work for Interpol."

Interpol? All I knew of them had been gleaned from Thomson & Thompson, the bungling detectives in the Tintin books.

"I was recruited in Paris, while we were travelling. We're not a police force, as such, but we help forces co-ordinate with each other across national boundaries. We've got all the gen on a host of topics that go on all around the world, too, so the police come to us for that. From missing passports and currency counterfeiting to stolen artworks and drug trafficking. Large crime syndicates are another speciality."

"I saw you smuggle something out of the Flinders' house at Verity's party," Bill said. "Which suggests that you are investigating Dave Flinders, right?"

I'd known nothing of this and glared at Bill.

"I forgot about it," he was apologetic. "After all, it hardly seemed relevant to our enquiries."

"Certainly, I was at work on the evening in question."

If everyone was going to start talking like [56]Dixon of Dock Green, I felt I should join in.

"Good evening, all!"

They both looked exasperated, so I shut up.

"I am only telling you all of this because I believe that you two might possess some information that may prove helpful to my case. I hope you realise that?"

"And because Bill and I are professionals now, working in the same business, Uncle Tristram."

He looked somewhat sceptical about my statement, but I wasn't going to let him put us down.

"Yes, we *are* professionals; that's right, isn't it, Bill?"

"Of course."

"Alright, alright," my uncle smiled, "let's set that to one side for the moment and see whether we can be of assistance to one another. Now, I am here simply to check that the police didn't overlook anything when they conducted their search. We enabled them to get a warrant extra-fast and have advised them to detain your brother for as long as possible, but, due to a shortage of evidence, that may not be for much longer."

I was stunned. The disloyalty of it. My uncle was putting his own nephew through hell, for no reason that I could discern. What a traitor. I opened my mouth, to give him a piece of my mind, but Bill got there first.

"Is it drugs?"

"Yes, and no. We believe that David Flinders has been employing your brother to drop off and pick up various substances around London, but that only makes him a courier, which is very small fry, indeed. What's more, to give your brother the benefit of the doubt, he may not have cottoned on to just what he's been delivering."

"That's right," I broke in. "Sam would have no idea. The way I see it, that Verity has recruited him to work for her father under false pretences and Sam, being the innocent boy that he is, has merely been a pawn in their devious game."

"Ha!" My uncle seemed amused by my outburst. "We have no indications that Verity Flinders has been involved. Rather the reverse, in fact."

"What do you mean by that? Either she has, or she hasn't," I shot back.

"We have reason to believe that Miss Flinders has been forced, against her will, to attend the clinic of a member of the medical profession, who is also a known associate of her father, David Flinders."

"Dr Ambrosia," Bill said, quietly.

"What do *you* know of Dr Ambrosia?" My uncle's attention was, instantly, focussed on him.

"He runs a fashionable clinic in Harley Street for people who are in danger of losing their marbles," I contributed.

"Thank you, Rosa. However, it's obvious that *you* are not in the loop here, because Dr Ambrosia is not a he, but a she."

"I didn't know that, either," said Bill. "All I know is that Verity has psychiatric problems of some sort and that her parents keep making her to go to Dr Ambrosia's clinic; she told me about it at her birthday party. Verity hates him, I mean her .. oh, and she said something else that might interest you. She said that when she pulled Sam out of the water at Dungeness with the big stick that may have been the murder weapon, she saw the body in the water. Mr Cole's corpse. She was terrified, but her parents – and the doctor, I think – convinced her that the body was a figment of her imagination. Brought on by her mental illness, I suppose."

Crumbs, how much more was Bill not going to tell me? We were meant to be in this together. I glared at him, but he ignored me and carried right on.

"I don't know whether you know, Mr Upshott, but Dr Ambrosia has been wiring Verity up to a machine and giving her electric shocks?"

"Well, well, Mr Hawking, Verity Flinders does seem to have taken you into her confidence."

Bill blushed, for some reason. I glared at him again, but he was determined not to look my way.

"She was upset. She'd fallen in the swimming pool and she can't swim and hates water. I suppose she just needed a friendly face to confide in and I happened to be there."

"Right. I do recall the swimming pool." My uncle looked thoughtful. "She said no more about the machine, Hawking?"

"No."

Aha! I was there before him, making connections between fragments of story that should have had nothing to do with one another.

"It was a brainwashing machine, wasn't it? Invented by Major Dyminge and tested out on his own brain after death."

Uncle Tristram stared at me, as if I were stark, raving mad.

"What, on earth, are you going on about, Rosa?"

Had I gone too fast? I stuck to my guns and brazened it out.

"You mean to say that you don't know about the Major's brainwashing invention and the letters? And I thought Establishment cover-ups were your speciality."

All of a sudden, he looked tired and rather old.

"I don't suppose either of you has a cigarette on you?"

"We don't smoke," I replied, possibly rather smugly.

"Sam's got some roll-ups," Bill offered.

"That'll do."

Bill got a packet of cigarette papers and some tobacco out of his jacket pocket, brushing away fragments of dried, green weed, as he did so.

"That's.." I stopped, mid-sentence.

"Sam's, I'm afraid," he apologised. "I took it before the police could find it. It really isn't much at all; nothing to write home about."

"I must say, I was surprised when they said there was nothing here," said my uncle.

"What did I tell you?" I said. "Sam may have had the tiniest amount of pot in the flat, for personal use, but he was no dealer. If Dave Flinders used him as a courier, I'm prepared to swear blind that he was totally ignorant of what it was he was carrying."

"I'm sure you're prepared to swear blind over all sorts of things, Rosa, but that has little bearing on the facts, and facts are what are important. They are the reality. I'm getting the impression that *you* .." he turned to Bill, "are the partner in charge of reality in your little set-up. Am I right?"

That was it, I'd had enough. The patronising, pompous, self-righteous.. I stood up, drawing my blanket around me.

"I used to think you were the best thing since sliced bread, uncle, but I was so very wrong. You are so in love with yourself that I can't bear to spend another minute in your company. You're not even worth saying goodbye forever to."

I ran out of the room and slammed the bedroom door as I went in, flinging myself onto the bed and pulling the covers so tight over my head that I might never breathe again.

4. THE FLAT OVER THE LAUNDRETTE

Mr Upshott polished his glasses with his sleeve and sighed,
"I keep finding myself on a sticky wicket with that girl," he said. "Is it just me, or is she getting even more irritating as she gets older? I find her constant interruptions play havoc with a man's train of thought."

I wasn't sure exactly what relationship Rosa had with her uncle, so I was wary of committing myself.

"She seems to me to have a refreshingly creative way of looking at things," I suggested, "which may not always be correct, but can let the light in a bit."

"Ah, well *you* will be in love with her, of course."

I felt the blush suffuse my face in the most horrible way and bent to study my notebook, so that he shouldn't see it.

"Sorry. It's just that she's always had young men falling at her feet. Sorry, Hawking."

He got up and drifted about, smoking his roll-up.

"To change the subject, if your friend Sam wanted to hide something, where do you think he'd choose to put it?"

I decided it was best to be honest with Mr Upshott.

"I don't know whether I should help you, or not, because I don't know what you're looking for. I mean, like you said, Sam's my friend; the last thing I want is to incriminate him."

He was in the kitchenette, lifting the lid of the teapot, which caused me a secret smile.

"I thought we'd established that Sam was, most probably, kept in the dark. Essentially, I'm not particularly interested in the boy; it's the bigger fish that I care about."

"Well.." I thought about it, ".. my guess is his room."

"But they turned it upside down and found sod all. You see, we know he took it, because he was seen with it. They even witnessed the handover."

"Took what, Mr Upshott?"

He didn't reply, just opened the fridge, gave a start of horror, and shut it, quickly.

"Look here, Mr Upshott," I got up from the settee, "you've got to give me more of a clue. I get that Verity and Sam's arrest may not have been to do with Harry Cole's murder, at all; that the arrest was a ruse to get them off the streets. I don't think you even care who killed Mr Cole, although Rosa and I could, quite possibly, put you on the right track where the murderer is concerned."

I was right, I could tell. Mr Upshott looked interested, but not that interested.

I persevered.

"As far as Hawking & Stone understand it, there are three strands to this. As I said, there's the murder, which doesn't interest you because it's not connected to your investigation. Then there's the drug trafficking, possibly masterminded by Dave Flinders, but even *that* isn't really what you're after. And there's number three. Number three is your holy grail. So, what is it?"

He sat down and started on another roll-up, slow and sure in all his movements.

"I may have been wrong about you, Hawking," he said, glancing sideways at me, while licking the cigarette paper. "You seemed rather too.. young; that's all."

"I'm a quick learner."

"So it would appear.

"Listen," he took a swift drag, "what we want is in a woman's case affair; the sort of job that they use for make-up and hairspray. It's pink in colour and has a small lock attached to it. Ring any bells?"

"No. Did Verity bring it here?"

"No, it was handed to Sam by Dr Ambrosia at a television studio in South West London last week. To the best of our knowledge, he hasn't transferred it elsewhere and it remains in the vicinity."

"You've been watching him?"

"Standard practice."

"Hmm. Do you think the police checked the communal bathroom on the landing?"

"Yes. I double-checked the cistern, etc, before I got here."

"The wardrobe and under the bed would be too easy, I suppose?"

"Don't be ridiculous; they'd have found it like a shot."

"There's nowhere else.."

"Yes, there is." Rosa was standing in the entrance to Sam's bedroom. "If it entered the front door, but didn't leave the building, then there's only one place that it can be."

"Where..?"

"The launderette, you pair of fools."

We went down with Mr Upshott when the laundrette opened at five in the morning, having had no sleep, at all. He wanted to go alone, but we wouldn't let him.

"If Rosa has found what you want, then you owe us, Mr Upshott," I said, as we followed him down the stairs.

"I'm just not fond of amateurs poking their noses in. If that sounds harsh, forgive me, but I can't emphasize enough how serious, if not downright dangerous, this business is. You could find yourselves in all kinds of trouble."

Rosa shook a fist at him, behind his back and mouthed something un-printable.

When we got to the laundrette, I went over to have a word with the manageress, who was already hard at work, despite the early hour, folding towels and sheets.

"Come for his washing, have you? It's over there in the checked bag. He's got you all running after him, eh?"

"How do you mean, 'all'?"

"Well, the young lady brought it in and now you're picking it up. Little Lord Muck. I took the case out just in the nick of time, by the way. Must've got mixed in with his bedsheets. Could've played havoc with my machines, that could."

The checked laundry bag contained a pile of nicely folded sheets and a pink case with a lock on it. I removed the case and handed it to Mr Upshott. As I did so, a scrap of paper fell out of the bag, addressed to 'Ver'.

Can you take my sheets to the laundrette downstairs? They're in the bottom of my wardrobe. Ta, S X

Rosa took it from me.

"See," she waved it at her uncle, "he wasn't trying to hide it at all. Verity just got it mixed up with his washing."

"Maybe," Mr Upshott took the rucksack off his back and stuffed the pink case into it.

"Either way, I'll be making tracks now. Thanks for the coffee."

"Oh, no you don't," Rosa grabbed one of his rucksack straps. "This isn't playing fair. You said we could both be of assistance to one another. You've done nothing at all for *us*."

"Rosa, for pity's sake; I've got a job to do."

"We've lost a whole night's sleep because of you; you can't just trot off now, as if we have no part in this. If you don't come back upstairs and give us some help with our investigation, I shall tell Aunt Kathleen all about it. I bet she doesn't even know who you're working for, does she?"

Rosa had a triumphant gleam in her eye that suggested she knew what she was at.

She did. Five minutes later we were back in the flat and spooning out the instant coffee once more.

"I'm not going to tell you what's in the case, Rosa, and that's that," Mr Upshott said, for the umpteenth time.

"But you *will* let Sam go now, won't you?"

"There's a distinct possibility that they will both be released later today, that much I can say."

"I should think so, too."

I brought the coffee in, knowing it would do us no good; I, for one, was jittery with caffeine and in need of some proper food.

"Thanks, Hawking," Mr Upshott took his, "I hope she's not making you do *all* the donkey work."

I found it difficult to tell whether uncle and niece liked, or disliked, one another. Either way, the relationship was too complicated for me.

"Right, Rosa," he looked at his watch, "I can give you just as long as it takes me to down this cup of coffee and not a second more."

My mind went blank. I couldn't think of anywhere that our interests overlapped. Why was she so insistent that he could help us?

"You said Interpol dealt in stolen artworks, Uncle Tristram?"

"That is correct."

"Ok, so I would like you to find out whether artworks were stolen from the Sultanate of Darfur, in Africa and the Emirate of Jabal Shammar, in Arabia, specifically in the period after the First World War. You might need to write that down. Can you rip a page out your notebook, Bill? Oh, and I would also like to know whether you find any connections with an antique shop in the Fulham Rd. It ceased trading last year, but it was called Summerby Antiques. Now, that's not too much to ask, is it?"

Claire Ingrams

◆ ◆ ◆

Halfway through the afternoon, they let us out, just like that. Sign a couple of papers, collect your belt, scarf and camera and don't let us see you here again. My lawyer, Latimer, and Verity's man were standing outside the front of the police station, rubbing their hands with glee at the money they were going to make. Nice quick buck for them for no graft, whatsoever, as far as I could see. I was out first, then Verity, still in the checked shirt that I'd lent her when we went out to listen to French songs. She ran straight into my arms.

"S.. am," she cried. "I've been so scared."

"There, there, Ver," I stroked her hair.

I guess it had been an ordeal for her, 'specially as she wasn't well to begin with. Personally, it had been a walk in the park; never a moment's concern. Yeah, the coppers had messed up, good and proper.

"We could sue for this, surely?" I asked Latimer.

He only blustered on about them being within their rights, lazy old sod.

I put my arm round Verity's shoulders and steered her away from the depressing scene, only stopping to pick some daisies sprouting from a gap in the pavement, and to throw them into hair, one by one. Then, we picked up some fresh bread, milk and croissants and strolled home to Cale Street in the spring sunshine.

I kissed her outside my front door.

"It'll all be fine, Ver, just you see."

She smiled up at me, her goofy, gap-toothed smile, while I put my key in the door.

"I'll finish off those shots for your dad. Another day another dollar."

"I wish you *weren't* working for him," she said, but I was too surprised by the sight of Bill Hawking, fast asleep on my sofa, to reply.

I went in and yanked at his socked feet, which were sticking out of the end of his blanket.

"Wha..what?"

He yawned and sat up.

"Hi Sam. Glad to see they've let you out."

He caught sight of Verity, behind me.

"Hi Verity, nice to see you again."

"Hello Bill. What are *you* doing here?"

"My thoughts, exactly," I said. "I was under the impression that you'd moved out, Hawking."

"Well, mate, if you refund me the rent in advance that I paid last time we met, I'll be happy to."

Bill seemed to have toughened up, somehow.

"Ok, ok, man," I headed into the kitchenette to dump the shopping, "let's be cool about this."

I'd spent the rent weeks ago and Flinders Associates were proving slow to pay up. I turned to Verity,

"I'm afraid you're just going to have to share my bed, Ver."

She started to giggle, but stopped, abruptly, at the sound of a voice from my bedroom.

"Not while I'm here, she's not."

It was my sister.

"What is this, a reception committee?"

Rosa came out, wearing her pyjamas. She bounded over and gave me a big hug.

"Hey Sam, I'm *so* relieved they've let you go. And you," she included Verity.

"The whole affair was beyond mad, in my opinion, but we sorted it out for you, which, I think, deserves a jam sandwich. Or.." she'd already nosed about in our shopping, "..one of these delicious smelling croissants."

"Oi! Hands off!"

"I don't think you can have heard me, Sam; *we* – that is to say, the private investigation firm of Hawking & Stone – were responsible for sorting out your troubles and springing you from prison. I'd say that was worth quite a lot more than one measly croissant, actually."

What was she going on about? If anything, the pair of them might well have got me busted by their meddling; just handing over my door key without even running it past me, was not cool. I had to assume that only a miracle of some description had prevented the police from finding my stash. Still, best to keep quiet about that.

Bill was already filling the kettle and putting my croissants on a plate, as if he was my mother. They were beginning to get on my wick.

"I have the familiar feeling that you might be exaggerating, Rosa. Verity and I got out because the cops had nothing on us. In fact, we were victims of police harassment and I'm seriously considering suing. Just because we're young and hip, the squares think they can do what they like. But, you know, the times they are a-changing.."

Rosa brushed flakes of pastry from her mouth. She was starting to go red and I wondered whether she was choking.

"I'm telling you, *we* did it," she began to shout. "Bill and me. Bill cleared your pot out of the flat before they could find it *and* he took the incriminating negative. Blimey, if they'd found *that* you really would be in the soup. Then, it was *me* who suggested looking in the laundrette for the pink case and, guess what, it was there. *God* knows where you would be without us, Sam."

She was spouting complete nonsense: incriminating negatives, soup, laundrettes. The only bit I could get a handle on was the bit about the pink case.

"Why the hell would Dr Ambrosia's pink case be in the laundrette? And whose business is it, anyway? That needs to go to Dave, so he can look after it while she's getting the decorators in. You haven't gone and given it to somebody else, have you?"

"Dr Ambrosia," Verity echoed, and then her eyes went funny and she fainted.

For a sec, we all gazed down at her small body on the floor. Then, Bill came charging in on his white horse.

"Take Verity to lie down on the bed, Rosa, and give her some water. Sam, I think you and I need a good, long talk."

"Since when did *you* start giving the orders, Hawking?"

"Shut up, Stone. And go and sit down."

I went and sat down.

5. BAD KARMA

Verity Flinders came to and stared at me.

"You've cut off your hair," she said. "I always think a girl's had bad karma when they cut off their hair."

While the whole 'karma' business tended to set my teeth on edge, I could see she had a point.

"You mean, they want to re-invent themselves because they didn't like what was there before?"

"Yeah, sort of."

"In my case, it was more the act of cutting, itself, that was important and not how I looked."

She nodded, as if she perfectly understood, and sat up on Sam's bed.

"That's sad."

Why had I told her that? How unbearable to have Verity Flinders pity me.

"Well, you seem to have half a hedgerow in *your* hair," I pointed out the daisies that were tangled in her yellow hair, as if she were a modern-day Ophelia.

"That was just Sam."

I didn't want to know any more and began arranging the pillows behind her back, all brisk efficiency.

"Anyway, my karma is doing wonderfully well, now. Just fab."

She nodded again, then swung her stick-like legs over

the edge of the bed.

"I think I'll get up."

"Stay. You've been through a lot. You should rest."

"No. I want to get up."

"Please stay."

She stared at me, pale eyes open wide. It struck me that I might have made a big mistake; what I'd taken for insolence might well have been fear. Curiosity, as ever, got the better of me.

"What did she do to you, Verity? At the clinic?"

"No," she whispered. "No, no, no, no."

It sounds odd, but I couldn't be sure that she was speaking to me. Yet, whoever it was that she was addressing, was hurting her.

"God, Verity, I'm sorry. I didn't mean to put you through it again. I can be so tactless. Please just forget I ever.."

She curled into a ball, her arms over her head.

"Get off me," she snarled.

"But, I'm not.."

"You're hurting me, you witch. I don't mind my voices, d'you hear? It's *yours* I don't like."

She had entered a place of her own. I didn't know whether to try to reach her, or to let her be. However, I did know that I might never have an opportunity such as this again.

"You don't like Dr Ambrosia's voice?" I asked.

"I hate Dr Ambrosia. But I hate the voices in the machine, even more."

"There are voices in her electric shock machine?"

"[57]*Put a tiger in your tank!*"

It was as if a man had entered the room. If I hadn't heard the words come from her own mouth, I would have tried to find him.

"Sorry, Verity?"

"[58]*Double good, double good, Doublemint gum!*" She sang out in a penetrating voice.

"[59]*A Mars a day helps you work, rest and..*"

"Play," I finished off for her.

I might have laughed, if it hadn't been so uncanny.

"Are these the voices in the machine, Verity?"

"*Put a Doublemint in your tank. A tiger a day helps you* [60] *Snap, crackle and POP!*"

She was sweating now, beginning to fling out her limbs and turn frantic. What had been merely uncanny was becoming truly frightening.

A calm, French voice floated into the air, singing:

Tous les garcons et les filles de mon âge
Se promènent dans la rue deux par deux..

"I've put on Françoise Hardy," Sam was beside me. "She helps her when she gets like this."

Sam climbed onto the bed and took Verity in his arms,

"It's alright, Ver. It's all gonna be alright. Nobody's gonna hurt you, sweetheart."

She nestled into him and juddered to a stop. Her cheeks were striped with mascara tears and she didn't look like any variety of insect; just a troubled, young girl who had been hurt.

"I'm so, so sorry to have put you through that, Verity."

A couple of squashed daisies had fallen out of her hair onto the pillow and I picked them off, uselessly. Far from helping her, I had brought more harm.

"Don't sweat, Rosa, this has happened a couple of times since she's been here. It wasn't your fault. She's just not well. She'll fall fast asleep, now."

It was true, her eyelids were drooping and her small body relaxing. Sam got up and pulled the blanket over her, tenderly.

"We need to get her to a proper doctor," I whispered. "I don't think you can deal with this on your own, Sam."

"Yeah, I thought I'd take her home to Kent. Let old Dr

Morris have a look at her."

"That's a good idea. I know a psychiatrist who might be able to help, too."

"I don't know about that, Rosa," he was alarmed. "No way am I letting them take her to one of those places again."

"No, no, I didn't mean that. Just get an independent opinion, you know. She may not want to see him, anyhow. With her experience, who could blame her? Maybe good food and rest might be all it takes. I wouldn't be surprised if she's been starving herself."

"Nobody's been looking after the girl, that's the trouble. But I'm going to do my best for Ver. It's me she needs."

I had been wrong in so many ways; far from corrupting my little brother, Verity Flinders seemed to have brought out the best in him. I'd seen how he had been with my babies – how kind he could be when he had somebody to look after – and I was glad that I had kept faith in him. We shut the bedroom door behind us, leaving Verity to sleep.

"Wow!" Sam exclaimed. "Do I need to chill. What have you done with my gear, Hawking?"

Bill took it out of his pocket, reluctantly, and handed it over.

"If you must do that, do it outside," I said

"Yes, Mum."

While Sam was out, I told Bill about Verity's bizarre behaviour.

"I don't care what my uncle thinks, Bill. Every instinct tells me that this *has* to be connected to Major Dyminge's brainwashing machine."

"Come off it, Rosa, you're taking strands from different investigations and knotting them together, whether they have any connection with each other, or not. Just because you *want* to build a case, doesn't mean that you have a case to build, if you take my meaning?"

"No, I don't 'take your meaning', not at all, Bill. You are

trying to make me out to be a storyteller, just like everyone else does. You think I have no proper grasp on reality, but you are wrong, and I'll tell you why. Because sometimes life just *is* extraordinary and co-incidences happen and stories prove to be true."

Bill sighed, seeming so very much older than his nineteen years.

"Ok, Rosa, have it your way. You want us to proceed on the assumption that Dr Ambrosia has, presumably illegally, obtained technical knowledge that British Intelligence pinched from Major Dyminge, either from his letters, or from his manuscript. Flimsy, but just *about* possible, I suppose."

"Then, we have to swallow the idea that Dr Ambrosia has been experimenting with this technical knowledge, having built a brainwashing machine, no less, and that the victim she has chosen to experiment upon is the daughter of – Sam tells me – her lover, David Flinders. Deeply bizarre, and possibly Freudian, but I'm willing to give it a go."

"*But* that this experimentation has involved well-known advertising slogans for petrol and sweets! Come off it, Rosa. Why would anyone wish to implant advertising slogans in another human's brain? So that vast amounts of money can be made out of people buying petrol? Out of people eating so much chocolate that they become grossly fat? Or, both, perhaps: fattening up the population to such an extent that they are forced to drive everywhere, thereby using up even more petrol. Some kind of capitalist dream *that* would be! No, Rosa. This is so far beyond wishful thinking that it's turned into complete madness, and if you really expect me to believe it, then I can see no future for Hawking & Stone."

◆ ◆ ◆

I went into the alleyway behind the laundrette and rolled a reefer such as had never been rolled before; the king of reefers, the bong of bongs. I emptied my lungs of all the unnecessary air, all the bad karma of the past two days and prepared to receive the holy smoke.

A man strolled into the alleyway, humming softly.

"Got a light, mate?" He asked.

"Yeah," I reached for my lighter, and he hit me.

He struck my cheek first, cracked the bone open with sharp metal in his fist. I didn't even have the space to scream, because he kneed me down in my groin and I doubled up with explosive agony and shock. He began to kick me, over and over again, until everything was pain and I could no more scream than I could breathe or save myself. I was mush and blood, scraped into the cracks in the pavement and I knew that if he kicked me one more time, I would die. He put the boot in again, just to make sure.

PART 5

1. BLUEBELLS

Millicent and Jerzy dashed out to their car and took off up the hill, as if there was a tiger on their tail.

"Golly," I said to Edwin, who was polishing my brasses, "whatever could be the matter at Shore House?"

Don't be nosy, Frances.

Edwin grunted and tipped up the Brasso, once more; he was rather an expert on obtaining a truly impressive shine.

I continued to peer out of the window, mind on all possible scenarios.

"I hope nothing awful has occurred in London. Young Sam can be a bit of a scamp, you know. Perhaps I should go over?"

Resist.

"Because the children will be all alone with Mr Tamang and they've only known him for a matter of days.."

Yes, I really felt I should go over.

"I take it he is their father?"

"Yes, indeed. Born out of wedlock, I'm afraid.. but one doesn't like to gossip."

So, don't, Frances.

"Can you, *please*, be quiet."

"I beg your pardon?" Edwin looked up from his task.

"Sorry, Edwin, I wasn't talking to you."

I let the lace curtain drop and went over to give his shoulder a pat. It was such a boon having him around to help with the heavy work, and he gave of his time so freely.

"Will you be putting up at the Red Dragon for much longer, Edwin dear?"

The inn offered quite a reasonable bed and breakfast, I'd heard, but I did feel that costs must be mounting.

"It suits me, for the moment."

"You haven't let out your flat in London?"

"No. I'm keeping my options open, as they say," he gave me one of those looks that had been preying on my mind, slightly.

I had no wish to toy with his affections, and yet.. I don't mind admitting that it *was* rather pleasant, and, well, flattering, I suppose. Guy, whom I had loved dearly, it went without saying, had never been.."

What had I never been?

"Yes, I think I *shall* just pop next door. You've done a wonderful job with my horseshoe, thank you so much. Please don't feel obligated to hang about; just close the front door behind you when it suits. Goodbye, Edwin."

I heard the noise before I'd even set foot on the path; two tiny children with really remarkable lungs, screaming at full blast. When Mr Tamang eventually responded to the doorbell, he looked as if he'd been caught in a raging storm, his black hair stuck to his forehead and his eyes wild.

"Mrs Dyminge," he exclaimed, "I was just going to ring you.."

It was rather gratifying.

"I don't know why they keep crying and nothing that I do seems to work.."

"Shall we try the pram?"

We managed, with the help of a box of rusks, and wheeled Benjamin and Jessica up the road to the bluebell woods, where they quietened in the most miraculous manner. Well, Mr Tamang wheeled, while.. I suppose, I talked. By the time that we were among the bluebells, I knew quite a bit about the Americans' lust for a moon landing.

"But, that's utterly preposterous," I said. "And far from desirable, I should have thought. Why can we never be happy with what we have?"

Mr Tamang smiled,

"I don't think that is how most people see it, Mrs Dyminge. Most people find progress an exciting prospect."

"Oh, I expect it is. I just feel that progress can so often lose sight of civilisation; it's so pleased with itself that it often forgets the most important parts of life."

"You have a point there, but it's an unusual one for the widow of an inventor, such as Major Dyminge."

"Hmm, and look at the trouble *he* managed to cause, one way and another. I should say that Guy was a prime example of short-term thinking; he could become so blinkered in his urge to discover – whatever he considered important to discover (and I was never quite sure *what* that was) – that chaos tended to ensue."

Chaos, Frances?

Yes, Guy, chaos.

I could tell that young Mr Tamang was rather shocked at my disloyalty, but I was getting too old for word-mincing. I didn't have the time not to get to the point.

"Shall we park at this bench?" I suggested. "Let the sea of blue lap at our toes?"

For what else can compare with a bluebell wood in full spate? It took me back to my youth, when I would fill my arms with the flowers. Quite suddenly – who could tell why? – Edwin Summerby popped into my head.

About time.

What do you mean? Guy?

"Anyway," said Mr Tamang, "the Programme will have to proceed without me. I have responsibilities," he glanced at me, shyly, "to my children."

"You will be moving down here?"

"I am considering posts at several universities."

I nodded, desperate to ask whether a wedding might be on the horizon. I resisted.

Well done.

"Will Rosa be coming back today?" I enquired. "One hopes she has been enjoying a nice, little break in London."

Intuition told me that, as so often, there was more to it than that.

"I believe she will, yes."

A cloud crossed over his charming face.

"May I ask, Mrs Dyminge, are you acquainted with this fellow, Bill?"

"Bill Hawking? I've known him since he was a baby, Mr Tamang. He's the sweetest, kindest boy. I believe that he and Rosa have set up a business in her mother's sewing room at the top of the house."

"And is he .. are they .. ?"

I couldn't think what he meant for a second.

"Bill and Rosa? Goodness, gracious me, no. He must be ten years younger than her. No, no, no, most certainly not."

Whatever had possessed him to get such an idea? I changed the subject, swiftly.

"I hope that the Red Dragon has been treating you well, Mr Tamang? My spies tell me that it's a nice, clean place, and most reasonable, to boot."

"It's ok for me; my requirements are small. I seem to be the only visitor, but it is a little run-down."

"The only visitor? What about Mr Summerby?"

"No," he frowned, "I have met nobody of that name."

"A well-preserved, elderly gentleman with pale, yellow hair and very blue eyes? *Edwin* Summerby? He has a dog; surely you have noticed *him*?"

"I'm afraid not, Mrs Dyminge."

How extraordinary. I hesitated to disbelieve Mr Tamang, who gave off an air of modest, yet keen, intelligence, however .. Why should Edwin pretend to be staying somewhere, when he wasn't?

Why, indeed?

What do you mean? Guy?

A small frisson of anxiety passed up my back and made me shiver.

"Are you cold, Mrs Dyminge? Shall we go back?"

"Sorry?"

He asked whether you were cold.

"Oh, right. Yes, spring sunshine can be deceptive. And the little ones probably need food, or.."

We arose and began to wheel the pram back home, trampling bluebells as we went. The green stems keeled over, oozing an unpleasant, white substance that I had not noticed before.

"I have enjoyed our conversation, Mrs Dyminge; it has set my mind at rest," Mr Tamang declared.

"Jolly good," I replied, wondering why the conversation should have produced the reverse effect upon myself.

I heard the taxi late that evening and may have just peeked around the door to ascertain who it was at that hour. It proved to be Rosa Stone, accompanied by an unknown girl in a very short skirt. Of Millicent and Jerzy there was no sign (for I barely slept a wink that night and would, undoubtedly, have heard them return).

The following day brought scant time to wonder about the comings and goings of my neighbours, as Rosa presented herself on my doorstep at first light. Indeed, it was so early that I was still wearing my dressing-gown and slippers and one, or two stray curlers in my hair.

"May I come in, Mrs Dyminge?"

There was an air of urgency about her, so I let her straight in, despite the curlers. In fact, I couldn't help noticing that she, herself, was wearing her scarlet blouse inside out and with the label showing.

"Tea, dear?"

"No, thank you," she replied, "I'll get straight to the point, if that's ok?"

Would it be about her parents' sudden departure? Or the mysterious girl she had brought back home with her? Or, indeed, the brief trip to London accompanied by Bill Hawking? But, no; the point turned out to be quite different from any of these. The point turned out to be about Edwin Summerby.

"Edwin, a murderer?" I was dumbfounded at the very idea. "You think he murdered Harold Cole? For a set of dominoes?" I had to sit down.

"Yes, we think that there's every possibility, Mrs Dyminge. Which is why I felt I had to warn you, as soon as possible. I hope you won't mind me saying this but, we've noticed that ever since the Major's sad .. absence .. Mr Summerby has been hanging around. That he seems to have a bit of a thing for you, in fact. A romantic thing."

I sensed my cheeks grow warm and my fingers pick at my old dressing-gown of their own accord.

"Gracious me, Rosa, I really cannot think what you are alluding to .."

"Involving bluebells."

There it was again, that frisson.

"Bluebells?"

Why did my breath balk at the word?

"Mr Summerby told me that the two of you picked bluebells together in the woods when you were both young."

"I can't seem to .."

Can't seem to what, Frances? Remember? Breathe?

"When you were the vicar's daughter, Frances Carlisle."

Frances Carlisle? Miss Carlisle from the rectory? I hadn't thought of *that* girl for a long, long time.

But it's *you*, Frances.

Please, Guy, stop it. It *was* me.

"Are you ok, Mrs Dyminge? I'm sorry, have I put my foot in it again?"

Me wading in long skirts through the blue, surprised to find Edwin Summerby from the village stepping out from behind a tree. Handsome as he was, I wasn't sure whether I entirely liked Edwin Summerby; didn't understand why he kept following me about, kept turning up in unexpected places. I didn't know what to say. Would it be rude to ask him to leave? A vicar's daughter should never be rude.

"You've gone very white, Mrs Dyminge. Would you like a glass of water?"

I smiled, I expect, so it must all have been my fault. It must have been the wrong type of smile. Dear Lord, but it was such aeons ago. How could it still have the power to shame? I believed that I had slipped it between the pages of a book, slammed the cover shut, set the book on a shelf, closed the door, locked the library and thrown away the key. I believed that I had forgotten that there had even been key, or shelf, never mind book.

"Edwin Summerby," I said, finally, "is a very bad lot."

At last, my love.

"Yes, that's what we're worried about, Bill and I. We are doing our very best to find proof that he was here on the night Harry Cole died, but it isn't easy."

I recalled my conversation with Mr Tamang, the day before.

"Well, wherever he was staying, it wasn't the Red Dragon, Rosa; not then and not now. It's my belief that he owns a property down here."

"Really? Now, that *is* interesting. Any idea where?"

"I'm afraid I couldn't say."

I arose, wrapping my dressing-gown around me. It was not yet eight in the morning, but I could have done with a stiff drink. What a fool I'd been to let that man back into my life. What an everlasting, prize fool."

No, Frances; nothing is everlasting.

"I can't think why *you* couldn't have said something."

Rosa Stone frowned.

"The thing is, Mrs Dyminge, we've only just found out. I mean, I was taken in by Mr Summerby, myself.."

"Oh, I wasn't talking to you, dear."

"Ah."

I went over and picked up her hand, giving it a squeeze. I was glad that she looked so much better than when we had last met, so much more like her old self.

"Thank you for telling me this, Rosa dear. It was kind of you to come here. Now, I think it's high time I got dressed and faced the day."

"But you don't seem to understand; we're worried about you."

"You think he means harm? To me?"

"We don't know .. it's just .. why is he still here? That does worry me, it really does. Why does a murderer hang about the scene of his crime? If I were him, I'd be back in the Emirate of Jabal Shammar, like a shot, and you wouldn't see me for camels."

I considered her questions at length (for I was not quite so foolish as to carry on believing that it was his ardent desire for myself that kept him in the vicinity).

"Has it crossed your mind that he did *not*, in fact, get whatever it was he killed poor Harold for?"

"The jade Chinese dominoes?"

I pictured Harry's set, as we had always called it. Guy had kept it wrapped up in a cloth inside a canvas bag, but I had seen it close to, once or twice. It had been a shade of palest celadon, with some pretty decoration in mother of pearl. Certainly, it had been old, but whether it had been precious, I honestly couldn't have hazarded a guess. What a dreadful idea, that poor, young Harold should have lost his life for the stupid object.

"Do you mean that Mr Summerby may still be searching for the treasure?" She asked.

"I suppose I do. Perhaps he thinks I have it."

Rosa whistled in alarm.

"Oh no, Mrs Dyminge. That could put you in the most terrible danger. If he's committed murder once, I can't see him hesitating to do so again. You must come and stay with us, this very minute."

At the precise moment that she uttered those words, a knock came upon the door. We both jumped.

"Don't answer," Rosa whispered.

"But, he may have heard.."

"No," she shushed.

"But.."

She made an unpleasant, slicing gesture across her throat, and I subsided.

It felt like a very long time had passed before there was the noise of a car engine starting up.

Rosa dashed to the window and parted the lace curtain.

"Yup, it's his Cortina. I'm going to follow him," she announced.

"Oh, no, dear, I don't think that's a very.."

But she had already left.

2. A DONE DEAL

The Ford Cortina turned right at the top of the hill, I noticed. It was still possible to catch glimpses through the delicate, spring growth of the trees. I sat at the junction and let a couple of cars pass between us, before I swung into the road. It was a weekday and there would be some traffic into Dover, but I intended to keep Mr Summerby – or, Hatchet, as I had come to think of him – within sight. It was important to keep my mind on the road ahead and not let it wander about in divergent directions, but there was so much to worry about, it was a tough job.

There was poor Sam, who was in hospital after having been badly beaten in the street. Our parents were at his bedside, and the doctors had said he would recover, but I hadn't wanted to leave. Only the thought of my children had sat me back on the train, accompanied, this time, by Verity Flinders. In all honesty, I hadn't known exactly what to do with the girl. She was clearly unwell and if, as seemed more than likely, it was her father who had set the heavy mob on my brother, I could hardly drop her back home. Besides, it wasn't safe for her there, not with the bizarre Dr Ambrosia situation . . and that was just London. In Kent, I had the unexpected appearance of my children's father, Jay, to deal with, on top of a horrible intuition that Hatchet might intend danger to Goose. I shivered; I must stop it and concentrate. Eyes on the road, Rosa.

Once past Dover, we sped along quiet roads, past the turning to Kingsdown and past Walmer Castle, then slowed down by the seafront at Deal. Just beyond the pier, he turned off into the warren of narrow roads, of quaint, picturesque old cottages that had once belonged to fishermen, in the oldest part of Deal. I hung back, sensing that he was about to stop, and parked by a churchyard, taking it on foot from there.

Sure enough, he stopped the car and got out. He let himself into the nearest house, one of the bigger dwellings, with a ship's bell above the front door and a painted mermaid carved into the overhanging roof. There was no side way in and, nor, once I'd walked past and round the end of the street into the one behind, was I able to discover a back entrance. The curtains at the front windows were closed. In a way, I was relieved that I couldn't get in, having been caught breaking and entering a strange house before, with awful consequences. Yes, it was just as well. Besides, I now knew where he lived and, more importantly, knew that he had lied about where he was staying. We had to be on the right track.

I was about to leave, when a thought came to me; I hadn't seen him lock his car. When given the opportunity, my natural curiosity knows no bounds. I didn't hesitate. I noted that nobody was about, crouched beside the car, opened the door and slid in. Hatchet kept a tidy interior, without an empty crisp packet in sight. There was a pair of driving gloves in, suitably, the glove compartment, along with a couple of folded maps and a London A-Z. A well-worn tweed jacket on the back seat yielded nothing in the pockets except a clean, linen hankie. There was a pair of binoculars beneath it, in a leather case. Whatever I had expected was notable by its absence. I checked for blood stains on the passenger seat, for the silver hip flask of my imagination, for stray dominoes, but there were none.

With one eye on Hatchet's front door, I edged myself over the gear stick and into the passenger seat, trying to commune with the spirit of Harry Cole. What did you do, Harry?

Did you sit there, drunk, and befuddled, simply glad of the lift? Did you even remember this man? Did you hold the Major's canvas bag on your lap, or did some indistinct memory, from a different world and time, make you place it down on the floor, beside your feet, where it might not be noticed? I reached down to feel the rubber mat, then probed beneath the seat. Crumbs, there was something there. I tried to pull it out, but it was difficult to get a purchase on. I had to turn it round and pull it out sideways, before I could see what it was; hardly able to comprehend what it proved to be. I opened the front cover, to see the library sticker, and then shut it again. It was a book about Woody Guthrie.

I hadn't been able to get out of that car fast enough, just leapt out and ran down the street, the book under my shirt. My heart was thumping like crazy, as I emerged on the seafront and scanned both ways for a red phone-box. There was one by the pier and I lunged at the door. My fingers shook as I rang the number of Sam's flat. It was still early in the day, but I couldn't be sure whether Bill would be there, or would have gone back to the hospital. Thank goodness, he was there.

"Bill?"

"Yes?" He sounded sleepy.

"It's me. Listen, I've found the library book, the Woody Guthrie one, and you'll never believe where. It was under the passenger seat in Mr Summerby's car."

"No!" The news had certainly woken him up. "But, that means.."

"Yes, Harry Cole *was* there. Hatchet gave him a lift to Dungeness and then he killed him, in cold blood."

"Have you got the book with you, Rosa?"

"Yes, I'm holding it under my top and trying not to get any fingerprints on it."

"Good for you. You will have to take it to the police and .. hey, I've just had a thought. What if Mr Summerby was in the Coastguard when the two of them were playing dominoes that evening?"

"You mean, by chance?"

"Or on purpose, it doesn't much matter. What matters is that he saw the set pass from Major Dyminge to Harry Cole inside the pub and he followed them out and . . my God, he could even be in Sam's photo. There were men in the background, weren't there, or is that just my wishful thinking?"

"No, you're right, Bill, there *were*. We've got to get it blown up. Can you do that? As soon as possible?"

"Well, Sam's got all the equipment here, but I haven't got a clue, to be honest."

"Ok, well, rush down to his college and get someone there to do it. One of his friends, or teachers, maybe.

"Brilliant thinking, Rosa. Where are you now?"

"I'm in a phone-box in Deal. I'll tell you all about it later, if you get the train down this evening. Come straight round to the house. Oh no . ."

"What is it, Rosa?"

"I think I just saw his Ford Cortina go past, heading in the wrong direction."

"The wrong . .?"

"He's going back . ."

I ended the call, then made one more; brief and to the point. After which I pushed the heavy phone-box door open and set off, running back to my car as fast as I possibly could; as fast as if there was a life depending on it.

The Cortina wasn't outside Coast Cottage, which threw me, although I was happy to think that I might have got it all wrong. But I found Jay Tamang pressed against the side door, like a slim shadow. I was thankful that Jay had been in when I'd rung. He had been a Gurkha when he was very young, and there was nobody on earth more professional than a Gurkha. He put his finger to his lips. I ran up to him, bending low so as not to be seen through the net curtain at the front.

"He's there?" I whispered.

He nodded,

"I think he may have brought a gun."

That was what Hatchet had gone back to his house for; he must have heard Mrs Dyminge and I talk and known that time was running out.

"I haven't got it, Edwin, I tell you," her voice rang out, strong yet shrill with anxiety.

He mumbled something and her voice rose another octave.

"I can't think why you should think so. Guy was dying and he knew it, can't you understand that? He gave it back to Harold as a goodbye present, I'm convinced of it."

"But it belongs to me," Hatchet bellowed, making Jay and I jump.

I took a step back, preparing to break the door down with my shoulder, but Jay grabbed and held me, with a grip of iron.

"I don't care who it belongs to. What's more, I don't mind betting that you stole it in the first place. I remember you, now, Edwin. It's all over." And then, "If you think you can scare me with that contraption, you are very wrong. Go on, shoot me, if you really want, I couldn't give a fig any more. Go on, do it."

There was a yelp and an enormous blast and Jay broke through the door.

Mrs Dyminge was sitting on the floor, holding her cheek, but I couldn't go to her because Hatchet still had the gun in his hand. It was a long, silver beast that looked as if it had come from the English Civil war and it was, literally, smoking, while black speckles of gunpowder had dappled Hatchet's face and white hair. The blackened hole in the cottage ceiling suggested that the aim was not entirely true.

"Don't come any nearer," he snarled, but he was far too late.

Jay had launched himself at him in one, balletic, movement and kicked him to the ground, where he lay, too winded to speak, or move. Some minutes later, after we had helped Mrs Dyminge up and assessed her injuries, a policeman emerged through the splintered door and got him to his feet. If it had been up to me, I would have left him on the floor.

After a scratch supper, I waited until Bill was absorbed in talking to Verity before I paid Mrs Dyminge a visit in my parents' spare room on the top floor. The minute that Bill had returned from London he had started issuing instructions about leaving 'Auntie Frances' alone to get over the shock (out of a sense of guilt, it seemed to me). But I seldom listen to instructions, and crept up the stairs in stockinged feet. I knocked, softly, and peeked around the door. She was lying on her back, the quilt drawn up to her chin and her long, grey hair running out over the pillow. I gazed at her thin, lined face, then went to go.

"Rosa, dear."

"I shouldn't have disturbed you."

"Nonsense. Come in."

She had a nasty bruise on one cheek, where he had hit her. I didn't know what else he had tried before finally resorting to his shotgun, but I hated to think that he had been cruel.

A cold, fine-boned hand emerged from beneath the quilt and took mine.

"Heavens, what a song and dance that was," she sighed.

"You were so brave, Mrs Dyminge; I couldn't believe how you stood up to him."

I sat down on the edge of her bed, being careful not to disturb her; she seemed so fragile, physically, as if she might be broken by one clumsy movement.

"Me? I haven't a brave bone in my body, Rosa. No, it's just .. rather different when one really doesn't care."

"I heard you say that to him. If you don't mind me asking, what did you mean?"

She gave an enigmatic smile and said nothing. I had to assume that she *did* mind me asking, after all.

"Where do you think that the dominoes set might have landed up?" I asked.

"Well," she sighed again, as if the question were beyond tedious, "I would suggest either the shingle, or the sea. That's generally the answer in these parts."

I thought about it, but couldn't see how that worked.

"Two old men running around Dungeness in the middle of the night, what an idiotic spectacle that must have made," she scoffed. "Jade is heavy, Rosa, and I doubt Harold could have hung onto it as he tried to escape across the shingle. I expect he dropped it somewhere as he ran; that's my view, for what it's worth. And good riddance to old rubbish, I say."

"Perhaps I should go back and take a really good look."

"If you must."

She yawned and removed her hand from mine, so I got up to leave her in peace.

"Sleep well," I said, but she didn't reply.

Just as I was closing the door, I thought I heard her speak.

"Where *are* you?"

"I'm just by the . ." I began, but it wasn't me that she was addressing.

"If I only knew where you were, Guy, I'd come and find you."

Downstairs, in the drawing room, Bill had put Dylan on the turntable; the [61]*Freewheelin'* album. *Blowin' In the Wind* was playing and no-one had bothered to switch the lights on, or draw the curtains, so that we were marooned inside black sea and sky. Verity Flinders was an ambiguous shape on the sofa, wrapped up in a blanket. Bill sat down beside her with the album cover; poor girl, it looked like he was going to explain the finer points of Dylan's acoustic technique to her.

I went and sat next to Jay. He had his eyes closed, letting the music wash over him.

"Have they worn you out?"

He opened his eyes and smiled. It was such a nice smile,

and one that I'd nearly forgotten.

"Are our children exceptionally noisy, or are they all like that?"

"Yeah, I think they're all like that, only you don't notice properly until you have them. There's a particular frequency, I think, that is designed to penetrate a parent's brain and re-arrange the furniture for ever more."

"Interesting. That might, actually, be the case."

"I was only joking, Jay."

"No, it might well merit proper research."

I thought about it.

"Major Dyminge would have been the man for the job."

"I heard that you were searching for his . ." he was embarrassed.

"His body, yes. Although it might turn out just to be his head, or, to be specific, his brain."

"Isn't that a little peculiar?"

He was so tactful; to say 'little'.

"It's *enormously* peculiar, of course it is."

I thought of my last conversation with Peter Upshott, and was thrilled to find that my old skill had returned; that I remembered it verbatim:

"But, *it's not just a body*, you see, Jay. *It's what's left of a brilliant, brave man who deserved to be treated with dignity and respect and not left on a laboratory table somewhere in Whitehall, his brain plugged into electric wires and whatnot, just so that some mindless bureaucrat can warm up the Cold War.*"

That startled him.

"Is that what you believe has happened to Major Dyminge? Do you possess any proof of this?"

"Well . ." I wasn't sure what to say because instinct wasn't proof and, as everyone kept telling me, stories weren't real. " . . We're at a tricky stage."

He nodded, and stood up.

"I shall walk back to the Red Dragon now, Rosa, but let me know whether you need any help with this . . problem, of yours. Anything that requires specific technical knowledge, I mean, because I know how experienced you are at these mysteries."

He leant down and kissed me on the cheek, and then he left.

I stayed where I was, sitting on the tapestry chair that my father's forebears had carried out of Russia on a horse and cart, away from the pogroms and their old life. I had a lot to think about.

Sleep was catching up with thinking by the time Bill came over.

"Our first case wrapped up," he said. "It's not a bad feeling, is it?"

"It isn't."

"I was wondering whether I *should* go back to Mum's tonight, Rosa. Only, I don't like to leave Verity alone."

"With me, you mean?"

"No, of *course* not," he said, with way too much emphasis.

Suddenly, I really was extravagantly tired.

"I'm going to sleep in my parents' room, with Jessica and Benjamin. There are a couple of other spare rooms, so just take your pick. I don't know whether they've got clean sheets on.."

"No problem; I'll sort all that out. Thanks Rosa. I'll just give Mum a call, if that's ok? In case she's worried."

But the phone rang before he could ring Sadie. I went into the hall to get it, before it woke up the children.

It was Uncle Tristram.

"Apologies for ringing so late, Rosa. I just thought you might like to know the latest."

"What latest is that?" I almost too tired to care.

"I'll be brief because you sound done in. The tip-offs you gave me vis-à-vis the Sultanate of Darfur and the Emirate of Jabal Shammar have perked up Interpol's art theft department. It turns out that both kingdoms picked the wrong side in the First World War and that both were subject to extensive looting afterwards. The art boys were interested to hear about Summerby Antiques and already had some connections with Edwin Summerby established. Now, given that the shop is closed down, I've been asked to enquire whether any more is known about his whereabouts."

I may have sniggered.

"Yes, it is, actually. He was arrested for murder earlier today, on information given by a little set-up called Hawking & Stone, so he's probably in police cells in Dover. What's more, there's a house in old Deal with a mermaid carved into the roof where I'd be astonished if you didn't find at least one missing artwork."

There was a brief silence, during which I very much hoped he was eating his words and finding them indigestible.

"Rosa Stone, it sounds like you've been busy. Jolly well done."

High praise from my uncle. There was a time when praise would have been more than enough to send me hurtling over the moon, but that time had gone. I needed more.

"Thank you. Now, as a quid pro quo, I expect you to count Hawking & Stone in on your investigation into Dr Ambrosia. Sam's been beaten up, which you may already know, plus we've got Verity Flinders down here recuperating with us; so, you can see that we're up to our necks in this case already. Actually, I know that you know that we will keep digging whether you count us in, or not. So, you might as well."

"Come off it, Rosa; it's not just me, is it? Interpol is a bloody big concern and there are much bigger boys than myself dealing with this case."

"Fine," I said, "Then I think it's time that Hawking &Stone were introduced to them. I expect to hear from you soon. Goodnight, Uncle Tristram."

I put the phone down, sank to my knees and crawled upstairs to bed.

3. WHAT SHALL WE DO ABOUT VERITY?

We didn't know what we should do for the best. Verity Flinders needed help but, at the same time, we were concerned about the type of help that she might be offered. The Stone family's doctor had given her a sedative, but little else. According to Rosa, Verity had a mild turn during the consultation, but she – Rosa – managed to convince him that they had, indeed, run out of petrol and that Verity's insistence on 'putting a tiger in the tank' was no more than plain common-sense.

"But, that's *why* you took her to see him; to help with those turns of hers," I protested.

"I just sensed that he might be about to make a call to the men in white coats," she explained. "I've been reading up on this, Bill, and I'm pretty convinced that she doesn't have what they call 'psychosis' and isn't seeing things."

"What about her voices?"

"*Her* voices are ok, so why get het up about them? I spent my childhood with an imaginary friend who wouldn't shut up, but so what, if it doesn't do any harm? That's her business and nobody else's, as far as I'm concerned. What we are dealing with here is deliberate experimentation with brainwashing and, actually, I think that may be beyond the remit of our local doctor."

So, we contacted Dr Robinson, or TL, as he preferred to be called.

At first, he prevaricated.

"At eighteen, this girl is still a minor," he said, "which means I would need the consent of her parents to treat her."

Rosa, who had her ear next to mine as I made the telephone call, snatched the receiver from me.

"I don't think you quite understand the situation, TL. It's her *parents* who pose a threat to her."

"I thought your partner said that it was a Dr Ambrosia."

"*They* sent Verity to her, even though Verity must have kept trying to tell them how terrified she was of the doctor. We don't know whether they heard the poor girl parroting advertising slogans, but it can't have been right to have kept forcing her back to the clinic against her wishes."

"Man," he said, obviously bemused, "you're telling me that an advertising man's daughter has been turned into a walking, talking slogan."

I took the receiver back from Rosa.

"Listen, Dr Robinson, we can't say whether the parents are directly responsible, because we know that they paid Miss Flinders very little attention. All we can say for sure is that they were, and are, negligent. So, in loco parentis, as her only grandparents are in France, apparently, we are asking you to help her. We have her consent."

He took his time to make the decision.

"Sure, I'd like to help, but .. you really think this might be connected to Major Dyminge's work on brainwashing?"

"We don't know," I replied.

"Yes, we do," Rosa interjected.

He booked Verity into his clinic later that same afternoon.

We got the last appointment of the day, in a run-down looking building on the outskirts of Dover hospital. It looked like a pre-fab that should have been knocked down a generation earlier. Once inside, the plastic seat covers were ripped and the whole place smelt of grime and Dettol. Rosa wrinkled her nose and got a bottle of perfume out of her handbag.

"The thing about the National Health Service," I explained, as it was clear Rosa had little experience of it, "is that it never has enough money for the extras. However, that doesn't mean that the folk who work in it aren't the best in the world, because they are."

I included Verity in my statement, because she was looking half scared to death.

"This clinic," I added, "has no connection with the ones in Harley Street. It's a completely different world."

"You can say that again," Rosa offered.

Fortunately, I didn't have to, because Verity's name was called and we all trooped in to see Dr Robinson.

"Good afternoon, Miss Flinders, please come in and make yourself comfortable," his voice had a gentler tone than before, and he was growing an impressive moustache.

I was surprised to see that Dr Robinson didn't wear a white coat, or have a desk, or, even, any chairs. Instead, he was still in his jeans and there were colourful bean bags and children's toys scattered over the floor.

"Do you want Mr Hawking and Miss Stone to remain during your session?"

"Would you mind awfully if I said not?" Verity replied, in a small voice.

"It's absolutely your call; this is your time and your space and you are in charge."

Rosa looked as if she was about to protest, but I took her arm and ushered her out.

We settled back on the plastic chairs and tried to avoid catching the receptionist's beady eye; it was obvious she was annoyed about having to stay late.

"I'm not sure about this, Bill," Rosa whispered. "What if TL is just *too* trendy? What if he makes her drop acid and starts banging on about cults?"

"That won't happen."

Of the two of us, I'd thought I was the square one.

"You trusted him, remember? He drives a Triumph Herald Convertible."

"That's true. I don't know why I'm so anxious," she got up and began to rifle through a stack of old magazines. "Maybe it's Verity bringing out the mother in me."

"Makes a nice change."

"What did you say?"

"Nothing."

We had a long wait and a bumper collection of Woman's Weekly didn't do much to help. Rosa was in the middle of displaying a long ladder in her tights - the chair's fault - when Dr Robinson called us back in.

"Hi Guys," he greeted us, "Verity and I have had a good talk and I have her permission to give you an outline of the points that have come up. Still okay with you, Verity?"

She was sitting, her chin on her knees, on a bean bag. Her black shoes were off and she looked the most relaxed I'd ever seen her. I cleared a space among some Corgi cars and joined her on the floor, as did Rosa and Dr Robinson. I couldn't help noticing that he was wearing pink socks.

"First and foremost, I see no signs of any entrenched mental illness that might require medication. In fact, Verity responds poorly to sedatives and to stimulants of any kind, and we have discussed what she can do to avoid situations where these might be on offer. I have a group of young people in London who like to come along and do their own thing in an open, non-judgmental space: artists, dancers, musicians – whatever floats their boat – and Verity is keen to give it a try."

Rosa narrowed her eyes at me, as if gurus were still on the agenda.

"Any problem with that, Miss Stone?"

"Gosh, *no*, TL."

"I can sing," Verity said. "I like to sing in French."

TL smiled,

"Sounds cool. Can't wait to hear you, Verity."

I could picture her singing, with her long, fair hair dangling over the guitar, that wistful way she had with her working like a dream with the French; so that you didn't need to know what she was singing about, in fact, it was better not knowing what it was, because then you were free to feel it.

"So .. now we come to a very different part of Verity's recent experiences."

He stood up and began to pace, as if on far less firm ground.

"When enduring stress, or strain, Verity is resorting to what we call an 'idée fixe' which, in her case, consists of repeating well-known advertising slogans. An 'idée fixe' is not, in itself, that unusual in my line of work and can attach itself to everything and anything. And the fact that her father works in this industry would, I'm sure, be seized upon by many of my colleagues. However.."

He definitely seemed far less sure of himself, maybe even troubled.

"Wow, I don't even know whether I should be saying this .. but, it's the eyes. Your eyes worry me, Verity."

Verity stared at him, while we stared at her. She, certainly, did have big, unblinking, pale eyes. I'd heard Rosa refer to her as a stick-insect, which was unkind. Only there was grain of truth about it. Her eyes were other-worldly. Not so much blank, as belonging to a different species.

"I have a colleague with some knowledge of hypnotism, and I'm wondering whether you would mind me including him in our next appointment, Verity?"

"Ok," she agreed.

"There *is* going to be another appointment, then?" Asked Rosa.

"Sure is. Verity and I have a way to go, but we'll get there in the end. I'm gonna ask you to do one more thing for me,

Verity. Again, feel free to say no. When you have a moment, I'd like you to make a brief sketch of the apparatus that we have discussed. I want you to do it when you feel calm and have friends around and I don't want you to give it a whole lot of thought. Got that? Make a cartoon out of it, if you like. Then give it to these guys and they'll make sure it gets back to me. What d'you think?"

"Yeah, I can do that."

"Fantastic. So, that about wraps it up. What are your plans for the time being Verity; are you staying with this couple of characters?"

She seemed unsure, although I couldn't tell whether it was because she didn't want to stay, or whether it was because she thought we might not want her.

"You're completely welcome to stay as long as you like," said Rosa. "My parents will be back soon and the housekeeping will improve, considerably. They love having guests to stay. Then, I expect Sam will come back here when they let him out of hospital, which should be any day now."

Verity brightened up at that.

"Oh, then that would be fab. Thanks, Rosa."

I took Verity for a walk in the village the next morning, while Rosa was busy with her kids. When it began to rain, I thought about taking her back to Mum's house, but I chickened out and we landed up in a tea shop, eating toasted teacakes dripping with butter.

"Do you think Sam will be here soon, Bill?"

"Next couple of days, I hear. Mr and Mrs Stone are bringing him. His handsome face may be a bit of a mess for a while yet, though."

"Poor Sam. I feel so bad . . is it true they broke his nose?"

"I'm afraid so. But, knowing him, it'll probably just add to his looks. Like, some rugged film star, you know?"

"Ooh," she brightened, "like [62]Jean-Paul Belmondo?"

"It's possible."

I poured her tea into a flowery, china tea-cup. She liked it black, as she liked most things. In her black jumper and tiny skirt, white lipstick and sooty lashes, she stood out like a sore thumb in the twee tea-shop, which was crammed with folk taking shelter from the sudden downpour. I'd acknowledged a couple of locals when we came in, and I admit that I was proud to be seen with such a pretty girl. I knew, also, that there had been talk in the village about Rosa and I. Which is village life, for you. So, it did no harm to be seen with a girl my own age. For her part, Verity seemed fascinated by the villagers.

"Wow, Bill, these people are just amazing," she was all wide eyes and giggles, "like, do children always dress like that in the countryside?"

She was referring to a party of kids with their teacher, who were rigged out in their May Day parade outfits. They looked like mini-Morris men in their straw hats and ribbons.

"Nah, of course not. You really take us for yokels down here, don't you? They've just been practising their bit of the May Day parade for the weekend after next."

"May Day? With a maypole?"

"Yes, all of that idiocy. It's quite a big deal here. My mother gets involved in the preparations, but I've always tried to avoid it."

I may have been trying to sound cool by distancing myself from it all.

"But, that's so gorgeous, Bill. Is there a May Queen and everything? I hope I'm still here for it."

"A May Queen on a float and a Jack in the Green – he's the Green Man with the leaves around his face – and over-excited kids and all that. Then, when it gets dark, there's a splinter group of Beltane fire worshippers, which is more Scottish, I think, but the local pagans have recently set it up. They parade down the hill to the beach and have a bonfire and set off fireworks, and then everyone goes to the Coastguard and gets pissed."

"Fab. I'm *definitely* going to that bit."

Which reminded me of something I'd been meaning to mention since our meeting with Dr Robinson the day before. It was probably going to blow any attempts I'd made to seem cool, but I felt I had a duty to say it.

"You will be careful, though, won't you, Verity? With alcohol and drugs and all that? Only, Dr Robinson was adamant that your system doesn't respond well.."

"Yeah, yeah. I get it."

She didn't sound that convinced.

"It's just that hanging out with Sam exposes people to certain.. temptations, and.."

"Jeez, Bill, what are you trying to do? Ruin my love life?"

"God, *no*, but.."

"I mean, what with Dave setting one of his guys on Sam, it looks like nobody wants us to be together." She was getting upset. "It's enough to.. put a frigging *tiger in your tank*.."

Now I'd torn it. I had to get her out of there before the whole village knew about Verity's problems. I flung the money for our tea on the table and tried to get her up.

"Cool it, Verity. There's no need to sweat, no need at all."

"*Snap, Crackle and POP!*" She declared, loudly and firmly, as if she expected to be obeyed, sharpish.

I hustled her out of the door, hoping that the general hubbub had drowned most of her declarations out.

She calmed down as we walked back to the house; I'd noticed that her turns were getting shorter in duration, which I took for a positive sign. The rain had cleared and we walked in silence, as the sun came out and the sea turned from grey to green to blue. I pondered over our conversation, reckoning that it might be better to speak to Sam about Verity's bad reaction to drink and drugs; I'd gone the wrong way about it, and spoken to the wrong person. I'd been a fool to upset her like that, except.. if I hadn't, I might not have learnt a, possibly, very important piece of information. For Verity knew that one of her father's hoods had beaten Sam. If she knew *that*, I pondered, what else might the girl know?

I put this to Rosa later in our office, as we were clearing up the case against Edwin Summerby (we had both given interviews to the police, had handed over the Woody Guthrie book and were now waiting for the blown-up photograph to arrive in the post).

"The problem is, Bill, that we can't talk to her properly because she keeps going doolally .. well, *I* can't, anyway. I'm not sure that she likes me, actually."

Verity was a highly sensitive girl and I wasn't surprised that she'd picked up on Rosa's earlier hostility.

"So, it'll have to be you," she continued. "You must approach her with extreme care."

"I'm aware of that, Rosa."

"Hoity, toity!" She glanced sideways at me, smiling.

Our relationship seemed to be changing. I supposed I wasn't the kind of mug who would be yearning after her forever; not when her kids' dad had just shown up. For all I knew, she might be packing them up and heading off to America with him on the next plane (although, I really hoped she didn't, because that would be the death of Hawking & Stone).

"I'm only going to touch on the subject of Dave Flinders' business," I said, "because I don't think there's any need to get her all worked up over Dr Ambrosia."

"God, no. That woman terrifies the life out of her. By the way, Verity hasn't given you her drawing of the brainwashing machine, yet, has she?"

"No. It really is jumping the gun to refer to it as that, you know."

"Oh, Bill," she sighed, "when will you ever stop being so boring?"

"When you stop being such a kook."

We both laughed.

That evening Rosa went up to bathe the kids, leaving Verity and I on the couch to watch [63]*Ready Steady Go!*

"I love it when they say *'the weekend starts here'*." Verity observed. "Even though I don't really have a job, which probably means I'm not entitled to a weekend."

"Yeah, it does make it more special when your time's not your own. But, what about your modelling career?"

"That's just Sam taking snaps," she seemed a bit downbeat.

"Well, you can say what you like about Sam Stone, but you can't knock his photography. The boy's got talent. He wouldn't be taking pictures of you, if he didn't think you had the goods, Verity."

That cheered her up and she chattered all the way through the programme. I wouldn't have minded if it had only been [64]Cilla, or [65]Tom Jones, but [66]John Mayall and the Bluesbreakers were ground-breaking.

"It's a shame [67]Sandie Shaw isn't on; they have her on a lot," she said. "I like her feet."

Just that minute, the commercials came on and I was so busy thinking about Sandie Shaw's feet that I left it too late to leap up and switch to another channel. It was those pesky cartoon elves in the hats, the ones with the breakfast cereal. Verity's eyes went all peculiar again, as she chimed in,

"*Snap, crackle and POP!*"

But then she did something different, because she seemed to come straight out of the trance-like state that the advert had caused.

"Why did I say that?" She asked, with a self-awareness that she had never had before.

I wasn't sure what Dr Robinson would have wanted me to reply, but it didn't matter, because she had more to say.

"I remember," she said, nodding to herself, as if she'd answered a question that had long been on her mind. "I thought I'd forgotten, but I remember now. I know what I saw and I know it was true, whatever they say."

My heart was in my mouth. Should I call Rosa downstairs, or would that take too long? Would Verity have forgotten whatever it was, again, by the time she'd made it down? I took the plunge.

"What is it you remember, Verity?"

"I saw them kill the old man."

I gasped with the shock of it. Yet, I was completely and utterly confused. It was as if Rosa had been right and all the stories in the world were entwined in unexpected ways and the only sense that made any sense was that there was *no* sense, none whatsoever.

"You saw *them* kill Harry Cole? Who do you mean by *them*, Verity?"

"Dave's men," she said. "I saw them do it at our house in France, in October. The old man brought a big crate with him, on a boat from England. Then, when they had the crate, they murdered him."

My head was swimming.

"But it wasn't Harry they killed, was it, Verity?" Rosa was standing by the open door. "It was some elderly official who worked for the Government, with connections to MI5. Somebody with a drink problem, or mental troubles, who visited a clinic in Harley Street in secret. No-one knew he was there, except the doctor who treated him. A doctor with experience in hypnotism and a lover – a bigshot advertising man – who she wanted to leave his wife."

Verity looked, blankly, at Rosa; as if she were seeing right through her.

"I don't know who the old man was," she said, "but I'm not telling *you* anything else. I want to speak to TL."

We prevailed upon TL to pay Verity an unofficial visit over the weekend. He wasn't too happy about it. He stomped up the stairs to our office, scowling beneath his moustache.

"This is way out of line, now that the girl's a patient of mine."

"Yes, but this is *murder*, remember. I don't think National Health Service guidelines apply to murder."

He shook his head, as if he still couldn't quite process how he'd got himself involved. Looking at things from his point of view, I could see his point. Simply by picking up his pen to reply to an old man, he'd been propelled from his little oasis of beanbags and plenty of disinfectant, to brainwashing, murder and the dangerous world of Hawking & Stone.

"Verity won't talk to us, Dr Robinson," Bill added. "You must see how vital it is to find out how much she knows. Quite honestly, there's not a moment to lose."

"Whatever happened to going to the police station?" He grumbled. "I thought the British loved their bobbies."

"Yes, I expect we will be going there at some stage," I muttered, "but not *now*."

Bill opened the door of our office, where Verity was waiting, and I pushed TL inside.

When he came out, an hour later, he was silent and grave. He pulled at his burgeoning moustache and answered my questions with monosyllables. I led him downstairs, while Bill went in to see Verity. The situation called for tea and whatever my father had baked earlier that day.

I sat him down by the dining room table with a large slice of coffee and walnut cake and tried not to pester him. Of course, that didn't last long.

"So? What did you find out? Tell me everything she said; there might be vital bits of info that you wouldn't recognise, but I would. TL?"

"I have to respect patient confidentiality."

"Of course, you do. Absolutely. We wouldn't want to make you do anything else," I lied. "However, this is a criminal case and I think you'll find that those rules don't apply. Have another piece of cake."

"Thanks."

"Not when there's *murder* involved."

"Yeah, I get that. I'd rather talk to the police, though, Miss Stone."

What was all this obsession with the police? Why go to them when you could have Hawking & Stone?

"Listen," I leant over the table, "the following is top-secret .. but I think you should know that my uncle is high up in Interpol and is investigating aspects of this very case. His name is Tristram Upshott and I can give you his telephone number, if you'd like to verify this."

"Interpol? Well, that certainly sounds official," he licked coffee buttercream from the edge of his moustache, thoughtfully. "However, what I think *you* should know is that I have a responsibility towards my patient's state of mind. I cannot say, this early on, whether Verity is conscious of the fact that she may be incriminating her own father, for example. That would come, naturally, with a tremendous amount of baggage. Which she's not capable of carrying, not now and, most probably, not for some time yet."

Bill came into the dining room, his hands in his pockets.

"She's doing ok. Just gone to sit at Sam's bedside."

"TL is being very cagey with me, Bill. I think he'd rather we were the police."

Bill sat down and poured himself a cup of tea, saying nothing.

"Man, this is hard," TL exclaimed, and then he sat back and put his hands on the table; as if he was going to put his cards there, quite literally.

"Alright guys, I'll give you some of what I've got. You can have *this*, for what it's worth."

He threw a scrap of paper on the table and I grabbed it. It was Verity's sketch and it appeared to be of an octopus. I turned it upside down, but it only looked like an octopus seen from below, perhaps when out for a swim.

"Yeah," TL clocked my expression, "it's like no ECT machine in existence. No kind of machine at all. If you want my opinion, this drawing says more about Verity's response to the apparatus, than to the thing itself. And, before you ask, I can see no connection to anything in Major Dyminge's letters, either."

He was wrong; I knew it in my bones. Some aspect of Verity's sketch was connected to Major Dyminge, but I couldn't think why. Was it something that I'd seen in his workshop? Something that might have provided the makings of a prototype?

"It's certainly strange," Bill said. "I agree, Dr Robinson; I think Verity may have given you a picture of her own fear. The octopus is her bogey-man in the night, if you like."

No, no, no.

"Yup. Now, if you turn the paper over, you can see I've noted down the address of a house in France. That's where Verity witnessed the first traumatising incident."

"Her parents' house, you mean? Where she saw the murder?" I pocketed the paper, swiftly.

"I'm not going to go into that, Miss Stone. You know that, so don't bug me."

TL stood up, as if the job was done. It was a shame that he couldn't give away more of Verity's secrets, but there was nothing more we could do. He nodded towards Bill and I and went to go. But he didn't.

"Dammit," he said, and turned back. "I must be as crazy as a loon, but I feel this weird loyalty towards the Major. I mean, the man's dead and all .."

I didn't dare utter a word, in case he changed his mind.

"Let me see .. I need to get this in order. Ok. So, the first traumatizing event happened last October, in France, after which Verity was sent to hospital. Not to see Dr Ambrosia, you notice, but to hospital. In fact, it was just after the day in Kent with your brother that Verity was first sent to Dr Ambrosia's clinic."

"Oh, no," I gasped. "It wasn't the bad trip was it? Please tell me this hasn't all been Sam's fault."

"The bad trip on the mushrooms was not helpful in any way, not for a girl like Verity, and you'd be doing her a favour by telling him so. However, it was the two events that sandwiched the trip that really did the damage, in my opinion."

"There were *two* events?" Bill was puzzled. "I can make an educated guess that seeing the corpse of Mr Cole – when she rescued Sam from the water – must have been the second. But what was the first?"

"The first was a very, very peculiar coincidence, Mr Hawking. One cold day, last February, Verity Flinders was taken on a trip to Kent by a boy who had been working for her father. He was a good-looking boy and she had high hopes of him becoming her boyfriend. On top of that, he was a talented photographer who thought that she had the potential to be a model. Naturally, she was thrilled when he suggested taking her to the countryside and photographing her. The only trouble was, that his scary (her words, not mine), elder sister told them they had to go to a funeral first and there was no getting out of it."

"Well, they went along and the church was very cold and gloomy and Verity felt her mood switch from complete elation at being with this handsome boy, to one of fear and dread. An outing that had promised so much of life – finally, after those long months of hospital – had brought her, once more, face to face with death. She became overwhelmed and left part way through the service to stand at the church door and cry. When, through her tears, she saw two men that she recognised, only too well, from her own nightmares. Two men, in actual fact, that she had been told had never existed. She saw the murderers."

"Sorry?" Said Bill. "I'm not sure I follow. Are you suggesting that she saw her father's hoods at the Major's funeral? The ones who killed the old man with the crate, in France? That's crazy!"

"Yeah, you said it. That was exactly what she took from it, too. She believed she was crazy, and part of her still does, to this day."

But I, being a woman who has no problem believing the

impossible (who knows, intimately, that stories and facts collide and merge every day of the year), saw nothing remotely crazy.

"Dave Flinders' men took the Major's body for Dr Ambrosia. She knew who the real inventor was because she'd hypnotised the old spy who had stolen his work and he had told her. She needed Major Dyminge's brain to discover more. So, Flinders and Ambrosia were collaborating on the brainwashing machine. End of story."

"You're jumping ahead again, Rosa," said Bill. "You can't know they were collaborating. Flinders may just have been doing her a favour."

"Considering that you accused me of telling stories, Bill Hawking, when practically everything that I foresaw has turned out to be the case, I really think you should start listening and stop preaching.."

"Hey, guys," TL interjected, "give it a rest. Save it for the office. Now, I'm done here, if you'll excuse me."

We walked to the front door and out onto the beach together, thanking him all the way. Bill even shook hands.

"You can give my name to the police, or your uncle, or whoever, but I hope you guys understand the situation. Verity is my number one concern. My patient is emerging from a traumatic episode. On top of that, we can see that there has been some infringement of personal liberty, possibly involving hypnosis, combined with a mechanical intrusion of unknown type. Weird as this may sound, people, most of this makes her very much the embodiment of all the psychiatric patients that I see. Verity is not an exception, but the norm. As such, I shall be treating her with the kindness and respect that should be the right of every human being, but seldom is."

He folded his flapping jeans into his Triumph Herald Convertible and left.

4. THE BIGGER BOYS

It was the next day, the Sunday, that my uncle rang to tell me he had arranged a meeting with the 'bigger boys' (his superiors at Interpol).

When we got off the train at Charing Cross on Monday morning, there was a car waiting. It drove us straight to New Scotland Yard on Victoria Embankment. Uncle Tristram came out to meet us, polishing his glasses, nervously.

"I hope you realise that I'm putting my job on the line for you, Rosa?"

"You won't be sorry, I promise. We have new information that we think your superiors will be interested to hear."

"Very well, then," he sighed, leading us up the stairs, "but it had better be within the realms of reality and not some nonsense dreamed up by a writer of half-baked fiction. This case has got the high-ups worried. We've got the Foreign Secretary, the Chief of Central Bureau and the Greek Ambassador upstairs waiting to talk to you two."

Bill and I looked at one another and swallowed, hard. When my Uncle had said there were bigger boys than him involved, he hadn't been kidding.

"I cannot stress highly enough that anything you may hear in the room is utterly confidential," he added, unnecessarily.

We were shown into the conference room and beckoned to sit down around a polished teak table, where we found even more big-wigs than we had been promised. The Commissioner of the Metropolitan Police had turned up, plus any number of Interpol agents, who all appeared to be French. I shouldn't have been surprised if Harold Wilson had strolled in, smoking his pipe. Bill – who was, after all, only nineteen – was looking scared out of his wits.

Fortunately, Uncle Tristram had been exaggerating when he said the bigger boys had been waiting for our arrival, because it was clear that the meeting was in full swing.

" . . and [68]a blue notice has been issued," declared a Frenchman.

The Greek Ambassador nodded, sagely,

"That is good news," he said, "but Athens wishes to make it clear that we have first claim upon any 'discovery' made by a Greek National."

"The British Government would just like to propose, in the mildest terms possible, that the nationality of the 'discovery's' inventor is still a matter of some dispute," said the Foreign Secretary.

I put my hand up and heads swivelled.

"Excuse me for interrupting," I said, "but is Dr Ambrosia Greek?"

"Yes, Anna Ambrosia is a citizen of Greece," the Ambassador replied. "May I ask," he addressed the top of the table, "who are these young people?"

My uncle introduced us,

"Miss Stone and Mr Hawking of the Private Investigation company, Hawking & Stone, Your Excellency."

How thrilling that sounded, especially coming from him; I felt as if I had grown a foot in my chair.

"If you look at Section 6, Your Excellency, the section headed 'Other', I think you will find further clarification," Uncle Tristram continued.

There was much rustling of paper as they all studied our credentials (or, whatever my uncle had told them that had given us access to the meeting).

"Ah, yes," said the elderly Chief of the Bureau, "Miss Stone and Mr Hawking are connected with your push for a [69] yellow notice, is that correct, Mr Upshott?"

"Yes, sir. The disappearance of a body from Kent earlier this year, sir."

Bill and I exchanged glances; it was news to us that my uncle was actively looking into Major Dyminge's disappearance.

"Also," the Chief continued, "it says here that they were in possession of highly confidential material at one point. The affair of the pink vanity case, is that correct?"

My uncle took off his glasses and began polishing them, madly.

"Yes, sir. The case and its contents fell into their hands inadvertently, through an unknown drugs courier employed by David Flinders. Hawking & Stone were instrumental in handing the intelligence over to Interpol."

"Ah, did you, at any time, read the information contained within the case, Mr Hawking? Ah, Miss Stone?" The Chief of the Metropolitan Police piped up.

We shook our heads with all the vehemence we could muster. Considering that we were telling the truth, it was amazing what a liar I felt.

The Chief Interpol man was still absorbed in the notes; the ones marked 'Other'.

"How extraordinary. Hawking & Stone also appear to have a personal connection with one of Dr Ambrosia's patients, a Miss Flinders. I wonder whether you would you be kind enough to explain how Hawking & Stone come to know this young woman, Mr Hawking?"

Bill actually began to stammer, so I took control. This was going to need careful handling, for, if my uncle had managed to erase Sam from the case, I most certainly wasn't going to drop my little brother right in it by telling them about his relationship with Verity. I decided to give them our new findings as fast as possible, thereby obscuring the facts about our 'connection'. I was working on the theory that if you give people plenty of pudding, they will forget about the biscuits and cheese.

"Verity is a family friend," I began, then moved swiftly on, "as was your yellow notice, Major Dyminge, who is at the heart of our investigation. Our client, Lord Peter Upshott, has employed Hawking & Stone to recover the Major's body and bring it back to his widow for a proper funeral and that is what we intend to do, isn't it, Bill?"

He nodded, opened his mouth to speak and started to stammer again, however nobody noticed because they were all busy digesting the unexpected arrival of the aristocracy.

"Lord Peter?" Inquired the Bureau Chief. "I didn't know the old boy was still alive."

"Your father, isn't he, Mr Upshott?" Said the Police Chief, dryly.

"Oh, I *do* beg your pardon," went the Bureau Chief.

"No need, I assure you," went my uncle.

They could have gone on all day, if I hadn't dropped the next bombshell.

"It was Major Dyminge who invented your 'discovery'."

The Greek Ambassador leant across the table,

"What grounds do you have for this assertion, may I ask?"

"That it was Major Dyminge? Well, the Major was a brilliant man, who was working on radar engineering and its application to the brain in his final years. I'm sure you will be interested to hear that we have his extensive notes on this project, which are stored in an extremely safe place. We also know that the Major was in contact with an influential medical professional, who has kept their correspondence on this subject, and would be willing to show it to the police. Believe me, we have plenty of proof."

The Foreign Secretary was moved to comment,

"I have to say that Intelligence have informed us that the 'discovery' was, indeed, a British one, but that it came from one of their own. We have been unable to confirm this, due to the gentleman in question's disappearance."

"We suspect that he was murdered," said the Chief of Police.

"No, no, no, my friend," responded the Greek Ambassador, ignoring the policeman's contribution. "As Dr Ambrosia was the first to build and operate the 'discovery' she must, therefore, claim the title 'Inventor'. There is no question but that the 'discovery' belongs to Greece."

I sat back in my chair, not caring whether my face gave away the sheer disgust that I felt, or not. Suddenly, I didn't want to give any more information to these men. They simply wanted the brainwashing machine for themselves, every last one of them. Nobody at the table gave a damn about Major Dyminge's body, Verity Flinders' fractured mind, or even the man who had been murdered. And, what would the brainwashing machine do for the world? Peter had been right, it would simply warm up the Cold War. I decided, there and then, that there was more to bury than an old man's body.

"C..c..can I ask?" It was Bill, who had screwed up the courage to address the Foreign Secretary. "Who was the murder victim, sir?"

The Foreign Secretary glanced over at an inconspicuous, little man who was loitering in the doorway behind the broad shoulders and helmet of a sturdy policeman. Aha .. I had wondered whether MI5 or MI6 would be present. The little man gave the most imperceptible nod of his head, at which the Foreign Secretary replied.

"Intelligence strongly suggests that Sir Neville Card, who, until his retirement last year, was a long-serving member of Her Majesty's Secret Service, was .. ahem .. persuaded to give away vital details of his 'discovery' under hypnosis. Hypnosis administered by Dr Anna Ambrosia at her establishment in Harley Street. As has been mentioned, there is a possibility that he may have been done away with after that, but a body has yet to be found."

"We have a witness to the murder, sir."

I kicked Bill's shins under the table, but it was too late. Now that he had mastered his nerves, it looked like he was going to spill all of our beans.

"Indeed? Now, who would that be, Mr Hawking?" Asked the Chief of Police.

I tried kicking Bill again, but he had moved his leg.

"Miss Flinders, sir. She saw this man arrive by boat at her parents' house in France last October, accompanied by a crate that may well have contained your 'discovery'. That same evening, she witnessed him being shot by one of her father's associates, an experience that has caused her a great deal of distress."

The spy in the doorway spoke up, with a lazy, mocking tone.

"This is the same Miss Flinders who has been diagnosed as being highly unstable? I cannot think that anything *she* has to say would stand up in court."

Of course, I realised, the spooks would want to discredit any eyewitness; they knew perfectly well that one of their own had stolen information contained in Major Dyminge's private correspondence and had then been 'persuaded' (whether through hypnosis, or greed), to give that information away.

"Interesting, though, that the young lady claims to have seen a crate arrive on the same boat as Sir Neville," mused the Chief of Police. "Not a detail that she would have any reason to invent, I'd say. It has occurred to us to wonder how Dr Ambrosia found the resources to actually build the . . 'discovery'. Now, somebody with Sir Neville's background and connections . ."

My mind was whirring. I had never considered the possibility that British Intelligence might have built the machine, themselves. Yet, why did they ransack his workshop, if they already had the knowledge? Why was this meeting even taking place? No, the policeman was wrong. Whatever

Intelligence might possess was partial and unusable. Be that as it may, they didn't want Hawking & Stone calling attention to their involvement. I noticed the spy slip up to the table and whisper something in the ear of the Interpol Chief, who glanced our way.

"Thank you for attending today, Miss Stone, Mr Hawking. That will be all. Can you find your own way out?"

We were dismissed and that was that. The bigger boys continued to talk amongst themselves, as if we had already gone. As if we had never been there at all. We found our way out.

The meeting had made me feel as if I'd been turned inside out and hung out to dry in a stiff wind. It was a surprise to find that it was still light outside and that the air was soft and warm and full of the familiar sound of London. I dragged Bill over to sit on a bench by the Thames and put my head in my hands.

"Sorry about that, Rosa," he said. "I haven't had much experience with that type of person."

"Who has? The Queen, possibly, but ... Damn it, Bill, I don't think that we got anything *whatsoever* out of that meeting. The men in that room couldn't care less about finding the Major's body. I don't think they even care that he invented their damn 'discovery' and that it was stolen from him. For all their blasted, multi-coloured notices, they none of them care about anything except claiming the brainwashing machine for themselves, so they can make the world an even more messed-up place than it already is."

"Yeah, it *was* pretty sickening," he agreed.

"And, *you* went and gave Verity away. They will turn up at our house any minute now and pick her up and interrogate her, and God knows what that will do to her poor brain. You just wait and see if they don't."

"Dr Robinson won't let that happen, Rosa."

"You don't get it do you, Bill?" My voice was getting louder and I could do nothing about it. "We're all absolutely enslaved to the Establishment. We think we're not, but we ARE.."

"Can you please stop shouting, Rosa?" It was Uncle Tristram, crossing the road at a clip. "They can hear you all the way from the corridors of power."

I sighed,

"How I wish they *could*."

"They heard more than you've been led to believe. They've asked me to get the address of the house in France from you."

"Have they?" I was surprised by that. "Why?"

"I'm not meant to reveal their intentions."

"So, you won't?"

"I didn't say that."

He got out a cigarette and lit it, staring at Waterloo Bridge, as if wrestling with a problem.

"Listen carefully, you two, because this is all I know. They will be commissioning a gunboat to take the police over to the house in France. Could be the army, I can't be sure, but not us, because Interpol don't make arrests. First and foremost, they want whatever was in the crate. If Flinders and Ambrosia turn out to be in-situ, then that's a bonus. Estimated time of arrival for the gunboat .. well .. I can't be sure, not at this point. Could be tomorrow, could be the end of the week, depends what the Navy have going spare. That's the best I can do, Rosa. Now, give me the address, because I've got to get back."

Bill tore out a page from his notebook, wrote it down and handed it over.

"Thanks Uncle Tristram, but .. why are you doing this for us?"

"Because I'm betting the Major will be there, too, and I don't trust those war-mongers to honour the yellow notice."

I nodded, thinking things through.

"You don't like the 'discovery', either, do you?"

"I didn't say that," he said, again.

"Because, whatever we might manage to do, there's a loose thread. What did your man call it?" I mused. "The 'affair of the pink case'. Could whatever's inside it be used to make more 'discoveries', in your opinion, uncle?"

He stared at me, blank of face to the last.

"I'm afraid that's it, Rosa; that's me done. Whatever you decide to do now, it's off your own bat."

He started back towards New Scotland Yard, but I ran and caught up with him, grabbing the sleeve of his expensive suit.

"Thanks for keeping Sam out of it, and for pushing for the yellow notice. I thought you didn't believe in me, I'm sorry."

"Oh, Gypsy," he sighed, "it's precisely because I've always believed in you that you drive me up the wall."

He did his odd, crooked smile – that one that only an Englishman does, as if a smile must be squeezed, surreptitiously from the corner of the mouth because they really aren't allowed – and then he disappeared into the traffic.

Later, when darkness had descended over the sea and the children were bathed and sleeping, I poured myself a small brandy from my parents' drinks cabinet and rang Peter. I told him everything.

"Right," he said. "We're coming down. Just give me a few days to arrange the necessary."

"The hotel?" I asked. "Why don't you both stay here? You know my parents would be delighted to have you."

"Hotel, be damned. I'll be hiring a boat. Keep your eyes peeled on the water, Rosa. Goodnight."

5. TO THE HORIZON

She was due to dock at Dover, but seemed difficult to spot from the Port car park, where Bill, Jay and I had been waiting in my old Hillman Husky for several hours, while lorries disembarked and the ferry came and went, and came again. Personally, I had cramp.

"Why do you keep calling the boat 'she', Rosa?" Asked Bill. "I think it has to be a large vessel for that."

We were getting hot and bothered, sitting there, and had begun niggling at one another. We were nervous, of course. Well, Bill and I were. Jay seemed remarkably calm.

"I'm not sure you are correct about that, Bill," he said, mildly.

"Does it matter?" I snapped. "Do you think they've given up? I mean, an old man in a wheelchair .. it's *so* utterly ridiculous. *And* we've waited until Saturday to sail. Who knows when the gunboat set off? And what are we trying to achieve, anyhow? We should just leave it to the professionals and go home."

To cap it all, I felt foolish in my old painting dungarees and a pair of wellingtons, which were the best I could muster for a day of action.

A car horn tooted behind us and we all tore our eyes from the sea. A Triumph Herald reversed, niftily, into the space behind and Dr TL Robinson got out, army-style jacket, flapping jeans, bushy moustache and all.

"What the..?"

"Hey guys," he boomed. "Thought I'd join you; maybe you could use an old marine."

It seemed more likely that we could use a psychiatrist.

"I mentioned our trip," said Bill, "but I didn't ask him to turn up."

"Good afternoon," Jay, extended a hand. "I don't think we have met. Jay Tamang."

The two of them shook hands, as if they were at a tea party. However, I was losing faith.

"This gets weirder by the second. I'm sorry, everybody, but I've got children at home and I'm wondering what on earth I'm doing here. Let's go."

I really was about to start the engine, when Bill gave a shout,

"Look! It's here."

He was pointing at a separate docking area, where fragile-looking yachts had been bobbing around their anchors in a decorous dance. The arrival of Peter Upshott's so-called 'boat' was whipping them into a frenzy.

"Blimey, would you look at the size of it? That's not a boat, it's a ship." Bill commented, unnecessarily.

She was multiple hands big, as white as snow and, most definitely, female. There would be no sneaking past Calais in that girl.

Standing at the top of the gangplank, waiting to greet us, was Peter's partner, the Air Chief Marshal, Sir Gabriel Adair. Even without a jacket-full of medals, Gabriel looked like a man of action. Which was reassuring, because Peter was immediately behind him, on deck in his chair, wearing a yachting cap at a jaunty angle, for all the world as if we were going on a merry day-trip to France.

"Ahoy there!"

I stumbled up the steep gangplank, lugging my rucksack.

"Why on earth have you hired this enormous bath-tub,

Peter? They'll be able to spot us from here."

In fact, that was no exaggeration, for on a clear day, which it was, the French coast was clearly visible on the horizon. If I used the binoculars that I was carrying in my rucksack, it felt as if I might be able to see the two Caps – Blanc Nez and Gris Nez – and the Flinders house, itself, nestled deep into the dunes between them.

Gabriel gave me a hand up the final bit and I jumped on deck.

"Hello to you, too, Rosa," said Peter. "Don't you like her? I think she's rather super. I hired her for the fridge, if you must know."

"The fridge?" I spluttered. "To cool the champagne?"

I'd never heard anything so ridiculous in all my life.

"Well, that does sound rather nice, but no . . . I thought we would need a big one for the old boy. Assuming he's still in one piece, I didn't like to think of us having to fold him in quarters."

That shut me up.

"Now, who are all these marvellous chaps? Introduce me, immediately, Rosa."

Once on board, we didn't hang about; I'd barely got through the introductions before a highly efficient crew had upped anchor and pointed the bath-tub at the coast of France. The sea was calm, the ferry had yet to set out again and we had a clear run to the horizon. For myself, however, I was not so calm; swarms of butterflies were looping the loop in my stomach. I went over to Bill, who was sitting up by the prow, flicking through his notebook.

"Oh, Bill," I whispered, so that the others shouldn't hear, "have we made a terrible mistake?"

"Perhaps, but it's too late now. One thing; nobody would be expecting a ship this size to show up. It's, actually, a pretty good camouflage. If the gunboat's already there and has us in its sights, they'll take us for tourists."

"But why should the gunboat be there *now*, Bill? Surely it will have been and gone?"

I was feeling so jittery that my hands had begun to tremble.

"I don't know . . ." He flicked a glance at Peter, who was still talking to Jay and TL. "I think Lord Peter may know more than he lets on. I mean, why go to the expense of hiring a ship, like this, just on the off chance? I reckon he may have been in contact with his son."

"But, they don't talk .."

Bill shrugged his shoulders.

"Best not to delve into it too much, Rosa. Let's get on with the job."

"Which is?" I squeaked.

I knew that I was letting anxiety get to me, but I didn't seem to be able to control myself.

"I think we should call a council of war. Right now."

❖ ❖ ❖

Rosa was losing her nerve. She'd been so impressive at New Scotland Yard, but now that it came to sailing across the Dover Straits, all of her confidence was seeping away. Strangely enough, I (who had never been abroad before), was experiencing the opposite reaction. Maybe it was the open air and the salt wind, the chug of the ship's engine and strong pull forward. It was such a dream – to be at sea, sailing into an adventure – that I didn't feel like shy, awkward Bill Hawking any more. It helped, too, to be among experienced, older men like the Air Marshal, like Jay and TL, and to be treated as an equal. There was a job to do and we were going to get it done.

When we were all gathered round on deck, I gave them a description of the Flinders house, having made sure to note down every last thing that Verity had told me.

"It's a modern, L-shaped building of glass and concrete. Single-storey. We'd call it a bungalow at home, but I don't suppose they do. Anyhow, no stairs to factor in. Now, it's set apart from a fishing village, Wissant, and is all alone in the dunes, so we don't need to worry about the neighbours. Verity said you're not supposed to build on Cap Blanc Nez, but they bribed an official. Mrs Flinders' family have been in Calais since before it belonged to England, so . ."

"Anywhere safe to land?" The Air Marshal asked.

"It's all fairly open, with low tide approaching in the next couple of hours," Lord Peter said. "But we've got two top of the range speedboats as part of the package, so I'd suggest firing them up from some distance away and running them straight onto the beach."

"*Both* of them?" TL enquired.

"One for the troops and one for the booty. We don't know the precise dimensions of the machine, of course, but . ."

"We are taking the machine, too? I had understood that we were here to bring back Major Dyminge's body?" Questioned Jay.

"Oh, I think so, don't you?" Lord Peter replied. "Heaven knows what kind of mischief people could get up to with a thing like that knocking about."

"We couldn't just disable it?" I asked.

"No, I'm with Peter, here," TL put in. He was surprisingly vehement, too. "Either we smash the critter into a million pieces, or we drop it so deep in the ocean that the fish can't find it."

I'd been wondering just why he had decided to join us. Did TL feel some sense of guilt that he had played a part, however small, in creating Major Dyminge's monster?

"I agree," said Rosa, "but let's not get ahead of ourselves. We have to find a way past Dave Flinders' henchmen, before we can take anything out of the house."

"Will they be armed?" Asked Jay.

"We must assume so," said the Air Marshal. "I've brought a pistol, but I'd rather not use it unless I have to."

"Jay can disarm anybody; he used to be a Gurkha," Rosa

boasted.

"I picked up a few moves in the Marines," said TL.

"Wonderful!" Went Peter. "I had no idea we'd have so many professionals on board."

I couldn't even offer up National Service, since it finished when I was fourteen.

"So, forget creeping up on them," Peter continued, "from the minute you get into the speedboats it's go, go, go. We've got time, but not that much of the stuff."

That was interesting news, but I didn't like to ask him how he knew, in case it put him in a sticky position. Luckily, TL asked for me.

"Have you got an inside track on this, Peter?"

"Let's just say, I have a sixth sense that the gunboat will be along later this evening. By which time, we should be well out of the way."

Rosa was wrong; the Upshotts *did* talk.

It wasn't long before we were sailing past the Port of Calais: the ferry docks and the white lighthouse, and the groins sticking out of the sea, where cormorants and seagulls perched, like bouncers at a nightclub, checking who went in and out. We weren't coming in. We were heading south, to the wild area of the Côte d'Opale, situated between Calais and Boulogne. They had wide, sandy beaches there and grass scrub and chalk headlands, much like we had on our side of the Channel but, already, on a grander scale. It was easy to identify Cap Blanc Nez because, from the sea, it looked like the white cliffs of Dover, but I did wonder quite how we would manage to find a bungalow nestled deep into the dunes.

In the end, it was the glass that gave it away. A beam of sunlight glanced off the frontage of the Flinders' house, like a flash of fire.

Rosa had her binoculars up.

"Found it!" She cried.

"Are you sure?" I asked, because I couldn't see a thing.

"Absolutely positive. The whole of the front of the place is built of glass, which is reflecting the sea back at us, like a giant mirror. But, when the sun strikes at the right angle, it catches light like a spark off tinder. See; there it goes again."

This time, we all saw it.

"Retreat and ready the speedboats," the Air Marshal hollered.

I had a moment of utter unreality. Was this really going to happen?

Rosa, though, possessed a good deal more imagination than me and had gone as white as those French cliffs. I threw her a life-line.

"You mustn't come," I said. "It's far too dangerous for a woman with children."

She said nothing, but I knew how relieved she was.

"I agree," Jay had overheard our conversation. "I insist you stay on the ship, Rosa. What if anything were to happen to both of us? Think of Benjamin and Jessica."

It crossed my mind to wonder whether this was the main reason that Jay had come along.

She opened and closed her mouth, like a floundering fish.

"Stay here with Lord Peter and the crew," I urged.

She didn't argue, for once in her life, and I was glad.

"Come on, guys," TL shouted, from across the ship, "all hands over here."

TL had taken the wheel of one speedboat, the Air Marshal, the other. I got my lifejacket strapped on as fast as possible and picked my way down the ship's ladder, before I jumped in with TL. I turned to watch Jay clamber down, with a tremendous agility that put me to shame, into the other boat. The motor revved, loud enough to drown out the wind, and I set my face to the shore.

"No!" A sharp cry carried across the water and I glanced back.

Rosa's head emerged above the side of the other speedboat; she had flung herself off the mother ship, without a life-jacket.

The sheer velocity was astounding to a land-lubber; we skimmed over the water and then seemed to fly upwards and into the air, beaching ourselves with a stomach-plummeting thud, upon the dunes. There wasn't a second in which to worry about whiplash, or Rosa, or anything extraneous to the present fraction of smashed time. We were out of the boat and running.

A gunshot cracked above us, but there was no time to scan for hidden marksmen, not when the angular conjunction of glass and concrete rectangles had risen from the wilderness and there was a long, Spanish-style patio with a lady sunbathing on a towel before an open door. The five of us charged past her, into the glass box, dimly aware of a screeching alarm, unseen male voices shouting and odd spurts of gunfire.

The Air Marshal got out his pistol and let out a round at the high, concrete ceiling, causing a grey-haired couple to emerge from a side room with their hands up, gibbering with fear.

"No need to get upset, guys," TL shouted, running into the room they'd just vacated, "we mean no harm."

"Anything there?" I asked.

"Just a tv, that's all. But, stick together, yeah? Don't let them catch you alone."

The main lounge area - involving a field of orange carpet and some peculiar mobiles that looked like they'd been cobbled out of drift-wood - was deserted. We tried all the doors off this, and found a number of empty bedrooms. There was one, however, where the door was locked fast. I tried putting a foot on it and wrenching, but Jay had a better idea. He picked up a solid piece of French furniture and battered it open.

"In here," he signalled.

The room had no window and was dark as a December night. Cold as winter, too. Even though we'd broken the door, little light filtered in there and the space felt close and slightly rank; in short, it smelt of a butcher's shop. I nearly gagged. Rosa's hand appeared from nowhere, gripping mine, hard. Terror, of a kind I had never known, froze me in the doorway. I could no more approach whatever was in that room, than I could remember how to breath.

Rosa released my hand and stepped forward into the darkness. One step. Two steps. Three, four, five .. and then I heard an intake of breath and a whimper, cut off in its prime.

"Rosa?" I called. "Rosa?"

There was no reply.

The others were at my shoulder.

"Have you lost her?" Asked TL. "What the hell is this place? It smells of.."

"She disappeared with her through an opening of some sort," Jay called out. "But I've been round the walls and I cannot feel a door."

"How about a trap door?" The Air Marshal suggested. "Get down on hands and knees; they must have gone through the floor."

I dropped to my knees, blinking in the dark, as I clocked Jay's words.

"She? How do you know a woman took her?"

"I caught a trail of sandalwood, like a Tibetan temple."

"Wasn't that Rosa?" I thought of the scent that she always wore.

"No, Rosa is all jasmine and peaches."

An unexpected spike of pure jealousy skewered me.

"Hate to break this up, guys, but that sure ain't what I can smell." TL commented. "Seems to me, old Major Dyminge may be hanging out downstairs."

"There's, most definitely, something going on down there," the Air Marshal spoke through the darkness again. "If one puts an ear to the ground, one can feel vibrations."

That much was true.

"I think I've located the trapdoor," the Air Marshal said. "Follow my voice, over here. Have you got it? Is that you, Mr

Hawking? Dr Robinson? Mr Tamang?"

We bumped into one another. I tried to crouch down, but the Air Marshal's arm came around my shoulder and he whispered in my ear,

"There'll be a bolt on it. What do you say, we all jump up and down at the same time? Might put enough pressure on the thing to break through? On a count of five?"

He began to count and we all entwined arms.

".. four .. FIVE."

The trapdoor splintered and we all crashed down a set of concrete stairs in the dark, hurting parts of ourselves as we collided with step and wall and body. I was just sitting up, the taste of blood in my mouth, when the lights turned on.

They were shockingly bright; dazzling enough to make you squint, involuntarily. When I could see, it was difficult to see straight, if that makes sense. I couldn't, immediately, grasp it. Light bounced off white walls and steel instruments in an immense, humming laboratory. Or torture chamber. For, the place could have been either. Two bodies had been strapped to steel stretchers, heads completely encased in steel suction cups, so that, if one hadn't been wearing denim dungarees, spattered with purple paint and the other, a formal army jacket and trousers, with well-polished shoes, nobody would have known that they belonged to Rosa Stone and Major Dyminge. Nor, that one was alive and the other three months' dead.

I was aware of intense cold. Somewhere a clock ticked and dials made bird-like clicking sounds and a metal apparatus, be-tentacled with those suctioned arms, breathed in and out with difficulty, like a wheezy old man who had smoked a lifetime's-worth of cigarettes. This was Verity's octopus come to life, but a thousand times bigger and more unpleasant. For the brainwashing machine had latched itself onto the faces of Rosa and the Major; as if to suck their brain matter from their skulls, like pop through a straw.

"What are you doing here? Go away, immediately. This

is highly important work," a blonde lady in a white coat spoke, making me jump because she had been standing so still that I'd failed to notice she was there.

This must be Dr Ambrosia, all alone in the laboratory that her lover, Flinders, had built for her.

"Please take that foul thing off Miss Stone's face," the Air Marshal stepped towards her.

"Back," she barked, in a deep, authoritative voice. "If you do not obey, I will be forced to turn up this dial, and you will not like what you see." She was holding a device in one hand, some kind of remote control that operated the machine. "If you do not want this woman to suffer, you must do as I say."

Only then, did I notice the screen. It was a giant television set that had been hung, like a picture, against a long, white wall. Colours played over it; a faint wash of green of many shades, and then red bursting over the green, like a rose opening in heat.

"I am a qualified doctor and psychiatrist," said TL. "If you don't stop whatever you're up to here, this minute, I tell you that Miss Stone could suffer irretrievable brain damage. Cause no harm, Dr Ambrosia. Cause no harm."

"You know me?" She seemed pleased. "Well, I don't know you, black man, and I don't believe you are any sort of doctor. Don't you tell me what I can, or cannot, do in my own laboratory. I labour for the great cause of science."

"Rubbish," I was surprised to hear myself sound off, as if my mum was talking. "A woman who experiments on her fancy man's daughter because he won't ditch his wife for her, is no kind of scientist, or doctor. You're just a bitter and twisted piece of work."

"Shut your mouth, boy," she shouted. "He will leave her once this has made enough money; this will make her fortune look like pennies."

"Well, he's not here to help you, is he? Hasn't even sent his hoods. It's looking like he really can't be bothered with you, Dr Ambrosia."

"No!" She screamed and turned the dial.

All four of us rushed at her, dashing the thing from her hand. TL had her pinned to the ground, the Air Marshal had run to try to release Rosa, and Jay had picked up the gadget, when I happened to glance up at the screen.

The swirls of green and red were retreating before a deep turquoise; the blue of the sea on a sunny day. Pictures formed like bubbles, then disintegrated: a small girl drowning in the sea beneath an up-turned boat. A great mass of seaweed fronds waving underwater in a cave. The sea turned to grey, and then sepia, and a young woman laboured to swim across a murky, brown river, her long, black hair trailing behind her.

I tore my eyes away and went to help the Air Marshal. The air-lock was so tight over her face that we struggled to shift the suction pad in any direction.

The screen went a bright, fluorescent yellow, as if in alarm and I, truly, began to panic.

We yanked at the suction pad, while trying not to hurt her, but .. the screen was turning black. What if she should die? Was she dying now? Dear God, don't die, Rosa.

There was a sudden, enormous squelching noise and the tentacle shrank off her face and retracted, with a whipping motion, straight back inside the machine. Jay had managed to switch it off. He ran to her,

"Rosa, are you alive? Please let us know that you are alive, my love?"

I looked at his face and took a step back. Which was when Rosa sat up, rubbing her scarlet cheeks. She took one look at the four of us, gathered around her like relatives around a death-bed, and sang out,

"Double your pleasure, double your fun
With double good, double good, Doublemint gum!"
We stared at her, in horror.

The clock ticked, and she burst out laughing.

♦ ♦ ♦

I certainly felt peculiar, sitting there in that vast fridge, but a good laugh improved the situation no end. The look on their faces. I considered the tiger and the tank, but I stopped, mid-consideration.

"Where's that unpleasant smell coming from?"

Bill glanced to my left, somewhat sheepishly, I thought.

"Oh, my .. we've found Major Dyminge!"

I tried jumping up, but was hampered by some strong straps.

"Yup," said TL, from down on the floor. "It's our guy, alright."

The Major wasn't looking his best, and no wonder. His skin was a nasty shade of grey, with circular, black blotches on his forehead where wires and pads had been attached.

"What, on earth, did they want from him?" I mused out loud.

"He has much to tell us. It is necessary to measure any damage to his brain," a woman said.

The infamous Dr Ambrosia was sprawled on the laboratory floor and TL was sitting on her, rather as if she were one of his beanbags.

"Is it catastrophic?" He asked.

"Surprisingly not. His brain seems to have been remarkably resistant."

That was the Major; resistant even beyond death.

Jay had unstrapped me and I got up feeling bizarrely light-headed; not in a bad way, but rather as if I'd plunged into cold water and been for a long, bracing swim. I shook out my legs and went over to where that doctor from hell was lying.

"I've got a few things I'd like to say to *you* .."

I was interrupted by a loud burst of staccato gunfire,

coming from somewhere alarmingly close.

"They are here," Dr Ambrosia said, a smug smile crossing her perfectly made-up face. "You will be killed, I am afraid."

"I'm not so sure," said Gabriel, pausing in the act of freeing the Major. "They've been shooting for a while, now. I just wonder *who* they're shooting at .. because it isn't us."

"The gunboat!" Bill and I chimed.

"Right, well, let's get a move on, shall we?" Ordered Gabriel, and he picked up the Major's body and flung it over his shoulders.

"See if we can disable the machine," I shouted.

"Don't you dare .." Dr Ambrosia writhed beneath TL, but he held her down.

Jay and I were trying everything we could think of to disassemble the brainwashing machine, when gunmen came charging down the stairs and into the laboratory. Not just one or two, either, but ten, or more. They could have been Dave Flinders' men, but, by the look of their smart uniforms, I thought they might be the French police. Either way, we were not supposed to be there. Jay vanished, while I slid down behind the machine, making myself as small as possible. I hoped Bill had managed to get away in time. TL and Gabriel, though, had nowhere to go.

"I say, stop that," I heard Gabriel shout, "he's a British citizen and you have no right to take his body."

There was the sound of a scuffle, and then TL spoke up.

"Easy does it. You can take *her* with my blessing. Look.. I'm not putting up any resistance. *Man*, there was no need for that .."

"Hey" said Bill, "that's completely unnecessary. It's her you want; he's on the same side as you .."

But, at that moment, Flinders' men must have appeared and it all got crazier. There was a thunderous explosion, as if a hand grenade had been lobbed into the lab and choking smoke filled the air. My eyes began to sting and my throat to close up and I had no choice but to break cover.

"It's tear gas," Jay appeared at the same time, his shirt pulled up over his face. "Come on, Rosa, forget the Major, we've got to get out of here."

We kept our heads down and ran through the smoke and the gunfire and up the steps, meeting no resistance, whatsoever. It seemed that Flinders' hoods had entered the lab by some other route. Even when we emerged from the dark room into the sunlit atrium, we met not a single soul, not until we got back to the beach.

The gunboat was anchored towards Cap Gris Nez and a flotilla of khaki-coloured dinghies were tethered on the dunes, where a couple of armed British soldiers were standing on watch. A third soldier had crossed the beach to talk to somebody sitting in the back of a rowing boat. That somebody was Peter. He waved at us.

"This fellow seems to think I'm mounting an invasion," he called out. "I'm almost flattered."

"He can't walk," I protested.

"Well what's he doing here, Miss? There's a dangerous operation being mounted in that house over there and I've been told to keep the beach clear."

"He's my grandfather," I said, "and we've just been doing a spot of sight-seeing .. I mean, my friend and I do the sight-seeing and then we come back and tell him what we've seen."

"And what would that be?" The soldier asked.

My attempt at a reply was interrupted by the sight of a hairy, middle-aged man in bathing trunks dashing out of the house to run, hell for leather, across the dunes. He was muscular and athletic and it took five French policemen to bring him down. Was this Verity's father?

While the spotlight was turned his way, Jay and I clambered into the rowing boat.

"Oh Peter," I wailed, "Major Dyminge is in there, but we have no way of getting him out, not now the gunboat's arrived."

"We've done our best, Rosa," Peter patted my knee. "They stole a march on us, pure and simple. As soon as I spied the gunboat, I had the crew lower me into this, but I had no chance to warn you."

"Look," Jay pointed. "Isn't that Bill?"

Bill's head popped out from behind the patio door, and then popped back again.

"Ssh," I whispered, because the soldier was still within hearing distance.

A final spatter of gunfire and then . . silence. The authorities had taken the house. A group of men appeared, hands in the air, and were ordered to drop to the ground while the police searched them. Several knives were removed and chucked in a pile on the sand. Gabriel and TL followed and were given the same treatment. Finally, Dr Ambrosia appeared, in handcuffs. She managed to make them look like the latest accessory from Paris. The woman hadn't a hair out of place and appeared as cool and in charge as I imagined she must be in her Harley Street clinic. When I thought of what she had done to Verity, it made me feel sick just to look at her superior face. It turned out that I wasn't the only one to have that reaction.

A thin woman in a bikini and sunglasses made a sudden dash from inside the house.

"You bitch", she snarled. "See what you have done to us, putain."

She pulled her arm back and slapped the doctor across the face, so hard that she nearly toppled over.

"Stop it, Clementine," her husband shouted.

"She deserves it," I hollered from the boat. "She used the machine on Verity."

"You did *what* to my daughter?" For a fraction of a second Flinders met my eyes, before his wife screamed; one of the most appalling sounds I'd ever heard.

"She did," TL spoke up. "I'm a psychiatrist and I can swear to what this so-called doctor did."

"I knew it," he said, "I fucking knew it."

What followed happened so quickly that I could hardly make sense of it for a long time afterwards. Flinders, who was a strong man, kicked out at a policeman and lunged towards his mistress. He was so fast, that I didn't see him grab the knife from the ground; I only learned of that later. He reached Anna Ambrosia and seemed to envelop her in a great, big hug, but my view was impeded by the bodies of the policemen, as they converged upon the entwined pair. And, then, by Bill and Gabriel and TL, thundering across the sand and jumping in the boat, which rocked as if it wanted to tip us all into the sea.

"Give me those," TL grabbed the oars from Peter and began to row, and if we hadn't known that he used to be a marine, we might well have guessed, because he pulled us through the water towards the ship with such force, such power.

Only when I looked back at the shore did I see the dying woman fall, and, even then, we were moving so fast through the sea, that I hesitated to believe the evidence of my own eyes.

6. THE SECOND FUNERAL

Sadie Hawking knocked on my door in the morning, to show me the hat that she had made for the May Day parade. It was a green straw hat smothered in florist flowers and she looked an absolute picture.

"You haven't seen my Bill, have you, Frances?"

"No, dear, I haven't."

"He's been that secretive lately, what with all this detecting he does with Rosa Stone."

Fly away, Bill. Fly away Rosa.

"Will you be coming to the parade later, Frances?"

"Oh, no; I've seen so many of them. I feel that spring and summer have been well and truly welcomed in by me, one way and another."

She seemed a touch puzzled by my reply.

"What does that mean?" She asked, in her lovely, straightforward fashion.

"Oh," I mused, "crocuses and daffodils, tulips and roses, Michaelmas daisies and snowdrops and back again."

Stop it, Frances, she may be the gardener's daughter, but you are confusing the poor girl with your everlasting flowers.

"Hmm," she said. "Is Mrs Stone in next door, by any chance? Only, I might just pop round and have a word. Goodbye, Frances."

"Goodbye, Sadie."

◆ ◆ ◆

I watched from the ship, through my binoculars. My uncle had been wrong to distrust the yellow notice, for Major Dyminge was on his way back to England. A cordon of dapper French policemen brought him out in a bag, before handing him over to the British Army at the shoreline. Soldiers stood guard over him as he lay in the dinghy, waiting for the machine to be dismantled and carted over the beach. The machine came out in several parts and filled several dinghies. One dinghy carried only silver tentacles. The operation lasted several hours and darkness fell as we waited out in the bay.

"If we can't bring him back, we may, at least, accompany him," Peter observed.

We sat together, Peter and I, watching over the procedure as if we couldn't bear the Major to spend a minute more without his friends.

"Oh, by the way," he said. "I forgot to give you a message from my wayward son. Something about a pink notice going awol. I couldn't make head nor tail of it, myself."

I was glad to hear it, although it couldn't make any difference now; not when they had their precious 'discovery'.

Bill came to sit beside me, his mouth swollen from where he had fallen down the steps into Dr Ambrosia's laboratory. He'd been lucky not to lose his teeth.

"Don't look so down, Rosa. We tried."

I felt like crying, but it may only have been a reaction to the day.

"Really," Bill patted my shoulder, kindly, "Good has triumphed, if you think about it."

I didn't want to think about it.

Hawking & Stone (1965)

❖ ❖ ❖

Millicent Stone knocked on my door in the afternoon.

"Any chance of a cup of tea?" She asked, holding up a brown paper bag. "Jerzy told me to bring these."

I had a peek inside; they proved to be flapjacks.

"Come in, dear."

I got waylaid between the parlour and the kitchen, but Millicent took control of the kettle and teapot, and so forth.

"Flapjacks and cake and crumpets."

"I beg your pardon, Frances."

"You must thank Jerzy, most warmly."

"That's alright, it's just what happens when you marry a baker," she laughed. "You stay right where you are, Frances, and I'll bring your cup over, nice and strong."

"How kind you are, Millicent, dear."

I might have a gin later. Nice and strong.

❖ ❖ ❖

It was dark by the time they'd finished, and the police vans had taken Flinders and his men ages before. Lights had been set up around the spot that Dr Ambrosia had fallen.

"Time to go home," said Gabriel.

"Yes," Jay agreed, "home to our families."

I leant over and kissed him, full on the mouth.

The engine started up and the sea lapped at the ship in the dark. It was possible that things might not be so bad. But, then again..

"I just cannot stand the thought of them having that damn machine," I said. "Of what they might do with it."

"Yeah," TL agreed. "But at least they can't get their hands on our correspondence. I ripped it all up and flushed it down the john."

"Ha."

"Good man," said Peter. "I burned his papers, too."

"Did you? When did you do that?"

"He did it weeks ago," Gabriel replied. "He stuffed them into the Aga, while I played the new Beatles album on the gramophone and cooked sausages."

"Ha."

❖ ❖ ❖

I could hear the jollity of the parade all the way from my cottage. They would be coming down to the beach soon to light their bonfires and set off fireworks. Those Beltane people with their pagan appetite for flames; I rather liked them. Especially after a most delicious gin and tonic.

Easy, Frances.

Oh, I don't think so, Guy.

There was a tap-tapping at the window, and I was afraid that it might be another visitor, but it was only my rose, my Rosa banksiae Lutea, straining against its bonds in the wind.

I opened the front door and stepped out to pick a spray.

Primrose yellow blooms. A dog howling in the distance. Fireworks beginning to speckle the sky. The sea; always the sea.

I daresay I fell and hit my head on something or other; it is of no account.

Guy.

Hallo old girl. What took you so long?

❖ ❖ ❖

The rocket soared into the blackness above St Margaret's Bay, sighing as it went. That long, drawn out sigh that makes the bang so startling when it finally comes, crumbling stars of red and green and purple and gold. A spark danced above the grey shape of the gunboat, as if it might not fall, might just fizzle away. It fell.

The boat went up in a crescendo of flames, as if it had been longing for the touch paper to be lit. It was so avidly hot that we had to shield our eyes, even though our ship was some distance away. It went up in gold and purple and green and red, and he went up with it, along with his last project; the one that he should never have invented.

Peter sat beside me in his chair, his yachting cap in his lap and his cheeks damp with tears. I bent to comfort him, but I was wrong.

"Marvellous," he murmured. "Simply marvellous."

He glanced up at me and smiled,

"Don't you see, Rosa? It's a funeral fit for a Viking. At long last, the old boy has got the funeral he deserved."

It was true; all the marching bands and military fanfare in the world could not have done it better.

"And . ." it dawned on me, "the explosion will have smashed the brainwashing machine into a million pieces."

"Yup," said TL, behind me. "Down so deep in the ocean that even the fish can't find it."

And they never did.

THE END

---

[1] Winston Spencer-Churchill (1874-1965). British statesman, politician and writer, twice Prime Minister, and leader of Britain during World War II. Churchill had died on 24th January.

[2] Dr Benjamin Spock, US paediatrician (1903-1998). Hugely influential childcare expert, who encouraged parents to be less rigid with the rules than previous generations (and more affectionate). Liberal-leaning in character, many have since complained that he helped to create the so-called 'permissive' society of the Sixties, onwards.

[3] Rosa is mangling *Life is what happens to you when you're busy making other*

plans .." Generally attributed to John Lennon, it was used by him in the lyrics of *Beautiful Boy (Darling Boy)* in 1980, a song written for his son, Sean. However, the expression actually goes back to a much earlier period; possibly an article in a 1957 issue of Readers Digest magazine.

[4] Sarah Bernhardt (1844-1923) Fabulous French stage actor, known for her intelligence, charm and passion. The daughter of a French courtesan, she lived life beyond the conventions of her time and has gone down in history as one of the best dramatic actors ever.

[5] Hattie Jacques (1922-1980), much-loved star of British comedy. She went from revue at the Players Theatre, London, where she excelled at traditional Music Hall, to being one of the team of British actors in the 'Carry On' films. Known for being a large lady, she was often cast as the butt of jokes, despite being a sensitive and accomplished actor.

[6] PL Travers (Pamela Lyndon Travers 1899-1996) wrote the first of eight Mary Poppins children's' books in 1934. Her Mary Poppins, while magical, was also acerbic and not particularly lovable. When Walt Disney brought out the film in 1964, he cast Julie Andrews as a serene, romantic Mary and added sequences featuring cartoon characters. Travers, herself, hated these sentimental additions, even though the film proved to be a smash hit.

[7] Mary Quant (born 1930), British self-taught fashion designer, enormously successful from the late 1950s onwards. For many, she epitomized the 1960's 'swinging London' scene, with her wearable clothes: tunic dresses and miniskirts, brightly coloured tights and fun accessories. She opened her first shop, Bazaar, with her husband Alexander Plunket Green, in the Kings Road, Chelsea in 1955.

[8] The BBC Wednesday Play was one of the jewels of 1960's television and ran from1964-1970. The plays were serious and ambitious and many leading British writers got their breaks working on them. They are still cited as examples of intelligent television, capable of reflecting their own era back to the viewer.

[9] "I'm in mourning for my life", is a line spoken by Masha, the middle sister, in 'Three Sisters' (1901), the play by Anton Chekhov (1860-1904), the wonderful Russian playwright, author of superb short stories, and doctor.

[10] The Hillman Husky was a British car manufactured by Hillman between 1954-1970. Rosa has a Mark 1 model from 1954, a three-door estate with two individual seats in the front and a bench seat in the back. Decidedly *not* a hatchback.

[11] Stirling Moss (born 1929), British Formula One racing driver of great talent and skill. He raced from 1948-1962, with particular success from 1955 onwards; although never World Champion, he was continuously up in

the top three.

[12] Stanley Spencer (1891-1959), English artist known for his figurative, mystical work – often showing scenes from the Bible as if they were taking place in his native village of Cookham, Berkshire. Spencer painted many versions of the Resurrection, but Rosa is referring to his early, best-known work, The Resurrection, Cookham 1924-1927. It is an astonishingly touching combination of the mundane and the profound, picturing Spencer's own acquaintances, lovers and friends, clambering out of their graves in a village churchyard. If you want to see it in the flesh, it's at Tate Britain.

[13] The Kinks, English band from North London, formed in 1964 by brothers Ray and Dave Davies. Gabriel was singing *Cadillac* from their first album Kinks (1964); the only album they had released thus far. *Cadillac* was originally released by Bo Diddley, influential US musician (1928-2008) in 1960.

[14] Upshott is referring to the oil painting 'Proserpine' (1874) by artist Dante Gabriel Rossetti (1828-1882), one of the founders of the Pre-Raphaelite Brotherhood in 1848. The painting features his model and lover, Jane Morris (1839-1914) as the goddess Proserpine who, having tasted six pomegranate seeds is condemned to spend six months of every year in the underworld with her lover, Pluto. Jane Morris, herself, spent half the year with Rossetti and half with her husband. While her luxuriant, dark hair and voluminous robes give Morris a monumental appearance in this painting, in reality she wasn't a large woman at all.

[15] Hammer Film Productions were founded in London in 1934. They went into the horror genre in a big way from 1955 onwards, after the X certificate had been introduced. Abominable snowmen, witches, vampires and zombies all emerged from Bray Studios, Berkshire, often portrayed by Hammer stars Peter Cushing, Christopher Lee and Vincent Price. The golden years of Hammer horror were to last until the 1970s, by which time the X certificate had become a far scarier (and less camp) proposition.

[16] US photographer Ansel Adams (1902-1984), known for his magnificent, black and white portraits of the panoramic American landscape.

[17] Norman Parkinson (1913-1990), British fashion and portrait photographer. Parkinson had been bringing whimsicality and informality to the previously rather stiff world of fashion photography since the Forties and Fifties. He often freed models from the studio and let them loose outdoors.

[18] *The Lord's my Shepherd* is a famous hymn based on the 23rd Psalm from the Bible. An extremely popular choice for funerals, the version used most often comes from the Scottish Psalter of 1650, set to the tune *Crimond*, which was composed in the 1800's.

[19] Frances is referring to *Kumbaya, my Lord*, a song associated with the US

folk revival and with the Civil Rights movement of the late Fifties, early Sixties. It was recorded by Pete Seeger in 1958 and Joan Baez in 1962 and was ubiquitous in this era. Its origin is disputed, but it may have begun life as an African American spiritual in the 1920's, sung by former slaves in a creole language.

[20] Graflex Super Speed Graphic, one of a series of Press cameras. The Super Speed was introduced in 1961, and much used until 1970. It had a faster shutter speed than previous models and, like the whole series, is now considered to be a classic.

[21] The 'new' nuclear power station Sam refers to was commissioned in 1965 ('commissioned' in the engineering sense of all checked and safe and ready to go, not in the artistic sense). It is now called Dungeness A because it ceased to provide nuclear energy to the National Grid in 2006 (de-commissioning will go on for many years to come, of course), and they then built Dungeness B (commissioned in 1983).

[22] Photographer David Bailey (born 1943), and model Jean Shrimpton (born 1942), beautiful British talents of the Sixties and beyond.

[23] The Topcon RE Super camera was a breakthrough camera of its time for professionals. It came on the market in 1963, used 35mm film and was both flexible and laden with gizmos, making it top of the range for the next five years.

[24] Bob Dylan, US musician (born Robert Zimmerman 1941). Came out of the American Mid-West, took Greenwich Village by storm as a principled folk artist, went electric, rest is history.

[25] *Heartbreak Hotel* was a massive early hit (1956) for 'the King of Rock and Roll', Elvis Presley (1935-1977).

[26] The Manchurian Candidate is a novel by American author Richard Condon (1915-1996). Written in 1959, it combines elements of the thriller and political satire to speculate about brainwashing.

[27] Frances is referring to Librium, one of the earliest of the benzodiazepine class of drug, which came on the market in 1960. It was widely prescribed for anxiety – perhaps too widely – given what we now know of the dangers of overuse of this type of drug.

[28] Frederic Truby King (1858-1938), New Zealand childcare reformer. His 1913 book, 'Feeding and Care of Baby' set out his draconian style of childcare, which was followed by many. Discipline was observed to a ridiculous degree: timed feeds, timed sleeps, even timed affection. Many are now horrified by his methods, although some modern childcare 'experts' have been influenced by him.

[29] The Beatles (band active 1960-1970). World-conquering British band

from Liverpool, John Lennon (1940-1980), Paul McCartney (born 1942), George Harrison (1943-2001) and Ringo Starr (born Richard Starkey 1940). John Lennon was married to his first wife, Cynthia Powell (1939-2015) in 1962, which was before the band really took off. They had been childhood sweethearts and had one son, Julian, but Cynthia was kept in the background throughout their marriage, so that fans knew practically nothing of her.

[30] *Beatles for Sale* was their fourth album in less than two years and came out in December 1964. Many now consider it their most uneven album.

[31] Harry borrowed 'Bound for Glory' (1943), the autobiography of US folk singer and prolific songwriter, Woody Guthrie (1912-1967). Born in Oklahoma, Guthrie lived through the Great Depression, followed by the terrible dust storms of 1935. Like many 'Okies' he left his family and headed for California, riding freight trains like a hobo, hiking and, eventually, living as a migrant in makeshift camps. All of these experiences influenced his music which, in turn, influenced a host of younger artists, such as Bob Dylan. What's more, as an archiver of old protest songs, slave songs and other music created by ordinary Americans, Guthrie provided a link between the past and present of folk music.

[32] The Pheasantry is a decorative nineteenth century (originally eighteenth) building located at 152 Kings Road, Chelsea. It housed a breeder of pheasants, an upholstery business and a ballet school, before the basement was opened as a nightclub, attracting various Chelsea Bohemians who also lodged upstairs. The nightclub was past its heyday by 1965 and the whole building was nearly torn down in the Seventies, only to be resurrected by the Pizza Express chain.

[33] Instant cameras with self-developing film had been around since the Forties, but the first inexpensive Polaroids appeared in the Sixties.

[34] Peter Rachman (1919-1962). Notorious London landlord operating in areas that had been slums – such as Shepherds Bush and Notting Hill – but which are now highly desirable. He profited from the Conservative government's Rent Act of 1957, which de-regulated rent control, thereby leaving tenants open to victimization from landlords wanting them out (so that they could charge more). His name has become a by-word for bad landlords, but didn't become widely known until after his death in 1962, when it cropped up in the Profumo case. Rachman had been involved with two of the prostitutes in that case, and it turned out that, as well as being the landlord from hell, he also ran a prostitution racket.

[35] The Labour government brought in the Rent Control Act of 1965 to reintroduce fair rent regulation (as it had been after the war), to be set by rent officers who were independent of private landlords.

[36] Dresses made from paper were a short-lived trend from the US. It was all over by 1968.

[37] Peter, Paul and Mary (Peter Yarrow, Noel Paul Stokey and Mary Travers), were another US folk band who became part of the American Folk Revival. They emerged from the nightclubs and coffee houses of New York's Greenwich Village in 1961 and became successful with songs such as *Puff the Magic Dragon* (1963) and *Leaving on a Jet Plane* (1969), as well as many Dylan covers. They broke up in 1970.

[38] Pete Seeger (1919-2014). As a near-contemporary of Woody Guthrie, Seeger was part of the older generation of US folk musicians, who influenced Dylan, Peter, Paul and Mary and many others. His influence went beyond the musical because he was a committed social activist all his life; involved in the Civil Rights movement, the anti-Vietnam war movement, nuclear disarmament and many other pressing causes. Having been subpoenaed to appear before the House Un-American Activities Committee in 1955, he refused to testify and was indicted for Contempt of Congress. Even though this was overthrown in 1962, he was effectively blacklisted for over ten years.

[39] By 1965 the Vietnam war had been raging for ten years and was to continue for another ten, only ending with the Fall of Saigon in 1975. Many now consider it to have been a 'proxy' war, in that a primarily local conflict – between North and South Vietnam – escalated when the world's Communist countries chose to support the North and the Capitalist West supported the South. The Cold War was, therefore, played out in the villages of a small country in Indochina, to appallingly destructive effect.

[40] 'Blue Hawaii' (1961) was a romantic comedy film starring Elvis Presley. The soundtrack was popular – including *Rock-A-Hula Baby* – but the film was the full Hawaiian cliché and as poor as most of Elvis' movie career.

[41] Francoise Hardy, French singer-songwriter, born 1944. Her hit song *Tous les Garçons et les Filles* came out in 1962 and she became internationally known. She was part of the 'ye-ye' (from yeah-yeah) pop movement of the early Sixties; singers from the Mediterranean countries – often female soloists – singing simple songs with innocent themes that were modelled on UK and US pop. However, Hardy was also influenced by French chansons and jazz, and has proved to be a more sophisticated and enduring artist than many.

[42] David Jacobs (1926-2013), British DJ and television presenter. The suave Jacobs presented the enormously successful tv show 'Juke Box Jury' – the British version ran from 1959-1967 – in which showbiz personalities (Rosa's glamorous Aunt Kathleen, perhaps) rated new records with a 'hit' or a 'miss'. The long-running BBC Radio panel show 'Any Questions?' (still on-air), was

also presented by him from 1967-1984, along with much else.

[43] If you *really* wish to know more about Frances Dyminge's unexpectedly adventurous life you would have to read 'The Perils of 1925' etc. (But you don't have to).

[44] Val Doonican (1927-2015), much-loved Irish crooner of light, popular music. Doonican was known for his casual style; often performing in comfy jumpers such as might be worn to play golf. He was so big in the UK that he was given his own show on the BBC from 1965-1986, where the relaxed vibe sometimes included singing while gently rocking in a rocking-chair.

[45] PI anti-hero from a series of classic detective novels by US writer Raymond Chandler (1888-1959).

[46] Elderly, but canny, amateur detective created by English writer, Agatha Christie (1890-1976).

[47] Bernard Katz (1911-2003), German-Jewish scientist who left Germany in 1935 for Britain. His work on neurophysiology (how nerve cells work in the body), especially during the 1950s, has influenced every aspect of the science. Of particular importance was his research on nerve terminals, or synapses (the junctions across which nerve cells communicate to the rest of the body's cells), which led to his being awarded a joint Nobel prize in 1970.

[48] The Cuban Missile Crisis was a very close call, indeed, at the worst period of the Cold War (1962). In 1959 Fidel Castro led a peoples' uprising on the island of Cuba, bringing down the right-wing despot Colonel Batista. Like Vietnam, what should have been a local matter became a Cold war confrontation involving America and Russia. For Cuba was only ninety miles from the coast of Florida and Batista had been propped up by the USA. Once in power, Castro nationalized American companies and the US, in return, banned the import of Cuba's main asset, sugar. So, Castro turned to Russia for help, becoming enemy number one for the Americans, who made several attempts to assassinate him, followed by a disastrous attempt at invasion on a quiet coastal area named the Bay of Pigs. It was in 1961 that the US discovered missile ranges on Cuba aimed at the US (provided by the Russians at Castro's request, in order to protect the island). The situation then escalated into the Cuban Missile Crisis. President Kennedy ordered a naval blockade and sent nuclear bomb carrying planes into the air. World War 3 was imminent, and this time it was nuclear. It took one terrifying week before Kennedy and the Russian leader, Nikita Khrushchev, managed a trade-off for peace.

[49] 'The Flower Pot Men' was a BBC tv programme, made for pre-school children, that was first shown in 1952. Bill and Ben were two puppets made out of garden pots who lived at the bottom of a garden and had gentle adventures with their friend, Little Weed (a daisy with a face and attitude).

[50] 'The Lion, the Witch and the Wardrobe' by British author CS Lewis (1898-1963), is the best-known of his 'Chronicles of Narnia', and is a magical story of ordinary children stepping through a wardrobe into a different world (while also being thinly-veiled Christian allegory).

[51] The Sultanate of Darfur incorporated a large area of what is now Sudan. It became a Sultanate in 1603 and remained so until 1874. The British re-instated a Sultan in 1898, however, when he became a supporter of the Ottoman Empire during WW1, they broke up the Sultanate and it became part of their Anglo-Egyptian Sudan. Upon achieving independence, it became, simply, Sudan.

[52] The Emirate of Jabal Shammar was the name for an area in NW Saudi Arabia, long ruled over by the Shammar family. It became part of the Kingdom of Saudi Arabia when that country was formed, in 1932.

[53] Nephrite is one of two mineral compositions referred to as 'jade', the other being Jadeite. Before 1800, the Chinese mainly used nephrite – generally of a paler, milkier look than jadeite – mining it from quarries and rivers to use for their delicate carving.

[54] 'The Avengers' was a UK tv series of hour-long adventures involving spies, bizarre villains and wacky Sixties fashion. It ran for 7 seasons from 1961 to 1969, with spin-offs coming later. Diana Rigg (born 1938), joined the series as athletic and sexy sidekick, Mrs. Peel, in 1965 (first episode aired October 1965), and became an overnight sensation. (Presumably, Sam had seen advance publicity for her).
She went on to show how accomplished an actor she was in a body of work including a Bond film, much serious theatre and Game of Thrones.

[55] Purple hearts were prescription drugs (primarily for tiredness) that became street drugs in the 1960's. They were half barbiturate, to calm and half amphetamine, to energise. As well as being part of Mod subculture, they were widely taken by teenagers for the speed effect.

[56] Dixon of Dock Green was a BBC tv series running from 1955-1976, starring the hugely popular actor Jack Warner (1895-1981) as PC George Dixon. The character was taken from a film, 'The Blue Lamp' (1950), in which Dixon was about to retire (so he was the oldest policeman in town by 1976). George Dixon was a sympathetic portrayal of a London bobby at the fictional Dock Green police station. When the series began, it was notable for showing a new level of social realism, even though it was exceptionally sympathetic to the forces of law and order. Dixon closed each episode with his reassuring catchphrase, "Good evening, all".

[57] *Put a tiger in your tank* was an advertising slogan that first appeared in 1959 in the US to promote Esso petrol and was used worldwide.

[58] Doublemint gum, made by the US company Wrigley's was widely advertised with the jingle *'Double your pleasure, double your fun with double good, double good, Doublemint gum'*. From the 1960's onwards, identical twins were also used, just in case the word 'double' hadn't sunk in.

[59] *A Mars a day helps you work, rest and play* was used as the advertising slogan for Mars chocolate bars from the late 1950's until the 1990's. Mars bars, themselves, were created in Britain in 1932 by Forrest Mars, son of US sweet magnate Frank C Mars.

[60] *Snap, Crackle and Pop* has a long history as the slogan for US company Kelloggs' Rice Crispies breakfast cereal. The cereal came to market in 1928 and the slogan was used from 1939 to illustrate the noise that's made when milk is added to your bowl of dry Rice Crispies. This was thought to be particularly appealing to children, so the illustrated elves that had been around to promote the product since the 1930's were named accordingly. The three little guys – Snap! Crackle! And Pop! – were updated in 1960.

[61] *The Freewheelin' Bob Dylan* was Dylan's enormously successful second album. It showed him at his best as a songwriter who could mix Folk and Blues heritage with powerful political, yet also poetical, lyrics. He addressed fears about nuclear war and civil rights on the album and it included songs that have been covered over and again, such as *Blowin' In the Wind* and *A Hard Rain's A-Gonna Fall*. The album went to number one in the UK charts in 1964.

[62] Jean-Paul Belmondo (born 1933), French film star and part of 1960's New Wave. His breakthrough came in 1960's 'À bout de souffle' (Breathless), directed by Jean-Luc Godard, playing a fool of a bad boy with a Bogart (Humphrey) obsession and a cigarette dangling from his lips. Attractive and louche, his broken nose only added to his appeal and he went on to star in many action films and comedies, mostly in European film.

[63] 'Ready Steady Go!' was a London-based pop and rock programme from the ITV company, Associated Rediffusion and was on-screen from 1963 until 1966. It provided a showcase for all of the up and coming – and already arrived – performers and bands of the day. Presented by Keith Fordyce and Cathy McGowan on a Friday evening, it opened with the phrase, *'the Weekend starts here!'*

[64] Cilla Black (born Priscilla White 1943-2015), singer and tv presenter. Born in Liverpool, she was friendly with the Beatles and made her singing debut in 1963. The auburn-haired, vivacious Liverpudlian was an instant hit and went to number one in the UK charts 1964 with *Anyone Who had a Heart* and *You're my World*. She went on to have her own BBC show for many years and became a fixture on British tv as a presenter. Always immensely popular, she was never really cool.

[65] Tom Jones (born Thomas Woodward 1940), is a Welsh singer who had a string of hits in 1965, starting with *It's Not Unusual*. He also sang the theme tune for the fourth Bond movie, 'Thunderball', later that year. Heavily influenced by Elvis and with a fine, deep voice, Jones began with rock and roll with a soul edge, but developed into a crooner and was a big hit in Las Vegas. He has remained successful to this day. (Again, like Cilla, he was always too populist to appeal to a serious boy like Bill!)

[66] John Mayall & the Bluesbreakers, an English blues rock band active between 1963-1970 and then 1982-2008. Born in 1933, John Mayall was heavily influenced by US blues and, in turn, became enormously influential himself to a generation of rock musicians who loved the blues. The Bluesbreakers had a changing lineup that included musicians such as Eric Clapton, Mick Fleetwood and Mick Taylor. His band, therefore, fed into key bands of that era (and on into the Seventies and Eighties), such as Cream, Fleetwood Mac and the Rolling Stones. Mayall's first album *John Mayall Plays John Mayall* was released in 1965, so his appearance on 'Ready Steady Go!' would have appealed to the cognoscenti. (Incidentally, the line-up that Bill and Verity watched was the one that appeared on the evening of 23rd April 1965).

[67] Sandie Shaw (Sandra Goodrich) was born in 1947. An English singer who epitomized the so-called 'Swinging Sixties', she sang barefoot, dressed in simple, little dresses with her hair loose. *(There's) Always Something There to Remind Me* was a big hit for her in 1964. She went on to win Eurovision for the UK in 1967 with *Puppet on a String*, the best-selling Eurovision single ever.

[68] Interpol issues colour-coded notices as international requests for cooperation (or alerts to the police forces of member countries). A blue notice is a request to 'obtain information on a person of interest in a criminal investigation'. (They want to know more about Dr Anna Ambrosia).

[69] An Interpol yellow notice is a global police alert for a missing person. (In this case, the person is most probably dead).

Printed in Poland
by Amazon Fulfillment
Poland Sp. z o.o., Wrocław